From Darkness Won

Blood of Kings
Book Three

Jill Williamson

PUBLISHING

From Darkness Won by Jill Williamson
Published by Enclave Publishing
24 W. Camelback Rd. A-635
Phoenix, AZ 85013
www.EnclavePublishing.com

ISBN (paper): 978-0-9825987-7-1

Published in the United States by Enclave Publishing, an imprint of Third Day Books, LLC, Phoenix, Arizona.

Cover Designer: Kirk DouPonce, Dog-Eared Design,
www.dogeareddesign.com
Cover Photo By: Kirk DouPonce
Creative Team: Jeff Gerke, Dawn Shelton

Printed in the United States of America

To Adele, Chris, Jacob, Leighton, and Ness,

for your enthusiasm, help, friendship,

and random texts of the day.

Advance Praise for *From Darkness Won*

"A satisfying end to a ground-breaking trilogy. Can't wait to see what Jill Williamson comes up with next!"

Kathy Tyers, author of *The Annotated Firebird*

"*From Darkness Won* had me up until 3:00 a.m. reading. It bonds to your hands the moment you pick it up, refusing to be put down until the last page falls."

Christian Miles, author of *The Scarlet Key*

"*From Darkness Won* is filled with action, romance, adventure and mystery. The storyline races forward, launching the reader through battle, loss, and victory. Just when the reader thinks all is known, Williamson twists the tale with one or two or five more surprises."

Amy Meyer

"My life wouldn't be the same without *By Darkness Hid*, *To Darkness Fled*, and last but *not* least, *From Darkness Won*. Jill Williamson held me a captive audience from 1st to last."

Adele Hajicek, writing as Adele Treskillard, 19

"Aside from finding a wife of my own and following God, I can say that one thing I would *love* to see/help with is making the *Blood of Kings* series into movies. *From Darkness Won* is the riveting conclusion to a series of epic proportions."

Leighton, 16

Map of Er'Rets
Ice Island
Tsaftown
Meitab Corner
Therion
Berland
Mitsarb
Zerab Rock
Carm
Carmine
LIGHT
Chowmah Mountains
DARKNESS
Zamar
Har Shaar
Sideros Forest
Gulf of Mayim
Melas
Sitna
Nesos
Barth
Melas Marsh
Albemtown
Arok Lake
Allown
LIGHT
Barth
Mirrorstone
Land's End
Nahar Forest
Mahanaim
Lebab Inlet
Walden's Watch
Cela
Meneton
Cela Mountains
Nabar Peninsula
Nabar Caves
Xulon
Nabar
Jaelport
Hamonab
Noix
Cherem
Shelosh Islands
Armonguard
Lake Arman
Magos
Arman
Erets Point

Prologue

Torch in hand, Sidal climbed behind his master up the spiral staircase of the Mahanaim watchtower. "But, sir, why is the teacher called 'Hadad'?"

Macoun sent his reply to Sidal's mind. *The title was chosen for its meaning and similarity to the royal name* Hadar. *And it is* the *Hadad, not simply Hadad. It isn't a name but a role, a human host for the keliy.*

"What does 'the Hadad' mean, then?"

God of rain, storms, and thunder. Division.

Sidal considered this as they reached a short landing then started up another flight of stairs. "Does the Hadad believe that claiming such a title makes him a god?"

No one claims the title "the Hadad," boy. For hundreds of years past, the keliy has chosen its host. Not the other way around.

"What *is* a keliy?"

The *keliy. There is only one. It is a powerful deity.*

That a god would take a human form intrigued Sidal. The chosen one must be a great man. "Will your master approve of me?"

Perhaps. If you hold your tongue and mind your place.

Sidal glanced over his shoulder. The torch cast light and shadow over the armored men walking behind him.

Sakin Magos. Black knights. Two of them.

Sidal had never accompanied his master on such an outing before. The presence of the black knights shot a thrill through his stomach. He picked up his pace. "How does your master decide who to train? Will it help if I tell him I've always wanted to be a Black Knight?"

It will help if you speak to me with your bloodvoice and not your audible one.

"Sorry, sir." *I mean, sorry, sir. Do you think it will help, though?*

The Hadad trains who he wants to train. Your prattling on will not make you more endearing.

Right. Curse his babbling tongue, anyway. Sidal had never seen a talkative black knight. If he wanted to join their ranks—to impress the Hadad—he would have to practice being serene and silent.

At the top of the stairs, Macoun stopped at a board and batten door. "Wait outside," he told the black knights. "Sidal, come with me."

Sidal slipped the torch into a ring on the wall outside the door and followed his master into a warm chamber.

The circular room was mostly empty, lit by a candle on the floor beside a narrow cot. There was nothing inside but the cot, the candle, and a birdcage on a fluted pedestal before a small window. A gowzal sat on the perch inside, watching them with its bead-like eyes. Sidal did not see the Hadad anywhere. The heat of the room warmed his face, though he did not know where the heat came from.

"How is it so warm, Master?"

Macoun shot Sidal an irritated glare.

Forgive me, Master. But there is no fireplace. I don't—

A voice sizzled out of the darkness. "We have nearly accomplished our goal, Macoun. Everything is in place."

Sidal jumped, for he had not seen the man standing before the window. His hooded black cape masked his body against the shadowed walls.

The Hadad.

Sidal stood beside his master, trembling in the presence of the great teacher.

The Hadad gazed out over the city. "So many years and it's nearly within my grasp."

"What is, sir?" Sidal asked.

Silence, boy! Macoun sent Sidal another glare.

The Hadad turned, his dark gaze falling on Sidal, who straightened under the teacher's scrutiny. "Who is this, Macoun?"

"One of my apprentices, Master."

"His name?"

"Sidal son of Lekim."

"Lekim." The Hadad drew out the m. "Lekim is a black knight, is he not?"

Sidal dared to glance up. "*Was*, my lord. He was killed during an attack against Sir Gavin Whitewolf and his prince just outside Mirrorstone."

The Hadad lifted his chin. "Yes, I remember. I daresay you have no love of our *king in waiting*."

Sidal pulled his dagger from his belt and squeezed the handle. "If I were to see Sir Gavin or his princeling, I would kill them both."

The Hadad chuckled. "He's precious, Macoun. Wherever did you find him?"

"His mother brought him to me after his father was killed."

"Hmm." The Hadad peered down on Sidal. "Seems to me the father was a failure. And so the son will likely be. You *do* find the lowliest apprentices, Macoun."

Fire shot through Sidal's veins. How dare this man call his father a—

Macoun gripped Sidal's empty hand. *Put the knife away, boy.*

Sidal obeyed, as if he had no choice.

Macoun lifted their joined hands. "I use what comes to me, Master, as you once instructed. See?"

A chill shot up Sidal's arm and pooled in his chest. He tried to pull away from his master's touch but found he could not move.

Macoun pushed his other hand outward, palm facing the Hadad. Green lines of light crackled around his fingers, swirled in his palm, and settled there like a ball of light.

"So this boy is your crutch," the Hadad said. "Very clever of you to find a way to make magic, Macoun, but I have more important things to discuss. What does Lord Nathak say his son will do now that—?"

"Not today," Macoun said, his voice a droning hum. "For you have tarried too long." He thrust out his palm, lobbing the ball of light at the Hadad.

The teacher caught it in a burst of sparks and wind that blew Sidal's hair back from his face. "Too long for what?"

Macoun's robes billowed around him as a new ball of light gathered on his palm. "The time has come for another to take your place."

The Hadad's eyebrows curled. "And you think it will be *you*?" He motioned to Sidal. "You can barely stand without stealing some poor fool's energy, and your strikes"—he lifted his hand and deflected Macoun's next attack—"are child's play."

Sidal didn't understand what Macoun was doing. They had never practiced such magic. He wanted the cold to stop. For his master to release his hold. But he could not move.

Macoun lobbed another ball of green flame. "The keliy tires of your pace, master. It came to me. Suggested I could do what you could not."

"Lies! The keliy has been loyal to me all these years. It would never betray me so." The Hadad threw a handful of green fire at Sidal.

Sidal wanted to duck aside, but he was still frozen by Macoun's touch.

Macoun disintegrated the fire with a pulse of green smoke from his hand. "That is where you are mistaken. The keliy is not your servant. It is your master. It wants what it wants, and you have taken far too long to deliver."

The Hadad sputtered. "How dare you! I have spent years setting everything up. The time is at hand. All my hard work—"

"Will become mine." Macoun shot a stream of light that singed the sleeve of the Hadad's robe.

The Hadad howled.

Macoun sent a second stream. "Did you not wonder why Esek did not call out to you when his arm was severed from his body?"

This time the Hadad dodged the attack. "The keliy told me he healed him."

"*I* healed him," Macoun said. "The keliy gave *me* the power."

The Hadad stumbled on his robe, and one of Macoun's streams of fire burned his cheek. He screamed, straightened, and conjured a shield of green light before him. "You cannot use your lies on me. Do not forget who taught you. Who raised you."

Macoun stilled, his hand suspended before him. "I will never forget the life you gave me, Master. But the end comes to us all. And when it comes to you, I am the *next* chosen. So the keliy has said. I feel it only wise to take my position posthaste. Esek is subject to me now, as is his father. Only you stand in my way."

"If you wish to die, you only need ask." The Hadad thrust both hands out before him. His shield broke apart like a hundred glowing knives flying their way. The gowzal in the cage shrieked.

Slivers of fire knocked Sidal to the floor, breaking his contact with Macoun. Heat flooded back into Sidal's body. He lay on his side, facing the open floor. His vision spun, everything a blur of flashing green light and dancing shadows. He blinked until his sight cleared. He wanted to get up, to slip down the stairs and flee the stronghold, but Macoun had taken all his strength.

The two sorcerers circled one another, throwing bolts of green lightning like spears. The bitter tang of charred wool wrinkled Sidal's nose. When the green light flashed, Sidal could see feathers floating in the air. Hundreds of gowzals circled the tower outside, squawking, shrieking, passing by the window in a tangle of black wings.

Macoun struck the Hadad with a blast of green steam. The Hadad's robe and hair blew back. He countered by flinging a glowing scythe. Macoun spun to the side, and the scythe cut through the back hem of his robe.

Macoun attacked again, as did the Hadad. Their power clashed between them. Knotted. Macoun pushed. The Hadad pushed. They stood on opposite sides of the chamber, the Hadad with his back to Sidal, his heels barely an arm's length from Sidal's limp hand. Peering around the hem of the Hadad's robe, Sidal could see only half of Macoun's face across the room.

They stood like that, grunting, pushing. The gowzals continued to screech and flap their wings. Sidal stared at his fingers, squeezed his fist. He could move again. His energy had returned. He sat up and backed against the wall.

"Haahh!" the Hadad roared. A blast shook the tower. Sidal looked around the Hadad in time to see Macoun's body fall.

A snare coiled around Sidal's stomach. His master! What could he do to—

Sidal's limbs turned again to ice. He stiffened, cold, yet mobile this time. Immense. Strong. Against his will, his body pushed to his feet, crept forward a step. And another. His hand slid to his belt, withdrew his dagger.

Watch and learn, boy.

The voice was Macoun's, yet it was Sidal's thoughts, deeper and more intimate than mere bloodvoicing.

The Hadad, lit now by nothing but the lone candle, stood over Macoun's body, kicked it. "Fool that you are, Macoun. As if you could ever defeat—"

Sidal plunged the dagger into the Hadad's back. The act horrified him, thrilled him, confused him. He still had no control over his own actions.

The Hadad screamed, turned to look at Sidal, but before he could speak, his body seized, his back arched, and a pale face rose out of his chest.

Tall and impossibly thin, a semi-transparent creature seeped out of the Hadad's body until it loomed over him, hunching under the ceiling. Its long limbs were corded in muscles. It had no hair, but cragged ridges ran from its chin, up its cheeks, over its head, then curled and darkened into black ram's horns. Charcoal veins bulged all over the creature's milky skin. Its eyes, mouth, and stub of a nose were blackened.

"No! Don't leave me!" The Hadad crumpled to his knees at the creature's feet. "I have nearly completed your task. Heal me. Let me finish what I started, I beg you!"

The creature roared, a sound that shook the tower and Sidal's bones. The Hadad whimpered and ducked his head under his arms.

The creature turned its black eyes to Sidal and spoke in a gravelly voice. "Set the snare."

Sidal wanted to run, but Macoun still controlled his body. He flicked Sidal's hand at the ceiling, conjuring a dome of light over the Hadad's body. The entire chamber glowed green, illuminating bits of feathers floating on the air from the birds flying outside

"Master, please." The Hadad sucked in a short breath. "If my body must die . . ." He wheezed. "At least let my soul serve you here."

But the creature glided over the Hadad and sank into Macoun's body that still lay lifeless across the room.

The Hadad, the great teacher, fell, choking in hitches of breath. Suddenly, a transparent image of the man floated out of his body, leaving a limp shell on the floor. Sidal started, not comprehending how any of this could be possible.

The misty form of the Hadad drifted low, staring at the dome of green light as if it were a sword to his throat. *Please reconsider, Master! I beg of you.*

Sidal thrust his hand at the Hadad's spirit. "I think not." Macoun's words came out in Sidal's voice.

The Hadad flew up. His scream cut off quickly as he passed through the dome and vanished. Sidal lowered his hand. The green light went out.

Sidal blinked a moment in the dull light of the lone candle, then staggered back as heat engulfed his body. He was himself again. By the time Sidal could see clearly, Macoun was sitting up on the floor.

"Don't just stand there gaping, boy, help me up."

Sidal lunged forward. His foot dragged through something thick and warm on the floor. He looked down to a pile of smoldering ash where the Hadad's body had lain.

Sidal leapt out of the ash and pulled Macoun to his feet. "What happened, Master?"

"The keliy has passed to me. *I* am the Hadad now. Unfor-tunately for you, boy. You've seen far too much."

A tremor of fear gripped Sidal's heart. He glanced at the door, but Macoun walked there and opened it to the black knights.

"Khai," Macoun said, "send the armies to attack Allowntown and Carmine, as planned. Bring me the prince. Dead or living, I care not. If you fail, bring me the girl, her mother, or one of her sisters."

"Sisters? What good are they to anyone, Master?"

"Bait for the girl and heirs should she die. Now, go!"

The black knight bowed. "Yes, Master." He descended the stairs, his companion at his heels.

Macoun closed the door and faced Sidal. "I no longer have use for your pathetic powers, nor need I stomach another incessant question from that mouth of yours."

Sidal stumbled back. "Master, please. You said I could train to be a black knight. You promised—"

A fist of green light gripped Sidal's throat. It lifted him and carried him away from his master. Sidal grunted, kicked his legs.

Promises are nothing but words, boy. Words that make people comply.

Sidal could not speak aloud. *I can be of service to you, master. I can help you.*

The keliy does not need your help. Only mine.

The fist pushed Sidal's body out the window. He struggled to cling to the side jambs with his hands, hook the sill with his legs. But the fist thrust him out. Gowzal wings swiped his back and head as they flew past the tower window.

Macoun stepped up to the window, a small smile on his lips. *Say hello to my master.*

The fist let go. And Sidal son of Lekim fell screaming, through the squawking birds, down the length of the watchtower, until he passed into Darkness.

PART I

ACHAN

1

Get the little pilfering prince!

The soldier's wooden blade whipped toward Achan's face. He lunged back a step in his heavy armor and threw up his guard. The wasters scraped overhead. His body ached, left thigh still sore from where Esek had stabbed him with Ôwr, right shoulder tender from the cham bear's teeth.

Achan tensed his muscles anyway, pushing against his opponent's blade. His elbow exploded with pain as a different waster slipped past his armor and struck true. Grinding his teeth at the fiery throbs shooting up his arm, Achan cut down from high guard at the man on his right and thrust his shield against the soldier before him.

Yet his attackers kept a steady pace. Dozens of boots pattered over the soft dirt around him. One waster clubbed his backplate. Another nicked his shoulder. He needed more space. They were crowding him. Even their thoughts and the cheers of the crowd seemed against him.

This was supposed to be a practice fight, not a real one. Good thing they were using wooden swords.

Achan stabbed one man's chest, thrusting against chain armor. He stomped on another's foot. Block to the left. Kick a man's thigh. Parry with his shield. Left-guard to cut at open shins. Elbow to an exposed neck.

And just when he managed to push back the last man, four fresh soldiers advanced.

They bore down hard, slashing for Achan's legs and head. He crouched, blocking his legs with his shield and parrying to high guard. Wood clubbed against wood.

Shung's warrior cry bellowed from behind, but there was no time to see whether Shung needed aid.

There were too many.

But Shung's yell reminded Achan that volume was strength. He released a hearty scream of his own and threw out his shield arm, knocking a soldier back. He cut across two men with his waster. One stumbled into the dusty soil. The other danced back and retreated to the benches. This won Achan a moment to breathe. He returned his blade and shield to middle guard and glanced at Shung.

His faithful Shield was surrounded by five foes. Shung blocked two strikes and caught a soldier square in the chest with his buckler shield.

The onlooking soldiers rooted for their comrades.

"Get 'em, men!"

Go low, Zin!

"Three cheers for Carmine!"

"Take him down, Grigio!"

Make him pay. For Rennan!

For Rennan? *Shung? Did you hear that?* Achan asked telepathically.

Shung glanced Achan's way. *Behind you!*

Achan spun around just as a waster pounded the top of his head, slamming his teeth together. His knees buckled. His head rang against his helm like the clapper of a bell. He sank to his knees—head throbbing, elbow and thigh screaming—and raised his shield to protect his head.

Little Cham! Shung yelled. *On guard!*

But Achan couldn't think. He needed a moment to—

A waster stabbed his left side. Another cracked against his shield. Achan cowered behind the slab of worn wood. He took several short breaths and jumped up. His shield struck his opponent's again, but this time Achan rammed it outward. The soldier fell and skidded in the dirt.

That won't do, Zin! We've got to show him a Carmine soldier is more man than he'll ever be.

Shut up, Grigio. You're distracting me.

Achan wanted to identify who Zin and Grigio might be, but he barely had time to crouch into position to deflect a blow from his latest opponent. This one came at his feet. He met it with his sword, and lifted his shield high, then brought the edge of his shield down toward his opponent's head.

Missed. The shields locked together. Achan's opponent tugged him close, their faces inches apart. The man's eyes were fierce, hateful. This was no training regimen for him. Why?

A shadow flitted across Achan's vision. Too late he saw his opponent's sword in high guard coming down. He jerked his head aside. The waster whipped the air beside his head, nicking his helm.

The helm twisted, blocking sight to his left eye. He ducked behind his shield as the weight of a man knocked against it. Leather scraped against wood. Achan fell. He kept his shield tight over his head and body. Kicked out a leg.

Useless.

Someone stomped on his wrist and jerked his sword away. A tug on his shield wrenched his right arm out straight. His cham wounds burned. He held tight until a waster cleaved against his arm. His shield flew away.

Three dark outlines hovered overhead, the sky clear and blue above them. A kick to his ribs felt like a playful nudge through his armor. A mailed fist to his jaw, however . . .

The air stung the raw flesh where he'd been struck.

That'll teach the lily-livered geck.

What in all Er'Rets?

Achan tried to roll away, but the same mail glove gripped his throat. Squeezed. "You yield?" the soldier asked, his voice a faint breath.

Achan pushed against the man's chest with his hands and managed to croak, "No."

Stubborn little pip, he is.

You've got him, Grigio. Make him regret it.

So this was Grigio, at least. The one choking him. The pressure increased, crushing Achan's throat until his cheeks tingled. The cheers of the Carmine soldiers warbled.

Shh-ung . . . a little help?

Coming.

Achan's vision spotted, but Shung's battle cry bolstered his courage. In one motion, the hand released his throat and his attacker fell away.

He gasped and lifted his head to see Shung dragging the soldier away by the cape. Five fresh men approached from the benches.

Pig snout. Would this never end? Achan pushed up onto one elbow and searched the dirt for his sword.

"Halt!"

Captain Tristan Loam stepped between the approaching Carmine soldiers and where Achan lay on the ground. The captain was tall and broad with reddish hair, a short beard, and a cushion of a belly, though Achan didn't doubt he was a formidable swordsman.

Captain Loam peered down on Achan. "Are you well, Your Highness?"

Achan licked his bloody lip and panted. "Aye."

"Take a moment before we go again."

Go again?

Achan let his head fall back on the ground. He swallowed a bit of blood and stared at the azure sky. It took several deep breaths to cleanse his strangled lungs. On his right, golden standards perched along the sentry wall, flapping in the wind, each marked with a bunch of plump red grapes. Achan watched their movement as his breathing returned to normal.

Captain Loam's voice muted as he addressed his men. "We'll give the prince a moment to rest, then get back to it."

Aww. The knotty-pated baby needs a rest, a soldier said.

Can't believe he's fighting us at all, another said.

Half-trained lout don't deserve Lady Averella.

Achan stiffened at the jeers, but then he finally understood. The soldiers were angry about his betrothal to Lady Averella. Bran Rennan, who had been engaged to her, was one of their number. In their eyes, Achan had taken Bran's woman.

Aw, pig snout. Achan had hoped to bond with these men by coming here this morning. But he'd been naive, as always. There had been too many factors to anticipate. Half-trained, indeed. Achan wanted to go back to the peace of his chambers. Hide there. Or leave Carmine altogether.

But that was not what a sovereign should do.

A shadow stepped before him. Achan squinted until Shung's hairy outline came into focus.

Shung extended an arm. *They are merciless warriors. Very brave. Glad they're on our side.*

Achan reached up and grasped Shung's forearm. *They wanted to beat me.*

Shung jerked Achan up. *That's the object of the lesson.*

No. Achan straightened his helm and wiped his sleeve over his bloody lip. His jaw and thigh stung. He met Shung's dark eyes and allowed anger to crush his self-pity. *They wanted an excuse to beat me without the ramifications of beating the Crown Prince of Er'Rets. They're cowards.*

No man had been willing to speak his mind. To confront Achan for taking Lady Averella from Bran. For such an act would be insubordination. Treason. Cause for discharge or at least a whipping. No. These men simply wanted an opportunity to vent their anger without backlash.

Achan found his waster and shield on the ground and picked them up. His armor pulled on his shoulders and trapped heat against his body like a forge. The rivets in his chain armor tugged at strands of his hair and grated against his shoulder blades through his sweat-soaked hauberk.

"Ready to go again?" Captain Loam asked.

Bet I take the sorry piglet down, a soldier said.

Yer full of dung, Zin. Keep to the plan. I almost had him.

Achan searched the crowd for Grigio, but either he'd vanished behind the observers or Achan hadn't gotten as a good a look at him as he'd thought. In hopes of discovering the gifted soldiers, Achan lowered the shields around his mind completely, as if he had forgotten everything he'd been taught. The act released the pressure of his bloodvoice. Anyone gifted would feel it like a blow.

When three soldiers sitting on the benches cowered, Achan knew he'd succeeded.

Your Highness? Sir Caleb's voice, panicked, burst in Achan's mind. *Are you injured?*

Achan snapped his shields back in place. *Sorry, Sir Caleb. Just a little experiment.*

"Your Highness?" Captain Loam awaited his answer.

"I thank you, Captain Loam, for a vigorous practice, but I have other matters to attend to." Achan returned his waster and shield to the racks, then walked to where his attackers sat, opening his mind to Shung. His heart hammered in anticipation. *Stay close, Shung. This might go badly.*

Shung walked alongside Achan. *What do you mean?*

Achan stayed open to Shung, but expanded his reach to the three soldiers, making sure Lady Averella's maroon dress sleeve that was tied to his left arm was displayed before the men. *Hey, you three. Did no one tell you the 'half-trained baby' could bloodvoice?*

Two of the men hung their heads, but the third—Grigio, the man with the angry eyes and unforgiving mail gloves—looked up, face flushed. Achan had no way of knowing if he were embarrassed, angry, surprised, or merely fatigued.

"What is your name?" Achan asked.

The man stood. "Grigio Franc, Your Highness."

Shung's six foot plus inched closer to Achan, causing Grigio to shrink a bit.

"Master Franc," Achan said. "You are loyal to your comrade, Bran. This is a deeply admirable trait. But have you bothered to ask his side of this . . . situation with Lady Averella?"

"I don't need to ask. I can see it on his face." Grigio glanced at Shung and added, "Your Highness."

Achan paused, curious whether Bran's broken engagement hadn't been as amicable as Duchess Amal had claimed. "Nevertheless, you should speak to Master Rennan before risking your life for his honor. While that in itself is an admirable way to perish, it is a foolish sacrifice when done under mistaken assumptions. Don't you agree?"

"I . . ." Grigio's brows wrinkled. "Perhaps."

Achan nodded. "Good enough." He walked away from the benches and the practice field, forcing himself not to limp on his sore leg. Shung tromped at his side.

You will not punish us? Grigio asked.

Achan turned back and met Grigio's wide eyes. *Should I? You're a worthy fighter, Master Franc, and fiercely loyal. Killing you would not help me take Armonguard. And I need such hearts as yours at my side. So I give you another chance to correct your misjudgment of me before I cast my final judgment upon you.*

• • •

Once Achan had cleaned up and changed, he and Shung went to lunch in the great hall. They arrived early for the scheduled meal, but Achan preferred it that way. He'd done his duty by confronting the men on the practice field, so he figured he'd earned a reprieve from making small talk with Duchess Amal's daughters and various other minor nobles.

Shung, as usual, stood against the wall behind Achan, staring ahead like a sentry guard.

Blazes.

"Sit with me, Shung. Surely no one here plans to threaten my life."

"Soldiers on field had motives Shung did not see."

"Don't punish yourself. You are Sir Shung, now. The brave knight who rescued the Crown Prince from a cham bear." Achan had knighted his friend their second day in Carmine. Shung was the first man he'd ever knighted.

"Shung did not slay the beast."

"You slowed it down and have the burn to prove it. And now the title too." Which would make Shung worthy to marry Lady Gali, should the man get up the courage to ask. "Now sit and eat with me."

"Forgiveness, Little Cham, but Shung must do his duty."

Achan slouched down in the chair and looked out over the elaborate great hall. They each had a duty, didn't they? And Achan's duty was to be king. King of all Er'Rets. If they won this inevitable war.

Sparrow had always sat with him for breakfast.

Sparrow.

With his bloodvoice, he found her instantly, sensed thick walls around her mind. He wanted to speak, but she'd been ignoring his messages ever since she left Mitspah. Likely still angry over his blunder the last time they'd spoken.

He tried and failed to look through her eyes. He could break into almost any mind with his bloodvoicing power. But not Sparrow's. Hers had always been impenetrable. He sighed. What good would any of this do? Pining away for Sparrow would not loosen the sleeve tied to his arm.

She had made her choice, and so had he.

Achan turned his chair sideways so he could talk to Shung as he ate. "I can think of no engagements set for this afternoon, can you?"

Shung tipped his head, and the circle of carved bone he always wore in his ear rocked. "I cannot."

Finally, some time to himself. One of his advisors would find him soon enough, make him study or drag him into another meeting. But if he could get out now, he might fill part of this day with his own will.

"We shall go to visit Gren and her family," Achan said, pleased with the idea. Months had passed since he'd seen his childhood friend.

Shung grunted.

For the next fifteen minutes, Achan ate his fill, and then he pushed his plate away. "I'm ready but will not leave this chair until you eat, Shung."

"Shung cannot shield when eating."

Achan switched strategies. "But a warrior must eat. At least carry some grapes with you as we walk."

The Shield shook his head. "Shung cannot wield sword with handful of grapes."

Achan blew out a long breath and stood. "Very well. I suppose you can eat at the Fenny home, though they are peasants and likely have little food to spare."

Shung looked over Achan's head, scanning the near-deserted great hall, then stepped toward the table and reached for a hard-cooked egg. His sleeve rode up his arm, and Achan caught sight of the scarred skin between sleeve and glove. A cham had breathed fire on Shung's arm. "Will eat this."

"Good enough."

After Shung ate the egg, Achan led him across the great hall to the foyer. His body ached with every movement, sore from his injuries and his exercise on the practice field.

"Good day, Your Highness."

To Achan's left Lady Nitsa Amal, the Duchess of Carm, stood at the foot of the brownstone staircase, her auburn hair sculpted up under a ruby-beaded caul. She wore a blood-red gown trimmed in black and gold embroidery. Her skin was ivory porcelain in the dim light.

He bowed. "Good day, my lady. Has your daughter returned yet?"

She fixed her moss-colored eyes on Achan. "She has not, Your Highness. You are not joining us for lunch?"

"I just finished. I planned to explore the grounds a bit, if you don't mind."

The duchess's small mouth curved into a smile. "Not at all. I shall not keep you from your schedule."

Achan bowed. "Thank you, my lady. Enjoy your meal."

"I am sure I will, Your Highness."

Achan and Shung exited Granton Castle. The sunny afternoon, chirping birds, and his destination made his burdens lighter. The blended smells of fresh-cut wood, dung, animals, and flowers tickled his nose.

"You ask Duchess Amal same question whenever you see her," Shung said.

Achan shot Shung a quick smile. "I want to meet Lady Averella if I'm to marry her. Is that so shocking?"

Shung grunted. "Duchess will tire of you."

"Good. Perhaps her fatigue will encourage her to draw Lady Averella out long enough to shake my hand." Achan couldn't stand not knowing what this woman looked like. He wasn't about to give up his quest to find out.

They passed through the gate to the outer bailey and into a throng of peasants, soldiers, and every sort of barn animal imaginable. Disdain from those around him flooded his senses. Achan met one soldier's frowning gaze and staggered at the hatred pouring from the man. He considered reading the man's thoughts, but Shung tugged his arm, pulling him aside. He narrowly missed treading on a boy carrying a basket of berries.

"Pardon, my lord." The boy bowed and scurried past as if Achan might beat him for being in the way.

Achan couldn't blame him. He'd been cuffed upside the head for the same many times in his youth.

They wove through the outer bailey. Disapproval continued to seep into Achan. He caught sight of two middle-aged women carrying buckets of water, scowling and whispering between themselves. Achan looked into the mind of the one whose eyes he met first and the words she whispered to her counterpart filled his head.

. . . has no right to come here and take over. I don't care if he's rightful king or not.

And when you consider— Her friend gasped. *Gods, no. Look who it is. There'll be a fight now, Kera, just you wait. Who you think'll win?*

Achan turned to where the women had focused their attention. A squadron of Carmine soldiers drew near, accompanied by more feelings of animosity. Perhaps Grigio Franc was among them.

A set of familiar eyes met Achan's from within the squadron. Bran Rennan. The squire left the formation, and the soldiers halted. One man glanced at the sleeve on Achan's arm but seemed content to wait and watch.

Achan's own feelings of anger and distrust mingled with those around him, not certain how to feel about Bran Rennan, especially after this morning's altercation.

Bran bowed low and smiled. "Nice to see you again, Your Majesty. Where are you off to?"

Not a shred of the animosity Achan sensed came from Bran. "I plan to visit Grendolyn Fenny," Achan said. "Sir Caleb keeps me busier than a squirrel in fall, and this is the first opportunity I've had since my arrival."

Bran's face tinged pink—at the mention of Gren's name, perhaps?—but he went on as if nothing were amiss. "Do you know the way? If not, I would be happy to take you there."

Achan glanced at Bran's companions and found their disdainful expressions fixed on him. Bran might not be angry, but everyone else seemed to be.

"You're not due elsewhere?" Achan asked.

"I ate in the barracks and was heading to my post."

"And your post is?"

"In the great hall, Your Majesty."

"Lead the way, then, Master Rennan."

Bran waved to the squadron. "I'll be along in a bit." He started toward the southeastern gate. His posture seemed to swell, as if walking alongside Achan were some sort of treat.

Shung followed on Achan's left.

"I'm glad to see you've embraced your calling since last we met, Your Majesty," Bran said.

"If I did not, someone else would have." Achan glanced at Bran. "When do you leave for Armonguard?" For this was one of the first orders Achan had given, that Jax mi Katt, Sir Rigil, and Bran return to Prince Oren to assist the southern troops and the Mârad rebels.

"In the morning." Bran led them over the drawbridge of the southeastern gate and followed a wide path through the surrounding vineyard. The nearly ripe grapes made the air smell sweet. Bees gathered around the bunches of fruit, helping themselves to a taste. Achan followed Bran past three women carrying baskets of grapes. All three glared at Achan.

"For Lightness' sake!" Achan stopped and turned to stare after the women. "What is the matter with everyone?"

"It's my fault, I'm afraid, Your Majesty," Bran whispered. "The people have heard whose token you wear and they feel you have . . . um . . . stolen my intended."

"Yes, I am aware of this." Achan huffed a dry laugh. "But Bran . . . *I* stole?" He set his hands on his hips.

Soldiers were one thing, but the peasants too? After all the debate over the best match for Achan—to find the lady who could unite the biggest army, the lady Achan was betrothed to nearly against his will—now the people of Carmine thought he had *stolen* Bran Rennan's love? It was almost funny, especially since Bran had broken his own engagement and stolen the heart of another. Gren Fenny's, to be exact, whom Achan had once longed to wed.

"Well," Achan said, "this is awkward."

Bran looked at his boots. "Yes, Your Majesty."

"I understood you severed your relationship with Lady Averella amicably. Was that not the case?"

"As well as I could. But the people were not told."

For who would tell them? Nobles did not make a habit of announcing their decisions to every peasant in their manor. Still. "Rumor has not circulated?"

"It has, but . . ." He lowered his voice. "Forgive me. The people think I'm covering for the duchess. That she withdrew her consent to make a better match for Averella."

Averella. So informal. A long history of friendship, likely. Similar to what Achan and Gren shared, perhaps. Achan struggled for words that would not insult Bran or Lady Averella. "It is not my wish to marry anyone. I—"

"Completely understood, Your Majesty," Bran said. "I know you did not choose Averella for yourself."

"*I* would never knowingly take another man's love."

Bran's complexion darkened. The comment had been cruel, perhaps. An unnecessary stab. Achan had no future with Gren Fenny—Hoff. He shook the thought away. But Bran had courted Gren, ignorantly perhaps, but still knowing that Achan had loved her.

Bran took a long breath and bowed his head. "You are a noble man, Your Highness."

In word alone. If Bran could bloodvoice, he'd sense how ignoble Achan's thoughts were at present. Oh, pig snout. He did not want an enemy in Bran. He had few friends, as it was. Maybe asking Bran's aid could soften this awkwardness between them. "I should like to meet Lady Averella. She has not returned from her latest hideaway, and the duchess thinks it a dangerous time for her to travel. Tell me, is she comely?"

Bran opened his mouth but did not respond. Then he blinked. "She is beautiful, Your Highness. But I do not know her whereabouts."

They walked again. Bran's claim of Lady Averella's beauty did not mollify Achan. Lady Jaira was beautiful. On the surface. "May I ask what happened between you?"

"We . . . grew apart."

"We? Don't you mean *you*?" In all his time spent *protecting* Gren.

"No, Your Majesty." Bran met Achan's eyes briefly. "It turns out, absence does not always make the heart grow fonder. Sometimes the opposite is true. Averella . . . She found someone else."

Wonderful. So Achan was now betrothed to a lady who loved another. "A lot of that going around."

"Yes," Bran said. "I . . ."

Achan waited, but Bran seemed reluctant to say what was on his mind. "You what?"

Bran swallowed and shuffled his feet on the dirt path. "Forgive me, Your Majesty, but I have no understanding with . . ." He glanced at Achan, then off into the vineyard, cheeks flushed worse than a scandalized maiden. "I made no promise to Madam Hoff. Though I may have unintentionally encouraged her affection, and for that I beg your forgiveness. It was never my motive to woo her."

Achan's jaw stiffened. He glanced at Shung, who stared at the castle as if Achan and Bran didn't exist. "And now?"

Bran straightened, full of courage. "Only with your blessing, Your Highness."

Achan had not expected Bran to be so courteous. Yet as much as he once wanted to strike him for his carelessness toward Gren's life and heart, his anger no longer burned. "I'll give no such blessing until I speak with Gren."

Bran's expression softened. "Thank you, Your Majesty." They continued along the dirt path as it passed into a vineyard. "What of the lady who traveled with you? I heard she dressed as a man."

Achan's eyes narrowed. "What business is that of yours?" Though even as he said it he saw Bran's intention. Bran had as much claim to protect Lady Averella's heart from Achan as Achan had claim to try and protect Gren's.

Bran shrugged. "I only point out that sometimes, when two people spend so much time together, it is difficult not to grow attached, despite how inappropriate the dynamics may be. I simply thought you might understand."

Achan smiled wryly. Bran was a clever one with his tongue. Achan might appoint him an ambassador to somewhere if he ever had peace in the land. "Point taken."

The path cut through the hedge wall that grew around the perimeter of the vineyard. It stretched across a grassy plain toward a group of cottages at the foot of a small hill. The sweet smell of grapes was replaced by that of grass and dust from the path. Asters sprinkled the green landscape in purple and yellow. More bees buzzed from blossom to blossom.

"Duchess Amal assured me that Lady Averella had no attachments. But you suspect she has a suitor?" Achan had believed every word of Duchess Amal's letter in which she had accepted Achan's—or rather Sir Caleb's—proposal. She had assured him her daughter's heart was free. He did not relish the idea of marrying anyone who would be pining for another man. It was bad enough he still longed for Sparrow.

His chest tightened at the thought. Sweet Vrell Sparrow. How he missed her.

Bran stumbled over a pebble on the path and barely managed to catch his footing. "I-I spoke in haste, Your Majesty, and perhaps out of my own chagrin. I beg you forgive me. I've no proof Averella loves another. I suppose my pride clung to such a scenario in hopes that someone had wooed her from me, rather than her simply losing interest."

Achan could certainly relate to a woman's rejection. "Peace, Master Rennan. If you still love the Lady Averella, I'll reject the alliance this moment."

Bran flushed all the way down his neck. "'Tis valiant of you to offer, Your Majesty, but . . ." For several steps neither spoke. Finally, Bran shook his head. "I do not think I loved Averella as much as I loved the idea of her." He took a deep breath. "I wish you both every happiness."

They had closed half the distance between the vineyard and the cottages when two women and a man stepped out onto the road. One of the women squealed and started to run toward them. As she neared, her short, curvy form and chestnut hair came into view.

Gren.

2

Gren collided against Achan in a combination of tackle and hug. He caught her, staggering back to keep upright and wincing as his thigh and shoulder screamed. He breathed in her familiar smell of cinnamon and bitter fulling water.

She looked no different but for her black dress, mourning for her deceased husband. Chestnut hair tied back in a braid that hung past her waist, freckled skin, deep brown eyes framed with thick eyelashes. Her figure had not changed. No lump yet to announce the child growing within.

Achan's chest heaved with a torrent of emotion. He fought it back, took her by the shoulders, and kissed her forehead, a brotherly gesture he forced himself to enact. "Gren, you look radiant. How have you been?"

She didn't seem a bit bothered by his controlled affection. "Terrible." She peeked at Bran, and a rosy flush crept over her cheeks. "Oh, I'm not complaining, Master Rennan. You've been so kind." She looked back to Achan. "It's just that people here think horrible things about me."

Achan held out his arm, but she either didn't notice or didn't know to accept it. "Might I visit your home? I should like to pay my respects to your parents."

"Of course." Gren pointed down the road. "Mother is just there."

Achan glanced up to see Gren's mother crossing the distance toward them. Sir Rigil, the knight Bran squired for, walked at her side. Again Achan offered his arm to Gren, then gave up and took her hand. "Let us save your mother some walking." He tugged her toward her mother, who was now jogging, arms outstretched.

Madam Fenny's fierce hug threatened to squeeze out his lunch. She slowly let go, stroking the back of his head, the sides of his face. "Dear boy. How the gods deceived us all." She took his hands in hers and stepped back. "My, how handsome you look. Gren, doesn't he look handsome?"

"I've always thought so." Gren smiled. "What a fashionable beard too. You've given up shaving?"

Achan grinned at the memory of Gren giving him his first shave after he had nearly killed himself trying. "It's but a mask, I'm afraid. To hide the marks Esek left on me, though I fear it fails." Esek had used Ôwr, Achan's father's sword, to cut a long gash on each of Achan's cheeks. The beard—nothing more than a short dusting of hair—managed to hide the humiliating scars somewhat.

Gren scowled. "That horrible man."

"Perhaps we should move this visit to the Fenny cottage," Sir Rigil said. "That would be most proper." He was dressed impeccably in a dark blue and black doublet, his hair and beard were trimmed short, but something about his swagger and grin reminded Achan of a marauder.

Achan nodded. "Thank you, Sir Rigil."

"Oh!" Gren's mother clapped her hands to her face. "But Jespa will be cross if Grendolyn is late."

"Bran can send word." Sir Rigil raised an eyebrow in Bran's direction. "Run tell Jespa the Crown Prince requested a visit with the Fenny family."

"Yes, sir." Bran bowed, cast a longing look at Gren, then turned and walked back toward the stronghold.

Sir Rigil led the way to the Fennys' cottage. It was a bit larger than their home in Sitna had been, but didn't look all that different. It was strange to see their old table and chairs in a different home. Master Fenny greeted Achan like a long-lost son, then he and Madam Fenny made excuses and left. Sir Rigil urged Shung to join him outside the front door.

Which left Achan and Gren alone. Achan marveled at the irony. The last time he and Gren had been alone in the Fenny home, they'd been scolded. Clearly Achan's station had changed enough that Master Fenny would give him Gren's hand now. Yet it was far too late for that.

Gren broached the subject herself. "You're engaged to Lady Averella Amal." She reached out and touched the bell edge of the maroon sleeve tied to his arm.

"Aye," Achan said. "Though I've never met her."

"Me either." Gren giggled. "As if the heir to Carm would be introduced to a peasant. But I never even saw her."

An awkward silence descended. Gren stood between Achan and the table and chairs. A footstool sat under the window. Would she think to ask him to sit? He scoured his mind for something to say. "Have you heard from Noam?"

She leaned back against the table. "Not since before I was arrested."

The memory of Gren in the Sitna cell filled his mind. "Gren, I'm sorry about this, about everything."

She waved her hand about. "None of it was your fault."

He glanced over her black dress. "It's because of me that Riga is dead."

This sobered Gren. "I do regret that, for Riga wasn't as bad a husband as I feared."

"You cared for him, then?"

"I didn't hate him, though it's a horrible thing to be married off against your will." Her eyes widened. "Oh! For a girl, anyway. I'm sure it'll be different for you."

Achan lowered himself to the stool under the window. A familiar sensation filled his mind. This very spot was where Bran had been sitting when Achan had looked in on Gren during Sir Gavin's lesson. He shook off the strange memory. "All I ever wanted in life was to be a free man, Gren. But it seems I've only exchanged one set of chains for another."

"But you'll be king, Achan. King of all Er'Rets."

He scoffed. "Being a king is not as pleasant as one may think. I never wished for finery and jewels, though I do like the food. You would think I'm free, but I dare not make a decision without consulting my advisors. I had to all but sneak away to have this moment to myself." He sighed. "I am glad to know who I am—who my parents were. But I'd rather not be king." Guilt nagged at everything so many had sacrificed to get him here. "Don't tell anyone."

Gren lunged to the floor beside him, kneeling at his feet. "Oh, Achan. Why have the gods been cruel to us? If only I'd listened to you, we might be living in the forest in that cottage you wanted to build. This might be your child I carry. We could've—"

"Let's not dwell on what was lost." Achan stroked her curls. "I must marry a noblewoman. My advisors chose Lady Averella, and Duchess Amal has given her consent. That's my lot now." He helped her into a chair. "The old Achan would have fled such chains, but the new Achan cannot. For if I were to be so selfish, all Er'Rets would suffer."

Gren smiled. "You're the best of men, Achan."

"'Tis kind of you to say so, Gren, with all I've put you through."

"You've done nothing."

"Your entire family uprooted, your husband killed, you in a cell—and only because Esek wanted to punish me."

"It's Lord Nathak I blame," Gren said. "And don't you blame another. He alone is at fault."

Achan cupped Gren's cheek in his right hand. "Do you care for Bran Rennan?"

She sucked in a sharp breath, eyes bulging.

He smirked. "Do not be frightened, Grenny. I only wish to see you happy."

A soft laugh wisped through her lips. "Isn't it ironic that you'll marry Bran's former love and that I might . . ." She sucked in a long, shaky breath. "You think there's a chance he'd have me? I'm far below his class. My virtue is gone. I don't think a man like him would choose a widowed peasant, yet I'm certain he cares a little. I see it in his eyes."

Achan almost laughed at Gren's babbling. "He asked for my blessing, Gren. Does that please you?"

She clapped her free hand over her mouth and squeezed her eyes closed. This didn't stop the tears from leaking past her eyelids and trickling down her cheeks.

Achan pulled a chair beside hers and sat. He took her into his arms and held her tightly. She sobbed and trembled. He stroked her hair with one hand and rubbed her back with the other. "You're more than what you see of yourself, Gren. Any man would be blessed to have you as his wife."

Gren pulled away, wet face beaming. "You've always been my hero. I've no doubt Lady Averella will love you."

Achan gritted his teeth and recalled Sir Eagan's words. Love was not taking because you wanted, he'd said.

Love was sacrifice.

Achan and Shung returned to the castle and entered his chamber to find Sir Caleb and a boy standing beside his bed, which was now covered in all types of armor and weapons.

"Ah, here he is, Matthias." Sir Caleb set his hand on the boy's shoulder. "Look who has arrived, Your Majesty. I'm sorry Master Ricks didn't stay to speak with you, but he was eager to return to Tsaftown." *Probably feared we'd go back on our word and refuse the boy*, he added silently.

Matthias? The lad's head barely reached Sir Caleb's belt. Big brown eyes peeked out from a shaggy thatch of hair the color of hay.

It all came rushing back. A man had given his youngest son to Achan at a celebration in Tsaftown weeks ago. Achan had refused the idea of taking a slave, but Sir Caleb had explained that a poor man with many children often sent his youngest to work in a noble household. Little Matthias could do no better than to serve his future king.

The boy wore a thin tunic that might have once been pale blue. A frayed hemp belt cinched his waist, accentuating his thin frame. His leggings were the kind Achan used to wear, brown and sagging in the knees. His face was dirty, his fingertips blackened. Odd that Sir Caleb had not yet bathed and redressed the lad. Appearance and decorum were Sir Caleb's specialties, if not obsession.

"Matthias will train to be your valet, Your Majesty," Sir Caleb said. "He will learn to choose your clothing and help you dress. When he is older, we'll teach him to groom you. For now, he can also serve as your page."

Achan should say something. Greet the boy, at least. "How old are you?"

"Seven, sir."

The soft voice melted Achan's heart. How could any man give up such a child, especially one of his own blood?

And seven. So young, yet it was the age most pages began training. Achan wanted to argue—he didn't need anyone to dress or groom him—but little Matthias looked him over with those wide brown eyes and rewarded Achan's silence with a trembling smile. So Achan swallowed his complaints. He was to have a valet.

"We are going to ready the prince for a meeting of the war council, Matthias," Sir Caleb said. "Tomorrow, you and I will have a clothes press and armoire brought up, and I'll show you how to store everything for our journey."

Achan glanced at Shung. *What do you make of all this?*

Shung likes the mouse. His eyes learn much.

A mouse. Did the man have an animal nickname for everyone? *If I am a cham, Sparrow is a fox, and Matthias is a mouse, what is Sir Caleb?*

A lion.

Achan chuckled. Sir Caleb did have a mane of shaggy blond hair. But his wild, penetrating eyes looked more like an owl's.

Sir Caleb waved Achan over. "Your Highness, come take off those clothes—which everyone knows you wore yesterday. Matthias and I will see you ready for dinner."

Achan sighed and began to unlace his doublet. He inched toward Sir Caleb, hoping to get the shirt off by himself, at least. With every other step, his left thigh cried out.

"It's imperative, Matthias, that the Crown Prince not wear the same ensemble in the same week. You must see that his clothing alternates and is clean and pressed, so that he always looks his best."

Achan snorted. "Even on the battlefield?" He envisioned men dying while he was busy changing into a fresh shirt.

"On the battlefield as well." Sir Caleb pushed Achan's hands away and finished unlacing the doublet. "As crown prince, and later, king, your presence must instill consistency and order. If you appear bedraggled, your men will feel all the more bedraggled. If you look sharp and rested, you will boost their spirits." Sir Caleb slid the doublet off Achan's shoulders and laid it on the table.

Achan rolled his sore shoulder. He wasn't sure he agreed with this logic. If he were a soldier, he'd want to fight alongside his king. And if his king looked like he'd been eating grapes all day, Achan wouldn't feel much like risking his life. Sometimes Sir Caleb's obsessions were just that.

Achan started to unlace his shirt placket, but Sir Caleb swatted his hands. Achan dropped his arms to his sides and glanced across the room. Movement below caused him to look down. Matthias now stood at Sir Caleb's side. Achan winked at the lad, earning a smile in return.

"Normally, we wouldn't dress the prince until he had bathed, Matthias, but since he is late and we have little time, we will not concern ourselves with that at the moment."

Matthias nodded as though he understood perfectly, yet Achan bet the boy hadn't bathed in over a week. Those rags he wore were probably his only clothes. Achan would have to see that Matthias got something new to wear.

Sir Caleb and Matthias dressed Achan in a green ensemble trimmed in gold ribbon and frills. Achan blew out a long breath and stared up at the frescoed ceiling.

When Sir Caleb finished cinching him into the fitted doublet, he patted Achan on the back. "Put on your brown boots."

Achan found the boots beside his bed. He sat down and pulled them on.

"Little Cham."

Achan turned to see Shung holding Lady Averella's dress sleeve in his scarred hand.

Oh, yes. Mustn't go anywhere without that.

"Do you know what this is, Matthias?" Sir Caleb snatched the sleeve from Shung and walked toward the bed.

"No, sir."

"It is a token from Lady Averella Amal, the prince's intended bride."

A yoke Achan must wear at all times, a reminder to all who saw him that he'd made an alliance with Carm Duchy, a promise to wed Duchess Amal's eldest daughter in exchange for Carm joining them in the battle for Armonguard.

Sir Caleb threaded the sleeve around Achan's left bicep and tied it snugly.

Achan glanced at the knight. "Have you met Lady Averella, Sir Caleb?"

"No. It's been twenty years since I attended court."

"Shung has seen her. First year squiring for Koyukuk."

Achan met Shung's black eyes. "You dog! Why didn't you say?"

Shung shrugged. "There is little to say."

"Tell me." Achan relished any word about his bride to be. He couldn't even find a painting of her in Granton Castle. With all the frescoes in this place, someone had to have painted the heir to Carm somewhere.

Unless she was too hideous. Yet Bran had said otherwise.

"A tournament in Nesos," Shung said. "Saw her from a distance. Sir Marken Hamartano remarked on the lady to the other knights."

Achan stiffened at the mention of the Hamartano name. "What did he say?"

"Shung will not repeat it. He favored her. Though not honorable, his regard. Sir Rigil rebuked him. Remarked on the lady's wit. And Shung could see the lady was fair. Small, like Duchess Amal."

Achan had heard this much. At least she wouldn't outweigh him. And if crude men thought enough of her to make crass remarks, she must be as beautiful as Bran had claimed. There was a chance he might like Lady Averella. Especially if she looked anything like her mother, for Duchess Amal, though twice Achan's age, was one of the most enchanting women he'd ever met, both in appearance and countenance.

But was that enough? How could he have pledged his life to a stranger?

He should be free to court *Sparrow,* to choose her as a bride. That Sparrow was a stray should not matter. But he'd already agreed to marry Lady Averella, given his father's signet ring as a token of his promise. It would be dishonorable to go back on his word.

Besides, he had decided to trust the One God, Arman, with his life. He had to stop worrying over things like this and serve Arman with each breath.

"Time to go, Your Highness," Sir Caleb said. "The men are waiting."

• • •

It was no use.

Achan opened his eyes and glanced around the table. He and the war council had assembled in one of the secret rooms outside Duchess Amal's study, a room only slightly bigger than the table they sat around. A small hearth lay cold along one wall. A lamp on the table cast golden light over the walls and the faces at the table. Achan sat at one end, Sir Gavin at the other. To Achan's left sat Inko and Kurtz. To his right, Sir Eagan and Sir Caleb, who had brought a pile of scrolls.

"I still cannot sense either of them," Achan said. "I've never been able to."

"Are you blocked from them the way you are with Vrell?" Sir Eagan's raspy voice pulled Achan's gaze to the man's lazy blue eyes.

"No. I can *sense* her, just not push past her shields. But of Esek and his father I find no trace. As if they don't exist."

"Esek is dead, then," Sir Caleb said, looking up from a scroll in his hands. "But what of Lord Nathak?"

Sir Gavin tugged the end of his braided white beard. "Lord Nathak has likely used some sort of dark magic."

"If so, I fear he would have been teaching his son to be doing the same," Inko said.

"The prince cut off the man's arm, he did." Kurtz chopped the edge of his hand against Inko's arm. "Can't have lived through that, eh?"

"Men have lived through worse," Sir Gavin said.

Kurtz's grin dimpled his cheeks under his trimmed blond beard. "Not much worse than losing a limb, eh?"

"Could we locate a personal item?" Sir Eagan asked.

Sir Gavin nodded. "Ôwr should be enough to bridge a connection. The sword belonged to Esek for years."

"I left it in my chamber," Achan said, drawing everyone's gaze back to him. "And I have nothing that belongs to Lord Nathak."

"Continue to try to access their minds, Your Majesty," Sir Eagan said. "It is likely one of them may let down their guard at some point."

Achan glared at the lamplight reflecting on the tabletop. "I thought the same of Sparrow, and *she* has not lowered her guard."

No one answered this statement, and Achan felt foolish for mentioning Sparrow yet again.

"We received another suggestion for a general, Your Highness." Sir Caleb passed a scroll to Sir Eagan, who passed it to Achan. "Lord Orson had requested that his son, Koyukuk Orson, lead Berland's army."

Achan glanced at the scroll, then around the table. "That seems like a reasonable request."

"Sir Koyukuk is being young for a general," Inko said.

Sir Gavin shifted, and the lamp in the center of the table blocked Achan's view of the old knight's face. "Aye, Inko, but he's well-trained."

"That gives us how many generals?" Achan racked his memory to recall all the names. "Five?"

"Six, Your Highness." Sir Caleb shuffled through his scrolls. "Prince Oren leads Arman Duchy. Tristan Loam is in charge of Carm. Baldwin Agros, Allown. Chaz Dromos leads the Mârad rebels. Keano Pitney leads Nahar. And now Sir Koyukuk over Berland. That's roughly . . . twelve thousand seven hundred men."

Achan sought a reaction from the expressions around the table. "Is that a lot? It seems like a lot." Many more than the three hundred or so they had freed from Ice Island not long ago.

"If we can get them all together, aye, 'tis a formidable army," Sir Gavin said. "Though at least thirty thousand more live in Er'Rets who are capable of fighting. Why they do not join us—whether they choose not to fight or to serve one of our adversaries—I cannot say."

"We should be finding one more general soon. Seven is a stronger number than six," Inko said.

Achan slid the scroll back to Sir Caleb and peered past the lamp to Sir Gavin. "Did we determine the location of Esek's army?"

"Our scouts last saw Captain Keuper in Har Sha'ar," Sir Gavin said. "Seems to be the same group Esek was with outside of Mitspah."

"But no sign of Esek with them?"

"No, Your Majesty."

"And the other scouts?"

"No reports as of yet. And I've not heard back from the man I sent to the Sideros Forest. We must be on our guard when we head that way."

"When will that be?"

"As soon as possible."

Achan frowned. He was just getting used to Granton Castle. "And what of this New Council?"

"Much news," Sir Eagan said. "Duchess Amal has discovered through Lord Levy that a man called the Hadad is the new chairman of the council."

A tremor squeezed Achan's chest. "The man who spoke to me in that pit in Barth! He took control of the Council?"

"From what Lord Levy claimed, the Hadad has had a longstanding relationship with him and Lord Falkson."

"So he has been plotting this overthrow with Falkson?" Inko asked.

"So it seems." Sir Eagan ran a hand over his thin, black hair and glanced at Sir Gavin. The men exchanged something between them, an understanding with their eyes.

"What," Achan asked. "Is there something more?"

Sir Gavin took a deep breath. "We simply wonder how long this man has been scheming. How deep and far his designs may go."

A silence hung over the table, as if Achan had suddenly lost his hearing. He glanced from face to face, taking in solemn expressions and averted eyes. Realization hit him like a fist to the jaw. "You think he killed my parents."

3

"We've always known someone else was involved, someone with a powerful bloodvoicing ability," Sir Gavin said. "This Hadad fits that description."

Achan's thoughts circled. The Hadad had bloodvoiced him not long ago, asking him to join him, to betray Sir Gavin, to turn from Arman. "Why would he want me to join him?"

"Because you are powerful," Sir Eagan said. "Because you are crown prince. And because if you join him, he does not have to figure out how to kill you."

Achan slouched in his chair and rubbed his face. "How can we know for sure he killed my parents?"

Sir Gavin lifted one shoulder. "We can't."

Achan slapped his hand on the table. "There must be a way. Sir Eagan, the trick with touch and giving me your thoughts—could I use that in reverse?"

"You cannot take a man's thoughts. Only receive those that are offered."

"I could ask him."

"Your Highness, please." Sir Eagan squinted, making him look all the more serious. "Do not toy with this man. His mystery hides his true power from us, but if you go to him, you make yourself vulnerable in displaying your weakness."

Achan wanted to yell but kept his tone civil. "Why is asking a question weak?"

"Because you reveal he has something you want. That gives him power over you. Do not let him suspect you have anything more than indifference for him."

"But if he killed my parents . . ."

"I know. Believe me, no one wants justice for the king and queen more than I." For Sir Eagan had been King Axel's Shield. "But vengeance belongs to Arman. We must focus on the path He has set before us and nothing else."

"But it won't hurt to pinch off the Hadad if we get the chance, eh?" Kurtz winked at Achan.

"Who serves on this New Council?" Sir Gavin asked.

Sir Eagan consulted Sir Caleb's scroll. "Lord Levy, Dovev Falkson, and an Eben named Rapha Gibbor. Duchess Amal suspects there are more, but the title 'Council of Seven' has not been mentioned. The New Council may have only four members."

"Lord Hamartano was not mentioned?"

"No," Sir Eagan said. "But if what you told us about his leaving Jaelport was true, he now serves Lord Falkson and the black knights. He would no longer hold rank of his own unless the Hadad gives him one."

"Which reminds me, Your Highness," Sir Caleb said. "You should begin lessons with Duchess Amal tomorrow, if she has time. The sooner you learn to storm, the better."

Achan's heartbeat quickened. He was going to learn to storm. Finally.

Achan shivered in the dark, stone passage. After the meeting, Anillo, Duchess Amal's steward, had offered to give Achan a tour of the hidden passages within the walls of Granton Castle. Shung, of course, had come along.

They had begun their journey in Duchess Amal's study, inched their way along the second level of the great hall, climbed a tower stairs, and were now stepping through a panel that slid to one side and emptied into Achan's bedchamber.

Achan stepped inside. The secret corridors had been cramped and narrow. He stretched his arms out wide now that there was space. "The stairwell we took. Does that lead to the first level?"

"It does, Your Majesty." Anillo slid the panel closed. His white hair belied his lithe body. "But you must promise not to go exploring without a guide. I would be happy to show you more."

"Perhaps another time. It has been a long day and I require rest."

"As you wish, Your Majesty." Anillo bowed and departed through the regular door.

Achan sat on his bed and pulled off his boots. It was not even time for dinner, yet he was ready to sleep.

A whimpering pup woke Achan. He blinked, found his surroundings dark, and sat up in a panic. The pale moonlight filtering through the privy door proved he was still in his chamber in Carmine. What hour was it?

Another whimper. The sound was coming from the far corner of the room. Not a puppy, though. A weeping child.

Understanding fell on Achan. "Matthias, come here."

The sound turned to sniffling. Bare feet padded over the floor until Matthias's silhouette stood at Achan's bedside. The moonlight shone on the lad's tear-streaked cheeks.

Achan's chest tightened. "You miss your father?"

Matthias sniffed. "Yes, sir. And Mama. And Linos. The bed is so big. I used to share one with my brothers . . . before."

"How many brothers?"

"Three, sir. But Armas had his own bed."

"So, three of you in one bed?"

"Yes, sir."

"Must have been cozy."

Achan got up and dragged Matthias's straw mattress across the room until it was beside his bed. "Get in."

Matthias scrambled onto the mattress and pulled the blanket up to his chin.

Achan climbed back into bed and propped his head on his fist, looking down on the boy's face. "Who's Linos?"

"My brother closest to me, sir. He's lived nine years."

"I'm sure you'll see him again."

Matthias turned wide eyes to Achan. "Father said I might never see any of them again."

"Oh. Well, I can't promise you will, Matthias, but I'll do all I can to see it happen."

Matthias hummed and squirmed. "Thank you, sir."

"Now go to sleep."

"Yes, sir."

The next time Achan woke, voices were coming out of the privy.

He sat up, squinting in the dim light. Shung's pallet, which had been dragged in front of the entrance to keep Achan from sneaking out alone, lay empty.

The distant sound of a trumpet tooted. He slipped out of bed and walked to the privy. Shung stood at one of the privy's arrow loops, an arm around Matthias's waist. The boy stood on the ledge of the hole. Both peered out the northwestern arrow loop.

The trumpet sang again, this time louder. Men were yelling. Horses whinnying. Achan stepped inside and wrinkled his nose at the rank smell. "What is it?"

Shung turned his hairy profile to Achan. "Castle under attack."

A prickle scuttled up Achan's neck. He lunged to the northeastern arrow loop and peeked out. Thick, black smoke filled the pale, predawn sky. The northern vineyards were ablaze, as was the roof of the stables. A man and woman were setting horses off at a run from the stable doors. Two other men stood on ladders fighting to get the fire out. One shoveled off the burning thatch with a pitchfork, while the other heaved shovelfuls of dirt up on the roof.

Movement beyond the stables caught Achan's gaze. Men dressed in black scaled the wall.

"They're using the fire as a diversion." Achan's heart raced. "We must dress for battle." He ran back into his chamber, opened the armoire, grabbed his padded stockings and jerked them on. They sagged around his waist. He snatched his gambeson and pulled it over his head. The satin felt cool and soft on his bare skin. "Shung, help me."

By the time Achan's eyes came through the opening of the gambeson, Shung and Matthias were at his side. Matthias fumbled with the points so much that Shung had to do them. The lad had memorized the order in which Achan's armor was to be attached, so now he went about laying items out in a row on the floor. Shung held up Achan's mail trousers.

Achan put a foot into one leg of the trousers. *Sir Caleb, the castle is under attack. The enemy scales the northern inner curtain wall while our soldiers work to quench the stable fire.*

We are aware of the attack. I'll tell Captain Loam about the men scaling the wall.

Achan seethed inside. *Sir Caleb, this is the second time the enemy has attacked while I slept. You will wake me next time, is that clear?*

Of course, Your Majesty.

Achan was dressed in all but his gauntlets, gorget, and helm when the doors burst inward and Sir Caleb strode inside. He fixed his owl-like eyes on Achan. "Oh, no, Your Majesty. You're not going out."

"Of course I am." Achan waved Matthias toward the gorget.

"Captain Loam and his men are meeting the threat. There is no need for your assistance."

Maybe not, but Achan felt he should still go out, make an appearance. He set his jaw and motioned for Matthias to bring the gorget. "Is it Lord Nathak? Esek? The Hadad?"

"Too early to say. No one has made any demands. It appears they approached under cover of night and hid in the vineyards, waiting until first light to attack. Shung, take the prince through the passageway to one of the secret meeting rooms until we know exactly what we're dealing with."

Achan stared Sir Caleb down. "What kind of ruler hides when the battle begins? Isn't this my war?"

"Do not argue, Your Highness. Matthias, you go too."

The boy set the gorget down on the bed. "Yes, sir."

Shung strode to the secret panel on the wall and tugged it open.

Achan drew a long breath in through his nose. He should be outside with his men, meeting this enemy head on. He glanced at Sir Caleb, knowing the man wouldn't relent. Should Achan continue to state his concerns? He felt like a child who must wait until he was older to play this game.

Only this was no game. It was war. His war. He would always be much younger than his advisors. He needed to take charge before they all got into the habit of ruling him.

Though his heart pounded like a hammer against iron, he said, "Sir Caleb, I will not hide like a coward. I am Arman's chosen. I will fight."

Sir Caleb raised his bushy blond eyebrows. "I am also Arman's chosen. My purpose is to protect you. In that one matter I am free to disobey you. I'm sorry, Your Highness, but Arman outranks you."

Achan shot a long glare at Sir Caleb and clomped toward the secret doorway, grabbing his helm on the way. He turned sideways to step through the narrow opening, but his breastplate scraped against the doorframe, knocking him off-balance. He stumbled against the far wall of the passage.

He took a few short breaths to calm his frothing nerves, then sidestepped toward the arrow loop and leaned into the V-shaped crevice, hoping for another glimpse of the battle.

The stable fire had been extinguished. No sign of fighting in the inner bailey, though a few peasants and soldiers lay injured. Beyond the curtain walls, the northern vineyard smoldered, clouding the hundreds of soldiers clad in red or black capes. It *was* the New Kingsguard—troops loyal to Esek. But was Esek or someone else their leader?

"Little Cham, come."

Achan pulled back from the arrow loop. The panel to his room was closed. Shung's shadowy form blocked the flickering light from the torch he held in the passageway. Matthias stood between them. At least the boy would be safe. But Achan would not start this war in hiding. He knew not whether Shung would obey him over Sir Caleb.

Best not to put the man in the position to choose.

He put on his helm and followed Shung down the narrow passage, slowing as they took the awkward steps that led underneath Achan's privy antechamber. Achan ran his gloved hand along the low ceiling so his helm would not scrape against the stone.

The end of Ôwr's scabbard tapped against each step behind him. Achan pushed the hilt down to keep it from hitting the steps. Shung paused in the small space at the bottom and looked back at Achan before starting up on the other side of the privy.

Did he suspect Achan wanted to slip away?

Once the passage leveled out, it was easier to move. Achan paused at each arrow loop and looked out on the distant battle. He should try again to use his bloodvoice to look in on Lord Nathak, see if he was out there commanding the New Kingsguard soldiers. Achan knew better than to walk and watch at the same time, though.

Shung stopped at the corner before the hidden tower stairs. He turned, waiting for Matthias and Achan to catch up. "Not far now."

Achan swallowed his regret and nodded, hoping Shung would understand why Achan needed to join the battle.

Achan's chambers were on the fourth level. The secret meeting chambers were on the third. Shung led them down one flight and stepped out onto the third level. He moved quickly along the western wall, south. Achan lagged behind, pausing at another arrow loop.

Three bodies lay on the inner bailey ground below. Two cloaked in black, one in red. Red-caped men crouched in clusters on the sentry walk behind each battlement. A good sign. Captain Loam's men must have stopped the infiltration and pushed the battle out to the vineyards.

"Little Cham."

Achan stepped back to see Shung waiting at the top of the next flight of steps that passed under another privy. If Achan's memory was correct, there were two such detours along this wall, then a long stretch leading to the secret rooms near Duchess Amal's study.

Achan moved on. "Captain Loam has taken the battle outside the fortress."

"Good. It will end soon." Shung took the steps slowly. Matthias followed, then Achan. When they reached the bottom, sure enough, Shung looked back to meet Achan's gaze before starting up the next flight.

Achan turned and practically crawled away up the steps. At the top, the light from the arrow loop lit enough of his surroundings that he was able to skip sideways along the corridor until he reached the tower. He took the stairs down too fast, stumbled, and slid down six or seven steps on his knees. He grasped at the wall and managed to catch his footing. He froze a moment, heart dancing, listening for Shung's voice.

Nothing.

He checked to make sure Ôwr was still at his side, then, with one hand on the wall, he took the steps one at a time, thankful for arrow loops and the pale light that seeped through them. Blessed sun. 'Twas dawn, and none could refute it. The curse of Darkness had not reached this place. Not yet, anyway.

Achan's temples twinged. *Shung Noatak.*

And there it came. Achan ignored Shung's knock and continued on until the light from the last arrow loop faded. He hesitated, weighing his options, unwilling to admit he should have stayed with Shung. He wanted the first floor. If there were no more arrow loops, did that mean he was underground? Or did the first floor not have arrow loops? He wished he'd been more observant when he'd last walked outside Granton Castle.

He pictured the layout of the castle in his mind. As long as he chose the right level to exit onto, he would need to turn south, or right, which should lead him to the great hall.

Unless the stairwell let him out in a different direction.

He inched down the stairs in the darkness, keeping a hand on the outer wall to be sure not to miss the opening. His leather glove scraped over the rough stone like a serrated knife cutting a loaf of bread. The wall fell away. Achan gripped the corner with his fingers and walked them around the edge to lead the rest of his body down the next corridor.

A soft beam of light shot out from the left a few paces ahead. Achan moved toward the light and found an indentation in the stone wall like an arrow loop, only this one looked in on a room. He hunched down and peered through the slot into an empty solar. Peek holes. A clever way to learn more about guests, though Achan's stomach clenched at the thought of anyone looking into his chambers. Perhaps later he and Shung could find any viewing places that looked in on his chambers and block them.

He stepped back, annoyed that neither Anillo nor the duchess had mentioned the peek holes. Surely they hadn't been spying on him.

Achan followed the dark passageway, keeping his right hand on the wall. Anillo had said a passage led into the great hall. Achan would likely have to turn right at some point to walk down the dais wall. Maybe the passage let out under the dais as it had in Tsaftown.

The wall under his right fingers vanished. He stopped and felt for walls around him. Yes. A corridor spilt off to the right here. Achan turned, walking slowly, scouring his surroundings for any sliver of light. Logic should put a door somewhere along the left wall, but he did not find one.

The wall disappeared again, as did the floor. His knees buckled and his right hand waved for purchase. His left hand and knees broke his fall, thudding against dirt. The musty smell had changed to the bitter scent of soil. He groped for the wall, stretched as far as he could until his fingers found a soft surface. Strange.

He popped back to his haunches and pulled off his gloves. He touched the wall again, scratched the ground beneath him with a fingernail. Packed dirt. Had he left the castle?

He took a deep breath, mind sifting through his options. The idea of following this tunnel blindly left him hesitant, yet so did backtracking when he obviously had the layout wrong in his head.

He could use his bloodvoicing power to leave his body and try to see what was above him, though that would be risky. Not only would there be no one around to wake him if he couldn't get back to his body, who would know to come looking for him here?

He should go back to Shung.

Failure vexed him. Sir Caleb would be cross no matter when he returned. Best have some manner of success to show for it. Prove he was right? That he could fight alongside his own men?

Stubborn man.

He smiled at the small voice in the back of his mind. Something Sparrow had said to him once. In fact, she had called him stubborn in one way or another almost daily. He had always thought it odd, coming from a boy. Though her odd words and ways were not so strange for a woman.

A crick in his ankles brought him back to the present. He would try the Veil. Since one should always sit or recline to enter the Veil, he twisted his sword out of the way and sat down. He shifted to lean against the dirt wall of the tunnel and stretched out his legs. A long breath filled his nostrils with the scent of soil. Straight up, then straight back down. No distractions. He focused and drifted up.

Through a black void. Memories from his time in Darkness chipped at his thoughts. He ignored the temptation to despair and held fast to his concentration.

Up. Straight up.

Light blinded him. He recoiled and found himself outdoors, floating a foot above a grassy lawn. A wide shadow darkened the grass a few feet away. He floated into the shadow, and the brightness of the sun dimmed, allowing him to take stock of his surroundings.

His mind's eye abided in the shadow of Ryson Tower, to the left of the stronghold and inside the inner bailey. Indeed, the tunnel had taken him out of Granton Castle. If he followed it, he would likely exit the stronghold altogether at some point.

He floated up to look over the curtain wall. Smoke billowed in the western fields and beyond. The invaders had set fire to the vineyards and several cottages. Both baileys were deserted but for some injured men and those caring for them. A couple dozen bowmen patrolled the curtain walls. Beyond, a fierce battle raged. Achan floated toward it.

Duchess Amal.

Achan let himself drift, momentarily shocked by circumstance. He had been expecting to hear from Shung or Sir Caleb, not Duchess Amal.

He opened his mind to her at once. *My lady?*

Your Highness. You have us all affright. Are you safe?

I am. I . . . got turned around in the passageway. A heaviness grew in Achan's mind. Never before had any lie—let alone such a small one—come with such instant remorse.

Going off alone is unwise, Your Highness.

Achan closed his mind, ashamed to treat the duchess so rudely, but unwilling to give up his attempt to help his men. If he could drift closer to the battle, perhaps he could see their leader. Why had he not tried this before?

But when he looked for the distant battle, he only saw sky. He whirled around. Nothing but sky in every direction. He looked down. All of Carmine stretched out like a map below, Granton Castle a speck under his transparent boots.

How had he gotten so far up?

The shadows of clouds dotted the land below in puffy shadows. How small the battle seemed from such a height. How small everything seemed.

Arman, you are great indeed to have created all this. To love each of us so completely when there are so many of us and we are so very small.

Achan stared at the awesome sight for a long time before jolting back to reality. He tried to float down but found he had no control of himself. He concentrated hard. Willed himself back to his body.

Nothing happened.

A gust of cold blew over him, raising gooseflesh on his arms. Sir Gavin had warned him not to leave his body. Why had he been so cocksure as to ignore the Great Whitewolf?

Stubborn man. What if he couldn't get back?

He called to Duchess Amal. *My lady, I am lost.*

Why did you close your mind? Are you in danger?

No, my lady. I mean, I'm not certain. I entered the Veil. I hoped to see the enemy, but I drifted up and can't get back.

Where is your body? Your physical body?

In an underground tunnel beneath the inner bailey, just outside the great hall.

One moment.

Achan's gaze locked onto a flock of birds below him. How strange to see flying birds from above.

I have found your body, Your Highness. You say you drifted straight up?

Very far up. I cannot control my movement.

I am coming.

Carmine seemed even smaller below him now. He saw movement. Another bird? The mist of a cloud?

Then he saw her. Duchess Amal, soaring toward him like an eagle diving for a fish. Her arms at her sides, her body straight, her hair and dress smooth from her apparent speed. Her eyes fixed on his. She stopped before him and her hair and gown billowed out around her, floating on air.

She held out her hand. *Shall we, Your Highness?*

Breathless, he took her hand in his. *Thank you.*

She tucked his hand around her arm and pulled them down. Slowly. Down. Through a misty cloud.

Down. Toward Granton Castle. The stronghold grew beneath their feet.

Achan could see the battle to the west. They drifted back toward the inner bailey, to the left of the great hall. The ground came closer. Nearer. His feet were almost there.

They passed through the dirt. The odd sensation choked Achan. All light vanished. Down. Down.

Darkness.

How far? Did Duchess Amal know exactly where his body lay? What if they missed it and traveled all the way to the Lowerworld?

He concentrated on his body, hoping that might help the duchess somehow. *Arman, help me find it.*

Achan's soul found its home in the wheeze of a sharp breath. He opened his eyes to blackness. The musty dirt and cool air were familiar, safe, reassuring.

This is one of the secret entrances to the castle, Duchess Amal said to his mind. *There are two ways out. Back the way you came. Or, if you continue on, you will come to a ladder that leads to a door in the ground. You are closer to the castle than to the trapdoor. Shall I inform Sir Caleb which direction you will go so he can come meet you?*

Achan heaved in another long, musty breath. *I will continue to the trapdoor, my lady. I must . . . complete my task.*

Fare you well, then.

Thank you, my lady.

Achan heaved himself up onto shaky legs, berating himself for such stupidity. The experience had drained his strength. At least he knew where he was headed now. He also knew there was no need to go there. The battle was far away, and Sir Caleb would likely be waiting, armed with a sour expression and hefty lecture.

Achan found his gloves on the floor and tucked them through his belt, checking again to make sure Ôwr was still there. He reached out until he found the dirt wall, then crept forward, keeping his right hand on the wall and his left hand stretched out to the blackness before him. Except for the occasional wooden post, the wall remained smooth dirt.

A needle pricked Achan's temple. *Sir Caleb Agros.*

Achan clenched every muscle. He should answer. He'd been foolish to sneak away. Even more foolish to leave his body. Sir Caleb's pointing that out would not change anything. It would only make Achan feel more inane. Perhaps he deserved such humiliation.

Sir Caleb did not enjoy losing control of a situation. Knowing Achan was safe would relieve his fears for a moment but—

Achan's hand struck something solid. He ran his fingers along wide, smooth wood. They traced a cobwebbed corner, slid down a few inches and met another horizontal bar that went back the other way. A square.

He patted the wood with both hands. Wooden rungs, thick with cobwebs, ran up the wall. His stomach danced. He had found the ladder.

He climbed slowly, pausing after each grip to raise one hand above his head and feel for the ceiling.

Sir Caleb Agros.

Achan would deal with Sir Caleb once he was outside and standing on solid ground. *I am well, Sir Caleb, I'll speak with you in a moment.* He sent the thought without opening his mind to a reply. He'd never done that particular feat, not to his knowledge anyway.

He rather liked it.

After a dozen rungs, his fingers broke through a crusty layer of cobwebs and touched spindly roots. He traced every inch of the ceiling until his fingers hit an obstruction. Iron. A ringlatch of some sort. He pulled it toward him. It barely moved, then suddenly snapped back.

The ceiling shifted, raining dirt and dry bits of grass over his armor. A sliver of white light increased his already-pounding heartbeat. When his eyes had adjusted, he pushed the door open and climbed up another rung.

He peeked out onto grassy ground. Thick vines hung overhead, heavy with plump red grapes. He let the door fall back against the grass. The air was cool in his lungs, but thick with smoke.

Achan wiggled and squeezed to get his armor through the narrow opening, thankful no one was around to witness his ungraceful movements. As he stood, his helm tangled in the vines overhead. His location was a vineyard, completely outside the stronghold. The outer curtain wall loomed a few yards ahead. He shut the trapdoor and could barely see the rectangular outline in the thick grass.

"This way!" a nasally voice said.

Achan straightened, ready to meet Sir Caleb, Shung, and whatever soldiers they'd brought along. But the voice had come from the opposite direction of the curtain wall.

A prickle scuttled up his spine. He crouched, hand on Ôwr's hilt, and listened to the crunch of leaves, the rustling of vines, every sound muffled through his steel helm.

A man screamed. "She bit me!"

"Stop her! She's getting away!"

Footsteps rained over the ground. Achan peered under the vines. A woman ran his way. He could see her from the waist down only, her red skirt a flutter of fabric as she ran. Mere feet from his location, she tripped and fell, skidding over the leafy grass and into the stand of a trellis. Her blonde curls tangled over her face.

Achan ran to her and grabbed her arms, but she screamed and crawled away. "Leave me alone!"

He recognized her immediately. It was Duchess Amal's second eldest. "Lady Gypsum. It's Achan. Prince Gidon, I mean." It was still difficult for him to claim *that* name. He smiled and held out his hand. "May I offer my assistance?"

She grabbed his hand. "Your Highness . . ." She panted and he pulled her up. "There are bad men . . ." She glanced back the way she'd come. "They are coming. They took me, and I . . ."

Achan bent down and spotted two sets of legs, one closer than the other.

"My lady," he whispered. "Your dress will give you away should these cretins think to crouch as I have. There is a trapdoor here." He scanned the ground. "Somewhere."

"Yes, under the marker." She stepped to the next row and reached up to the trellis where a piece of faded, frayed cloth was tied. She crouched underneath it and ran her hands over the grass. Her finger hooked around something, and she pulled. The next row away, the trapdoor popped open.

"I see her! Who's got her?"

"Hurry, my lady." Achan grabbed her hands and lowered her into the hole. Her dress billowed on the grass like a tent. "Have your feet found the ladder?"

"Yes. You may let go now."

He released her hands and started to tuck her skirt down the hole, but her quick descent dragged her dress with her. "How will you see, my lady?"

She smiled and Achan saw Duchess Amal's beauty in her young face. "This is my home, Your Highness. I know my way."

"Arman be with you then."

She frowned. "You are not coming?"

"You there?" A man's deep voice yelled. "Have you seen a little lady?"

Achan kicked the trapdoor closed. A burly man dressed in black armor stood on his row at least ten yards away. Achan ducked under the trellis on his right, and under the next few trellises, hoping to lure the man away from the trapdoor.

"Soldiers!" a voice yelled in the distance. "Retreat!"

Likely Sir Caleb come to fetch his headstrong prince. Achan stopped, listening for the big man's footsteps. He squatted and looked toward the castle. Sure enough, a dozen or more sets of black boots charged into the vineyard near the trapdoor, which was now rows down from his position.

Achan spun slowly on his toes and met a set of thick legs. The man in black armor stood over him, swinging a mace above his head. Achan popped to his feet and reeled backwards. He tried to draw Ôwr, but stumbled. The man sent his mace flying.

Achan ducked, yet the mace struck his helm on the left side, just above his ear. Pain exploded in his head. He hit the ground on his back, nauseated. Trying to get up, he bumped against a trellis. Sick. Dizzy. Unable to sit. Death was coming. Yet . . . Where had the man gone?

Achan rolled to his back. The sky spun above him. Strange to see it from below now. He sucked air through his nose so he wouldn't vomit.

His vision blurred. He should bloodvoice someone. Tell them of Lady Gypsum. Hot pain swelled over him like a wave in the delta. He held his breath. Was he burning? He reached up to feel the fire, but his hand did not move.

He finally released a long breath. The pain overtook him, darkening his vision like a door closing out all light.

Part 2

Vrell

4

"Are you sure it's wise, m'lady?"

"What are you so worried about, Syrah?" Vrell brushed past her maidservant and turned to the door to the receiving room, squeezing her hands together. The room, wallpapered in elegant paintings, held only a sideboard, four chairs, and a short table. She hoped Jax would be comfortable, despite the diminutive nature of the chairs. "There is nothing clandestine about receiving an honorable soldier when a chaperone is present."

"I'm hardly a reputable chaperone, m'lady. I doubt the duchess would approve."

"My mother will not find out, Syrah, because you will not tell her."

Syrah curtsied. "Yes'm."

Vrell sighed, frustrated she had spoken to Syrah so. "Forgive my tone, dearest. My daily dance on a pincushion is making me behave badly. But without this opportunity, I do not know what I shall—"

A knock rattled the door. Vrell smoothed her skirt and straightened, aggravating the wound in her side. She held her breath against the pain, weighing whether or not she could handle such a posture for the entire conversation.

What was she thinking? This was Jax, her friend. She nodded at Syrah and slouched, instantly relieving her side.

Syrah opened the door to Jax mi Katt, a giant man who stood over seven feet tall. He ducked inside, and his long braids swung out before him. As always, he wore a red scarf over his head like a marauder. A bushy beard covered his face. Even indoors he wore daggers and axes strapped to his legs in leather sheaths.

Jax's large brown eyes settled on Vrell, and a rangy smile parted his beard. "Hello there."

Vrell beamed at her old friend until Sir Rigil entered behind him. What was this? Why bring Sir Rigil along?

Sir Rigil, a knight in his early thirties, looked small next to Jax. He wore blue and black, the colors of Zerah Rock, his home town. His hair was blond and cut short, except for the top, which swooped back in a lazy wave over his head. His short sideburns and beard were red.

Until Achan's true heritage became known, Sir Rigil had been the most eligible bachelor in all Er'Rets. Years ago, Vrell had mistaken Sir Rigil's chivalry for romantic interest. But over time he had become like an older brother. And now, being Sir Eagan's half-brother, she realized he was her half-uncle.

All this was unbeknownst to him, of course, as Sir Eagan had not publicly claimed Vrell as his child.

Jax laid a hand on Vrell's shoulder heavily.

She hugged his waist. "I've missed you, Jax."

"Well, bless my belt! Lady Averella home at last." Sir Rigil took both Vrell's hands and squeezed. "I've asked your mother about you time and again, but she would not—"

"Sir Rigil, Jax. Please, sit." Vrell motioned to the chairs. "Are you thirsty? Syrah, offer the men something to drink."

Syrah rushed forward, but Sir Rigil waved a hand. "We've just come from the great hall. Why have you not eaten there? I hope you are not ill."

"Please, Sir Rigil. There is a reason I invited Jax here, and I will speak if you give me a chance."

Sir Rigil bowed. "But of course, my lady. I apologize."

The men settled in two chairs beside each other. Jax's chair creaked under his weight, but he looked comfortable enough. Vrell sat in one on the other side of the table. "I have heard you leave first thing for Armonguard. Since I shall be going—"

"Forgive me a moment, my lady, if you please." Sir Rigil pointed between Jax and Vrell. "When did you become acquainted? I was under the impression you had not met."

Vrell stifled a sigh at Sir Rigil's interruption, but Jax answered before she could.

"Not officially," he said. "We spent a week together last spring when Khai and I escorted her to Mahanaim."

"Mahanaim?" Sir Rigil's lips pursed, as if his mind searched for an answer he could not recall. "I heard you were there, my lady. I also heard rumors of an abduction, but Prince Oren said it had been resolved. Since none of us ever saw you, I figured your presence had been rumor, as well."

"Vrell was dressed as a boy," Jax said.

"Wait." Sir Rigil's gaze fixed on Vrell. "Surely not!"

Vrell cringed, wishing Jax had not opened the door to that henhouse.

"My dear lady Averella, please tell me that it was not *you* traveling with the prince as his squire and healer?"

Vrell's stomach clenched. She should not allow Sir Rigil to shame her. None of this was his concern. She straightened, which made her side throb. "If you do not wish to hear the truth, Sir Rigil, then do not ask questions."

Sir Rigil balked. "Your mother knows of this?"

"I thought you did not want to know."

"That all this time . . . ? Does Master Rennan know?"

She sighed. "He did not. But I assure you he now—"

"How very like a woman, constructing a fortress of falsehoods." Sir Rigil looked away, brooding. "No thought as to what poor soul might be ensnared along the way."

Bitter anger surged up in Vrell. "And what poor soul have I ensnared by my *fortress of falsehoods*, Sir Rigil?"

"Besides our future king? Master Rennan is my charge. I must ask why you did not tell him of this charade."

"It was not my charade, Sir Rigil. Not at first, anyway. My mother and *your* aunt arranged it. Mother sent me to Walden's Watch, and Lady Coraline dressed me as a stray boy so Prince Gidon—so *Esek*—would not be able to find me. I had but one instruction: tell no one of my true identity until it was safe to do so. Yet no one foresaw that Macoun Hadar would sense my bloodvoice and claim me as his apprentice. Under the circumstances, I have done my best."

"But in Mahanaim! Master Rennan and I stood beside you. We spoke to you! You needed only look our way. We would have . . . My lady, I should have known. How could I have missed it?"

Vrell relaxed and took a deep breath, easing the pain in her side. For Sir Rigil was not scolding her but himself. "I do not blame you for not recognizing me, Sir Rigil. I am plain as it is. This helped me escape notice. And without a dress, it seems, I was not at all feminine."

"I hear the prince pines away for you. Whilst he is engaged to . . . to you!" Sir Rigil's eyes were wide. "Why let him suffer so? My dear lady, I never thought you so heartless."

Now he *was* scolding her. His stern expression stung like shards of glass on the backs of her eyes. She sought a dignified response, but emotion took over. "Your opinion of my heart is nothing I care to hear, Sir Rigil."

"Please, my lady. If you have no feeling in your heart, I pray you have mercy on his."

"His heart flutters about as much as yours. How am I to trust the word of a man who is enamored with a different woman every day?"

"Such accusations are beneath you, Lady Averella."

The truth of Vrell's heart? It felt like it was being wrung like a wet rag. This was not fair. She had known Achan only three months, and his head had been turned more times than she could count. How could she believe he truly loved her?

None of that mattered at the moment. "Your opinion has been noted." She shifted on the chair to face Jax. "Shall I bring my own armor, Jax? Do you expect any resistance on your journey?"

Jax's eyes shifted away. "Forgive me, Vrell, but Prince Oren requests you remain here with your mother."

Vrell stood, which put her at eye level with Jax. "That is impossible. I wish to use my healing gifts to assist in the coming war. I cannot do that from Carmine."

Jax would not meet her gaze. "Prince Oren says the coming battle is no place for a lady. He said with all you've been through, he's surprised you'd ask to leave again."

"Leave?" Sir Rigil stared up at Vrell. "Lady Averella, what are you thinking?"

"I am thinking of serving my prince."

"To serve your— My lady, the truth would serve him best."

"Sir Rigil, you are *not* my father. You have no right to lecture me so."

"Well, someone must. I've always known you were headstrong, my lady, but not so selfish. Perhaps I mislaid my opinion of your character. For at this moment, you are no better than any spoiled young noblewoman I've met."

"It is not my fault I was raised in Granton Castle, given everything I wanted—even things I did not. I am tired of having my life lived for me. *I* choose my path, not Mother, not any prince, and certainly not you. Who invited you to this meeting, anyway?"

"Forgive me, Vrell," Jax said. "I asked Sir Rigil to come. I hoped—"

"That he would talk some sense into me? I see now that I have put my hope in the wrong comrades."

Sir Rigil stood and circled the table to stand before her. "Now see here—"

Vrell turned her back to him. "Please leave, Sir Rigil. And I trust you will keep this conversation—and my identity—to yourself."

"I would never betray your trust, but the prince—"

"Need not know. You yourself have given your opinion of the attributes of my heart. He would be better off without such a deceitful woman in his life, would he not?"

"You put words in my mouth, my lady. And whether or not he would be better off should be his choice."

"My choice, Sir Rigil, and I have made it."

"I will not lie to my prince and future king. Should he ask me of Lady Averella's whereabouts . . ."

"You will not know them."

Sir Rigil sighed. "But you will inform Master Rennan of this, will you not?"

"I have already spoken with Master Rennan. He is aware of my situation."

"And what did he say?"

Vrell averted her eyes.

Sir Rigil snorted a knowing laugh. "That's what I thought. Good lad, Master Rennan."

Vrell swallowed another retort. She did not wish to quarrel with Sir Rigil. "Won't you change your mind, Jax? I can take care of myself. I have my own horse."

"I cannot go against Prince Oren, Vrell. I'm sorry."

Sir Rigil gripped Vrell's upper arm. "Lady Averella, whether you can protect yourself is not the issue. Prince Oren knows that your presence would still be a distraction to our men."

She pulled away. "I am plain enough that most men pay me no mind."

"Regardless, while your beauty would fluster many, all would be distracted by their need to protect you. Our men train to a certain code. We swear to protect women and children above all. No man would be able to focus on his task when you were nearby, vulnerable, without an escort."

"Your men need not concern themselves. I can—"

"Forgive me, my lady, but it is not a question of need. It is simply the way Arman made men. We cannot, in good conscience, ignore the presence of a woman. Like it or not, you would be a great distraction."

The chivalry she had hoped for during her time as a boy had come too late. "I thank you both for your counsel. Good day."

Jax reached out for her again. "Please, Vrell, do not be cross."

She stepped back to avoid his touch. "Not cross, only disappointed. For I very much wish to serve as a healer."

"If your duchess mother should travel south," Sir Rigil said, "I am certain Prince Oren would covet your assistance with any wounded."

"Thank you, Sir Rigil. I shall inquire as to whether she plans to make such a journey."

When the men had left, Vrell fell back into her chair. "Oh, Syrah, I am such a fool."

Syrah ran to Vrell's side. "No offense, m'lady, but I'm glad Prince Oren said no."

For months Vrell had longed for home, and now she wanted to leave again. What was the matter with her? "But I can help, Syrah. I am a gifted healer."

Syrah released a shuddering breath. "The idea of you on a battlefield, m'lady, it terrifies me. Stay here where I can care for you."

"You are sweet. But there is no honor in doing nothing."

"There is plenty of honor in taking care of your sisters and the people of Carmine. There is much to be done here."

"And plenty of sisters to help Mother do it." Sisters who were true heirs to Carm. Vrell was tired of hiding in her own home. She had changed. She was no longer content to marry and wear pretty dresses all her life. She wanted—no, needed—to participate, to be of use in the coming war. And if doing so took her away from Achan . . .

Syrah offered her a glass of water. "'Tis only a few days until the prince and his men leave. Then you won't have to see any of them for a long time."

That was what Vrell wanted, right? But the thought of never seeing Achan again brought tears to her eyes.

Vrell slipped along the cool, stone passage. She knew her way so well it was hard not to run the straight stretches. She forced herself to walk slowly, watching the flame on her candle flicker with each step. It took ages to move about the castle using only the secret passageways, but she could not risk being seen until Achan was gone.

Vrell was still furious Mother had permitted Anillo to show Achan the passages. Of course he should know of the secret meeting rooms, but not that he could walk to his chambers.

No doubt Mother hoped Achan and Vrell might stumble upon one another in the dark corridors. Mother did not understand Vrell's reservations. The sooner Vrell could find a way to leave Carmine, the better.

At the northwest tower stairs, she started up. Her room was on the sixth floor, but she paused on the fourth. Achan had gone out to practice with the soldiers. She had seen him and Shung from Ryson Tower.

No. Enough time had been wasted spying on Achan. She continued to climb. Her dress scraped along the stone steps and walls. She did not bother to lift her skirts and protect the fabric. She would have no need for such gowns on the battlefield.

By the time she reached the sixth floor, her lungs were tight. She passed the first arrow loop and held the candle high until she spied a strip of white fabric. She had tied the swatch on the entrance to her sister's room to make the door easier to find. She knocked once and pushed the door in.

Gypsum sat before an embroidery stand, plump lips turned down. Baskets of colorful thread sat around her feet. Eyes on her work, she said, "By all means, Averella, enter."

Vrell ignored her sister's tone and sank down on the foot of the bed. In many ways, twelve-year-old Gypsum acted older than Vrell. The girl had been an exceptional seamstress since she had first touched needle and thread, an admirable skill for a young noblewoman. She never disagreed with Mother, never climbed trees, and never argued with squires or knights. Vrell doubted she had ever touched a weapon in her short life.

Gypsum's room was always spotless, of her own accord. Maids had little to clean here. Gypsum had chosen lavender and deep purple floral bedding and matching solid upholstery on her chaise lounge and chairs. Frescoes of children and angels covered the ceiling, but the walls were white. Framed tapestries hung every two feet, most of which Gypsum had crafted herself. Vrell spotted a new one near the door and heaved herself off the bed to examine it more closely.

Two sheets of silk, one black, one white, had been sewn together with raw, jagged stitches. The outline of a map was embroidered in gold. On the white silk, happy people danced among the ripe vines of Carmine and full orchards of Allowntown. On the black side, Vrell's gaze stopped on a small boat in the water west of Mahanaim. Five figures sat in the small craft. Three men in red Kingsguard capes, a young man, whom Gypsum had stitched with a golden glow over his head, and a girl, staring out from a hooded cape with wide eyes, her black hair blowing out from the side of the hood.

Vrell shivered. "This is amazing, Gypsum. When did you do this?"

Still absorbed in her latest masterpiece, Gypsum pulled the thread with an easy rhythm. "When you were gone. Mother told us much of what you relayed. Your journey spoke to me, so I made that."

I made that. As if the girl merely whipped the piece out in an afternoon, which, for all Vrell knew, she had.

"Do you want something, dear sister?" Gypsum asked.

"Just your chatty company."

Gypsum rewarded Vrell with a fake smile. "Do not mock my silence when I am concentrating. Besides, Mother says men prefer silent ladies."

Vrell blew a wry laugh out her nose. "I do not doubt that most do."

"If you have no news to lighten my mood, go away."

Not this again. "I am sorry your mood is sour, but you are too young to understand. I cannot do what I feel is wrong."

Gypsum's hands stilled and she looked up. "You feel the truth is wrong?"

"Not the truth part. The other part."

"You can do both, Averella. You simply refuse. And who is to pay for your disobedience to Arman and to Mother? I am. For I will do my duty, even if I have to marry this prince of yours."

"He is not *my* prince."

Gypsum rolled her eyes and continued stitching. "You mope about the castle, scuttling within the walls like a spider. I do not have to be as old and wise as you to see that he owns your heart."

Vrell crossed the room, toward the tapestry of the kittens that hid the secret entrance. She did not need yet another lecture, especially from her little sister—half-sister, though Vrell had not shared that secret with anyone. Maybe she should. Maybe then Gypsum would understand.

She turned back to spill the truth, but Gypsum's tear-filled eyes pleaded. "Normally I would be ecstatic about marrying a prince, especially the real Prince Gidon Hadar. Imagine it! He is handsome and kind, good-mannered. And he is only four years my senior, which is nothing compared to what most girls suffer in marriage. After what happened to Tara, how could I refuse such a match?"

Vrell lifted the kitten tapestry aside. "It appears that you cannot. Congratulations."

"Vrella, please do not force me to marry him."

Vrell set her jaw. "I will not force you to marry anyone. Nor will Mother."

"No, but she will lose honor if the agreement is not fulfilled. I will not put her in that situation."

Vrell dropped the curtain and folded her arms. "It has been said that some make an idol out of obedience. Such perfect standards cannot bring you joy at all times. I suspect that even you sometimes rebel in your heart."

Gypsum's wide-eyed glare was all innocence. "I am simply doing what Arman asks of me."

"Is that so? And have you consulted the Book of Life? I recall this printed in its pages: 'Anyone who loves his father or mother more than Arman is not worthy of Arman.'"

Gypsum straightened. "'Children, obey your parents in Arman, for this is right.'"

"'Our fathers disciplined us for a little while as they thought best; but Arman disciplines us for our good, that we may share in his holiness.'"

"'In the same way be submissive to those older than—'"

"'Do not be yoked together with unbelievers. For what do righteousness and wickedness have in common? Or what fellowship can light have with darkness?'"

A stream of tears ran down Gypsum's cheek. "Please, Vrella. I do not want to marry the man you love."

"Then refuse. But until I see his heart set on Arman and not on a whim or on any pretty face that walks by, I will not give him my heart."

"Rubbish." Gypsum withdrew a handkerchief from the thread basket under her embroidery frame and dabbed her eyes. "You already have."

"Maybe partly . . ." Vrell blinked away her own tears. "But not all of it. Which is why I cannot confess now. He would forgive me, then be sweet and charming and steal more of my heart no matter how I tried to keep it from him. And then he would turn to some tavern wench, and I would be destroyed. My heart is already weak. Staying away is my only defense."

"But Mother speaks so highly of him. You truly believe he would play with your heart?"

"Not intentionally. He would be sincere at first. But it would not be long before temptation whisked him away. And even if he remained loyal and true all his days, he does not live for Arman. How can I—"

"Mother says he has met Arman."

Vrell frowned, wishing it were so. "I cannot trust Mother's word of late."

"For shame, Averella! How can you say that? When has she ever deceived us?"

"Oh, you want to know . . ." But Vrell could not bring herself to destroy Gypsum's good impression of Mother by telling her about Sir Eagan. "It is not your concern. Simply know that Mother will not make you marry anyone if you tell her your heart."

"She is not making me marry anyone. She only suggested I think about it in case she is unable to change your mind. I do not think she intends to make a final decision until after this coming war."

"Then we both have time to consider the situation."

Gypsum picked up her needle. "I suppose. But I pray you make the right choice so I do not have to."

5

Vrell looked down on the training fields from the top of Ryson Tower. The wind whipped her loose hair about her face as she watched the soldiers practice drills.

Achan's shiny breastplate and Shung's black armor made them stand out from the soldiers dressed in red. It reminded Vrell of when she used to watch her father, Duke Amal, train from this tower.

Tears flooded her eyes. The innocent memory had come so naturally. But the wave of sorrow, confusion, and guilt that followed nearly brought her to her knees.

Duke Amal, dear father he had been, was not her blood. Just as Carmine had never really been her home. Months of trying to get back, and this was the truth she now faced.

Where did she truly belong?

She swept down the spiral staircase, filled with such confusion and uncertainty. She pleaded with Arman to set it right. She knew better than to petition Him when she refused to obey. But she hoped Arman understood her heart. She barely understood it herself.

Vrell pushed through the secret door into Mother's study and peeked out from behind the changing screen. The room was empty, so she went to the door, rang the bell, then stood at the window and looked out on the practice field again.

She had no intention of living a lie any longer. To be true to who she really was she had abandoned her birthright and sought out a place with Prince Oren and the Mârad. But he had refused her services as a healer—suggesting instead that she reconcile with her mother. As if it were that simple.

And now that Jax had refused to take her along, her last hope rested with her former fiancé, Bran Rennan. Their relationship had been strained since they had parted ways. He disliked her plan to serve the Mârad, but she hoped she could convince him to take her along to Armonguard.

She wanted—needed—to assist in this war. If she were on the battlefield, there was little chance she would run into Achan. He would be kept safe, protected by his guard. Months, maybe years, would pass before she saw him again. She hoped so, anyway, for she had promised Arman that when she did see him again, she would tell him the truth.

Bran could not refuse her. He had courted another woman while he and Vrell were engaged. That alone should indebt him a bit, should it not?

The door to Mother's study swung inward, and Anillo entered. Mother's steward was thin and old, but had bested men on the practice field as young as Vrell. "Yes, my lady?"

"Anillo, I require a visit with Master Rennan. Here, as soon as possible. It is an emergency."

"Emergency, my lady?" he asked, his expression blank.

"Well . . . it is very important."

"An emergency of great importance, then?"

"No, just that . . . Oh, well. Go on, then. That will do, thank you."

"Of course, my lady." Anillo bowed and left the room.

Vrell's side ached. She wished it would heal quicker. She sat at Mother's jade desk and let her thoughts drift. She grew tired of hiding from Achan. Of spying on him. She needed distance. The sooner the better. She did not wish to fulfill her promise to Arman anytime soon.

Fiery pain gripped her skull. She grasped the edge of Mother's desk to keep her balance.

Your Highness? Sir Caleb said. He was one of the knights who advised Achan. *Are you injured?*

Achan's mellow voice answered. *Sorry, Sir Caleb. Just a little experiment.*

And the pain subsided.

Vrell released the desk, her breath shaky. An experiment? Merciful heart! Did he have to experiment in such a way that brought all bloodvoicers to their knees?

She rested her head on Mother's desk and dozed off, until a knock sounded on the door. She sat up. "Yes?"

The door cracked open, and Anillo slipped inside. "Master Rennan has arrived, my lady."

Vrell stood. "Thank you, Anillo. Please, show him in."

Anillo bowed and pulled the door open. "Master Bran Rennan, my lady."

Bran swept into the study, black boots clomping on the redwood floor. He looked a fright, face flushed and sweaty, hair matted to his forehead and cheeks. His Old Kingsguard uniform was wrinkled and dirty.

"Are you well, Master Rennan?"

"Yes, my lady. I've come directly from the practice fields. I was told it was an emergency." His deep brown eyes regarded her, filled with concern that quickly led to impatience. "What, Averella? What is so urgent?"

She hesitated at his tone. If he was already angry, how would she obtain his help? She held her chin high, employing every ounce of her training as a future duchess, and gritted her teeth at her aching side. "I require your assistance, Master Rennan. I wish to journey south to Armonguard and would like to—"

"*This* is your emergency?"

"I require an escort."

His mouth fell open. "I will *not* be your escort."

She wilted. "I only wish to ride along. No pomp or protocol. No one need know. I will even dress as a boy to—"

"No," Bran said. "You ask me to lie to Sir Rigil? To Jax? To Prince Oren? I beg you, stop this ridiculous plotting and go talk to the prince."

She stifled a whimper. Was everyone against her? "I most certainly will not."

Bran tipped his head back. "But why, my lady? He will be thrilled to discover that you are you."

Would he? Vrell was not so certain. "I will not marry him."

"Why ever not?"

"He does not follow Arman."

"But he is Arman's chosen—"

"Not good enough. Many a king has been *Arman's chosen*. I recall not one truly righteous man among them."

"You did not know the kings of old. Do not judge based on rumors of history."

"My fath— Duke Amal knew King Axel. I heard much from him about the former king's philandering ways. And what is that saying? 'For where the father stumbles, the son falls?' I have seen Achan tempted, *heard* his thoughts on the subject. It is only a matter of time."

"Averella." Bran propped his hand on his hip. "That is hardly fair."

"I do not trust Achan with my heart."

Bran all but snorted. "He already has your heart. You love him."

"Do not say that! It is not true."

"You are a poor liar, my lady."

"Am I? I went almost a year as a man without anyone suspecting I was not."

"The prince discovered it."

"Only when he looked into my mind, where he had no right to be, and saw things he should not have. His mischief with bloodvoicing is another reason I do not trust him."

"Well, *I* trust him."

"Good for you, Master Rennan. You marry him."

Bran rolled his eyes.

How could she make him understand? "Achan is my friend, Bran, but that is not enough to pledge him my life."

"My lady, you are too hard on our future king. He did not have your sheltered childhood. And he has turned out remarkably well, considering. He is fair and kind."

"But he is unscrupulous with his gift. He uses his power for his own devices. He had no right to look into my mind."

"Though doing so saved you from a terrible fate."

True. Polk would have succeeded in his attack if Achan had not been watching. She shook the thought away. "I do not wish to speak of him again. Stop bringing it up!"

"But you are engaged to marry him."

"I am not. I relinquished my birthright. If Mother has not announced it yet, she soon will. The prince can marry Gypsum to earn his army. Mother is already preparing her."

Bran's mouth gaped, his dark eyebrows pinched as if he were thinking very hard. "Averella, *Gypsum*?"

Vrell's voice came softly. "She is heir to Carm now."

"Why would you renounce your birthright?"

She could not tell him that Duke Amal was not her birth father. "The prince signed an agreement with my mother. Carm gives full support for his campaign if he agrees to marry Mother's heir."

He rubbed his face as if exhausted by the conversation. "I don't understand."

"It is a private matter. But please do not misunderstand me. I do believe Achan will make a good king. I support his claim to the throne and want to help him take it. I can do that best by serving as a healer in Armonguard. Please, Bran?"

Bran sighed. "The duchess forbade you to come with us. Prince Oren has told you no. As has Sir Jax. And Sir Rigil is in agreement. I will not defy them."

Vrell stewed a moment. Truly, she had known all along that Bran would not help her. She sighed dramatically. "I suppose I should give you leave to bid your peasant girl farewell before you abandon her as well."

His expression tightened. "Ugliness does not suit you, Averella. I know you to be a lady above such petty insults. The truth shall set you free. Think on it." He opened the door. "I shall find my own way out."

And Bran left.

Vrell slumped into her mother's chair and pressed a hand against her aching side. She did not doubt Bran's wisdom. And she did need to speak with Achan someday.

She imagined going to him now. He would show his joy, scold her for leaving, perhaps an embrace . . .

No. She would not accept any affection until she spoke her mind. She would remove his hands and say, "I am Lady Averella Amal. I am sorry for deceiving you."

And he would say . . . ?

Dash it all, she did not know what he would say, but her stomach knotted just thinking on it. Or perhaps what truly upset her was the thought of his embrace.

• • •

Vrell led Kopay out of his stall and toward the stable doors. Dawn had not yet broken. Dressing as a boy would have allowed her to leave at daybreak, but the guards would not permit just anyone to ride Kopay through the gate.

She patted his neck. "I have missed our rides together, boy. I am sorry I have not come to see you until now. I could not risk it. But I also could not leave you behind this time."

Kopay dropped his head and snorted, plodding alongside Vrell. He was a sleek white courser with a white mane and tail and flecks of black on his hindquarters.

Her desire for taking Kopay meant she couldn't afford leaving in daylight. Everyone in the castle thought she was away still. Rumor of her "return" would spread like wine on linen. She needed to be on the road by the time word reached Mother. Or Achan.

She would leave as Lady Averella, ride south under cover of night, and wait near the fish pond. She could change her clothes there. And once Jax's party passed, she would trail them as a lagging soldier.

Vrell had Kopay three paces from the stable doors when one side creaked open. A young woman carrying a lantern slipped inside. Vrell froze, hoping this girl would not think Vrell a horse thief and call the watch.

The girl lifted the lantern above her head, took two steps before her eyes locked onto Vrell, then screamed. She dropped the lantern, which tipped on its side, igniting bits of hay strewn across the dirt floor.

"Oh!" The girl lunged for the lantern, but pulled back when the flames licked at her shoes. "I'm sorry!"

Vrell jumped forward, righted the lantern, and batted at the fire with her skirt. The flames died, and Vrell breathed out a long sigh.

"Thank you, miss!" The girl lifted the lantern, casting light over her black gown. "I'm so clumsy."

"All is well now, since nothing—" Vrell stared, for Gren Fenny stood before her, the girl Achan had pined for in his youth. The girl whose husband had been recently killed, leaving her widowed and with child.

The same girl Bran found so pretty.

What was Gren doing in the stables at this hour? At any hour, for that matter?

Before she could ask, a distant yell distracted her. She cocked her head to the side. "Did you hear that?"

"I didn't hear nothing, miss."

Kopay whinnied. Vrell could hear other horses dancing in their stalls. A thump overhead drew her gaze to the ceiling. "Something is on the roof." She ran to the doors and opened them. The light from the torch stands greeted her. Men's voices drifted from beyond the curtain wall. Yelling. She listened hard to make out any words.

A trumpet blared. A man yelled.

"Raise the drawbridge and close the gate!"

Heat flooded Vrell. Something was happening. A quick glance at the roof of the stables confirmed it. A coil of grey smoke drifted against the black sky. Fire!

She ran back inside. "The roof is on fire. We must get the animals out. Now!" She grabbed the lantern from Gren and hung it on a hook by the door. "Take the east end. Open all the stalls and send the animals out. Go, hurry!"

Vrell ran past Gren and reached for Kopay's reins. "Outside, boy." She twisted the reins loosely around the saddle horn, pointed him toward the open doors, and slapped his rear. He lurched and trotted toward the exit.

Vrell ran down the west end, opening stalls and ushering horses out. Most broke free from their leads and ran. She hoped Gren knew to keep out of their way. By the time Vrell had emptied the stalls on the west end, burning bits of thatch were falling from above. Thick smoke curled down from the roof. It hadn't rained in days. The roof would go quickly. Vrell ran toward the exit and met Griscol halfway.

The stable master, though grey-haired and aged, had the build of an adolescent boy with a voice to match. "My lady! How many more?"

"I have cleared everything on the west end, Griscol. I sent a woman to the east end. Would you check on her?"

Griscol took off at a run.

Vrell kept back as several more horses jogged out from the east wing. Smoke grew thicker, pulling ragged coughs from her lungs. Chunks of smoldering thatch fell around her. Finally, Griscol and

Gren returned. Griscol pronounced the stables empty, and they all hurried out into fresher air.

"I thank you both for clearing the stables." Griscol wiped soot from his forehead. "That trumpet was what woke me. I stepped outside, saw the smoke, and came running. Something sure has the soldiers in a tizzy."

Vrell gazed at the top of the curtain wall. Soldiers crouched low, aiming their bows out at the vineyards. Her words came out in one breath. "We are under attack."

As if in agreement, an arrow slammed into the side of the stable.

Gren shrieked.

"Best get inside, my lady," Griscol said.

But Vrell had other ideas. She ran a few yards, scanned the outer bailey, then turned back to Gren. "Help me find my horse. He was the only one saddled. He's a white courser. And take care not to get trampled. The fire has upset the horses."

Gren's eyes widened, but she ran off to the east of the bailey in the direction the last of the horses had gone.

Vrell went the opposite way. But before she could see a single horse, a groan pulled her away. A soldier Vrell did not recognize lay on his back alongside a cart, gripping his stomach and moaning.

Vrell knelt at his side. She tried to move his hand, but he fought her. "Let me help you." She looked into the man's eyes. He was young, Bran's age, perhaps.

"My lady? You've come home?" The man's eyes rolled back. The tension left his body, and he fell limp.

Vrell leaned close and felt his warm breath on her cheek. He had only fallen unconscious. She moved his hand and examined the dark patch of blood that had soaked his uniform. Unfortunately, he wore no armor to protect him from injury, but that made it easier to get to the wound.

A shadow fell over her patient. "What happened?"

Vrell twisted around to see Gren clutching Kopay's reins. "Thank Arman. Unlatch the left saddlebag. You'll find a small, leather satchel. Bring it to me."

Vrell pulled the cape over the soldier's head and pushed up his shirt. A jagged shaft of wood protruded from the wound on his side. Vrell winced. He must have broken off the arrow.

Gren crouched beside Vrell, holding the healing satchel. Vrell took the bag and set it on the grass beside her so that she would have easy access to the contents.

"I need some water, Gren. Fresh water. Do your best."

Gren loped away.

Vrell used linen to mop away some of the blood. Gren returned with a bucket of water with leaves floating in it. Vrell shot her a scowl.

"It's all I could find."

Vrell fished out the leaves and cleaned the wound. Using a set of arrowspoons Sir Eagan—her real father—had given her, she withdrew the arrowhead, cleaned and packed the wound with yarrow, and bandaged the man up.

A boy ran over. "Please, miss. My pa's hurt. Can you help?"

"I shall try." Vrell grabbed her satchel and followed the boy.

Gren trailed along. "Where'd you learn to do this?"

Vrell increased her stride to keep up with the boy. "Practice."

The boy scurried toward a shack behind the chicken coop. Part of the roof was charred and had partially collapsed. "The soldiers put out the fire, but they couldn't stay to help my pa." The boy ducked inside and knelt on the dirt floor. "He's here."

A man sat on a straw-covered pallet, cradling his arm. It was Fredic, the man who tended the chickens and brought eggs into the kitchens each morning.

Vrell knelt in front of the man. "May I see, Fredic?"

"By this day, my lady! What are you doing out here?"

Vrell ignored the question. "What happened?"

"Broken, I think." Fredic held his arm out. His forearm was swollen abnormally, his tanned skin bruised purple atop the bump. "Piece of timber fell from the roof when I was chasing old Bessol. That old rooster's a rascal. Heard something snap. Know how to fix a broken arm? Didn't think noblewomen learned healing arts."

"Most do not." Vrell ran her hands along his arm. Her thumb could feel the broken bone, right below the swelling. "Gren, I need a piece of kindling, no thicker than my wrist, a smooth piece if you can find one."

"How 'bout an axe handle?" The boy jumped up and snagged a worn length of wood from the end of the pallet.

"That will do fine." Vrell removed a roll of linen and took the axe handle from the boy. She wrapped it in linen until it was completely covered. She handed it to Gren and rose to her knees. "Gren, hold this under his arm. Fredic, I'm going to try and move the bone into place. It's going to hurt badly. Would you like something for the pain?"

"Nay, my lady. For my pain is only a reflection of Câan's pain. I shall bear it well and give Him praise for it."

Vrell smiled. "You are a brave and faithful man."

Once Gren had the handle in place, Vrell molded Fredic's arm until she felt the bone fall back in place. She ignored his screams, for they only agitated her, and she needed to concentrate to do the job well.

When she finished, she rubbed yarrow salve on the bruise, then wrapped his arm to the axe handle with strips of linen, tight enough to hold, but not so tight that Fredic's fingers would purple. She made a sling from a larger strip of linen to hold Fredic's arm close to his body.

"You are to visit the castle daily to have this checked by the duchess's healer. Tell Anillo I sent you, do you hear?"

"Yes, my lady. I thank you for your kindness."

Vrell smiled, then turned to the boy. "You be a help to your father, now. He must not lift anything for a while."

"Don't you worry 'bout me, my lady. I'll take fine care of Pa. I'm strong enough to lift anything he can."

Fredic winked at Vrell. "My boy thinks he's ready for the Kingsguard already."

"Or your personal guard, my lady, should you need another man." The boy grinned.

Vrell gathered her bag and curtsied. "Why thank you, young man. I shall inform Anillo to keep watch for you."

When Vrell and Gren walked away, Gren asked, "Do you *have* a personal guard, my lady?"

"Not since I returned." But her mother would assign one if she discovered Vrell had been planning to leave.

Gren and Vrell continued to help wounded peasants and soldiers until pale, predawn light filled the smoky sky. When they had assisted everyone inside the stronghold, the need took them outside the sentry walls. Soldiers on their way inside the castle told Vrell the battle had ended. She was helping a man with a cut on his leg when Captain Loam approached.

He bowed. "My lady, I did not know you were in Carmine. Does your mother know you have returned?"

"She does." Though Vrell had no desire to speak with Captain Loam about her mother. "Is the battle truly over?"

"For now. Sir Gavin would like to take the offensive as soon as possible. I can't help but agree. Carmine will only be safe once we eradicate these traitors for good. To attack peasants under cover of night. It isn't right."

"Darkness has been their master for years, Captain Loam. They do not hold true to your high standards of conduct and chivalry."

"My lady, I am grateful for your care of my men."

"I consider them my men as well, Captain."

"That they are, my lady. But I'd feel better if you'd return to the castle. We have other healers out now."

"I can help a bit longer. The outer gates will keep me safe." Vrell changed the subject, hoping to glean some knowledge that would help her. "If Sir Gavin does take the offensive, will Sir Jax and his party ride south with the army?"

"Sir Jax departed last night, my lady. I pray they got through without running into the enemy."

"Last night?" The blood drained from Vrell's face. Had Jax changed his plans because of her? And what if the enemy had intercepted them? What if Jax and Sir Rigil had been killed? What if Bran had been killed? Vrell nodded to Captain Loam. "Good day to you, Captain Loam. I must continue my work."

"I'll send some soldiers to assist you."

Guard her, he meant. There was nothing to be done about it now. The whole stronghold would know she was home. "Come, Gren." Let the guards seek them out.

Vrell stumbled toward the southwestern vineyard. The wounded needed her now. She could worry about Bran later. "We shall walk along the road and check each row of the vineyard, since that is where our men found the enemy."

Gren plodded alongside Vrell. She sniffled and heaved in a deep breath.

"Are you well, Gren?"

"I—" Gren turned her tear-streaked face toward Vrell. "How do you know my name?" She curtsied. "If you please, my lady."

Vrell pursed her lips, scrambling for a suitable answer, then stopped herself. No need to fib. The truth would do fine. Some of it, anyway.

"You are the prince's childhood friend. My mother brought you here to keep you safe. My knowing your name cannot be the reason for your tears."

Gren's eyes widened. "Oh. No. I . . . the battle, I suppose."

Vrell doubted Gren was giving *her* the full truth either.

They moved along the road, peering down each row they passed. Vrell wanted to use her bloodvoice to check on Bran, but she needed to be sitting down to do that, for watching made her weak. It would not be wise to try until she finished assisting the wounded and was safely indoors.

"There!" Gren pointed past Vrell, down the next row. A young soldier lay on his back, writhing.

Vrell ran toward him. Upon seeing his condition, she bit back a cry. He had been hit with a mace in the neck and chest. Blood had completely soaked his scarlet Kingsguard cape to a deep maroon. Vrell crouched at his side.

The man's eyes focused on hers. Deep brown eyes, pleading for help. He sucked in short, strangled breaths and grunts, as if trying to speak. From the wound on his neck, Vrell feared he could not. His entire body trembled as if he were freezing. The shock of pain to his body had taken control. Vrell began to tremble herself as she considered what, if anything, she could do to help.

Gren's footsteps approached. "Sorry, my lady. I can't keep up. I'm queasy most mornings and I— Cetheria's hand! What happened to him?"

Vrell spun around, fixing the deepest scowl she could muster. This man would not live, but there was no reason he need know. "He fought bravely, Gren—that is what happened. Now, hold your tongue and get me some fresh linen." Vrell turned back to the solider and smoothed his sweaty brown hair back off his head. "Do not try to speak. Just blink. Once for yes, twice for no, all right?"

The man blinked once.

"Good. I know you are in pain, but try to relax and lie still. You are bleeding. I would like to stop that, but it might hurt some. Are you ready?"

One blink.

"Very well." Vrell took a bundle of linen from Gren and tore it in two. She rolled half into a wad and handed it to Gren. "Put pressure on his chest."

"Me?"

"Now, please."

Gren crouched beside Vrell, her black skirt puffing around her. Arms shaking, she set the linen on the man's chest and pressed down with her fingertips.

"Harder."

Gren's hands shifted a bit. Vrell pushed her hand over Gren's to show how much pressure.

The man groaned. His body stiffened.

"Shh. You are very brave." Vrell laid her linen over his neck and pressed down lightly, concerned about his breathing. "Are you thirsty?"

The man's face turned pink. One blink.

"Good. We'll get you a drink in a moment."

The man sucked in short gasps. Vrell lifted the linen from his neck, uncertain where to press to stop the bleeding and not cut off his air. She pressed down with two fingers where the blood seemed to pool. Better.

She reached for her water jug with her free hand, wedged it between her knees, and pulled out the stopper. "Here is a drink." She tipped the jug over the man's lips. His chin quivered as he lapped the water. "Tell me, sir, do you know Arman, the One God?"

The man blinked once.

Joyous heart. Arman would save his soul, then, if she failed to save his body. "I would like to ask Him to ease your pain. Would that be acceptable?"

The man gurgled an intelligible response. His eyebrows sank, and he blinked.

Vrell took hold of his hand and closed her eyes. He squeezed until her fingers pinched. "Arman, You are aware of this man's pain.

We ask for Your healing touch on his body. We know You are able to mend these wounds." The man's grip relaxed. Vrell forced her voice to remain even, though tears tightened her throat. "We also know You will choose what is best. Bring this man comfort and strength. Be glorified in his life. May it be so."

Vrell opened her eyes. The man's eyes remained closed. He had stopped trembling. She laid his hand over his chest and set hers on top of Gren's.

"Thank you, Gren. That will do."

Gren pulled her hands away. "Is he dead?"

"I'm afraid so."

Gren sucked in a short breath. "I knew him. Not his name. But up until a few weeks ago, he served night duty between the great hall and the kitchens."

"And he joined the Kingsguard?"

"Captain Loam assigned him to personal guard. The man was mighty proud. I heard him bragging to his chums."

"A personal guard to whom?"

"Lady Gypsum."

Vrell met Gren's gaze, no doubt exchanging the same curiosity, but neither willing to voice it aloud. Why would one of Gypsum's guards be in the vineyard at such an hour?

Vrell called to Anillo. *Lady Averella Amal.*

Yes, my lady?

I am in the southwestern vineyards helping the wounded. I found a man who I believe is one of Gypsum's guardsmen. He is dead. Would you send someone for his body, please? He lies in the tenth row thereabouts.

Right away, my lady. Should I inform your mother of your location?

If you must. Vrell stood and gathered her satchel and water jug. *But why might Gypsum's guard be out here?*

It would be best if you returned to the castle.

Fire sparked in Vrell's chest and spread quickly through her limbs. *Tell me now, Anillo.*

Very well. Lady Gypsum was abducted from the courtyard. Do not fret! She is back in the castle, well and safe. Her abductors took her through the vineyards. She will be saddened to hear that Arne did not survive.

Vrell glanced down at the soldier named Arne. *He gave his life to save my sister.*

He tried, my lady. Lady Gypsum says that Arne was struck down long before she escaped. My lady, if you don't mind looking . . . The prince helped Lady Gypsum into the southwestern tunnel. Yet he did not follow her and is no longer responding to the duchess's calls.

The prince? Achan had been here? Was he here still? She couldn't let him see her. And yet . . . Her eyes strayed to Arne's ruined body.

Please, Arman. Let him be well.

Vrell crouched and scanned the ground under the vines. She counted three bodies at various distances away. *I will find him, Anillo.* Vrell bounced back up and ran to the road. The tunnel's entrance was not far. "Come, Gren. There are more wounded."

Vrell's heart pounded as she jogged down the road, scanning each row for the next body or the scrap of fabric that marked the trapdoor to the secret tunnel. She spotted a downed man and ran to him. It was not Achan, however, but an enemy soldier—dead from an amputated leg.

Vrell backpedaled, bumped into Gren, and darted past.

Gren cried out, "He's dead too?"

Vrell turned back and gripped Gren's shoulders. "Gren, please. I am sorry that you are seeing this, but we must keep moving. Besides, he was one of the enemy."

She sniffled. "How can you tell?"

"He is wearing a New Kingsguard cape. Black. Not red." Vrell jogged to the road and waved Gren to follow.

Gren stumbled after her, sobbing. "I didn't even notice his cloak. I'm just so sad for that other soldier. He was so excited to be a guardsman. I don't even know his name."

"Arne." Vrell gripped Gren's hand, tugged her along.

Gren panted. "How do you know?"

"Anillo told me. I bloodvoiced him to ask him to send someone for the body."

"Oh."

Down the next row, a leg stuck out from under a clump of vines. "Wait, Gren. Here is another." Vrell ducked under a broken trellis and made her way down the row. The vines on her left were a mess. Some had come loose from the trellis and hung like fallen garland. Some were broken and hung like the branches of a weeping willow.

The man lay on his back, arms spread out as if he could fly. His body appeared to have knocked down the trellis, for pieces of wood and bunches of red grapes lay on the ground around him. His head, covered in a gilded helm, was turned away. The helm was twisted slightly and dented with the star-like imprint of a mace.

Vrell stopped, dumbstruck by the etching on the glided breastplate that had once belonged to Moul Rog the Great.

Achan!

6

Vrell knelt at Achan's side and studied the dent in his helm. Only one spike had pierced the steel. A thin trail of blood trickled through it. There did not appear to be an abundance of blood on the grass.

She carefully pulled off the helm. Some of Achan's black hair frizzed, wanting to stay with the wool cushioning of the helm. The rest was stuck to his temple with blood. An odd tingle started in her belly and ran up to her head. She could almost hear the sound of his voice saying, *"We need you as much as you need us. If not for you, who would patch us up when we're half dead?"*

Indeed. She parted his hair with her fingers, looking for the wound near the large lump on his head. Only a small hole had been pierced in the flesh, just above his ear. The spike could not have gone too deeply.

She cupped his cheek and turned his head. Tears flooded her eyes, blurring his face. She leaned over him, placing her cheek in front of his lips.

She could not feel his breath. She needed to get his armor off so she could see his chest. "Gren, help me!"

Footsteps crunched over leaves, and Gren knelt on Achan's other side. "Oh! 'Tis Achan." Gren grabbed Achan's shoulders and shook him. "Achan! Wake up!"

Vrell seized Gren's wrists and squeezed. "Stop! You could make him worse shaking him like that. Help me untie the points on his breastplate. We must get it off."

Gren let go. Vrell began to untie the points on Achan's right side. Gren stared for a moment, then mirrored her movements.

When Vrell finished, she looked to Gren. "Almost done?"

"No! I-I can't do this. My hands are shaking."

Vrell stood and stepped over Achan to his other side. She crouched beside Gren and loosened the points. As she untied the last one, the waist of the backplate fell to the grass. Vrell reached across and grabbed both sides. Gren leaned over her shoulder.

"Back up, please, Gren. I need some room."

Gren's presence vanished, and Vrell lifted. The breastplate was heavier than she expected. She gripped it tightly and passed it to Gren.

Achan's eyes shot open and he sucked in a loud, croaking breath that morphed into a yell. He panted and yelled again, sucking short breaths between his teeth. "What!" He gasped. "My head. Ahh!"

Vrell leaned over him, catching his gaze, thrilled to see him awake. "Shh. All will be well."

Achan's eyebrows sunk low over his eyes. "Sparrow? Sparrow, are you here?" He gripped her arm. "Am I dream . . ." His eyes fell closed then flashed open again. He lifted his head and groaned, his gaze roaming over her. "A dress, Sparrow? You look lovely. I miss you."

Vrell's cheeks flamed. "Shh. Be still."

His eyes widened as his gaze flitted over her. "You're . . . bleeding?" His head thumped to the grass. Unconscious.

Vrell sighed, pushing back her emotions. Dried blood was smeared on her skirt, hands, and sleeves. Probably her face as well. She sent a knock to Sir Caleb. *Vrell Sparrow.*

Vrell? How have you been? Are you—?

Achan is hurt. In the southwestern vineyard, about eighteen rows west of the eastern gate, six paces in. Bring something to carry him on.

Right away.

Vrell unlaced Achan's surcoat. His necklace caught her attention. A cham's claw as long as her index finger hung from a cord of braided leather and red twine. She fingered the cord. The twine had been hers. She had used it to decorate the jar of rue juice she had left to help Achan with his fleas. Her chest tightened.

She could not deny her feelings for this man.

She squeezed the cham's claw in her fist. "Oh . . . I'm such a fool," she whispered. "What do I do? What do I—?"

Vrell?

She jumped at Sir Caleb's voice in her head and dropped Achan's necklace.

We are not far, Sir Caleb said. *How is he?*

She smoothed Achan's fly-away hair. *He is asleep, Sir Caleb. He was struck in the head. A mace.*

Blazes. That boy.

Gren crept up beside Vrell. "Is he . . . ?"

"He should be fine."

Gren knelt at Vrell's side, perusing Achan's body with a doe-eyed stare. "When will you two marry?"

Vrell's gaze left Achan's face and settled on the burgundy sleeve tied to his left arm. Her sleeve. Gren would have heard that Achan was betrothed to Lady Averella Amal. All of Carmine knew. "I know not."

"But you said he'd be fine."

"He will be. But no date has been set . . ." She threaded her fingers through his and squeezed his limp hand. It was sweaty and cold. The words of a song flitted to her mind. The song Yumikak had sung to Achan and Vrell in Berland.

View not my face, I am undone beside you
    The beating of my heart will not cease
Whilst I am near you, whilst I am near you

Tears flooded Vrell's eyes. She blinked them back to no avail. The sun had risen now, bathing the vines and grapes in a golden glow and warming her face.

Arman, what do I do? What can *I do?*

Footsteps crunched over leaves. Sir Eagan, Sir Caleb, Shung, Kurtz, and two servants bounded down the row. One of the servants carried two poles wrapped in canvas over his shoulder. A healer's litter. Vrell dropped Achan's hand and backed away, pulling Gren with her.

Sir Eagan, her father, nodded to Vrell. A calm warmth wrapped around her. Sir Eagan's bloodvoicing specialty, no doubt.

The servant dropped the litter beside Achan's body and unrolled it. Shung and Sir Eagan crouched by his head. The servants crouched on either side of his legs.

"On three," Sir Eagan said. "One, two, three."

The men lifted Achan off the ground and set him on the litter. He groaned but did not wake. Shung walked back out of the row, as if to clear the path. The servants hoisted the litter and carried Achan away.

"I shall care for him now."

Sir Eagan's voice tore Vrell's gaze from Achan's body. She met his piercing blue eyes and nodded. "Thank you."

Sir Eagan held her gaze a moment, which only added more weight to the pressure in her chest. Then he walked away, following the men carrying the litter.

"Well now, Vrell Sparrow. You look fetching, you do, even covered in blood." Kurtz stood before her, brown eyes grazing her as if she were an apple tree. Kurtz, one of the soldiers freed from Ice Island, knew how handsome he was. Tall, blond, burly, and more shameless than a boy in the sugar jar. "You know, now that the prince is set to marry that stuffy young noblewoman, perhaps you and I could—"

"I think not."

"But we're closer to the same rank, we are. And I can show you things our young prince hasn't dreamed of."

Vrell wanted to slap the leer off Kurtz face. She picked up her satchel and walked to the road. "Good day, Kurtz."

"Aw, don't be cross, Vrell. It was just an idea, it was."

Sir Caleb remained on the road. He looked haggard, like a father whose son had not returned from war. He ran his hands through his shaggy blond hair. "How did you find him, Vrell? What are you even doing here? We thought you'd gone elsewhere. And forgive me, but that dress." He looked her up and down. "Where did you get such a gown?"

Say it, she urged herself. *Say, "I am Lady Averella Amal."* That would put Kurtz in his place. But words would not come. Instead, she curtsied and ran after the litter.

She stifled her tears. She would not allow herself to cry until she made it inside the castle. Now that the sun was up, she felt exposed. She stopped suddenly, remembering Kopay, and veered toward the stables. Where had she left her horse?

"My lady!"

Vrell spun around at Gren's voice. The girl hastened toward her, her ample bosom bouncing, face pale and clammy. Vrell melted. Gren had done far too much this morning for a woman with child. She should rest.

Gren stopped before Vrell, chest heaving. "Where are they taking Achan? How will I know he's well?"

"Word will spread through the servants. If not, you could ask Remy. He is Anillo's assistant."

"But," Gren panted, "I can't stand not knowing."

"I told you, he should be fine."

"*Should be*, you say."

Vrell closed her eyes, angry that this peasant dared ask such a thing of a noblewoman, yet her anger was only pride. She no longer cared about classes. After all she had endured living as a stray. Bran was right. She hid behind her title as much as she had hid within the walls of Granton Castle.

Bran!

Vrell sat on the edge of a trough and closed her eyes.

"My lady?" Gren said.

"A moment, please." Vrell reached for Bran.

The sun beat down, but the wind of flight on horseback blew his hair away from his face as he traveled down a dusty road behind Sir Rigil's black courser. Grassy plains stretched out all around him. All was well. No fear clouded his thoughts. No concerns.

She opened her eyes, relieved that Bran, Jax, and Sir Rigil were safe. And Achan too.

Praise You, Arman. And thank You.

Vrell reached a hand to Gren. "Help me find and stable my horse, and I shall take you to Achan."

Gren pulled Vrell up and released a shaky sob and a stream of tears. Vrell wished she could afford such transparency.

They found Kopay back in what was left of the stables. Nothing but a corral inside the stone walls. The roof and all the stalls were gone. At least the animals could not roam free. Griscol had started to gather saddles and tack on a cart outside the stables. Vrell found her pack there. She hoisted it over her shoulder and led Gren around to a servant's entrance on the east side of the castle.

They followed the corridor that stretched along the north side of the courtyard. Vrell picked up a low-burning candle and ducked inside Mother's receiving room in the north wing. She closed the door, thankful they had not run into anyone.

The dark room slowly took shape around them in the low light. Vrell left her pack here. She moved the candle to her right hand and reached for Gren with her left. "Take my hand."

Gren's hands clasped hers. "Where are we?"

"My mother's receiving room. Trust me, please, and would you mind closing your eyes?"

"My eyes? Why?"

"If you want to see Achan . . . Mother would not like that I've brought you here. You must promise not to tell a soul what you see today. Do you?"

"Sure. Close my eyes now?"

"Please." Vrell held the candle aloft so the light fell over Gren's face. Her eyes were shut. The rest of her body melted into the darkness, black dress and all. "Thank you, Gren." Before Vrell turned to go, she looked kindly on the girl's face. "Gren, you did very well helping me today. You are a good friend."

Gren smiled, and Vrell pulled her slowly across the room to the painting of her mother. Her fingers found the latch on the upper left side of the frame. She pulled until it clicked and the painting bounced out from the wall.

"Only a moment longer." Vrell helped Gren inside the passageway and pulled the painting closed behind them. "All right. You may open your eyes."

Gren studied the corridor. "Where are we?"

"In one of the secret passageways in Granton Castle."

"There are secret passageways?"

"Yes. But you must be absolutely silent, or we will be discovered."

"I can keep quiet."

"Good. Follow me."

Vrell led Gren all the way to the peephole that looked in on Achan's chambers. She glanced inside and saw that the men had already put Achan in his bed. Sir Eagan was smearing something on his head. Yarrow salve, likely. Shung stood behind Sir Eagan. A young boy stood at Shung's side.

"Is he dead, sir?" the boy asked.

"Sleeping."

"Will he sleep forever?"

"No, Matthias," Sir Eagan said. "He will wake when he is ready, once his body is rested."

Vrell stepped back from the peephole, motioned for Gren to look, then reached up and felt for the stone ledge she often used for her candle. When her fingers found it, she set the candle down and leaned against the opposite wall.

"Is he well?" Sir Caleb's voice carried through the wall.

"He should recover fully," Sir Eagan said, "though we must make sure that he wakes every few hours."

"He went out there to spite me," Sir Caleb said. "If I had acquiesced, Sir Shung would have been with—"

"He is old enough to make his own choices, Caleb," Sir Eagan said.

"But that's just it. He makes the wrong ones. Continually. How can I stand by and let him kill himself?"

"He will not learn to make the right decisions if he is coddled."

"I don't mean to coddle him, but . . . why does he insist on his way? He is so willful."

"He is merely trying to be a leader, I suspect."

"It would have been better for him to disobey me outright and take Shung along. But he sneaks off alone." Footsteps tapped over wood and echoed along the stone wall of the corridor. "I don't know how to control him."

"You cannot control him, Caleb. Nor should you. He needs to know that we believe in him. We must advise him, build up his confidence, not command him."

"I never intend to command him, but I've seen too many hurt. Killed. It's a cruel and brutal world. My fears are well-founded."

"That they are," Sir Eagan said, "but your fears will not give him the insight of experience. He must learn that for himself. I daresay the headache he will wake with will teach him a strong lesson in heeding your advice in the future."

"But he didn't learn from the cham attack." More footsteps. "Why is Vrell here? I thought you said she was going to Allowntown."

Vrell nudged Gren away from the peephole and looked inside.

Sir Eagan put the lid on a jar. "I never said I knew where she was going."

"Someone said it. Perhaps Gavin. I don't understand why she's here. And dressed so well. You spoke with her. What did she say?"

"Only to give me her assessment of the prince's injury."

"Should we be concerned about her? It's good she left, don't you think? I don't want her becoming a distraction now that the prince is betrothed to Lady Averella."

Sir Eagan turned away from Sir Caleb, faced the peephole, and winked. "Ah, Caleb. I would not worry about Vrell Sparrow. Arman will work through her thick skull in his timing. All will be well."

Vrell pursed her lips. Sir Eagan knew of the secret passages as well? If Mother continued to tell people, they would no longer be a secret.

Sir Eagan drew a blanket over Achan's waist and walked to the doors. "We must let the prince sleep. At least *two hours*." He winked in Vrell's direction again. "Sir Shung, stand outside and let no one enter. Come Caleb, let us take this discussion elsewhere. Matthias, you as well."

The men and the boy left.

Vrell nudged Gren. "Come."

She inched down the corridor, running her hand along the wall until her fingers felt the crack in the surface. She slid the panel open. Lamplight streamed through the doorway. She ducked inside and tugged her dress past the narrow opening. Gren followed, and Vrell slid the panel closed.

Vrell hurried to Achan's bed and sat on the edge. His skin had purpled over his right temple. Sir Eagan's yarrow salve had slicked his hair flat around the wound. The thick paste smelled like fresh flowers. She smoothed the loose hair back off the other side of his forehead and studied his face.

What was she to do about Achan now?

"Go visit him."

Vrell sat on Gypsum's bed, the skirt of her peach gown billowing around her like a mushroom. "I have, Gypsum."

Her sister sat at her embroidery frame, already half finished with a new tapestry depicting her abduction, Arne's death, and her rescue by Achan, or as she called him, Prince Achan. How she could create new embroideries so quickly bordered on magical powers.

"He saved my life, Vrella. Those men meant to take me to Esek's camp."

The very idea horrified Vrell more than she cared to admit. "Truly, Gypsum, you heard them say Esek is alive?"

Gypsum glanced up from her work. "The ogre man, the one who killed Arne, he said, 'If yer sister won't marry the king, you will. Once she's dead, you'll be heir to Carm.'"

Vrell's stomach churned. "Maybe someone else is planning to be king now."

"Vrella, are you listening?" Gypsum stood and walked to the foot of her bed. "They plan to *kill* you. Are you not concerned?"

"Not nearly as much as I am about them taking you."

Gypsum slid her hand around the bedpost and hugged it with one arm. "Well, if you will not marry Prince Achan, I shall. I still do not wish to marry a man who loves you, and I *am* frightened of marriage, but Prince Achan is so kind and attentive . . . and handsome." She straightened her arm and swung around the bedpost as if dancing. "I know he would not hurt me."

Vrell scowled at the dreamy expression on Gypsum's face, as if Achan were the bedpost. Her sister's eight minutes spent alone in the company of Achan Cham had apparently made her an expert on his countenance. "Why ever would you think your husband would hurt you?"

"Well, that is what some say about their husbands."

"Who says?"

Gypsum sat on the edge of her bed. "Halley married a soldier who is very brutal. And Meglan says that her husband only ever wants to make babies and that it hurts her but he doesn't care. And even Havella, my maidservant, has a fresh bruise every now and then. She never said outright Marden struck her, but I can tell it was him. Oh, and Suzelle—"

Vrell wrinkled her nose. "No more, Gypsum, please. You depress me. I had no idea how many wretched men lived in Carmine." Yet her comment brought to mind the men who had attacked Gren. She shook the thought away.

"It's not only Carmine men. Lady Melita Thorvald married Derno Sigul of Hamonah, and he is a *hideous* man. You wouldn't believe the things he does and says and—"

"The Siguls are pirates, Gypsum. They are hideous at birth. Really, for all your tales of horror, I can tell you as many tales of joy. Think of my Syrah. Jonol has courted her this past year and has only ever kissed her hand. And Princess Glassea and Keano Pitney."

"But they are not yet married. Things are different then."

"Prince Donediff and his wife, Lady Yulessa. I've heard from her mother that they are blissful. And Lady Katiolikan and Lord Eli seemed to get along well enough. And the priest Trajen Yorbride and his wife Ressa . . . They were sickly sweet to one another."

Her sister sighed, a long, sing-song sound, and tucked a strand of Vrell's hair behind her ear. "All I am saying is that it seems to me a smart lady would seize the chance to marry a good man."

Gypsum's eyes were shining. Had Vrell been so dreamy about romance at Gypsum's age? Yes. And pining after Sir Rigil. She felt the need to give her sister some wisdom, as if she knew anything at all about romance.

"A lady should consider a man's goodness before she agrees to be courted, not married," Vrell said. "She should know him very well by that point."

"And you do not dispute Prince Achan's goodness?"

"Every man—and woman, for that matter—is capable of doing good or evil. So, yes, dear sister, *Prince Achan* is a good, kind man. But he does not follow Arman as you and I do. So when temptation comes to him—and it will—how will he choose good? That is my question of *Prince* Achan. He snuck to the battlefield this morning. His idea of doing good was following his own pride. Even Mother agrees with that. Until he conquers what hinders—"

"And how did *you* come to be on the battlefield, dear sister? You dare judge his pride when your pride is equal to his? You claim to follow Arman, but still you go your own way. None of us are perfect, Vrella. Least of all you."

"But I am trying to follow Arman."

"You follow your own will first. Arman's will second. And if Prince Achan hadn't done what he did today, I would be lost to

Esek. Arman used Prince Achan's pride to put him in my path. It is not too late for Arman to make good of your bad choices either."

The words shocked as much as a slap to the face. Heat welled up inside, for Vrell recognized the truth in Gypsum's words, though she could not admit it aloud. "You know not what you . . ." Her voice hitched. "There is more to it than—"

"I am saying, sister, that I *will* marry Prince Achan should you not. And I will be happy to do it. So you had best figure out what you really want before it is too late."

Again Vrell led Kopay through the clusters of horses and toward the exit of what remained of the stables. The fire had cost her a day. And the last time she had looked in on Bran, he and Jax's men were already nearing the Sideros Forest.

A girl in a black dress stepped out from the shadows as Vrell approached the brand new plank doors.

Gren Fenny again. This time she clutched a burlap sack in her hands, wringing the fabric as if she might squeeze water from it. The sack twisted gently, full of something that made it bulge like a teardrop.

"Whoa, boy." Vrell and Kopay stopped. "Good morning, Gren. You are up early. Again."

Gren fidgeted with her bag. "I wanted to thank you for taking me to see Achan yesterday."

"You are welcome." Vrell eyed Gren's sack. "I never asked why you were in the stables yesterday. You work in the kitchens, do you not?"

Gren's face flushed. "I was going to steal a horse."

For some reason, the very idea tickled Vrell. She giggled in spite of the seriousness of Gren's confession. "You do not strike me as a horse thief."

"I can't stay here. The people of Carmine hate me."

Vrell's mind filled in what Gren had not said, what she knew had happened this past summer when Gren had been attacked. "They blame you for my broken betrothal. I thought Master Rennan had made an announcement."

Gren approached until she stood right before Vrell. "He did, but some think it's a lie, that your lady mother forced him to say it. And now that he's gone, I won't stay with no one to watch over me."

Vrell stroked Kopay's neck. "Master Rennan cares for your welfare. I am sure he would not have left you here had he believed it dangerous."

"He didn't say nothing like that. He said he'd be back after the war. But I don't know what that means."

"That he did not want to risk your heart. To ask for your hand or to marry you before he left would be irresponsible."

"I don't understand you nobles and all your rules. All I know is he's gone. What if his master bids he stay in Armonguard after the war? If I'm not there, he may forget me. But if I follow him, I'd be there when the war's over."

"I know that you care for Master Rennan, but you will cause him nothing but trouble to follow him now. How can he assist his king if he is worried about you?" Vrell winced at how much her words mirrored Sir Rigil's. But that was different. Vrell was not chasing after a man. She was running from one.

Gren gazed up at Kopay. "Oh, I don't wish to worry him. Only to be near when all this is over. Plus, I have to look out for my child. And it's not safe here."

"My mother will see that you are cared for."

Gren turned her eyes back to Vrell. "I don't doubt your mother's kindness, my lady, but she can't watch me always. I'll be safer in a war."

"After all Master Rennan and Jax and Sir Rigil went through to bring you here?"

"Achan said he isn't worried for me no more. He figures Lord Nathak has his hands full with other things. And if Achan's not worried, I'm not worried."

"But what of your parents? I am certain they would want to go with you."

"They're happy here."

"But they will want to see their grandchild."

"They can visit once the baby comes. But I can't put my baby's life in danger because Bran might come back someday. Please, my lady. Can't I come with you to Sitna? I have friends there who'll take me the rest of the way."

The very idea stunned Vrell. "I do not plan to travel through Sitna."

"It can't be far out of your way. Please? I'll serve you. I'll cook for you."

Vrell would not mind a companion or a cook. She was so far behind Jax and the others that it was dangerous for her to travel alone, though it was the road from Sitna to Mahanaim that truly frightened her. And she wouldn't be able to ride as fast with Gren along.

"I am sorry, Gren, but I cannot take you with me. I must ride like the wind to catch up with Jax. As it is, they are a day ahead of me."

"Then I'll tell your mother you've gone."

Vrell's chin dropped. "You would blackmail me?"

A tear streamed down Gren's cheek. "I don't want to, my lady. But I'm desperate. Have mercy, I beg you."

Vrell sighed. "Oh, very well. Run and get your things and meet me back here."

Gren held up her sack. "I've no things to be getting. Just tell me which horse I can ride and we'll be on our way."

This foiled Vrell's plan to ride off while Gren was packing her bag. Vrell was worried enough for her own safety. Two women riding alone—and one with child. It was more than foolish.

She heaved a long sigh. Vrell's stick-like frame made her a believable boy, but it would take a masterpiece of disguise to make Gren's curves look like those of a plump man. And that black dress would never do. Still, if anyone saw them from afar . . . She released her hold on Kopay. "We should find you some trousers and a man's tunic before we go. It will be safer that way."

PART 3

LESSONS

7

Achan lay on his back in a vineyard. The sky draped overhead like a cerulean tent. Leaves and vines rustled in a cool breeze that blew his hair across his face. He felt no pain.

Hadn't he been wounded?

Perhaps he was in the Veil again. He tried to float off the ground, and he suddenly stood on the platform in Berland. Drums beat a low cadence that rumbled deep in his belly. Bodies danced around him in a blur of slow motion. All but one. A woman, clear and close, sang in a haunting voice.

View not my face, I am undone beside you
    The beating of my heart will not cease
Whilst I am near you, whilst I am near you.

A jeweled tiara held her silky black hair in place. She wore a green gown as fine as any of Duchess Amal's. Her skin was soft and white like the petal of a daisy. Her green eyes drew him in.

Vrell Sparrow.

He reached out for her but grasped nothing but air. Why couldn't he get to her?

He opened his eyes to the frescoed ceiling of his chamber in Granton Castle. Pain stabbed his head like a gowzal's bite. He took a deep breath and the stabs struck again, sharp and angry.

Trying to sit made it worse, so he lay still, gasping shallow breaths. His stomach churned, threatening to expel whatever might be inside. Nothing, if he went by memory, for he had not eaten before sneaking out.

He lay in his bed, shirtless, a blanket pulled up to his waist. The stripe of sunlight that spilled through the door of his privy proved it daytime. But what hour? And what day?

Footsteps padded across the wooden floor, and Matthias's brown eyes came into view.

"Matthias . . ." The room blurred, taking the boy's face and blond hair and twisting them with the colors of the frescoed ceiling above. Tingles danced behind Achan's eyes. He closed his eyes, breathed deeply, then opened them to a clearer view. "What's happened?"

"You were struck down in battle, sir."

The mace. Achan ran his fingers over the side of his head. It felt swollen, tender. "How long have I been sleeping? What of the battle?"

"The battle has ended, sir. Though Sir Caleb says we leave soon to fight again. You've been sleeping two days."

Two days? No wonder his stomach ached. He blinked at the boy and realized he was wearing a new red tunic and black trousers. "You have new clothes."

Matthias smiled. "Yes, sir. Thank you for them, sir."

"You're welcome." Achan took a deep breath and smelled a hint of roses on the air. "Did someone bathe in rose water, Matthias? Or was a woman here?"

"Aye, sir. Three."

"*Three* women? All at once?"

"No. First come the duchess with her man, the scarred one. What happened to his neck, sir?"

"Anillo? Lord Nathak's men tried to kill him. What of the other two women?"

"They came together."

"Maids, you mean?"

"Oh, no, sir. Not maids. One wore a black dress. The other looked like a cornsilk doll and sang like an angel."

Achan perked up. "One of them sang? As she worked?"

"She didn't work. She sat with you and held your hand."

"Did she?" Sparrow. It had to be. Hope spread through Achan, coiled around his chest like armor.

"Who was she, sir? The one who sang?"

"The woman I love," Achan said, almost to himself.

Matthias's snicker turned Achan's head.

"You find that funny?"

Matthias sobered. "Do you kiss her?"

Achan sighed, fighting a laugh he suspected would make his aching head worse. "No, Matthias, I do not. We are not permitted to be together."

Matthias seemed to mull this over. "Armas loves a lady not of his station."

"And who is Armas, again?" Matthias spoke of so many siblings, Achan couldn't keep them all straight.

"My oldest brother. He's lived nineteen years."

Right. The son who would inherit Master Ricks's net-making enterprise. "Is the lady above or below him?"

"Oh, far above, sir. She is Lady Lathia. Her father is captain of the *Brierstar*."

Achan's eyes widened, recalling his dances with Lady Lathia the night before her grandfather, Lord Livna, had been killed. "I'm familiar with Lady Lathia. Has she ever spoken to your brother?"

"Oh, yes. They kiss when they think no one is looking."

"Do they?" Achan tried to imagine Lady Lathia kissing a peasant man. "Does she strike him or get angry?"

"Never, sir." Matthias wrinkled his nose. "I think she likes to be kissed."

Achan grinned. "From your report, Matthias, I gather she does. Perhaps I can help your brother make that match. It is good for people to marry the one they love. Arman knows I will not have that pleasure."

The door opened and Sir Caleb entered. "Ah, I see you are awake. Praise Arman. How do you feel?"

"Hungry. And my head hurts."

"I do not doubt it, Your Highness. Why you insist on disobeying simple instructions, I'll never understand."

Heat rushed through Achan's chest. "Really? You can't imagine why I might make a decision every now and then?"

Sir Caleb's eyes shut as if trying to control his temper. He opened them slowly. "I know you desire to be a good leader. But it's selfish to risk your life. Er'Rets needs you."

"Why do you decide how I serve Er'Rets?"

"I'm a Kingsguard knight, appointed by your father. And your advisor, appointed by you."

"*Advisor*, Sir Caleb, not father."

"I never meant to imply that—"

"How can you expect me to lead—to ever have confidence to do so—if you continually override me? True, I am but sixteen years of age. I have not your wit, experience, or skill with politics and war. Still, Arman chose *me*. And I am trying to obey His call. If you refuse to be reasonable, to accept any authority from me at all . . ." Achan paused, hating to say what he felt he must. "I will replace you."

Sir Caleb's shoulders sank. "Understood."

"Thank you." Achan wanted to forget this conversation had ever taken place. "Now is there something you needed?"

The knight's tone grew distant. "No, Your Highness. I only wanted to see how you fared. Since you are hungry, I'll have a tray brought up." He bowed to his waist, causing his wild hair to fall forward and reveal a balding patch of skin. Then he strode out the door.

Achan rubbed his eyes. The pain in his head was now accompanied by an ache in his chest. He hadn't meant to berate Sir Caleb, especially in front of Matthias. He should have held his ground in the first place and demanded to go to the battle. It would take time to prove to Sir Caleb that Achan wasn't completely hopeless as a leader, but he could never prove anything without a chance to try.

He felt trapped in his bed and desperately wanted to sit. He turned his head and met Shung's gaze. The Shield sat on a chair in the dark corner, shadowed in his black clothes.

"Why, hello, Shung. Nice of you to announce yourself."

His Shield raised one eyebrow. "Shung was sleeping until Sir Caleb spoke. The lion's voice haunts my dreams."

At least Achan wasn't the only one under Sir Caleb's careful eye, though he felt even more embarrassed knowing that Shung had also overheard his lecture. "He means well."

Shung leaned forward in his chair and clasped his hands. One of his thick braids fell over his shoulder and dangled with the charmice tails that decorated his jerkin. "Still, the lion needed taming, even if the little cham is a willful cub."

"I'm sorry I left you, Shung. Next time I will fight for my choice instead of sneaking off."

Shung's smile caused his cheeks to ball above his hairy sideburns. "Shung saw Little Fox."

"Sparrow?" Achan's pulse rose at the idea of her in this room, holding his hand. "She was really here?"

"Aye. Shung sees now why you named her fox."

"*I* named her? I thought you named her as you do everyone else."

"No. When Little Cham came to Berland, said, 'That one is fox.'"

Achan tried to remember when he first considered Sparrow a fox. It could have been the time he caught her bloodvoicing her supposedly dead mother. Or even earlier, like the day she'd read Gren's letter.

Aye, Sparrow deserved her title. Deceiving him seemed to be her favorite game.

But she was here, in Carmine. She'd been inside the castle—inside his chambers! "Who let her in?"

"Shung did. She came with the fawn yesterday."

"I am an injured man, Shung. Have mercy on my head and speak plainly."

"The widow works in the kitchens, sir." Matthias still stood at his bedside. "Jespa calls her Gren."

Achan balked. Sparrow and Gren had come to visit him? Together? What madness was this?

A knock sounded on the door. Shung answered it.

Could it be Sparrow and Gren again?

No, only Anillo. He walked to the foot of Achan's bed and bowed. "Your Highness, Duchess Amal would like to pay you a visit. Would now be an appropriate time?"

Now? Achan wasn't even dressed. He pushed himself up onto one elbow, holding his breath at the ache in his head.

Shung's boots clomped across the wooden floor. "Little Cham should stay down." He pushed on Achan's shoulder, agitating the place where the cham had put its teeth.

"No." Achan met Shung's scowl. "I need a shirt."

Matthias was already padding toward the bed, shaking out a long green tunic. "It's not pressed, sir."

"It's fine," Achan said as Shung helped him sit. "Anillo, give us a moment?"

Anillo bowed. "Of course, Your Highness. But there is no need to hurry. We can return later."

"No, no. I just need a moment."

Matthias slipped up to the bedside. The boy had already gathered the tunic in his hands just as Sir Caleb had done for Achan ever since the cham attack. Matthias threaded the sleeve over Achan's right hand and slid it gently up his injured shoulder. "Tip your head, sir."

Achan leaned his right ear toward Matthias, who pulled the tunic over his head in such a way so the fabric didn't touch his head wound. Achan shoved his left arm through. Matthias laced the shirt and padded away.

"All right, Anillo." Achan sucked in a short breath. He tucked the long hem under the blanket. "I'm ready."

"Wait!" Matthias ran across the room with a comb and length of green ribbon. "Your hair, sir. It's a fright."

Achan looked to Shung. The hairy man nodded once, smirking. "One moment more, Anillo," Achan said.

Achan sat still, suffering through the pricks while Matthias tugged snarls from his head. The boy took care with the hair over Achan's head wound and combed it all back into a tail. He held the hair with one hand and stretched the other out over Achan's shoulder, blackened fingers clutching the green ribbon. "Sir Shung, can you help?"

Shung snagged the ribbon. Together, he and Matthias managed to secure Achan's hair. Matthias arranged the pillows into a small mountain, then Shung helped Achan lie back, so he was somewhat reclined.

Achan smoothed the covers over his lap, making sure the Duchess would in no way suspect he wasn't wearing trousers. "All right. I'm ready."

Anillo opened the door and poked his head out. "The prince is ready, my lady."

Duchess Amal entered, wearing a bronze gown that swept the floor as she walked. Achan couldn't say why the lady sent a wave of heat over him whenever he saw her. Though small, something in her regal stature made him want to cower at her feet.

She walked up to the side of his bed and curtsied. "Pardon my intrusion, Your Highness. I hope I did not wake you."

"No, my lady. You did not wake me. You bring news of Lady Averella?" He flashed a wide smile.

Her pursed lips curved into the faintest smile. "I see you are your charming self again. Did you forget your pledge that you would not wander my castle alone?"

Her green eyes penetrated to his heart, igniting it like parchment. Heat spread over his body like wildfire, tingling his cheeks. He wanted to look away, but found he could not.

"Ah, yes. You have that look in your eyes. You are not the first man I have seen felled by his own pride."

At this Achan did look away. Leaving the castle alone *had* been foolish. But if Sir Caleb hadn't overruled him, Shung would have come along. He turned back to the duchess but looked over her shoulder to avoid her eyes. "Thank you for bringing me back from the Veil."

"You have already thanked me, Your Highness. No need to do so again. I hope you see now that men in high positions play a different role from most. Though your heart wants to fight like the average man, you must not risk yourself in such a way. You understand that better now, do you not?"

Would every elder lecture him his whole life long? He didn't need to be set afire when he was already burning. Yet he said in a small voice, "Yes, ma'am."

She didn't move or speak for so long that Achan was drawn to look in her eyes. When he did, she smiled and tipped her head, pulling his gaze to the swaying brown gems that dripped from her ears. "And now I shall thank you."

"Me, my lady?"

"You saved my daughter from a terrifying ordeal. Lady Gypsum is most grateful and has asked permission to visit when and if you are willing to receive her."

"Oh, sure." Achan had forgotten all about Lady Gypsum. "She made it back safely, then?"

"She did. I am glad you used the tunnel that morning." She stepped so close to his bedside that her gown crinkled against the mattress. "Though your body is weak, I suspect your mind is still strong. Might you permit me to check?"

Check his mind? "Uh . . . Of course, my lady."

"Sir Eagan assured me my venture should not aggravate your head wound. But I warn you, Your Highness, this may hurt in a different way."

He did not relish more pain, especially in his head. But as Duchess Amal lowered herself to sit on the edge of his bed, he did not stop her.

Her intense gaze locked onto his again. "Do you trust me, Your Highness?"

His hands trembled and his voice came out a near whisper. "With my life."

She smiled wide, and he felt as if he could jump out of bed that moment and challenge Esek to a duel.

The duchess reached for his face. Her icy fingertips slid across his cheek and rested just before his ear.

He clenched his teeth and shivered.

"Close your eyes and open your mind."

Achan obeyed instantly, as if he had no other choice. He had a choice, didn't he? He felt nothing but her touch on his face and the ache in his head. He sat there, breathing shallowly, waiting.

"Your gift is stronger than mine, but as your body is weak and I am touching you, I could destroy you. Did you know that?"

Achan's eyes flashed open. He drew up his shields, and what felt like the bite of a cham bear bit down on his head. He gasped.

"*Relax.* I will not hurt you. Open your mind." Her gaze was focused on her hand. "And close your eyes."

It went against all logic, but he blew out a short breath and obeyed. He had no reason not to trust this woman, but blazes, she had a shocking way with words.

"Touch, skin to skin, increases the connection between gifted minds. Like having a key to one's soul. You may have other defenses to keep me out, but touch reduces the biggest obstacle." Her fingertips shifted. "Let us play a bit."

Achan swallowed.

"Sir Shung, stay close to your prince as we practice. Keep the connection open between your minds. Listen to his conversation with me, though he could block you from our words should he wish to. If you do not hear from him often, speak to him. If he does not respond, or you suspect he is in danger, wake him. Do not leave his side until he returns to his body. Should you wait too long, it is possible he will never wake. Do you understand your responsibility?"

Achan opened his eyes to see Shung bang his fist against his chest. "Shung will not fail, my lady."

"And please make sure I do not fall off the bed."

Shung lunged to the bedside, hands out.

Duchess Amal smiled. "Not yet, Sir Shung. First connect your mind to the prince's."

Shung's knock came almost instantly. *Shung Noatak.*

Achan opened his mind to his Shield. *Any clue what she's going to do?*

None, Little Cham. She is her own kind of warrior.

Achan took a jagged breath. *That she is.*

The duchess caressed Achan's cheek. "Relax, Your Highness, and please, close your eyes."

He obeyed, willing his hands to stay still, his heartbeat to calm, his breathing to slow. Suddenly, he was flying up through the ceiling, through the rooms on the levels above his, out the roof, and into the sky. Hovering over Castle Granton, he could see the stronghold beneath his bare legs.

Bare legs?

His heart leaped into his throat. They were in the Veil. He did not want to be here again. And in his undershorts!

Trouble, Little Cham? Shung asked.

Achan looked to his left and found Duchess Amal holding his hand, floating in the sky beside him. Oh, horror. He couldn't breathe. *I am well, Shung. It's just . . . She took me into the Veil and . . . No pants, Shung! No pants!*

Yet Achan would knight Matthias for having chosen such a long tunic. It hung to his knees like a nightshirt. He prayed the duchess would assume it was just that.

To Duchess Amal, he said, *How did you . . . ?*

She flashed her disarming smile. *I have stormed you.*

Achan squeezed her hand. *Isn't that a bad thing?*

Not how I have done it, for I mean you no harm. But you understand why this is dangerous?

Achan shuddered at the memory of not being able to get back to his body. *Aye . . . I mean, yes.*

When our mind is away from our body for too long, it yearns for the world beyond and drifts to one of the gates.

Gates?

The Pearly Gate or the Fiery Gate.

How does the mind know where to go?

It doesn't. It is pulled by Light or Darkness. Only Light can go to Shamayim. All Darkness goes to the Lowerworld.

Achan considered this. *You must know Câan to reach the Pearly Gate, for Câan is Light.*

Precisely. When you storm someone in battle, you push their mind from their body and strip it of its recent memories. This way, the mind is lost, drifting until it reaches one of the two eternal destinations.

How long does that take?

That varies, I think, depending on Arman's will. Some go within days, some linger for years.

That's . . . horrible.

No more horrible than being run through by a sword and left to bleed to death. As you can see, it is a peaceful, ignorant death. I suspect many believe they are dreaming.

And some would know that they are not?

Those trained to navigate the Veil would know. If you found yourself here, you would know—now that I've told you. You would know to try and return to your body.

So that's possible then? I could get back on my own?

Certainly. As long as you have not passed through one of the two gates, you can will yourself to move.

And if I cannot? Like before when I was drifting?

You merely require practice, Your Highness. But if you could not, Sir Shung could come for you, once he's trained.

And pull me as you have done?

As long as he knew where to find you, which is why it is essential to keep in contact with him, maybe even let him watch through you so he knows your location.

Achan thought again to the day he had found himself drifting. *If he didn't know where I was, how would he know where to look?*

It is difficult. When a person is stormed, I message them first. If they have lost their memory, I might look where I knew they last were and hope their mind has not drifted far. Touching their physical body would help. And if I could not do that, I would hold something that belongs to them.

Before, when I was drifting, what if you had not come? Could I have gotten back on my own?

Without a partner's aid, it can be difficult. Only Arman could help you then. You would be completely at His mercy.

Do you have a partner now? Like I have Shung?

I do. Anillo's connection to my mind anchors me in Er'Rets. Without that connection, I might drift as you did.

Achan recalled the time he had gone into the Veil to help Gren when the Carmine peasants attacked her. The knights who had been with his body had thrown water on his head to wake him. *Shung doesn't have to enter the Veil to bring me back.*

Usually, all it takes is a shake of your shoulder. If he cannot wake you, he can message you. But if you were stormed, your memory would be altered. And it would be difficult for Sir Shung to find your location.

I see. Achan's thoughts tumbled until one came to the surface. *How is it you can touch me now? For every time I've been in the Veil, I drift through people and solid objects.*

The rules of nature are different in the Veil. We can touch each other, but we cannot touch objects or people in the physical world. That is why we passed through the roof. Now, you are to take us back, Your Highness. Concentrate and use your connection with Sir Shung to draw strength.

Achan did as she asked. He pulled Duchess Amal by the hand down toward the roof. He smiled. It was working. They passed through several rooms until they were floating in his chamber. Anillo and Mathias were talking over by the armoire. Shung stood at the foot of his bed.

Now take us back to our minds, Your Highness.

How?

Simply return.

Achan opened his eyes and found himself in bed. Something heavy pressed down on his legs. He glanced down and saw Duchess Amal's limp body lying across the foot of his bed, one arm draped across her waist.

"Shung! What has happened to the duchess?"

"She went limp. But Shung did not let her fall."

All is well, men. Do not fret. Duchess Amal's voice boomed in Achan's mind. *I chose not to return to my body, for I wanted you to understand, Your Highness, that you cannot force me back. Only I can make that choice.*

But I could force you out by storming? Achan asked.

Not exactly. Storming is a trick. It's all about making the other person lower their guard enough so you can pull their mind away from their body the same way you pulled me to this room. If you keep your shields up, you can resist.

The door opened and Sir Eagan entered.

Duchess Amal's body shifted. She sat up, her delicate complexion tinged pink. She smoothed her hair, stood, and shook out her wrinkled skirt. "That is enough lesson for today. Next you will learn how to storm in battle."

Achan wanted to ask when she would return—he couldn't wait to learn how to be a Veil warrior—but Duchess Amal walked to the door and curtsied. "Good day, Your Majesty. Sir Shung." She met Sir Eagan's gaze and her voice softened. "Sir Eagan." And she left.

Sir Eagan approached Achan's bedside. "I am pleased to see you awake, Your Highness. How are you feeling?"

"Oh, fine." Recovering from Duchess Amal's presence. "How is all that going?" He gestured to the door. "You know, you and Duchess Amal?" For Sir Eagan and Lady Nitsa had loved one another in their youth but had been parted for nearly eighteen years.

Sir Eagan glanced at the door and smiled. "Very well, thank you." He took Achan's chin in one hand and set his other hand on his head. "This is healing quickly. You are a fortunate man." He pressed on the lump.

Achan gritted his teeth at the pressure. "Shung tells me Sparrow is here." He hitched in a short breath. "Perhaps she could serve as m[illegible] healer again?"

Sir Eagan raised an eyebrow. "You think she would not hav[illegible] determine the level of your pain?"

Achan grunted, for Sparrow took healing just as serious[illegible] Eagan. "She's nicer to look upon, at least."

"True." Sir Eagan ran his fingers over Achan's [illegible], neck and stomach, pushing down and asking how muc[illegible] everythi[illegible]

Nothing hurt but his head, though his cham[illegible] wounds [illegible] were still tender.

"My assessment is that you are fine," Sir Eagan said. "We should be able to depart as planned."

Depart. "Will Sparrow visit again? Has she returned for good?" Would she come back to him? Could she, now that he was betrothed to Lady Averella?

"I have not seen her since the vineyard."

"So that wasn't a dream?"

"Not a dream, Your Highness. She found you, called us to bring you in, and so we did."

Achan closed his eyes and reached for Sparrow. He found her mind impenetrable, as always. A giddy thought grew within. If the duchess taught him more, he might somehow be able to find Sparrow in spite of her shields.

The little fox could not hide from him forever.

8

Vrell had hoped to ride out at dawn amongst the harvesters, but Gren's joining her delayed their departure until after breakfast. To Vrell's frustration, Gren had never ridden a horse. How the girl thought she would steal one and make it through the gates unnoticed—black mourning gown and all—Vrell would never guess.

After a lesson in how to ride, they left the stronghold behind a group of wagons headed to the orchards. They rode through the partially burned vineyards that the enemy had destroyed and out of Carmine.

The air smelled sweet and fresh as they passed by hay fields. Dozens of men waded through the timothy grass, swinging scythes against the golden hay. Boys with pitchforks scurried behind, spreading it flat so it could dry.

The day passed slowly. Vrell stopped at a creek to water the horses, and she and Gren changed from their dresses into dingy blue tunics and brown trousers. Though this time, Vrell did not bother with fake bellies. Once Gren's black mourning dress and Vrell's green travel dress were packed away in their saddlebags, they continued their journey more comfortably. Men's clothing was much cooler to wear.

When night fell, they made camp in a grove of olive trees at the foot of a grassy knoll not far from the road. The trees sheltered them and their horses from any passersby. They sat on bedrolls under a bushy olive tree, munching on dates and cheese. Gren inhaled her food like a man.

Vrell supposed the child within wanted his or her share, so she gave Gren a bit more. "When is your child expected?"

"Mother guesses the end of winter."

"That seems so far away."

"I think so too."

"Does it hurt? Being with child?"

"I get sick in the mornings, and I seem to live with a never-ending headache."

"I have feverfew in my satchel." Vrell pointed to her things propped against the tree trunk. "Help yourself."

"Thanks." Gren lifted the satchel and dug inside it.

Vrell closed her eyes and sought out Bran. He, Jax, and Sir Rigil were sitting on bedrolls in their own camp, hashing out their suspicions as to whether or not Esek was still alive.

Gypsum seemed to think so. But the only way Esek could have survived the loss of a limb was if a skilled healer had been present. Perhaps one had been.

Vrell fingered the chain at her neck that held Achan's signet ring. She wanted it close until she decided what to do.

"Is this Achan's hair?"

Vrell glanced up to see Gren clutching feverfew leaves in one hand and a lock of black hair in the other. "It is."

"I cut his hair so many times . . . It looked familiar." Gren twirled the lock in her fingers. "Did he cut this for you?"

Vrell laughed heartily. "Does that sound like something Achan would do?"

A small smile curved Gren's lips. "I guess not."

"*I* cut it," Vrell said, "back when he was wounded in the Mahanaim dungeon. I was learning to bloodvoice at the time."

"Locks of hair help with bloodvoicing?"

"Personal possessions increase the ability of connection. I thought hair would be personal enough."

"So you met Achan in Mahanaim?"

"I did."

Gren's tone hardened. "Then how come he's never met you? For he confessed as much to me only days ago."

"I . . ." Vrell would never escape her own lies if she could not prune herself of all deceit. What was that Bran had claimed? That the truth would set her free? "When we first spoke, Achan believed I was a boy."

Gren studied her. "A boy? But you're so beautiful."

Vrell's cheeks warmed. "I am not shapely like you. Once I put on a tunic and trousers like these, no one suspected a thing."

"But why dress as a boy, my lady?"

"It is the same as what we're doing now, Gren." Vrell sighed. "Back when we all thought he was Prince Gidon, Esek wanted to marry me. When Mother refused, he tormented us. So Mother sent me to Walden's Watch to hide under the guise of a stray boy. But a man sensed my bloodvoice and brought me to Mahanaim to train as his apprentice."

Gren's eyes were saucers. "You must've been terrified."

"I was." Vrell went on to tell about her journey to Mahanaim with Jax and Khai, her training with Macoun Hadar and his obsession with Achan.

Gren frowned. "I don't understand bloodvoicing. You mean that people could feel Achan's mind?"

"Before he learned to contain it, his power released a painful pressure into every bloodvoicer in Er'Rets." Vrell recalled Achan's experiment the other day. "So, Master Hadar, hungry for another apprentice, sent me to fetch Achan. I found him injured in the wake of a battle. Once he was transported to Mahanaim, I cared for his wounds. And when he woke, he thought I was a boy named Vrell Sparrow. That is how we became friends."

Gren's eyes widened. "He called you Sparrow in the field. He knows you're a woman?"

"He knows now," Vrell said. "But he does not know that Vrell Sparrow and Lady Averella Amal are one and the same."

Gren rolled onto her knees. "Yet you are betrothed."

Vrell tugged at her necklace. "The betrothal is a political match Achan's advisors planned with my mother."

"But why didn't you tell him you are Lady Averella?"

Why indeed? "Things are complicated, which is why I needed to leave."

"But . . ." Gren stared, mouth flapping. "You love him. You sang to him. He looked so forlorn when he spoke about his engagement." She gasped. "It's because he loves Vrell Sparrow and thinks he will never have her. The poor dear."

Vrell looked at her hands. "I do not know what to do."

"Tell him the truth and marry him," Gren said.

"If life were *that* simple, you and he would be married."

"I suppose." Gren nibbled at a feverfew leaf. "But from a woman who was forced to marry, believe me, to marry for love would be worth any complication."

Even breaking Arman's laws? "I grow weary of this discussion. Please, I would like to sleep now."

Gren rolled her eyes and leaned back against the olive tree. "Must be nice to order your problems away."

Vrell lay down on her bedroll and pulled the blanket up to her chin. "It is *not* nice. Ordering them away only prolongs the pain of indecision."

"So make a decision," Gren said, as if Vrell were choosing which dress to wear.

Vrell rolled on her side, putting her back to Gren. "I have. That is why I'm following Jax."

"You won't marry Achan?"

"No. I will not." Though even as she said the words, she did not know if she meant them. Tears pooled in her eyes. She did her best to stifle the sound of her crying.

The following day passed as slowly as the first. Sitna was a two-day journey on horseback, but Gren, not used to riding, refused to allow her horse to do anything but walk, claiming faster movement jarred her queasy stomach.

Vrell's boredom tempted her to look through Achan's eyes. She had never been capable of such, and the last time she tried he had sensed her. Instead, she looked in on Mother several times and found her busy coordinating supplies for Achan's army or strolling around the castle with Sir Eagan.

It did not appear that Mother had noticed Vrell's absence yet. Not surprising.

While they stopped for lunch, Gren urged Vrell to check on Bran's progress.

"From the look of the land, they are still north of Allowntown. I pray Jax will linger there a day or two. For that is the only chance I have of catching up."

Gren set down her figs. "If you're so set on deserting Achan, it makes no sense for us to part in Sitna. I have two friends—strong men—that'll escort me the rest of the way. Why not come with us? It'll be safer."

Vrell met Gren's reproving gaze and wrung her hands. Stopping in Sitna would likely waste another day. But Jax was already so far ahead, perhaps travelling with Gren and her friends would be wisest.

It was late afternoon on the third day when Vrell and Gren arrived in Sitna, a small, brownstone castle surrounded by a dingy moat. Gren led her over the drawbridge to a long clapboard stable. They dismounted and took their horses in.

"Hello there." A stray, tall and thin, walked toward them. The sight of his orange tunic brought back memories of Vrell's time as a stray. How quickly she had forgotten the orange tunic in her weeks of comfort in Carmine.

"See here now," Gren said, faking the low voice of a man. "We two men wanna put up our horses, and we want you to be quick about it, see?"

"I'd be happy to, sir." The man stopped and squinted at Gren. "Gren?"

"Noam!" Gren rushed forward and embraced him.

He bent awkwardly to hug her short frame. "What are you doing here? Has your family returned? Why are you dressed like a man?"

Gren's eyes glittered. "I'm in disguise. And I came without my parents. I couldn't stay in Carmine any longer. It was horrible, Noam. You won't believe what happened to me."

"You must tell all." Noam studied the mare beside Gren. "Including where you got such a fine horse."

"Oh, forgive me!" Gren slid back to include Vrell in the conversation. "Lady Averella Amal, this is Noam Fox. The horses are hers, Noam. She's in disguise too."

Noam stared a long moment, his gaze taking in Vrell's clothing, then he jerked into a low bow, his spine pressing against his thin tunic. "An honor, m'lady."

Mercy. Did the poor man ever eat? Vrell hoped this was not one of the men intended to escort Gren to Armonguard. He did not look able to stand up to the weakest soldier.

"Noam is Sitna Manor's stableman."

"Don't say such things, Gren. Oster will hear you." Noam glanced around as if expecting this Oster person to charge out from one of the stalls and reprimand him. His worried gaze shifted to Vrell. "I'm the stable hand, m'lady. Nothing more than a stray."

Vrell opened her mouth to speak, but Gren said, "You're more of a stableman than Oster. You do all the work."

Noam shifted his feet and lowered his voice. "Gren, please. Can we speak of this later?"

"We need to talk to you about why we've come. Can you take a break?"

"You know I can't. What if we meet at the Corner tonight?"

Gren clapped her hands and jumped. "Oh, yes, we must. A brilliant plan, Noam. We need speak with Harnu too."

Noam raised a dark eyebrow. "Reconsidered his offer, have you?"

Gren shoved Noam with both hands. "I most certainly have not, Noam Fox, you take that back!"

"Calm yourself," Noam said, rubbing his chest. "It was just a question."

"Which is all I want with Harnu. To ask a question. Where is he?"

"The armory, as usual." Noam's gaze bounced between Vrell and Gren. "Did you know Lord Levy has come?"

"To visit?" Vrell asked.

"To stay, it seems. Lord Nathak is preparing to move to Armonguard to assist Prince Gidon's rule. Lord Levy came to replace him and govern Sitna."

Gren shoved Noam again.

He clapped a hand to his chest. "What now?"

"*Achan* is Prince Gidon, not that pigheaded . . ." She pushed Noam. "Evil . . ." She pushed him again.

He grabbed her arms and pulled her into a hug. "All right, Grenny. I know it, you hear? It just slipped out. I meant Esek. He's who Lord Nathak plans to help rule."

"You have seen Esek recently?" Vrell asked.

"No, m'lady. Not here. Not for months."

Praise Arman. "But Lord Nathak is here?"

"Aye. And I urge you take care, m'lady. There's a ransom on your head. They seek a woman dressed as a lad. You'd both be wise to change and fast."

"A peasant's dress," Gren said, approaching Vrell. "I'll do your hair in pigtail braids."

Vrell felt queasy. People were hunting her. Stopping in Sitna had been a mistake. "Is my hair long enough?"

Gren fingered Vrell's stubby tail. "Just."

"Stray!" a man yelled from the back. "Put those horses up and get on with the stalls!"

"Yes, sir!" Noam took the bridles of both horses. "Until tonight, then."

"Farewell." Gren pulled Vrell by the hand, outside and across the crowded bailey. Vrell kept her head down and pulled her hand away. Men holding hands would surely seem odd.

In Carmine, the armory had its own building. Here it was a shelter with two walls on the back corner and the front corner open, held up with a wooden post.

An old man wearing a leather apron held a stick of white-hot iron with tongs and swung a hammer on it again and again. Each strike sent dozens of sparks into the air.

Vrell did not want to remain out in the open. "What are we doing here?" she whispered to Gren.

"Looking for Harnu."

"I thought we wanted to change? Pigtail braids?" Vrell's nerves tingled at the idea that Lord Nathak was so near.

"Stand behind me if you're worried." Gren walked up to the old man. "Master Poe, have you seen Harnu?"

"Grenny girl! Haven't seen yer father. When yeh get back?" The man set down his hammer and brushed his hands on his apron. "How's the baby comin' along? And why yeh dressed like a man?"

"Father's not here, Master Poe. Just me and my friend. And please keep your voice down. We're trying to blend in."

Vrell's lips parted, breath frozen in anticipation. Surely the girl would not introduce her to *every* old friend in Sitna. These peasants likely needed money enough to turn her in.

The old man looked Vrell up and down. "I've seen *yeh* before. Not 'n the flesh, but on Nathak's scrolls. Ever' day some soldier comes sniffin' fer yeh an' the pawn. S'prised I was to hear yeh stole the pawn's heart. Didn't think that boy'd ever get over losin' Grenny to Riga Hoff."

"The pawn?" Vrell's apprehension grew. If there were scrolls bearing her likeness, she needed to hide her face.

"That's what the people in Sitna call Achan now that the truth is known," Gren said. "There's even a song."

"Beg yer forgiveness, m'lady," Master Poe said. "It ain't fittin' speak ill o' the dead." He nodded to Gren. "An' I mean no disrespect to yeh or yer unborn child. But Harnu was always a simple lad. Did what he was told. Followed that Riga like a lost pup. Ever' idea'r those two got into sparked with Riga Hoff. My son's changed since the pawn's days here. Like to think I beat enough sense into 'im."

"Master Poe." Vrell kept her voice low and her eyes on the people passing by the armory. "I harbor no ill will toward you or your son. And I assure you, Achan is kind and forgiving. I am certain he would be willing to pardon your son for any wrongdoings in the past."

The old man laughed. "Well, I'll be forged. She calls 'im Achan."

"Gren?" a man's voice said.

Vrell spun around. But instead of a soldier holding a scroll, as Vrell feared, a strong young man stood outside holding two buckets of water, frowning at Gren. He had a plain, pock-marked face and dark hair. He too wore a leather apron over a brown tunic and trousers.

"Hello, Harnu." Gren's cool tone lacked the familiarity she shared with Noam and Master Poe.

Vrell looked between Harnu and Gren, intrigued by Gren's behavior. Was it Harnu's past treatment of Achan that angered Gren, or had these two shared something more?

"These fine young *men* wanna talk to yeh, son." Master Poe gripped Harnu's shoulder and chuckled. "Go on an' see what's so urgent."

Harnu's dark eyebrows arched as he took in Vrell. Then he stomped off toward a cluster of thatched cottages. "Come."

Gren stared after him, her expression pinched.

"Thank you for your good company, Master Poe." Vrell dragged Gren after Harnu, but when they reached the cottages, Harnu had vanished. "Gren, do we trust this man?"

Gren nodded, staring off into nothingness.

"Good, for at least he looks capable of protecting us. Now, help me find him, for I cannot guess where he went."

Gren heaved a deep breath and came back to herself. She wove through the maze of cottages until stumbling to a stop before a small dwelling nestled between two older ones and the curtain wall that loomed above.

The door opened and Harnu stepped out.

When Gren did not move, Vrell asked her, "Is something wrong? Should we not enter?"

Gren jolted, her gaze settling on Vrell. "This was Riga's home. And my home. It's . . . strange to be back."

Oh. Vrell took Gren's hand and squeezed. "Let us go in, then, before we are seen. All will be well." Would it not?

Gren led Vrell over the threshold and into a small room that held a round table, two chairs, and a hearth. Two doors split the wall opposite the entrance. Harnu stood before the hearth, facing them, hands behind his back. His size made him an imposing figure in such a small place.

Gren's gaze danced along the shuttered windows, walls, and furniture. "You've done all this?"

Vrell looked over the room again, for it looked very bare in her opinion.

"In case you came back." Harnu shifted his weight from one leg to the other. "In case you changed your mind."

Now Vrell felt like the imposing figure who had intruded upon some private conversation.

Gren shook out her hair. "I have a different reason for returning, Harnu. Come with us to Armonguard."

"Armonguard?" His dark gaze shifted to Vrell. "Who's she, anyway?"

"That's not your business. Will you help us?"

Harnu's ominous posture gave out, and he looked every bit a chastened little boy. "I can't go to Armonguard, Gren. My father. I'm his only son. I—"

Gren rolled her eyes. "What's *that* matter?"

Harnu's neck bobbed as he swallowed. "Well, I—"

"It needn't be forever. Just to get us safely there. Then you can return."

"I would if I could, but—"

"You swore on Riga's grave you'd protect me and the baby."

Harnu seemed to shrink further. "I will if . . . if you'd let me."

"Your oath to protect me does not include marriage."

Vrell wanted to leave, yet her gaze flickered between Harnu and Gren.

"I know that," Harnu said. "But see? I've taken care of the house. Finished the windows. Divided the bedchamber in two." He walked to the back of the cottage, pushed open the doors. "That way, should you want to live here, the child will have his own room for when he's older."

"Who says the child is a boy?" Gren asked.

"I'll check on you every day. And if you change your mind I—"

"I won't change my mind!" Gren growled a scream, paced to the door and back, then softened her voice. "Two women traveling alone . . . so far . . . we won't be safe."

Again Harnu's gaze took in Vrell, his eyes seemed to grip her soul and plead, as if Vrell somehow could give him what he needed in life. Vrell suspected what he thought he needed was Gren.

He looked back to Gren, forehead puckered. "My father . . . He sometimes forgets things. Things he never forgot before. I worry he'll hurt himself. And if I'm not here to keep watch . . . Gren, I'm all he's got."

Vrell looked away from the torment on Harnu's face. She did not understand Gren's cruelty toward this man. He clearly cared a great deal for her and her unborn child.

Being here seemed all wrong. Vrell and Gren were two confused women trying to manipulate their destinies. Gypsum's words came back to Vrell. *It seems to me a smart lady would seize the chance to marry a good man.*

Yet Vrell and Gren both denied good men.

Could her sister be right? Vrell meant to trust Arman, but what if He wanted Gren to stay in Sitna with Harnu?

What if He wanted Vrell to marry Achan?

Arman, am I mistaken? Does Achan follow you?

ASK HIM.

Vrell gasped and sank to one of the chairs at the table. Never before had she heard such a clear word from Arman. It brought an overwhelming wave of heat and humility.

Had Achan committed his heart to Arman? Accepted Câan's sacrifice? The heat faded, and goose bumps popped over Vrell's arms. When would she have the chance to ask him now?

She could always . . . No. Not that.

Gren's raised voice drew Vrell back to the present. "We're leaving in the morning. May Cetheria deal harshly with you if you let us go alone and we're killed." Gren stormed out of the cottage, slamming the door behind her.

Vrell jumped. Her gaze shot to Harnu. The man's face had paled, and he gripped the mantle as if he might fall over without its support.

Vrell stood and smoothed her tunic. "Master Poe, had I known the details of your situation, I would have encouraged Gren toward another plan. I would never ask you to abandon your father for our foolish quest. Do not burden yourself further. I shall see that Gren is safe. Forgive us for wasting your time." Vrell curtsied and walked to the door.

Harnu crossed the room, his steps three strikes on an anvil. His strong hand gripped her wrist. "Who are you?"

She swallowed, her pity for him lost in her sudden fear. "I do not know that I can trust you."

He released her, stepped back. "You've nothing to fear."

"Very well." Arman help her if this was a mistake. "I am Lady Averella Amal of Carmine."

He bowed his head. "Forgive me, m'lady. I should not have touched you so."

Vrell relaxed, thankful for the sudden appearance of manners. "You are forgiven, Master Poe. I can tell your mind is on other matters at present."

"You're not safe in Sitna. Soldiers are looking for you."

"We have made plans to meet Master Noam this evening. At a corner, I believe it is called."

"Noam?" His dark gaze searched hers. "Why?"

"I think Gren plans to ask him to accompany us on our journey as well."

Harnu laughed. "Noam knows nothing 'bout protecting two ladies."

"Be that as it may, we hope to leave tomorrow."

Harnu stepped to the door. "I must return to Father. Stay here 'til tonight. No one will bother you here."

"I thank you, Master Poe, for your kindness. We are indebted to you."

Harnu left. Vrell peeked out the door to see him stop before Gren, who stood in the lane between the other two cottages. Harnu spoke to her, bowed, and stalked off.

Mercy.

Gren glanced to where Vrell stood in the doorway. "What'll we do if Harnu won't come? Noam's the one I expect to say no, him being a stray and all."

"Gren . . ." But what could Vrell say? Lecture the girl for being heartless to poor Harnu? As if Vrell had any right to comment on that. "Come inside before you are seen."

But Gren turned the other way. "I'll fetch us some dresses first."

"Harnu said we should stay hidden, and I agree."

"But if we're going to the Corner tonight, my black dress and your fancy gown won't do. I'll find plain ones that'll help us blend in."

"I suppose you must." For Vrell could not go looking for dresses, nor could she parade about in her green one.

Vrell shut the door and paced the cottage, admiring the little touches she suspected were from Harnu's hands. Polished clapboard shutters covered each window and were held in place with decorative iron hinges molded into scrolls and leaves. A circular iron candelabra with vines and flowers hung from a thick iron chain overhead. And a dozen intricately painted pewter toy figures stood on the mantle. Vrell picked up a white lamb and smiled at his tiny black face. There were horses, cows, sheep, and pigs. A chicken and rooster. Vrell picked up the figure of a girl with chestnut hair and knew immediately that it was Gren.

How did Harnu find paint the color of Gren's hair?

A noise sent Vrell spinning around. Harnu walked in the cottage, arms laden with bundles. "Sorry for startling you, m'lady. Thought you might be hungry." He set his bundles on the table. "Where's Gren?"

"She went to find us dresses." Vrell held up the figure of Gren. "Did you make this?"

Harnu shrugged. "A boy or girl will play with animals, don't you think?"

"You made them for Gren's baby?"

"Metal is all I'm good with."

"Oh, I disagree. I've never seen such colors of paint on toys. And the construction of the cottage too. You are quite gifted, Master Poe."

"Thank you, m'lady. I'm, uh . . . not proud of how I was before. To Achan."

Vrell did not want any details of cruelty to Achan. "Yes, we all have dust under our beds, do we not?"

Harnu retreated to the door. "I'll come back later." The door clumped shut behind him.

Vrell sighed, knowing exactly what dust was hiding under her bed. Ask him, Arman had said.

As much as Vrell did not want to be queen, feared confessing her lies to Achan, loathed the idea of women throwing themselves at her husband, and the small snag that she was no longer the true heir to Carm—the only legitimate reason to deny Achan had been his indifference to Arman.

But if Achan believed . . . If he truly followed Arman . . .

She set the figure of Gren back on the hearth.

She would have to ask him.

The first thing that came to mind when Vrell approached the corner of the outer bailey with Gren was *The Ivory Spit* in Tsaftown, the inn where Kurtz and Achan had gone dancing with women of questionable repute.

This "Corner" was dark, though they'd posted rushlights around the perimeter. A man stood singing on the end of a small wagon parked against the curtain wall. Three musicians accompanied him with lute, flute, and tabor drum.

Vrell sat on a wooden stump beside Gren on the perimeter of the clearing. They wore simple peasant dresses made of scratchy brown wool with no petticoats. Vrell could barely hold still with the itchy fabric against her skin. She berated herself for not bringing a separate corset. This gown had no structure at all. She felt completely exposed.

She scanned the dark mob of people, but Noam had not yet arrived. Dozens of couples danced. Vrell could not bear to watch, for several were kissing in public. The very idea.

Two young men approached. One had bright orange hair and a short beard with freckles to match. The other was towheaded with a smile that covered half his face.

The towheaded man addressed Gren. "Grenny Fenny, when did yeh move back to Sitna?"

"Cap!" Gren's smile lit up her face. "I'm not back, just passing through."

Cap turned his wide smile to Vrell. "Who's yer friend?"

Gren gave the alias Vrell had chosen. "This is Ressa."

Cap bent down and propped his hands on his knees so his face was level with Vrell's. "My, yer a pretty thing, Ressa. Dance with me?"

Vrell's eyes widened. She would most certainly not dance in such an environment. And with no corset? "Thank you, no. I do not mean to dance this night."

Though it seemed impossible, Cap's grin widened. "My my. Aren't yeh a proper little princess. Ol' Cap ain't good enough for the likes of yeh, that it?"

"That is not what I meant to imply, sir. But I do not—"

"It's fine." Gren jumped up and grabbed the redhead's arm. "May as well enjoy ourselves 'til Noam gets here."

"That's the spirit!" Cap took Vrell's hands and pulled her off her stump. He dragged her into the dancing crowd. But just as he jerked her close, the music stopped.

Vrell stepped back, pulling her hands from Cap's as she went. "What a shame. The music has ended." She turned toward her stump, but a new song began.

Cap circled Vrell and cut off her path. "This is one of my favorites." He grabbed her hand, wrapped his other arm around her waist, and propelled her through the mob.

Vrell stumbled to keep up as he skipped back and forth and spun her around. Onlookers clapped and sang along.

Hail the piper, fiddle, fife,
The night is young and full of life.
The Corner teems with ale and song.
And we will dance the whole night long.

Hear the pretty maiden sing,
Hair and ribbons all flowing.
She can take my heart away,
By her side I long to stay.

Grab that maiden, kick your feet
Laugh and spin and keep the beat
If you're too shy to ask a dance
Another man will take the chance.

When the song ended, Cap kissed Vrell on the cheek. "Thanks for the twirl, Ressa."

Vrell squeezed her hands into fists, shocked at Cap's audacity. But before she could scold him, he lunged up to a golden-haired woman and whisked her into a dance. Vrell retreated to her stump, dropped onto the unyielding surface, and folded her arms, hoping to look vexed and unsociable.

Yet another man approached from her side. Vrell looked away. If their eyes never met, perhaps he would give up.

But he sat on the stump beside hers. Vrell stiffened, wanting nothing more than to return to Gren's cottage.

"Where is Gren?" a familiar voice asked.

Vrell turned, delighted to see that it was Noam. "She is dancing."

Noam squinted at the crowd, his eyes dark under his messy brown hair. "You really going to Armonguard?"

"Who told you?"

He flashed his dark eyes her way. "Harnu questioned my ability to protect two women and bid me think hard before agreeing to help you."

Vrell laughed silently. "He has a way with words."

The rushlights elongated Noam's narrow face. "I'm not brave, like Achan. Thought he was mad for the reckless way he lived. But I'd like to see him again. Think he'd see me?"

"Of course he would! But we are not going to see Achan. Not right away, at least."

"But if I made it that far—if *we* made it, I mean. You think he would pardon my crimes?"

"What crimes have you committed, Master Fox?"

His face went slack. "None. But if I leave my master . . ."

"I can assure you, if we make it to Armonguard, you will be safe. Achan will not continue to imprison strays."

"Then I'll come," Noam said. "Though I'm too scrawny to be much help, I'll do my best to look forbidding."

The song ended. Gren returned arm in arm with the redheaded man. The band segued into another song.

Noam chuckled. "Ah, the new favorite of Sitna Manor. Have you heard this one, Lady Averella? I bet you'd like it."

Vrell winced and hoped the music had drowned out Noam's use of her real name.

He grew up here in Sitna Town,
    The hand his life was dealt.
He milked the goats and fetched the wood
    Or Poril gave him the belt.

The pawn our king, sing merry, merry, merry.
    The pawn our servant king.
For he was once the lowest of all strays
    And now claims to be king.

Then the Great Whitewolf took him up,
    Taught him to use a sword.
He fought quite well, his blade struck true,
    And blood from Esek poured.

Remember us, sing merry, merry, merry.
    Remember us, O king.
For you were once the lowest of all strays
    And now you'll be our king.

Vrell smiled at the lyrics. Achan had become a legend in Sitna. What would he say if he heard this song?

The band continued to play. But the minstrel jumped off the cart and broke up a dancing couple. He twirled around twice with the maiden, then left her standing and interrupted another couple. Men from the crowd roared with laughter, as if such rudeness was hysterically clever. Two men from the crowd ran into the mob and copied the minstrel, breaking up couples and dancing with the ladies.

Cap suddenly appeared before Vrell and dragged her back into a dance. He spun so quickly her head tingled. She pulled back, trying to slow them down. Their connection broke. Vrell stumbled. Someone caught her and threw her into a jig. She squealed and held on for fear she might fall.

Yet another man ripped her arm away from her partner. The minstrel! He spun Vrell round and round and round before releasing her. She staggered a few steps and fell to her knees, her surroundings whirling around her.

The minstrel's voice sang out again.

For he and we were all deceived,
By our own Lord Nathak.
And now the Pawn King marches south
To take Armonguard back.

O rescue us, sing merry, merry, merry.
O rescue us, O king.
For you were once the lowest of all strays
Save us, our precious king.

Vrell still sat on her knees. Couples twirled around her as if she were not there.

"Brazen animals!" a voice said to her left. "Don't know how father abides them. Look how they treat their women."

Vrell scanned the crowd for this critical onlooker who was bold enough to judge but unwilling to assist a lady in need. He stood with two much taller men. He was young, not yet a man, and horribly familiar.

Reggio Levy's gaze locked onto Vrell the moment she recognized him. She pushed herself to her feet and ran.

"Stop that woman!" Reggio screamed, like a boy throwing a temper fit.

Vrell darted past dancing couples, toward Gren and Noam, then thought better of it. For Lord Nathak might try and capture Gren too. Then what would become of her child?

Vrell veered left around a cottage and collided with a soldier, who clapped his arms around her like irons.

"Let me go!" She kicked the unyielding oak of a man.

"Not on yer life, missy." He dragged Vrell back to the Corner. The music stopped. Everyone stood staring.

Reggio strutted across the clearing, a nasty smirk upon his face. "Why, Lady Averella. What brings you to Sitna? Or do you go by *Vrell Sparrow* these days?" Reggio yelled "Vrell Sparrow," as if he were hoping the minstrel might make a song of him catching the infamous lady-turned-stray.

Vrell straightened her posture in the guard's grip. "Good evening, Master Levy. I hear Sitna has the best blacksmith in Carm Duchy. I am in need of a new sword."

He snorted. "You expect me to believe you came to Sitna for a sword? There's a price on your head, in case you were unaware. One my father will be pleased to accept."

"I hear your father has been demoted to Lord of Sitna Manor. My, how well evil men are rewarded. When I get my new sword, Master Levy, I shall test its sharpness on you."

Reggio's cheeks pinked, but he chuckled as if she had made a joke. "You, my lady, are going to the dungeon. There will be no swords for you to wield there."

9

The overwhelming smell of tobacco woke Achan. A lantern hung on a hook at the foot of his bed, blinding him to anything beyond the canopy. His stinging eyes led him to believe it was still night. But he had stayed up far too late the past few nights, seeking a way around Sparrow's shields. Maybe it was nearly morning. Or perhaps a dream?

He sensed excitement. Another lesson from the duchess?

"Achan Cham," a man said.

Achan jolted and rolled over. With the lantern at his back, he could see better. Sir Gavin, Sir Eagan, Sir Caleb, and Shung stood in a line beside his bed, dressed for battle.

Achan sat up so fast his head spun. "Another attack?"

The men simply stared past him. Achan turned to see what they were looking at, but saw nothing strange but Matthias's empty pallet. Where had the lad gone?

Sir Gavin's voice pulled Achan's gaze back to the men. "As a male Er'Retian past sixteen years, you are a man. You received no manhood ceremony to commemorate such a momentous occasion. Tonight we will rectify that."

Achan's head tingled. Manhood ceremony?

Sir Gavin peered down upon Achan. "Do you wish to become a man?"

Achan looked from face to face, the night air cool inside his gaping mouth. All four men now fixed their gazes on him. He felt underdressed—he was wearing only his trousers. The beating in his chest drew his eyes back to Sir Gavin's. "Aye, sir."

"Stand then, Achan Cham."

Achan crawled out of bed and stood, facing the knights.

"As to your achievements," Sir Gavin said, "these past months I watched you train harder and withstand more pressure than any man of any age."

Then Sir Eagan spoke, "I witnessed your mercy as you pardoned prisoners. Your tenacity as you sought out a traitor."

"You felled Esek." Shung stomped one foot on the floor. "Killed the great cham bear." Another stomp.

"You surrendered to Arman," Sir Caleb said, "accepted Câan's sacrifice and plan for your life. I say you are a man."

Achan's chest tightened.

"As to your character," Sir Gavin said. "You are smart, the quickest study I've ever seen. And I find your perseverance under trial inspiring."

"You are good-natured and moral," Sir Caleb said.

"Brave and honorable." Shung stomped again.

"You have a high regard for all people, no matter their social status, circumstance, or past errors," Sir Eagan said. "I say you are a man."

"As to our advice for this journey through manhood," Sir Gavin said. "Always be teachable, willing to learn."

"Remember that every man is a slave to something," Sir Eagan said. "Let no one or thing master you but Arman."

"Set goals and boundaries to protect yourself. Resist the hosts of temptations that await you," Sir Caleb said.

"Always carry weapon." Shung banged a fist on his chest. "And Shung says the little cham is a man."

Achan trembled through a silent laugh.

Sir Gavin lifted a diamond-shaped shield off Sir Eagan's back and hoisted it before Achan as if he were going to use it. "We had this made for you."

Blood tingled to Achan's fingertips as he inspected the shield. Slightly pointed at the top, the bottom edges tapered like a stemless arrowhead. The wood was covered in dark brown leather edged with a band of thick gold plating. Two more strips of gold crossed over one another, dividing the shield into four sections. A gold symbol was mounted in each section: a castle, a tree, a crown, and a cham. A two-headed hawk covered where the strips crossed in the center.

"It's identical to the shield your father carried in battle but for one difference," Sir Gavin said. "We put a cham bear on this shield in honor of the life that made you who you are. A cham stands for ferocity and protection. Its presence on your shield should remind you always to be courageous."

"The crown stands for authority," Sir Caleb said. "You are responsible for leading Er'Rets."

"Fortress means stability," Shung said. "Unshakable."

"The tree will remind you to remember your creator," Sir Eagan said. "Always be reverent."

"The two-headed hawk is the symbol of the Hadar name," Sir Gavin said. "The Hadars, the line of kings, are men of action, not idleness. While one head looks to the kingdom, the other looks to Arman, always on guard, always vigilant. As you walk through life, be courageous, responsible, steadfast, reverent, and vigilant. No longer will we treat you like a boy. We say you are a man." He passed the shield to Achan.

Achan took the weight into his arms with a fierce pride.

"Because of my continual concern for your safety, you feel I don't respect you," Sir Caleb said. "Nothing could be further from the truth. I'm proud of who you are and what you've accomplished. From this day forward I shall strive to respect your wishes, whether I agree or not."

The words lightened Achan, lifting a yoke he hadn't realized hung so heavily over his shoulders. "Thank you."

"If ever you have need, come to any of us," Sir Gavin said. "For we have lived many years."

"Some of us more than others, Gavin," Sir Eagan said.

Achan laughed and examined his shield, enthralled by its beauty, its significance, its weight—the amount of gold. "How was my father's shield different?"

"King Axel's shield bore a stag instead of a cham," Sir Gavin said, "for the stag and the name Axel stand for peace. But your shield, had your father given it to you as Gidon, would have born a lion, which represents a warrior."

Achan's chest swelled. His father had named him *warrior.* "What now? Is that the end?"

Sir Gavin clapped him on the back. "By no means. Now you must hear three old men—and one young one—tell of our greatest triumphs and follies."

Sir Eagan and Shung dragged chairs over from the wall and sat in a half circle around the side of Achan's bed.

"Do not judge us too harshly, Your Highness," Sir Eagan said, sitting on his chair, "for some of us have had much greater and many more follies than we have had triumphs."

"First," Sir Gavin said, digging something out of his pants pocket, "take this. Since your father cannot be here."

Achan accepted a smooth gold coin. He had never held money in his life. He examined the coin and saw the two-headed hawk on one side. He flipped it and gasped, for what looked like his own profile was molded onto the other side.

"You and your father look a lot alike, but someday your own profile will mark Er'Retian coins," Sir Gavin said.

Achan laughed. "I never even thought of such a thing as my face on a coin."

"Yes, well, now that King Axel has arrived," Sir Caleb said with a glance at the coin, "we can get on with it."

Each man took a turn sharing personal stories about their own journeys to manhood. Sir Gavin's proudest moment had been when King Paxton knighted him and appointed him Prince Axel's Shield. His biggest failure had been King Axel and Queen Dara's deaths and losing Achan.

Sir Eagan's intense blue eyes focused on Achan. "I have had many failures, Your Highness. Too many to confess in one night. Some I have already shared with you. The differences with my father. Losing King Axel on my watch." Pain flashed across his face. "But none has plagued me as much as dallying with a young woman days before her wedding."

Stunned, Achan averted his eyes to the floor. Sir Eagan didn't seem capable of something so low.

"I don't doubt the young woman was partially to blame," Sir Gavin said.

Sir Eagan growled like an irritated cat. "Whether or not she was willing, it is a man's duty to protect a lady's honor. In that I failed. And though I regret my actions, I would not change them if I were able to live through it again."

This admission caused Achan to look up. "Why?"

Sir Eagan's expression lightened. "My failures, no matter how painful, brought wisdom. And Arman, by his infinite grace and mercy, bestowed blessings through my failures that, over time, made the pain bearable."

Sir Eagan shifted on his chair, looking as if there were more to confess, but he switched topics altogether. "Now, my best moment, I'm afraid, has yet to be lived. Should I survive the coming war, I shall waste no time making amends with those I have wronged. Forgiveness and reconciliation will be, I have no doubt, the greatest moments of my life."

"Why wait?" Achan asked. "Can't you do it now?"

"Why, indeed? It is always best to wait on Arman's timing. The battle for Er'Rets must come first. I pray Arman will give me opportunity to reconcile after the war."

Then it was Shung's turn.

Of all the men, Shung's voice was the lowest. "Each year Shung's village sent one young man to Berland for tournament. Winner would become squire. During tournament, Shung fought too hard. Wanted to impress Father. Shung's friend Arluk fell."

Even the knights were staring at Shung, surprise evident on each face. Achan recalled how horrified he'd been to kill his first deer, and later, the Poroo soldiers. He could not imagine having killed a friend. "How old were you?"

"One and ten."

So young to deal with such guilt. "Were you arrested?"

Shung snorted. "Not in Therion Duchy. Not for that. Shung tried to withdraw from tournament, but Arluk's father made Shung swear to become great warrior. To bring honor to Arluk's death. When Shung became Sir Koyukuk's squire . . ." He banged a fist on his chest. "Proudest moment. Until Shung became Shield to future king and was knighted." He nodded to Achan and banged his chest again.

"You *are* a great warrior, Shung," Achan said. "You have brought honor to your friend's life."

Shung glanced to Sir Caleb. "The lion's turn."

"Very well." Sir Caleb released a shaky sigh. "My brother's wife, Ambrosia, liked to walk in the forest and often went alone, despite

Baruch's pleas that she take care. As the head of her guard, he often sent me to fetch her when she was gone too long. Until the day I found her half dead. Poroo had attacked, beaten her to within an inch of death. To this day she cannot speak properly, and she limps . . ." Sir Caleb's eyes were glassy and wet, staring into the past. "I was responsible for Ambrosia's safety. I was to blame. It is still the most horrible experience of my life."

A deep breath seemed to bring him back to the present. "When I saw Esper's husband strike her that day in the marketplace in Armonguard, I lost all sense. I saw a chance to save a woman from Ambrosia's fate and took it. Some believe I stole a married woman from her husband, but I never believed Esper was that man's wife. Not of her own will. She was his prisoner. His slave. His pell."

No wonder Sir Caleb obsessed over safety. "Do you miss your wife?" Achan asked.

"Very much. When Sir Gavin called me to Mahanaim to free you from the dungeon, I did not know I would be gone so long. May Esper forgive me. I do send letters, but it is not the same as my return."

"May you forgive me as well," Achan said. "It never occurred to me you might rather go home than be one of my advisors."

"I am called to serve my king. Esper knows that. Besides, none of us have any sort of life to return to until your rule is settled."

Achan sat in awe of the men around him. Each one had shared so freely, encouraged him in ways he had never expected. It made him wonder what bits of wisdom King Axel might have shared had he been present. Achan took the coin in his hand and studied it. These men, as honorable and good as Achan knew them to be, had all struggled in some way. Surely his father had, as well.

Achan only wished he knew if the mysterious Hadad had killed his parents. Every time he heard his family name "Hadar" he thought of that faceless man from the pit in Barth. He frowned, brushing the troubling thought aside. This was a celebration. He had been a man for months, but tonight, for the first time, he truly felt like one.

• • •

When Achan awoke the next morning, he found Matthias standing beside his bed. Achan yawned long and hard. "Good morning, Matthias."

"You've lots of wounds, sir."

Achan glanced down to see that he had, as usual, kicked off his blankets in his sleep. He rolled his sore shoulder in an attempt at a stretch and yawned again. When he looked back to Matthias, the boy held his hands before his face, knuckles facing Achan, fingertips blackened with soot.

"I've wounds too, sir."

Upon closer inspection, it was clear that Matthias's fingertips were not covered in soot, but black for another reason. "What happened?"

"I was hunting with Father but got lost. A long while passed 'fore he found me. I was frozen."

Achan recalled Master Ricks's words when he'd offered the boy to Achan back in Tsaftown. *He's a good boy, but took a bad frost to his hands. He can use them fine, just not for the detail of tying knots.*

Frostbitten fingertips? "Is it painful?"

"No, sir. Can't feel a thing."

"And here I thought you'd been playing in the fireplace."

Matthias giggled. "I know better than that."

The boy's contagious laugh made Achan chuckle until Matthias pointed a blackened finger at Achan's chest.

"What happened to you, sir?"

Achan glanced down. "Oh, a host of things."

Matthias's expression fell. Everyone who had seen Achan's scars was always fascinated—or horrified. Why would little Matthias be any different?

"Pick one," Achan said, "and I shall tell you the tale."

Matthias's eyebrows lifted into a pale arc, and his eyes flickered over Achan's chest. He pointed to the still purpled scars on Achan's right side and shoulder.

"Good choice. Those are bite marks," Achan said in as eerie a voice as he could muster. "A cham tried to *eat* me."

Matthias's eyes widened and flicked to Achan's neck. "Is that why you wear that?"

Achan fingered the claw. "It is."

"You killed it?" These words were whispered with awe bordering on disbelief.

"With a knife to its throat." Achan couldn't help but enjoy the look of admiration on the boy's face.

"That's why Sir Shung calls you Little Cham?"

"No. He calls me that because Cham is my surname. Was." Achan frowned. His answer had clearly confused the boy. Matthias may as well know the full tale if he'd be working with Achan for the rest of his days.

"I grew up as a stray in Sitna Manor," Achan said. "Worked in the kitchens as the cook's boy. I milked the goats, got firewood, and kept the hearths hot. One day Sir Gavin offered to train me as a squire. It's against the law for a stray to serve in the Kingsguard, so I trained in secret. But Lord Nathak found out and banished Sir Gavin. I'd learned enough of the sword by then that Lord Nathak made me one of Prince Gidon's squires."

Matthias's brow crinkled. "But you're Prince Gidon, sir."

Achan smirked. "Aye, but only Lord Nathak knew that. And with Sir Gavin gone, I had no choice but to travel with the fake prince to Mahanaim. On the way, Poroo attacked."

"I've never seen a Poroo, sir."

"Well, they're ugly to look at, but not the best warriors. Still, they struck me down." Achan touched a white knot on his shoulder, one of the scars from the Poroo arrows. "I woke in the Mahanaim dungeons. Lord Nathak had accused me of trying to kill the prince, but of course I'd been protecting him. A week later, Sir Caleb broke me out of prison. He and Sir Gavin dressed me in a lot of finery, took me to Council, and revealed the truth."

Matthias was mesmerized. "What truth, sir?"

"That I was *the* Prince Gidon. That when I was just a babe, Lord Nathak switched me and his son, Esek, branded me a stray, and gave me to his cook to raise." Achan turned to show Matthias the mark of a stray, an "S" still branded onto the back of his shoulder. "So, though my real name *is* Gidon Hadar, I've always been known as Achan, and those closest to me call me such."

Matthias's lips turned into a grin. "Father says 'achan' when he's angry."

"Does he?" *Achan* meant "trouble" in the ancient language. It had humiliated him for years, but now he rather liked it. For Achan planned to cause trouble for any foe who stood in Arman's way. "It's never been the kindest of names, but it's mine." Achan's stomach rumbled. "You hungry?"

Matthias nodded.

"Fetch us some breakfast, then. But first we must wake the door-stop. I'd have you pounce on him, but he's a mean one in the mornings and might wring your neck."

Matthais's eyes went wide as he regarded the lump of furs on the pallet by the door.

Achan jumped up in a crouch on his bed and waved to Matthias. "Reach under his pillow and take his knife."

Matthias hesitated, then padded to Shung's pallet. Quiet as the mouse Shung had entitled him, he pilfered the knife and backed up against the wall, clutching the bone hilt to his chest with two hands, the shiny steel blade pointed down.

Achan winked at the boy and bellowed a war cry.

Shung sprang into a crouch on top of his straw mattress, arms tense and bulging, brown eyes wide and bleary. He wore black trousers and nothing else. Curly black hair covered his muscled chest.

Achan pounced from his bed to Shung's. They slammed into the door, slid along the wall, and tumbled to the floor in a tangle of arms and legs. Achan pinned Shung for two seconds before the hairy man flipped him onto his back and pressed his forearm over his throat. "You think you can beat Shung, Little Cham? Where you hide my knife?"

Achan's eyes rolled back to where Matthias stood.

Shung looked up and laughed. He pushed off Achan and sat with an arm propped over one knee. "Mouse is your new ally, Shung sees."

Achan scowled. "The lad is hungry, Shung. How is he to eat with your bed in front of the door?"

Shung fumbled along the side of his pallet until he found his shirt. "You must wait for Shung."

Winking again at Matthias, Achan said, "If I wait for you each morning, I'll never eat breakfast again."

"A warrior must sleep." Shung tugged a white shirt over his head and laced it up. "Sleep renews strength."

"Fine. But must you sleep in front of my door?"

"Shung swore to protect the little cham. Promised—"

The door opened against the pallet. "Your Highness? Are you well?" Sir Caleb's voice.

Achan bloodvoiced his answer. *I am fine, Sir Caleb. Matthias and I were only trying to wake Shung.*

Shung stood, pulled on his black leather jerkin, and pushed his pallet away from the door.

The door swung in, and Sir Caleb stepped inside, followed by Sir Eagan, Sir Gavin, Inko, and Kurtz.

"What in flames is going on?" Sir Caleb asked. "We thought you were being attacked."

"Not him." Shung walked to Matthias and snatched his knife away. He pointed the blade from Matthias to Achan. "They attack Shung." He tucked the blade into the sheath on his boot.

"The troops have arrived from Berland and Tsaftown," Sir Caleb said. "Matthias, choose the prince's best ensemble and see that he's bathed and dressed. Once the soldiers from Zerah Rock arrive, the war council will meet one last time. During the meeting, pack the prince's armor and clothes. We hope to leave this day."

"Yes, sir."

Achan might have glared at Sir Caleb at the mention of the boy bathing and dressing him, but the idea of leaving Carmine banished the thought from his mind.

"Until then, Your Highness, put on a shirt and get back in bed. The duchess wants to share her strategies for storming in the meeting and would like to give you a lesson before then so that you have at least experienced it."

But the duchess didn't visit Achan's chambers this time. He was sitting in bed eating breakfast when her knock came.

Duchess Amal.

Even her voice tangled his nerves. *Yes, my lady?*

Good day, Your Highness. Since you will be leaving, I think it wise to begin our instructions in this method, as that is how we shall work together in the future.

Whatever you think best, my lady.

I understand you once stormed someone.

Achan hadn't thought her statement was a question, but when she didn't speak, he fumbled for an answer. *Yes, I stormed Sparrow.*

Uh, Vrell Sparrow, my lady. We were learning to shield our minds. Sparrow knocked without giving her name. Since I didn't know who she was, I tried to . . . He searched for words to describe what he had done. *Push her away.*

That is the basics of storming. You combine your push with the element of surprise. I gather Miss Sparrow was surprised when this happened?

She fainted. Bloodvoicing sometimes makes Sparrow weak. Sir Gavin said that's what saved her from the Veil that day.

How fortunate for her.

A silence stretched on. Achan shifted in his bed, wondering where Duchess Amal had gone. Matthias shuffled around the end of Achan's room, stacking mounds of folded clothing into the clothes press Sir Caleb had brought up.

Her voice came again, suddenly, as if she had never left. *The trick to storming is to utilize the moment of surprise. First you must enter the Veil and approach the person you want to storm. Is someone there with you?*

Matthias is here. And Shung is on guard outside.

Call another guard so Sir Shung may sit with you.

Achan reached for Shung's mind. *I need you in here. Find someone else to guard the door and come in.*

Shung grunted, and the connection vanished. Shung was the only person Achan had met who grunted with his bloodvoice. The idea made him smile.

His Shield entered the chamber and closed the door.

"Pull up a chair, Shung. You're to guard my body so no one kills me while I learn to storm." *Shung is here, my lady.*

Good. Your Highness, your responsibility whenever entering the Veil is to be wise. Overconfidence has killed more men than I dare recount. Do not ignore your man. He is there for your safety. Unless it is imperative, do not shut him out. If he is going to help you, he must hear you. Now, I am in my study. Do you remember where that is?

I do, my lady.

Come to me through the Veil. It may take you a while as this is your first attempt alone.

What is the trick to moving faster?

Concentration, mostly. And practice. I am going to sever my contact with you. When you find me, try and storm me.

Isn't that dangerous, my lady?

I am prepared and fully trained.

Achan's nerves knotted in his chest. *Very well.*

The duchess's presence vanished from Achan's mind. He glanced at Shung, who raised a bushy eyebrow.

"Off I go, then."

Achan closed his eyes and pictured Duchess Amal's study. He instantly saw the room from the door to the secret chambers. Straight ahead, Duchess Amal sat at her desk, writing on a scroll weighted with an iron figure of a puppy. Anillo stood at the wall behind her. Before Achan finished his thought of getting closer, he was looking over her shoulder.

> Lord Levy,
>
> Best wishes on your reassignment. I pray you will be a more hospitable neighbor than Lord Nathak, though I daresay if you are in league with this New Council I doubt your integrity grows stronger.
>
> Your offer to make Sitna the ruling city of Carm is ridiculous. Carmine has ruled Carm since its inception. I see no reason to change that for a usurper who will soon be defeated. I beg you reconsider where your loyalties lie, for soon the true Prince Gidon Hadar will sit on the throne in Armonguard. You would be wise to cast your support with his claim.

"You are to storm me, Your Majesty, not read my correspondence," Duchess Amal said aloud. She lifted the puppy, and the scroll coiled up on her desk.

I thought maybe you'd be writing to Lady Averella to tell her to come home and meet her intended.

She chuckled.

Her laugh filled him with such warmth that he wanted to make her laugh again. Instead, he asked, *How did you know I was here?*

"I can sense when I am being watched. A lesson for another time. You arrived faster than I anticipated. I suspect you have been entering the Veil more than Sir Caleb is aware of."

Achan had no answer for this. He concentrated on Duchess Amal's face, her flawless skin, her auburn hair. He rushed forward, hoping to knock her mind from her body like tackling Shung. He entered her head—

And flew right through her. He'd glided halfway into the wall behind her desk before he could stop himself.

"That will not do, Your Highness."

Her criticism filled him with heat. *When I stormed Sparrow, she was trying to penetrate my mind. I sensed her, so I had a target. How can I find you if you're not attacking?*

"If I'm not attacking you, where is my mind?"

In your head. Which was why Achan had tried the tackle approach.

She folded her hands on her desk. "Do not make this more complicated than need be. Seek my thoughts. Should my shields keep you from seeing them, you have my shields to focus on."

Of course. Achan sensed strong shields around her mind, yet he pushed past them with little effort.

Her private thoughts filled his head. *—is such a bright young man. I expect he shall have me stormed before I can—*

Achan flew against her voice. He made contact but this time took the duchess with him, through the wall and into the bright sunlight.

Duchess Amal's deep laughter filled his head. *"Before I can finish my thought," was what I had been thinking. Well done, Your Highness!*

Achan floated over the inner bailey in almost the same place he'd come up from the underground tunnel. He held Duchess Amal around her waist, his head tucked under her arm. He released her at once, cheeks burning. His body floated up and back from hers.

And there you have stormed me. Duchess Amal shot up to Achan's height. *Though in battle, you would throw me up as far as possible. If you recall, the sky is disorienting in the Veil. If your target does not have a partner, it only takes seconds for them to forget and get lost.*

Duchess Amal vanished.

Achan floated back through the castle wall and found her whole again, sitting at her desk.

"That is enough lesson for today, Your Highness. This is how we shall practice from now on. Should you need me, message at any time. I am your servant." She bowed her head.

Dismissed, then. *Thank you, my lady.* Achan opened his eyes to the frescoed ceiling above his bed and smiled. He was getting faster at this. He raised up onto one elbow to see Shung slouched down in the chair beside his bed, eyes closed.

"Are you sleeping?"

Shung's eyes flashed open. "Listening."

Achan narrowed his eyes. "You expect me to believe you were focused on nothing but Duchess Amal and my conversation? All this time?"

His Shield's dark eyebrows wrinkled low over his eyes.

Achan continued to needle him. "That your thoughts never once drifted to a certain tall woman with dark hair and a cheerful smile?"

Shung bared his yellow teeth in a wide smile. "Berland soldiers arrived this morning. Eager to see Lady Gali."

Achan sat up and swung his legs over the side of his bed. "Lady Gali travels with Sir Koyukuk's army?"

"In Berland, female warriors are not prohibited."

This did not surprise Achan. Lady Gali was as forbidding as Shung. "I'm glad Berland is on our side. For I would not wish Lady Gali's wrath upon any of our men."

Shung banged his fist over his heart. "You honor Lady Gali to say so."

Achan bit back a smile. "You must go to her and give my greetings right away, *Sir Shung Noatak*."

Shung stood and stomped one foot. "As you wish, Little Cham." He bounded to the door and opened it so fast he almost ripped it off its hinges.

Kurtz, who'd been on guard in the hall, swung around to look inside the door, one hand on the hilt of his sword. He met Achan's gaze through the open doorway. "Hello, Pacey."

Achan grinned at Kurtz's use of the nickname he'd given him on their visit to a tavern in Tsaftown. They had pretended to be sailors just into port. Achan had been an oarsman. "Hello, Kurtz."

Shung darted past Kurtz. The floor shook lightly as his footsteps pounded down the hall at a run.

Kurtz turned to watch Shung. "Where are *you* going, eh?"

Achan stood and stretched. "I've sent him on an errand, Kurtz. I'm afraid you'll have to guard the door a bit longer. For Lady Gali awaits."

10

A whip cracked. A man screamed.

"It weren't me. I swear! Ask Murgon. Ask him, I say!"

Vrell pushed her fingertips into her ears and squeezed her eyes shut. Her hands trembled, creating a hum that only agitated her distress. Closing her eyes could not stifle the stench of urine, dirt, and moldy bread.

Reggio Levy had no right to put her here. A noblewoman should *not* be kept in a dungeon. Reggio's audacity had always been borderline insane. But to take her from the Corner at Sitna Manor and throw her here? Had the man no sense of propriety? More importantly: did he really plan to give her to Esek? Could Esek truly be alive?

The muted screaming stopped. Vrell released her ears and opened her eyes. The torchlight from the corridor painted stripes of light across the dirt floor of her cell. Her skirt had fallen to the ground again, and she wrapped the rough fabric around her knees as if bundling something precious. Or keeping something hideous out. That fear had kept her from sleep. Was it morning yet?

Her cell was dark and, thankfully, vacant, though a cot, stool, or some kind of blanket would have been nice. The front of her cell consisted of a half wall of stone with iron bars running from the top of the wall to the ceiling. She sat against the stone, knees to her chest, just to the left of the barred door. Full walls of iron bars divided her cell from others. Hers looked to be in the middle of a dozen or more along this row, for she could see men at various distances on both sides, trapped behind the bars like the teeth on a comb.

Vrell tried not to look at the back wall, but her gaze continually flitted to the iron rings hanging from the stone. She shuddered at the memory of Achan hanging from such rings in his cell in Mahanaim while Lord Nathak's guard whipped him. She prayed she would not meet the same fate.

If she had followed her own instincts instead of caving to Gren, she would be in Allowntown by now. But what was done was done, and fuming would not change her circumstances. She should contact Mother, she supposed.

Mother would be furious.

She prolonged the inevitable tongue-lashing by focusing on Bran's mind instead. She found him in an even darker room than her dungeon cell. The hairs on Vrell's arms tingled. Something was wrong.

Bran's wrists stung. *What did Prince Oren say, Sir Jax?*

That he can do nothing for us at present. Jax's voice boomed from the darkness on Bran's left. *Promised to inform Sir Caleb of our plight, but I told him I can manage that. He's got enough to worry about.*

Quite right. Sir Rigil's voice came from Bran's right. *Do take care, Jax. Lord Agros is Sir Caleb's brother.*

I had forgotten, Jax said. *Do you think I should message Sir Gavin instead?*

No, Sir Rigil said. *Sir Caleb is Prince Achan's closest advisor, and we were returning to Prince Oren on the prince's orders. I'm afraid you must message Sir Caleb.*

Jax did not answer again, and Vrell suspected his message to Sir Caleb was being sent. What could have happened? Were they in a dungeon too?

We were too lax, Sir Rigil said. *I should have had Jax bloodvoice Lord Agros before we approached the gate.*

That conniving old blackguard! Bran's slang shocked Vrell, for she had never heard him use such language. *Does that mean this "New Council" has taken over?*

It appears so, Master Rennan.

What do you suppose they've done with Lord Agros?

I dare not say. It is clear he is not down here, unless he is too injured to speak.

Bran shifted his hands. Scratchy rope bit into his wrists, bringing tears to Vrell's eyes. *Can you loose your bonds at all? Mine are cutting through the skin.*

As are mine. That old man is a smart devil. Even had his guards check my boots.

Mine as well. If only you'd taught me to hide a knife somewhere else.

We must not give up hope. Arman will provide.

Bran sighed. *Unless He is ready to take us home.*

Do not get sentimental, boy. We may be here a long while. It would be better for Sir Caleb to leave us than risk men in a rescue attempt. I should have had Jax tell him so, though he will likely come to that conclusion on his own.

At least by our capture the men will know not to bring Achan this way, Bran said.

Good man, Rennan. That's the way to look at it. See? Arman has already used us, and we almost missed it. But I've told you not to refer to the prince as "Achan."

Bran was about to respond, but Jax spoke.

The army moves out today. Sir Caleb was grieved to hear about his brother but thankful to know of this trap.

Vrell pulled away from the men, heart heavy. A trap in Allowntown? There was no time to waste. *Mother? It is Averella. I have news.*

One moment, dearest.

Vrell squeezed her hands while she waited. A prisoner in the cell on her left sang a slurred tune.

What is it, Averella?

I'm in Sitna. I thought I could catch up with Jax but—

Mother sighed heavily. *I am in a meeting, Averella. Unless you are in mortal danger, we shall speak of this later.*

I am in the dungeons. Reggio Levy had me arrested.

A dungeon? Averella, why did you leave Carmine?

Gren wanted to go home.

The peasant widow? And you *are her escort?*

Yes, Mother. I—

Of all the ridiculous . . . Really, Averella. We are in a war for the throne of Er'Rets. I cannot be rescuing you every other day. For all that was sacrificed to see you safely home . . .

I am sorry. This would not have happened if I had used my head. And gone on without Gren.

That much is true. What did Lord Levy say to you?

I have not seen him. Reggio put me here.

Has anyone hurt you?

No, but they put me in the dungeon, Mother! It's horrible here.

Averella, it is you who seem to want to be treated like one of the men. If you insist on this lifestyle, you should get used to dirt and manhandling. I love you and will do all I can to see you freed. Let me speak with your father.

Mother, wait! Allowntown is a trap. Vrell explained what she had heard from Jax, Sir Rigil, and Bran.

Sir Jax just informed Sir Caleb of this. Do not despair, Averella. I shall send help. But rest assured, once you are back under my roof, you will be living in another kind of prison. Do you understand my meaning?

Yes, Mother.

Vrell exhaled a shaky breath. Something moved across her cell. Her heart jolted, and she drew the peasant skirt tight around her knees, no matter how much the fabric itched.

Feathers rustled. Odd. How could a bird have gotten so far underground?

"Greetings, favored one," a low voice purred.

Vrell glanced to the cell on her left. The man had stopped singing and lay asleep. The cell on her right was vacant. Who had spoken?

A sound came from the corner of her cell, like a boot scraping over dirt. A rat, perhaps? Digging at the dirt?

Vrell swallowed and stood, wanting to climb the walls.

A hooded figure stepped into the stripes of torchlight. "Many years have passed since I have seen a woman garner such attention from men."

Vrell pressed against the half-stone wall. The bars that rose to the ceiling cut into her shoulder blades. "Who are you? How did you get in here?"

"First, Lord Nathak asked for your hand."

Vrell's mouth went dry. No one but Vrell and her mother knew Lord Nathak had also asked to marry her. "Lord Nathak had no right to ask for my hand. He is already married to Lady—"

"When he could not obtain your favor, his son set his sights on you. You refused him as well." The man's voice was a soft hum, horribly familiar. "Yes, many a suitor found himself not good enough for Lady Averella Amal. Why, half the male population of Carmine asked the duchess for your hand, not to mention nearly every nobleman in Er'Rets. And then there was Bran Rennan. Poor fellow was beneath you as well, wasn't he? No, you wanted the stray. Of course, he turned out to be much more than a stray, didn't he?"

"You twist words, sir. Most of those men wanted my dowry, not my heart."

"My mother was like you," the man said. "So beautiful she couldn't see it. Women don't understand how beauty is more than a pretty face and figure. Men like those things, of course, but most prefer a woman with spirit, who stands for something and is willing to fight for it.

"Katine was like that, you see. Hated her husband's magic, his gods. Tried to fight him, which only made him control her more. Yet her spirit drew the attention of the king. He told her to leave her husband, promised to keep her safe. But her husband was stronger. He killed the king, and eventually, Katine too. She didn't know her place. Pushed things too far. As have you."

Vrell could not breathe. Was this man saying he knew who killed King Axel? But the name Katine made her think of Lady Katine, a distant relative who lived far before King Axel's time.

The man glided toward her as if floating, though his steps scraped over the dirt floor. He stopped an arm's length away. In the distant torchlight, she could just see the outline of his face beneath the black hood. A face she recognized.

Macoun Hadar. The man who had been her master in Mahanaim, who had taught her to bloodvoice, then tried to trade her to Esek for Achan. How in all Er'Rets did he do this magic? He had never been strong enough.

"My master hoped to take Achan Cham under his wing, mold him into a powerful sorcerer. Yet the stray turned him down. When I killed my master, I had no desire to give that boy a second chance. For I received a better offer. And now the stray must die, for he alone stands in my way."

Vrell trembled, unhinged by the evil in this man's very presence. How had he become so powerful?

"Esek still wants you, girl, though I'm not convinced I want him in Carm. Perhaps I shall wed you to Sir Jabari instead? Put him over Carm Duchy."

"You cannot wed me to anyone," Vrell said.

"Oh, but I can. Carm is a necessary duchy to control. And you are the key to that."

So everyone thought. But Gypsum was the true heir to Carm. Yet Vrell could not publicly announce that, at least not until Achan assumed control of Er'Rets. For she could not allow this wicked man to go after Gypsum. Her breath caught as she wondered if he had been the one who had tried to abduct Gypsum days ago.

Macoun lunged forward and gripped Vrell's neck with his wrinkled, coarse fingers. His breath smelled like rotten eggs. She kicked him, but her leg passed through his body. Solid hands but vaporous legs? Was he a black knight now too?

Vrell closed her mind. Pain stabbed the base of her skull and swelled until it engulfed her entire head. She screamed, slapped his arms and head but found no purchase. Tears streamed down her cheeks. She ground her teeth, sucking short breaths, but her shields crumbled under the pain.

Macoun's voice boomed in her mind. *You are still quite strong. You could be useful for more than what you will inherit. Now, tell me what you know of the prince's plans.*

Vrell focused on squirrels and herbs and the waves in the sea, but her mind betrayed her. Jax said Achan was leaving today. Mother was training Achan's mind. Vrell saw herself sitting at Achan's bedside, singing to his unconscious form.

Ah, he's hurt, is he? the old man said.

"No!" Vrell focused on Kopay in the Sitna stables. Of Gren's baby. Would it be a boy or a girl? Would Bran marry Gren? Be a father to the child? Or would Harnu?

The old man's oily chuckle brought her gaze to his shadowed face. *Clever girl. But what of the prince? What of the young man called Achan?*

Against her will, Vrell pictured Achan, fallen in the vineyard.

Good, good. His fingers rubbed her neck like sandpaper.

Vrell sobbed. She had to break away from his probing mind. She had to protect her thoughts.

Arman, help me!

As if thrown, her perspective soared out of her body and through the bars of three cells. She screamed, startled by the motion. She could see all the way back into her cell, where her body crumpled to the floor.

Macoun glanced around. "Don't be a fool, girl. Leaving your body is a good way to die." Macoun spoke aloud, as if he could not see where she was now.

So Vrell stayed put. She knew the dangers of the Veil. But she could not return to her body. Not until Macoun left.

Footsteps drew Vrell's attention. Three men walked down the narrow corridor that separated one row of cells from another. They stopped before her cell.

Macoun Hadar vanished, leaving behind a flock of squawking shadows.

Gowzals?

"Hear that?" a man said. "Sounds like birds."

"There ain't no birds down here, fool. Just rats." Something banged against the bars. "Lady Averella?"

Vrell tried to drift closer, wanting to see who they were, but she suddenly realized she was drifting near the ceiling. She circled her arms, as if trying to catch her balance, but the action only made her lift higher until she passed through the ceiling and lost sight of her body completely.

11

"My brother and his family are safe, for now," Sir Caleb said. "They are being held in one of the outbuildings."

"But not with Sir Jax?" Achan asked.

"No. Sir Jax and his men are in the dungeon."

Achan sat at the head of a table in one of Granton Castle's frescoed assembly rooms. To his left sat Sir Caleb, Sir Eagan, Inko, and Altair Bentz, captain of the contingent from Zerah Rock. Sir Gavin sat on Achan's right. Beside him, Captain Tristan Loam of Carmine, Sir Eric Livna of Tsaftown, and Sir Koyukuk Orson of Berland. The duchess sat at the opposite end of the table. Anillo stood by the door.

Achan wished Sparrow were here. Given the heavy nature of this meeting, he could use her bloodvoicing quips. Plus she made a tea that could quell any headache. "How many were lost in the attack?" he asked Sir Caleb.

"Baruch fears it was a slaughter," Sir Caleb said. "They attacked at dawn the same day they attacked here."

Pig snout. "How many men did Allowntown have?"

"Just over one thousand."

A thousand men. Lost to the devil who might have killed Achan's parents. He rubbed his throbbing temple with the heel of his palm.

Are you well, Your Highness? Duchess Amal's voice soothed his pain. Perhaps Sir Eagan had taught her the trick.

Only a headache, my lady.

"Anillo?" Every head at the table turned to face the duchess. "Some chamomile tea, please?"

Anillo nodded and slipped from the room.

Thank you, Achan said.

"Berland will help destroy this enemy, we will," Sir Koyukuk said to Achan. Like Shung, the young general from Berland was hairy and dark. He wore needles of white bone through each ear lobe.

Achan worded his reply to fit Berland customs. "Your presence and offer honor us."

Sir Koyukuk smiled and bowed his head to Achan.

Sir Gavin stood and rolled out a leather map that covered their end of the table. The bitter smell of tanned leather filled Achan's nostrils as he leaned forward to examine the burned lines that depicted roads.

Sir Gavin set his finger on the word *Allowntown*. "We now know that at least part of the enemy army is gathered in Allowntown. That there will be a battle before we reach Armonguard, none now can deny. I can't guess whether they intend to wait in Allowntown in hopes of blocking our path south or if they will advance north. If we move now, we may be able to avoid both those options—at least make it a battlefield of our own choosing."

"How so?" Achan asked.

"If we can pass the Sideros River before they reach us, we can move south over the Allown plains, perhaps bypass Esek's army altogether."

Achan examined the map. "Why Allowntown? Wouldn't they make a stronger stand in Mahanaim since it is the only way through to the south?"

Sir Gavin grinned, but his thin teeth made it look more like a grimace. "'Tis not the only way, Your Highness. And the enemy is greedy, trying to take every town at once. My scouts tell me their forces are divided, with the majority of their men south of Mahanaim. The northern troops are going to do all they can to keep us from reaching Armonguard. And while they distract us, the southern troops will march against Armonguard. Prince Oren's Mârad is scattered throughout Arman and Nahar duchies. Without our aid, Armonguard will not be a difficult victory for Esek.

"So our first objective is to bypass the enemy army in Allowntown. After that, to cross the Lebab Inlet into Southern Er'Rets in hopes of reaching Prince Oren before Armonguard is lost to the enemy."

"What if Armonguard is lost before we can reach her?" Achan asked.

"Then we take her back."

A silence descended over the table. The idea of such battles twisted Achan's stomach. Duchess Amal's voice distracted his dark thoughts.

"I received a letter from Lord Levy." The duchess glanced around the table. "He informed me that the Hadad has made Sitna the ruling city of Carm Duchy until he appoints someone to replace me. I, of course, am not leaving."

"What else does this Hadad say?" Altair asked. He was a man with a long neck and sunken eyes.

Duchess Amal's expression sobered. "He placed Lord Levy to rule Sitna, Macoun Hadar over Allowntown, Dovev Falkson over Barth, and Rapha Gibbor to rule the giants and Nahar. Esek is set to rule Armonguard."

Esek was alive. Truly? Achan couldn't believe it.

"Who is the Hadad, anyway?" Sir Eric, Duchess Amal's nephew and Lord of Tsaftown, was dressed in black that matched his trim black hair and beard. "I thought at first you'd meant to say *Hadar*, our line of kings."

The door opened and Anillo entered with a pot of tea. He carried it to Achan's end of the table, and poured a steaming mug.

"No," Duchess Amal said, "the two are quite different. *Hadar*, as you say, is the family name of the line of rightful kings in Er'Rets. The prince's true name is Gidon Hadar, for instance. But the Hadad is something supernatural. Something evil." She looked like she didn't want to say more but lifted her chin and continued. "There is a dark legend of a creature that feeds off men. Just as our service to Arman gives us the strength of His light, men who serve this creature are strengthened by its darkness. It is called the *keliy*."

Sir Gavin cast a knowing gaze at Sir Eagan.

"Unlike its master, Gâzar, who abides in the Lowerworld, the keliy lives among men," Duchess Amal said. "Its purpose is to influence events through one man at a time. The keliy has always chosen its host, and that person, that host, takes the title *the Hadad* and sets out upon a life of utter destruction, depravity, and evil. I believe this name, so similar to that of our kingship Hadar, was chosen to confuse, mock, and steal loyalty away from the throne."

Achan realized his mouth was hanging open and closed it. The Hadad had done just that to him. Confused him with a name being so similar to Hadar.

Duchess Amal continued, "The last suspected keliy was a man named Jibhal Hamartano. He ruled Jaelport with his wife, Katine, during the reign of King Johan. It was suspected that Jibhal murdered King Johan. I believe that this act of evil was what drew the attention of the keliy."

Sir Eric cast a stricken look to his aunt. "Surely not. Jibhal Hamartano died young. And Lady Katine lived in Tsaftown for years, a lonely old widow. She was mad. Crazy Katine, the people called her."

"She was not crazy, Eric," Duchess Amal said in a firm voice. "Once Jibhal killed King Johan, he banished Lady Katine and relocated to Land's End, where he began training young men in dark magic. We now know them as black knights. Years later, Jibhal, host of the keliy, took an apprentice: a young boy cast off for his illegitimacy. Macoun Hadar, whom I have recently discovered was King Johan and Katine's son."

Sir Eagan's complexion paled.

The duchess continued, her piercing green eyes fixed on Achan. "Lady Katine was not mad. She was telling the truth about the creature who stole her husband and murdered the king. It took a while to uncover this mystery, Your Highness, but I believe it is the truth."

Achan let out an audible moan. His great, great grandfather murdered for taking another man's wife? How long did men in his family usually live? Had every king been murdered? He looked around the assembly room as if an assassin might've appeared from the shadows.

"I am believing it," Inko said. "When I was serving Macoun Hadar in my youth, I always was knowing that he was serving someone who was being even more powerful."

Achan shook off the shock of the story. "How does knowing any of this matter?"

"Because it always helps to know your enemy's past." Duchess Amal's eyes lost focus, and she pursed her lips.

"We now know we face an enemy greater than Esek and Lord Nathak. And I do not speak merely of numbers of men in our armies." Sir Gavin's moustache arched into a frown. "The keliy is an enemy of Arman himself. So, Your Highness, just as you are Arman's chosen, the keliy—and its human host of the hour—is Gâzar's chosen."

That statement so took Achan off guard he couldn't form a reply. So now, not only must he push back darkness, he must fight one of Gâzar's supernatural creatures?

"Surely Jibhal Hamartano can't still be living," Captain Loam said. "He'd be over a hundred years old."

Inko turned his grey, pockmarked face toward the captain. "If he has been practicing dark magic all these years, he could easily be prolonging his life."

Duchess Amal stood. "Please excuse me a moment." She strode from the room, Anillo at her heels.

Achan watched her go, curious at her departure.

"Jibhal Hamartano would only be one hundred twenty-some years old, Tristan," Sir Eagan said to Captain Loam. "Dark magic could have kept him alive this long."

"He uses gowzals," Achan said.

Altair looked at him, confused. "What are gowzals?"

"A cross between ravens and bats," Sir Gavin said. "Weak-minded creatures that black knights use to wield their magic."

"Berland will help destroy these creatures, we will," Koyukuk said. "Fowl is best roasted on a spit."

Achan fought a smile. "You honor us with your offer, Sir Koyukuk." Yet even Koyukuk's eagerness to roast gowzals did not keep the Hadad—whoever was the current Hadad for the keliy—from coming back to his thoughts. The man—creature?—had killed his great, great grandfather, and perhaps Achan's parents. "What if the Hadad is watching through me right now? Shadowing me with his bloodvoice?"

Sir Eagan's keen blue eyes locked with Achan's. "Do not give in to paranoia, Your Highness. You are wise to be concerned and on guard, but no one can watch through you when your shields are up. None can hear your thoughts."

"But it's been weeks since he spoke to me, and I've lowered my shields at least once during that time. If he's not trying to see through me now, why did he stop trying?"

"He has not spoken to you since you swore fealty to Arman," Sir Caleb said. "Is that correct?"

"Aye, right." Arman was with him now. How could Achan have missed that vital difference? *Arman, help me withstand this foe.*

A flash of heat welled up in the pit of Achan's stomach.

FEAR NOT, FOR I AM WITH YOU. THE ENEMY SHALL COME IN LIKE A FLOOD, BUT I SHALL LIFT UP A STANDARD AGAINST HIM.

Relief chased after the heat, bringing a peace over Achan. *Thank You, Arman. Thank You.*

The door opened, and Duchess Amal returned to her seat at the foot of the table. Was it Achan's imagination or did her eyes look red?

They discussed the plans to depart. Sir Eric mentioned that his brother, Captain Chantry Livna, was bringing a fleet of battleships to Armonguard, but they had not passed Zerah Rock yet. The army would have to march south without their aid and face whatever enemy it met along the way.

When no one had further business to discuss, Achan adjourned the meeting.

He was in his chambers, making sure all of his things had been gathered, when Sir Eagan entered.

"Your Highness, Duchess Amal is in need of your immediate assistance."

Achan glanced past Sir Eagan and out the open door. He could see the emerald sleeve of Duchess Amal's gown in the corridor. "Certainly."

Sir Eagan opened the door fully, and the duchess strode to the chair beside Achan's bed and sat down. She held her own hands, fidgeting. "Your Highness, please sit a moment."

Achan sat on the edge of his bed. "My lady, are you well?"

"I bring sad news. It has come to my attention that your friend, Miss Sparrow, has found herself in an unfortunate situation."

Achan's stomach seemed to slide into his boots. "What has happened?"

"She was captured and imprisoned in Sitna. Lord Levy holds her there for Esek Nathak's bidding."

"So Esek really is alive?"

"According to Vrell," Sir Eagan said.

"She contacted you, Sir Eagan?" Achan felt passed over by Sparrow. But after all, Sir Eagan had helped her before.

"Regardless," Duchess Amal said, "neither of us are able to contact her now."

Achan reached out for Sparrow and found no sense of her. He forced himself to ask. "You think she's dead?"

"I know not." Duchess Amal's voice was barely a whisper. "I hoped to discover whether you had ever been in the dungeons of Sitna Manor. I have not, nor has Sir Eagan, so neither of us can look for her . . . body."

"I-I have." Achan shuddered at the memory of Myet, Lord Nathak's head torturer, flogging Achan in the darkness under the Sitna Manor keep.

"Will you look for her there?" Duchess Amal asked. "Tell me what you see, and I shall watch your body."

"Of course, my lady." He scooted back on his bed and lay down, eyes closed, unhinged that he had been hoping to seek out Sparrow in such a way, though under vastly different circumstances.

Arman, please let me find her. Please let her be safe.

Achan found himself in an open space at the foot of a stairwell that led up the southeast tower of the Sitna keep. Barred cells ran along every wall except the eastern one, which was solid stone and covered with various saws, knives, pikes, iron spiders, whips, cat tails, racks, and other torture devices. How he knew this place. Thankfully, Myet was absent. Achan did not want to see him again.

Achan drifted to the right, down the path on the southern wall. The thick smells of mildew, urine, and body odor made him gag. He passed a cell where a man keened, rocking back and forth, clutching his side. In the next cell a man slept. In another a man sang to himself, scratching his finger in the dirt floor. Achan drifted, scanning the ground for Sparrow. A large rat chased a smaller one across the corridor.

Achan reached the end of the row and circled down the next. Two men stood in the aisle halfway down where a cell door hung open. Achan drifted closer, concentrating on the men's soft voices.

"Well, they're diseased, aren't they?"

"Even so, Reggio, she wouldn't pass out instantly if a rat bit her. There is something about this I don't understand."

"Black knights?"

"Perhaps, though I would expect to be informed before they used their magic on my prisoner. Where are those blasted men with the litter?"

"Probably stopped to drool over some woman. I declare, Father. The peasants of Sitna Manor are the most wayward bunch. You should have seen them reveling last night. You should put a stop to it at once."

Achan slowed his approach beside Lord Levy and his son, Reggio. Lord Levy was a man of medium height with small, brown eyes. He had short, white hair and a matching beard that he'd oiled into a point. Reggio, Levy's son, hadn't grown an inch since Achan had last seen him. Scrawny, brown-haired, and no older than thirteen years, the boy acted as if all Er'Rets was his to command.

Achan drifted through the doorway and into the cell. At first it appeared empty, until he realized he had glided right over a woman's body that lay on the floor near the entrance. It was Sparrow, all right. He dropped down beside her, overcome at the sight of her still form. She wore a peasant's dress of brown linen. Her hair had been braided in two short plaits. Both were frizzy. One had lost its thong and was half unraveled.

A cham raged in Achan's chest. That any man would treat a woman so. She should not have been put in a cell like a man. Though knowing Sparrow, she had likely demanded it. He hated being here without his body. He wanted to lift her in his arms and carry her from this place.

His mind raced through the things Sparrow would say if she happened upon an unconscious person. Had anyone thought to try smelling salts? She had likely only fainted. Probably saw one of the huge rats in her cell.

He reached for her mind, elated to find no shields blocking his way. *Sparrow? Wake up. It's me, Achan.*

No answer came, nor could Achan sense her sleeping mind. His heart rate doubled. *Sparrow!* Her chest rose and fell steadily. So why couldn't he sense her?

Duchess! I have found her. She breathes, though it's as if she isn't there. What could that mean?

Duchess Amal's voice whispered in his mind. *That she has been stormed.*

Achan glanced around the cell, looking for Sparrow's transparent mind. *I will find her. She cannot be far.*

Footsteps shuffled down the corridor outside the cell.

"What took you so long?" Lord Levy said.

Two men pushed their way inside and lowered a litter beside Sparrow.

"Hurry up, now," Lord Levy said. "Put her in the eastern chamber on the sixth floor. And stand guard at her door until I tell you otherwise. Let no one inside."

"Not even the healer?" one of the soldiers asked.

"He said no one!" Reggio yelled. "Are you deaf or just daft?"

"No, my lord."

The men lifted Sparrow's limp body onto the litter. Achan wanted to push them all away. He didn't want anyone to touch her. The men carried Sparrow from the cell. Achan drifted along after them. He needed to see the room they were taking her to.

Duchess Amal's voice came again. *Your Highness, do you see her?*

They are taking her body. I want to see where they go so I can bring her back to her body.

Very well. As soon as you see, return to yours.

Achan followed the men up the tower stairs. If only he could knock their heads together for the careless way they carried the litter. Sparrow nearly slid off the litter twice and her skirt had ridden up to her knees.

They exited on the sixth floor and into a spacious chamber. Fat arrow loops looked out over the delta where the Sideros River met the sea. The guards set the litter on a bed tented in a thick sheet of burlap. They left Sparrow there and went outside, closing the door behind them.

Achan scowled at the door. The brutes hadn't removed the cover from the bed or lifted Sparrow off the litter. Achan hovered over her, staring at her face. How badly he wanted to touch her cheek. Her ivory skin, usually lustrous, was milky, almost greenish. He worried that her blood had stopped flowing. Her chest still rose and fell. There must be something more he could do. She looked so stiff and awkward, one hand caught under her back.

Your Highness? Have you arrived? the duchess asked.

I have, my lady. They threw her on a dusty bed. She looks so uncomfortable. Her dress is twisted around her legs. You're sure there is no way I can move her?

Not without your body, no. Come away, Your Highness.

But Lord Levy is going to come. I should stay and hear what he has to say. Maybe I will learn something—

No. You must come back now.

Achan tensed. He didn't want to leave Sparrow alone with these people who intended to harm her.

Please, Your Highness. We must hurry if we are to bring her mind back from the Veil.

Of course. Sparrow still needed him, but not here. She was out there, drifting, alone. Frightened.

He opened his eyes to find the duchess staring down at him. He took a deep breath. "Do you think she knows about the Veil? About what can happen there?"

Duchess Amal shook her head slightly. "I know not."

"Macoun Hadar might have taught her."

She pursed her lips. "Perhaps. It matters not to fret over it. We must go and look for her."

Achan wanted to pace, but he needed to enter the Veil and look for Sparrow. "How will I know where to look?"

"Message her."

"I tried. I couldn't find her mind."

"I suspect that was because you focused on her body and her mind was not there."

Achan closed his eyes and sought Sparrow's mind. This time he sensed her. And her shields were down! *Sparrow? You must return to your body.*

Hello? Her voice sounded far away. Confused. *Is someone there?*

Sparrow. It's Achan. You've been stormed. Return to your body right away.

Who are you?

Achan. Achan Cham.

I cannot see you, Master Cham. Where are you and why do you jest? It is a lovely day. I cannot imagine it would storm.

Sparrow! Achan tried to enter her mind, to see through her eyes, hoping to hear her thoughts, but he was unable to see anything. How could that be?

He growled and looked at Duchess Amal. "She's not herself. She called me Master Cham, and when I mentioned her being stormed, she thought I was talking of rain."

The duchess sighed and closed her eyes.

Sir Eagan set a hand on her shoulder. "Nor must you fret, Nitsa. We will all reach for her and, in time, convince her to return."

Duchess Amal's eyes flashed open, wild with fright. "We must not. Only one person should speak with her. Too many and she might close us out. If her memory is gone . . . If she does not know what bloodvoicing is . . ."

Achan knew too well how frightening it was to suddenly hear voices and not know why. "I will talk to her."

Duchess Amal's eyes filled with tears. "But I do not think you are ready, Your Highness. I should be the one—"

"But you don't know Sparrow at all, my lady. And Sir Eagan has only known her a few weeks. She was closest to me. I should be looking for her."

A tiny sob escaped Duchess Amal's lips. Achan did not understand why the duchess was so upset over a missing stray girl she'd never met. She knew Achan cared for Sparrow, and clearly Sir Eagan had brought the matter to the duchess's attention. Perhaps she was simply a compassionate woman.

Sir Eagan gripped the duchess's hand and turned her face to his, looking into her eyes. "We will find her, Nitsa. But we will not decide this now. Since Achan has already spoken to her, he will keep messaging until we decide how to proceed. All right?"

She nodded, a calming breath restoring her regal posture and demeanor. "Of course you are right, Sir Eagan."

"And now we must go." Sir Eagan helped Duchess Amal stand. "The army is waiting for the prince so it can depart."

Achan scowled. "I cannot leave when Sparrow is lost!"

"You will have nothing to do but search, Your Majesty," Sir Eagan said, "for you will not be riding a horse. And I will ride with you should you wish to enter the Veil, but we must move south today. You understand that, do you not?"

"Aye." It wouldn't be so bad as long as Achan could keep looking for Sparrow. "But I'm not riding in a litter, am I?" He recalled Esek's fancy portable bedchamber.

"Duchess Amal has given us three litters, which will be filled with supplies. Decoys, you see? You will be riding in one of five covered wagons. No one will know where to strike. I did not start taking care of royalty yesterday."

Duchess Amal locked eyes with Achan. "Please continue to speak with . . . Miss Sparrow, Your Highness. Sir Eagan and I will stay in contact. Should we discover a better way to find her, Sir Eagan will advise you. Will that do?"

"Yes, my lady. Thank you. I will not rest until she is found."

She nodded. "I will assist in battle from here. I dare not leave Carm unguarded with Lord Levy's orders to take over. And I must stay with my daughters." She reached out and cupped Achan's cheek. "Worry not, Your Highness, for Arman will guide you. When next we meet it shall be your wedding day."

His wedding day. Pig snout. Here he was going on about Sparrow when he was betrothed to Duchess Amal's daughter. "My lady? Might you tell me where Lady Averella resides at present? If we were to pass near, I might take the opportunity to—"

Duchess Amal dropped her hand from his face. "I am sorry, Your Highness. But taking an army to my daughter's location would not be wise. Besides, she is not along your path. Arman give you patience until she stands before you." She lifted her skirts and stepped past Sir Eagan toward the door.

Sir Eagan reached out and gripped her elbow. "A moment, my lady, please?"

She stopped, her gaze locked on the floor.

Sir Eagan stared at Achan, one eyebrow quirked. "Shung is waiting for you outside, Your Majesty. I shall meet you in the foyer momentarily."

Oh. Sir Eagan and Duchess Amal wanted a private farewell. Achan's cheeks burned. "Of course." He grabbed his belt and sword and exited his chamber for the last time.

Achan walked toward the stairs with Shung, buckling Ôwr around his waist as he went.

Shung's heavy footsteps matched his stride. "You are bothered."

"It's Sparrow. She's . . . stormed."

"How?"

"I don't know."

They walked downstairs. Every step of the way Achan wanted to reach for Sparrow. He fought the urge, for a pair of broken legs would not provide her a worthy hero.

When Achan and Shung descended the grand staircase, they found Kurtz, Sir Caleb, and Inko waiting in the foyer. Lady Gypsum and one of her little sisters stood beside a broad-shouldered man dressed in a surcoat that had once been white. Three interlocking circles were embroidered on the front in dull red thread. His brown leather boots resembled the tattered pair Noam had given Achan for his coming-of-age gift. He stood with one hand on the curling end of the balustrade, slouched as if he'd rather be elsewhere. He had short, dark hair, and a scruff of a beard and mustache, as if he had forgotten to shave for several days.

Achan reached the foot of the stairs, expecting to be introduced to the mysterious stranger, but Lady Gypsum stepped forward and curtsied.

"Good day, Your Highness."

"My lady." Achan nodded to Lady Gypsum, then to her little sister, who grinned, revealing two missing front teeth.

Lady Gypsum met his eyes then looked away, a flush darkening her cheeks. "I wanted to . . . to thank you again for helping me in the vineyard the other morning." Her gaze continued to dart to and from his. "If it weren't for you, I . . ." She dropped her focus to the marble floor, her eyelashes casting curling shadows on her cheeks.

Achan couldn't be certain, but Lady Gypsum appeared to have dressed differently this day. She wore a more womanly gown and what he first thought had been flushed cheeks, now appeared to be pink powder of some kind. He pushed the awkward realization from his mind and sought a formal and honest way to respond to her appreciation. "Think no more of what the consequences might have been, Lady Gypsum. Arman spared us both that day."

The dark-haired man raised his eyebrows and smirked. Achan glanced at the door, wanting only to be in his wagon. Sparrow was lost. He didn't have time for these niceties.

"We'll miss you, Your Highness," the small Amal girl said.

Achan berated himself for not recalling her name. *Sir Caleb—?*

Lady Terra, the duchess's second youngest girl.

Thank you. He bowed. "And I you, Lady Terra."

"Your Highness," Sir Caleb cut in, to Achan's relief. "Please welcome Toros Ianjo to our company. He will serve you as a priest of The Way."

Achan tried to keep his face passive, but Sir Caleb's words were the furthest from what he had expected this man to be, though the interlocking circles should have tipped him off. He nodded at the priest. "Pleased to know you."

Sir Caleb ushered them out into a sunny day. It was the first time Achan had stepped outside since he was struck down. He glanced at the fluffy white clouds, wondering if Sparrow were lost among them. They hurried through the inner bailey, the outer bailey, and finally out the gatehouse. Achan sensed conflicting emotions in the surrounding crowd. He kept his shields firmly in place. At the moment, he didn't have time to worry about whether these people liked him or not.

North to south, thousands of soldiers on horseback and hundreds of wagons and carts stretched out in a line from one horizon to the other. Flags dotted the line, waving in the breeze. Most were banners of Armonguard, though Achan could see some Zerah Rock standards to the north.

Achan's wagon waited directly outside the gatehouse. Actually, it was less a wagon and more a small cottage on wheels pulled by two horses. It had plain clapboard walls and a timber roof painted red. An entrance was cut into the center of the side facing the castle with a linen drape for the door.

Cole, the stray stableboy Achan had weaseled from Lord Yarden in Mitspah, stood behind the wagon, patting the nose of a small, black and white rouncy that was harnessed to a cart filled with trunks. Dove and Scout, Achan's horses, were tethered to the back of the cart. Dove was a white festrier warhorse that stood a full head taller than any other. He had been a gift from Sir Eric Livna. Scout was a sleek black courser Achan rode for speed or recreation.

"Who's your new friend?" Achan asked Cole.

"This is Bart, Your Highness. He's a piebald, and your new packhorse. But he gets to pull instead of carry this trip, since we've got the cart."

Achan shook his head at the number of trunks in the cart. "What's in those? I don't own anything."

"You do now." The jingle of chain drew Achan's gaze to Toros Ianjo, who stopped to pat Bart's nose. "You're a prince, after all, and princes never travel light."

"Are you wearing chain armor?" Achan asked.

"We're going into battle, aren't we? I'm no fool."

Achan smirked, unsure what to make of his new warrior priest. "Have you fought in many battles?"

"Enough that I'd rather not fight in another. Though Arman is not opposed to calling us to what we dread."

Achan took a deep breath. "Sometimes it feels as if Arman has made a game of putting me in dreadful situations. I wonder if my life will ever be normal again."

"Not for a king, I imagine."

"Well, I never asked to be a king."

"I hear you, Highness. Change isn't my game, either."

"Your game?"

Toros shrugged one shoulder. "My game is dice. One Hundred or Passage. I'm also fond of hawking."

"You have a bird?"

"No. Point is, Highness, Arman uses change to stir us. Clarify priorities. Supply direction. The battle comes and we face it, for that is where Arman wants us to be. Normal is tedious, Highness. Don't long for blissful lethargy. Long for change."

Long for change?

Achan stared at the interlocking circles on Toros's tunic. No matter what would come, Arman was in control. He would not allow Achan to fail. He would help Achan find Sparrow, defeat the Hadad, and push back Darkness.

Achan raised his gaze to Toro Ianjo's scruffy face. "Thank you, Toros. Your outlook has raised my spirits a great deal. Now I must go." For Sparrow was lost and needed to be found.

12

Averella reached out toward the tea rose again, and *again* her fingers passed through the two-tone petals. How could that be? Was she invisible? An apparition? Had she died? The knowledge evaded her mind, just out of reach.

She studied her body, intrigued that she could see through herself. She did not feel sad or frightened. But why was she wearing this peasant dress? It was hideous and itchy and stained and had no corset.

Confused, she continued to admire the garden. Not even the beauty of the courtyard in Granton Castle compared to this place. There were lilies, irises, rosemary bushes, sunflowers, daffodils, and more types of roses than Averella had ever seen.

Over the last year, she had missed her garden greatly. She had spent so many days there with Bran. But that had been fall. It was clearly summer now. Why had she neglected her garden all this time? Where had she been?

Averella drifted closer to the temple along a worn dirt path. Her transparent feet floated inches above the ground.

How very strange.

A man's voice boomed, as if spoken in her ear. *Sparrow? You must return to your body.*

Hello? She spun around, pressing a hand to her heart. *Is someone there?*

Sparrow. It's Achan. You've been stormed. Return to your body right away.

Who are you?

Achan. Achan Cham.

Cham? Why would a stray address her so familiarly? Averella cocked her head to the side and listened. Distant sounds of chickens and children's laughter drifted from beyond a nearby sentry wall, but she saw no man. *I cannot see you, Master Cham. Where are you and why do you jest? It is a lovely day. I cannot imagine it would storm.*

Sparrow! A moment of silence passed, then the invisible man growled.

Averella jumped at his angry tone. Sparrow, indeed! How peculiar. She continued to the temple and approached a guard dressed in a black New Kingsguard cape.

Good day, sir. May I—

"You there! Where do you think you're going?"

Averella turned toward the voice. Two guards dragged a burly young man out of the inner gatehouse. She drifted closer. She did not believe she had ever seen this young man before, yet his familiar pockmarked face drew her near.

He struggled between the two guards. "I must get inside! You don't understand!"

The guards pushed, the man pushed, back and forward like a game of reverse tug-o-war. On one of the tugs when the guards had the man back in the outer bailey, two peasants—a man and a woman—slipped through the gate and scurried toward the keep without looking back.

A diversion?

She breathed out a laugh. A diversion, indeed! Listen to her. One would think she had been cavorting with soldiers all her life to have such assumptions quick to her mind. Still, she drifted after the peasants, curious why they snuck about. Peasants came and went from Castle Granton. Why not here?

Wherever here was.

Averella followed the peasants inside. The stone structure cut off the heat and light from the sun, bathing her in cool shadow. The peasants stood inside a small foyer. A stone corridor led off on the left and right. Two flights of stairs lay ahead, one going up, the other down.

The man started up the stairs.

The woman stepped to the right and whispered, "Noam! Not that way!" She waved the man to follow and ducked into the dark corridor on the right.

The peasant girl's brown dress was identical to Averella's. She drifted behind Noam's lanky form. Torches crackled every ten paces or so, lighting the corridor in a bronze glow. The peasant woman took the first left and strode through the dark halls as if this were her home. "No one will question us on the servants' stairwell."

"But someone will question us eventually," Noam said. "Gren, please stop. We need more of a plan."

Gren spun around, her chestnut hair twirling over her shoulders. "Fine. If anyone asks, Shelga sent us to mend a ripped canopy in Lady Marah's chamber."

Averella's memory surged at the mention of Lady Marah, mistress of Sitna Manor, wife to Lord Nathak.

Then this must be Sitna's keep. It was very cold and drafty compared to Granton Castle in Carmine.

Gren continued down the dark corridor and turned up a spiral staircase. Noam and Averella followed her to the top floor and exited on a well-lit passageway that stretched along the outer wall of the keep. Sunlight stabbed through dozens of arrow loops. Averella soared into a sunbeam and let the warmth soak into her.

Gren stopped where another corridor shot off on into the keep and peeked around the corner. "There are guards posted at the door," she whispered. "Listen."

" . . . guess he's a god now," a man's voice croaked, low and slow, like a bullfrog. "Traded his soul for a new arm."

"To who?" Another man's voice. High-pitched.

"To Nathak's sorcerer, I guess."

Averella drifted around the corner. Two New Kings-guardsmen stood before a door. One had bushy brown hair and a beard. The other was younger, though his face was creased as if he had not slept in weeks. He also was missing four front teeth, two on the top and two on the bottom.

"This sorcerer collects souls?" The bearded man's high-pitched voice sounded almost like a critical woman.

The toothless guard grinned, baring a black hole where his teeth should be. "Guess so. Guess that's how he gets stuff done. Binds people to him."

"You think that's something to smile about, do you?"

"Nah, just that Prince Gidon was—"

"*Esek.*"

"Oh, you know who I mean. He was a thorn to serve, wasn't he? Sent me to Myet twice for his own bad temper. Guess I can't help but smile thinking of him being tethered so. To a master of his own, you know?"

Averella drifted to the door and reached between the men for the latch. Her fingers passed through the wooden surface. She moved slowly, unsure, but curious to know who or what was being kept behind this door.

She turned her head so her face was the last thing to pass through the dark wood. She soon found herself in a spacious chamber. On the exterior wall, the sun shone through a narrow balcony. A canopied bed stood in the far corner. Linen draped over the furniture, suggesting the room was not being used. No one was here. Why guard an empty chamber?

On her second survey of the room, she caught sight of a limp hand dangling over the bedside. She drifted closer. A body came into view, sunk into the linen drape that covered the mattress. A woman in a plain brown dress. A peasant. The woman's face was twisted away, her thin black hair tangled in a pile that covered her face.

Averella did not know why, but a dark fear pressed in on her heart as she studied the woman. She skirted to the foot of the bed, trying to get a better view of the woman's face.

The chamber door burst open. Averella pressed against the wall and sank to her haunches, falling partway into the next room. Then she remembered that no one could see her, so she steadied herself and looked to the doorway.

Lord Nathak entered with Lord Levy, Lady Fallina Levy, and their son Reggio. Averella froze at the sight of Lord Nathak and his horrible mask, fear curling the ends of her nerves like ribbon. She built an imaginary wall around herself. What such an act did, she did not know, but she felt more secure after having done it.

Lady Fallina gripped her thick brocade skirts in both hands and ran to the bedside. "Really, my lord. Could you at least have chosen a room that had been aired? A fresh bed?"

"She can't feel anything, right, Father?" Reggio asked.

"I know nothing of this magic," Lord Levy said, puffing on an ivory pipe.

Lady Fallina brushed the hair off the unconscious woman's face.

Averella screamed, a soundless, heart-wrenching act for her ears only. For it was *her* face under all that hair. *Her* body lying limp on the bed like a discarded shawl. She leaned over the foot of the bed to get a closer look. Was she dead? Why was she dressed as a peasant?

"She is warm," Lady Fallina said. "She breathes still."

"Of course she does," Lord Nathak said. "She has been stormed, not stabbed."

Stormed. The invisible man in the garden had spoken of a storm. *Master Cham! I have found my body*, Averella said. *Please tell me how to return to it.*

But Master Cham did not answer.

"Regardless, Lord Nathak," Lady Fallina said. "This whole situation is horribly improper. I will not allow this lady to be without a chaperone. Think of her reputation." Lady Fallina moved Averella's arms, folding them over her stomach so that she truly looked like a corpse.

Reggio snorted. "Her reputation is soiled of her own instigation. Cavorting all over Er'Rets in the company of men. No one held her hostage, Mother. She chose her lot."

"Still." Lady Fallina smoothed Averella's hair. "I will have no one say that I contributed to her degeneracy."

Averella's jaw dropped. Never in her life had she been so brutally slandered. On what grounds did they accuse her of such poor conduct?

"None of this matters, my dear." Lord Levy set a hand on his wife's shoulder, bringing with him the strong smell of tobacco and vanilla. His pointed white beard reminded Averella of a goat. "Lord Nathak is moving the lady to Mahanaim in the morning."

Lady Fallina regarded her husband with wide eyes. "Moving her how?"

"She is being transported with my procession," Lord Nathak said. "My master can do with her as he likes."

"I will not have it! Her mother must be notified." Lady Fallina sat on the edge of the bed and glanced to her husband, who was sucking on his pipe. "Think of Jacqueline, Abidan. She and Lady Averella are the same age. Could you allow our daughter—"

"Jacqueline has not broken the law, my dear." Lord Levy blew out a stream of smoke. "Lady Averella is a criminal by her own volition."

"And she should be tried as such," Reggio added.

Averella gasped, hands trembling.

"*Really*," Lady Fallina said. "Just because she would not marry you, Lord Nathak, or your depraved son?"

"Fallina!" Lord Levy snapped. "You *will* respect Lord Nathak in his own house."

"Sitna Manor is *your* house now, my lord husband. You should remind Lord Nathak to respect you." She shot a haughty glare at Lord Nathak. "And your wife."

Lord Levy sighed. "Lord Nathak, would you allow my wife to sit with Lady Averella until you are ready to transport her?"

"I care not what your wife does. But Lady Averella will be taken to Mahanaim at first light tomorrow."

Lord Nathak left the room.

Lady Fallina stood and smoothed out her skirt. "He intends to send an ill noblewoman to Mahanaim with a bunch of soldiers? And no escort? Can nothing be done?"

"What does an unconscious woman need with an escort?" Reggio asked.

"Lord Nathak will make certain nothing vile happens to her, my dear, I assure you," Lord Levy said.

"You vouch for Lord Nathak's character, Abidan? Since when have you trusted him?"

"Mother, Lord Nathak is loyal to our cause. It's *Lady Averella's* character that's the issue here," Reggio said.

How Averella wished she could speak aloud and give Reggio Levy the scolding of his life.

"Reggio, please!" Lord Levy turned back to his wife. "Lord Nathak said his interest in the girl is strictly political. She's to marry his son."

Lady Fallina scoffed. "To think all this began because her mother is the Duchess of Carm."

"She is only Lady Nitsa now, for *I* am Duke of Carm. And Lady Nitsa could have avoided all this trouble by making the betrothal herself. Her stubborn ways have done her and her daughter no favors. Both women have brought their fortunes upon themselves. Dâthos has weighed their behavior of the scales of justice and made his judgment."

Lady Fallina peered at her husband. "I find it odd that Dâthos always agrees with *your* judgment, my lord."

"Because I know my god well."

His wife huffed. "So you agree with Dâthos's decision to send us to Sitna? That the Levy rule of Mahanaim is to end with you? I would think that Dâthos would condemn Lord Nathak for all his years of deceit. You did, at first."

Lord Levy's eyes smoldered. "I cannot see Dâthos's full plan, but I assure you my years of loyalty will not be overlooked. Would you have me rebel, as Lady Nitsa has? Would you have our daughters used against us as pawns?"

Lady Fallina whispered, "Of course not."

"Then do not question my judgment. I am loyal to Dâthos, as is the Hadad. I support his takeover, as should you."

Lady Fallina looked back to Averella's body.

"I would hate to think my own mother a traitor." Reggio stood by the door with his arms crossed, glaring at his mother as if she were a vandal.

"That will be enough from you, my boy." Lord Levy shooed Reggio out the door and pointed his pipe at Lady Fallina. "We shall see you at dinner, I hope?"

"As long as two women sit with Lady Averella in my place. Send me Tylia now, please."

"As you wish, my dear."

The door clumped shut behind Lord Levy and Reggio. Lady Fallina stepped back to the bed and sat down. She ran the back of her hand along Averella's cheek. "I am sorry, child. I can only keep you safe under my roof. Once you leave . . . May Dâthos find more good in you than evil."

• • •

Averella stayed with her body all afternoon, flitting about the room like a ghost. Two maids came when Lady Fallina went to dinner.

Lady Fallina returned shortly and sat in a chair beside the bed, dozing restlessly into the night.

Averella drifted about the room and went out onto the balcony to look at the moon, high over the glassy sea.

Sparrow? The stray man's voice boomed in her head again. *You've closed your mind. Are you back in your body?*

Averella paused, intrigued by his words. *How do you know I am out of my body? And why call me Sparrow?*

Sparrow, please. You have to lower your shields to talk to me. At least say something so I know you are well. I promise to leave you be after that, but I must know that you're not hurt.

I am here, Master Cham. And I feel no pain, though I am out of my physical body.

Averella's ears itched. She tried to scratch them, yet her fingers passed into her head, finding nothing solid to scratch.

Achan Cham.

What do you want, Master Cham? You said you would leave me be. Can you not hear me? Averella did not know what else she could possibly say. This man had heard her in the temple garden. What could have changed?

Master Cham spoke to her several more times through the rest of the night, but he never seemed to hear her responses. She did not understand anything. What had happened to her? What was storming? How could her mind be outside her body? Why did she have no memory of how she came to be this way? Why did the Levys slander her name as if she were a wanton woman?

Her ears itched. *Duchess Amal.*

Joy surged inside her. *Mother! Where are you?*

Duchess Amal.

Yes! I am in Sitna. Lord Nathak holds me captive. He plans to take me to Mahanaim tomorrow. Without an escort!

Duchess Amal.

Averella's joy fizzled. *Mother?*

Silence stretched on. Crickets chirruped outside. Lady Fallina's soft breath held a steady flow at Averella's bedside.

Merciful heart! Why could no one hear her? Averella started to cry, though no tears left her eyes.

• • •

"Be gentle!" Lady Fallina scolded.

"We won't drop her, m'lady," the toothless guard said as he and the bearded guard heaved the casket off the floor of the bedchamber.

Averella shuddered, knowing her body lay inside the sanded pine box. She must truly be dead. But where, then, was Arman? For this could not be Shamayim. All believers went to Shamayim when they died. It was written.

Not knowing what else to do, Averella drifted along with Lady Fallina and the men, staying with her body as they carried the casket down the spiral stairs and out of the keep to a wagon in the inner bailey. Two more guards helped lift the casket into the back.

"There are three more crates to be loaded," Lady Fallina said. "I will show you where they are."

The guards followed Lady Fallina back into the keep, leaving Averella's body alone with the driver sitting on his bench.

"What took you so long, boy?" the driver said. "We're set to leave soon."

Noam, the lanky peasant who had snuck into the keep yesterday, approached the wagon, leading two horses. But today he wore the orange tunic of a stray. "I had to wait until they were shod."

Averella watched the young man so closely that she didn't see Gren until the peasant woman was crouched by the wagon's wheel. A beefy man squatted down beside her. The same man who had caused the diversion so Noam and Gren could sneak inside the keep.

"Can you help me?" Noam asked the driver.

"You want me to do your job?"

"Just hold the reins of this one while I hook up the other. I'll be done faster and out of your way before Lord Nathak arrives. I'm sure you'd like Lord Nathak in good spirits for the long journey."

"All right." The driver climbed down, but before he could take the reins from Noam, both horses took off at a run toward the temple.

"Help me!" Noam cried, leading the driver in a chase that took them both away from the wagon.

The beefy man dropped two bulging linen sacks into the wagon then hoisted himself over the side. With a quick flick of his wrist, he pried up the casket's lid with a knife. He slid the lid back and lifted Averella's body out. Holding her close, he jumped off the wagon and carried her to a small cart. He dropped her inside, covered her with linen sacks, and pushed the cart toward the inner gatehouse.

It all happened so quickly, Averella could only stare.

Gren lifted one more heavy sack into the back of the wagon. She pulled herself up, loaded all three sacks into the casket, and slid the lid back into place.

"What's this Poril sees?" a man's voice said.

Averella turned to see an old man with a dusting of white hair standing on the other side of the wagon. He was as tall as the beefy man who had taken her body, maybe taller, though his hunched posture made it difficult to tell.

"Master Poril." Gren jumped down off the wagon.

"Poril heard yeh went away, Madam Hoff. But now Poril sees yer back and causing more mischief."

Gren threaded her arm with the old man's and led him away from the wagon. "Remember what you said to me the day Sitna heard the news. That you'd do anything to go back and make it right?"

Poril's eyes grew wide and glossy. "Poril would have never laid a hand on the boy had Poril known the truth, I'll tell yeh that. Poril's a kind soul, he is."

Gren patted his hand. "I know you are, Master Poril. But Lord Nathak is deceiving you again. For the woman in that casket is not dead. And Lord Nathak wants to hurt her."

"What does Poril care of the master's business? It's only 'cause Poril is the best cook in Er'Rets that the master be taking Poril to Armonguard. And Poril can't be left behind." The old man lowered his voice to a raspy whisper. "Poril needs to see the boy again, he does. How else can Poril set right all that's been done?"

"But that's just it, Master Poril. Achan loves this lady."

Averella straightened at this.

"Bah!" Poril waved a hand. "The boy loves yeh alone."

Gren shook her head. "Not anymore, Master Poril. He's betrothed to Lady Averella of Carmine now. Wears her sleeve on his arm, even as he marches into battle."

Icy fingers stroked the back of Averella's neck. That Master Cham would love her, wear her sleeve, and she not know him. How?

The old man's eyes misted. "Poril heard he killed a cham."

"Yes, he's very brave, Master Poril. But Lord Nathak means to force Lady Averella to marry Esek."

Surely not! She suspected Lord Nathak of vile things, but that he would kidnap her and force her to marry . . .

Poril sneered. "Poril never did like the master's son. Pompous brat. Criticized Poril's pastries and pies, he did."

"Please help us. Help Achan. Keep silent about what you've seen. Let us take Lady Averella back to Achan. I'll make sure he knows you played a part in her rescue."

Poril's thin lips stretched into a smile. "Yeh'll tell the boy Poril helped?"

"The moment I see him. I promise you."

He patted Gren's shoulder. "Yeh have Poril's silence, yeh do. Poril's a fair man, he is, and owes much to the boy."

"Thank you, Master Poril. You are indeed good and fair. I must go." Gren walked casually toward the gatehouse.

Poril returned to the cart and climbed up on the driver's bench. The driver was still assisting Noam with the horses.

Averella floated after Gren. She caught up with her in the outer bailey. Gren was now walking with the beefy man, who pushed the cart past a barn and around dozens of cottages with thatched roofs. He stopped before one such cottage and lifted Averella into his arms. Gren opened the front door, and they went inside.

Averella floated through the wall in time to see the man carry her body through a doorway in the back of the cottage. Averella shadowed Gren into a bedroom. The man stood beside a wide bed where Averella's body now lay.

Gren stopped in the doorway. "Is she . . . dead?"

"No. She breathes. We should fetch a doctor but—"

"Harnu, we can't!"

The pockmarked man turned his brown eyes to Gren. "But that would be unwise, I was going to say. We shouldn't even keep her in the stronghold. Once they learn she's gone, it won't take 'em long to search every cottage in the manor."

Gren swallowed. "What can we do?"

"Get her out of Sitna before they come looking."

"Should we put her back in the cart?"

"Let's wait for Noam. If Lord Nathak and his men depart as scheduled, we'll be able to leave without anyone suspecting us."

Averella waited in the cottage with Gren and Harnu for what seemed like hours before Noam arrived.

"They've left," Noam said, a wide grin plastered across his narrow face. "We've done it!"

Gren squealed and embraced Noam.

Harnu stared at Gren and Noam like a jealous lover. "My father has a cottage in the Sideros Forest. We could keep her there 'til she wakes. Then we can journey south."

Gren stared at Harnu. "You're going to help me?"

He nodded. "You can't stay here. Word will spread that you've returned. And when they discover Lady Averella's body is gone, they'll question you."

Gren squealed. "Thank you, Harnu. Thank you both."

"Why do you and Lady Averella need to go to Armonguard?" Noam asked.

Averella waited for Gren's answer, for she could not imagine why she would travel alone with a peasant woman, especially such a great distance.

"Our reasons are our own," Gren said. "Lady Averella's things are out here." She ducked out the door, but her voice carried into the bedroom. "How will we get the horses?"

"I'll take them out to exercise them," Noam said, following her. "No one will question that."

"Until Oster realizes they're gone," Gren said.

"I'll tell him the guests departed," Noam said.

Averella drifted back into the main room.

Gren wrung her hands together. "So much is left to chance."

"It's left to Cetheria," Harnu said, stepping out of the bedroom. "She's noble and just. She'll protect us."

Averella wrinkled her nose. Cetheria?

A bird cawed, drawing Averella's attention away from the discussion. The eerily familiar sound plucked a string in her heart. She stuck her head through the wall of the cottage and glanced around for the source.

A black bird perched on the edge of the cart that Harnu had carried Averella's body in. It cawed again, revealing rows of sharp teeth in a bat-like head. A gowzal. Averella could only stare, knowing she had never seen such a creature outside of paintings and tapestries.

Yet certain she had.

13

Achan squeezed his hands into fists, overwhelmed with frustration. All day he had tried and failed to contact Sparrow. He looked to Sir Eagan, who sat across from him, the only other occupant of the wagon beside Matthias, who lay sleeping in a pile of blankets at Achan's feet.

"How can Sparrow close her mind?" Achan asked, unable to mask the tinge of desperation in his voice. "If she lost her memory, how can she bloodvoice at all?"

Sir Eagan's pensive eyes met Achan's. "She would not lose her abilities and has likely closed her mind instinctively. I suspect something frightened her."

The whole situation frightened Achan. But he needed to be strong to bring Sparrow back from the Veil.

Then back into his life.

The wagon traveled over a bump on the road, and he put a hand down to steady himself. This wagon was as fine as any room in Granton Castle. The interior was walled in colorful tapestries. Two couches upholstered in red silk filled the front and back walls. A narrow table stretched down the long wall facing the door, which was covered in a thick linen drape tied shut to keep out dust from the road.

The impending battles nagged at the back of Achan's mind, but he pushed those thoughts aside to focus on Sparrow. "Why can't I see through her eyes?"

"You cannot see through her eyes, because her eyes are in her body." Sir Eagan's calm bled into Achan.

Achan wanted to tell Sir Eagan what to do with his calming tricks, but gave himself over to it. He took a deep breath and released it slowly, clinging to Sir Eagan's peace. When he spoke again, his voice sounded normal. "But isn't her mind in her body?"

"Her brain is in her body, but what you refer to as her mind is really her essence, her spirit and soul. That is in the Veil. And the Veil is where Vrell truly is. She has been pushed from her body before her time."

This was almost too much to fathom. That sweet Sparrow, who had so wanted to end her adventuring, had been forced into another. "If Lord Levy cannot bloodvoice, who could have stormed her?"

"I cannot say."

"How much farther to Sitna?"

Sir Eagan studied his hands. "Tomorrow evening."

"I don't suppose Sir Caleb would approve of my being included in the rescue party."

"I think not, Your Highness. Nor would I."

Achan gritted his teeth. "How did you survive in Ice Island after losing the duchess? I tried to forget Sparrow, but she shadows me like an old wound. And now this."

"You may try and convince yourself of all the reasons you should forget her, but forgetting is not the answer. You care for her. She matters to you. And it is painful to lose her. But pain, in time, brings strength and wisdom. Arman makes good of all things, if you give Him leave. Do not blame Him for what's happened to Vrell."

"I don't blame Arman. I blame myself. If I hadn't pushed so hard she—"

"*If,* Your Highness, is a word that will steal your soul. Do not waste your thoughts on ifs. What is done is done. Look to the future."

Achan met Sir Eagan's pale blue eyes. "What future?"

A soft smile spread across Sir Eagan's face. "Despair does not become you, Your Highness. Do not lose sight of the goal."

Achan looked at his lap. "Armonguard."

"Precisely. Focus on Armonguard. Leave the rest to Arman."

From the corner of Achan's eye, he could see the dark maroon fabric tied to his arm. Another shadow that followed him everywhere. "But Câan told me if I submit to Him, He would give me the desires of my heart." He glanced at Sir Eagan. "I thought He meant Sparrow."

Sir Eagan chuckled. "Câan is not a wishing stone, Your Highness. What you think you desire now is not necessarily the most important thing. Câan has seen places in your heart that no man or woman will ever see. He knows your hopes for next year and thirty years from now. And He does not operate on man's schedule. He will bless you in His time. But not necessarily in the ways you think you want now."

No sense fretting, then. But for Achan, being calm never came naturally.

That night they made camp in a field. The soldiers in Achan's division circled the wagons, creating a sentry wall around the camp with hundreds of tents erected inside.

Achan sat on the bed inside his tent, which was round and held up in the center by a single pole with dozens of spokes jutting out like a wheel. Solid brown on the outside so it would not appear special, the inside walls were covered in thick tapestries depicting vineyards and forests. It reminded him of Esek's tent. The tent where Achan had found Sparrow unconscious and bruised, lying on Esek's bed, dressed in that ridiculous gown. Achan's tent had no hole in the center roof for the smoke of a fire, but it was big enough to hold a large bed on one side of the pole and a round table, three chairs, and all his new trunks on the other.

Esek's tent. Just what had Esek been planning for Sparrow if Achan had not gotten there in time?

A darker idea crossed his mind. What if Esek had already done something vile to Sparrow before Achan had arrived? Esek had struck her, but Achan had not thought to inquire as to anything else. He hung his head. No wonder Sparrow had left. What woman would want a man who forgot to ask of her well-being after she had been kidnapped by a maniac? What woman would want a man who thought of taking her as a mistress along with his wife?

He was an insensitive fool.

A fool who would marry Lady Averella. Achan hoped to find her as agreeable as her mother, for that would be good fortune indeed.

Perhaps Sir Eagan was right about the desires of his heart. Perhaps in time Lady Averella would become just that.

Achan walked to the entrance of his tent and lifted the flap. Shung and Kurtz stood under a square valance that covered the entrance. They turned toward him.

"I feel like a bird in a cage," Achan said.

"Come out then, Pacey," Kurtz said, "so long as you don't mind two extra shadows trailing after you, eh?"

Achan mumbled, "I suspect I'll have extra shadows trailing me for the rest of my life."

"Is that so bad?" Kurtz threw an arm around Achan's shoulders. "Some of the men are reveling, they are. Shall we join them?"

The weight of Kurtz's arm on Achan's shoulder shocked his cham wounds. "I don't feel like reveling. There is much on my mind."

"And reveling will help you forget it for a few hours. What could be better, eh? Come on."

Kurtz led Achan around a large double pole pavilion, past a series of triangular tents, around a round tent with a dome-like roof, and past three tents that looked like tiny cabins. All were dark, solid colors—maroon, navy, emerald, brown—not striped or bright like the tents Achan had seen at the tournament in Sitna. Armonguard flags flapped in the wind atop each tent they passed. The image reminded Achan of his new shield. His inheritance. His future.

What would it bring? If they succeeded, if he lived, what kind of legacy might he leave? Could he truly be responsible, steadfast, reverent, and brave at all times? Could anyone? He stumbled over a guy line anchoring a green tent.

Kurtz gripped his arm to steady him. "Easy, there, Pacey."

The raised voices of dozens of men, a lute, and laughter drifted on the cool night breeze. As did the smell of something meaty. They skirted the edge of a bronze tent and entered a clearing.

A tide of negative emotions crashed into Achan. Something he would have to get used to, he supposed. Men sat on the ground in circles, stood in clumps, a few danced by a bonfire. One sat on a barrel, playing the lute. Several faces turned toward him, though most the men chattered on. The scene took him back to the night Esek had demanded he fetch a jug of water and Silvo Hamartano had attacked him.

A length of glossy black hair drew his gaze to the bonfire where the men were dancing. He squinted, looking closer. "There are women here?"

"Aye, from Berland. They train women soldiers there. Berland women are more brawn than I like, eh, Pacey? But if you want to meet them—"

"Lady Gali has come then?" Achan asked Shung.

Shung nodded. "Aye. She travels with Sir Koyukuk's army."

"And how did Lady Gali find *Sir Shung Noatak* when you saw her?"

Shung's grin filled his face. "She found honor in Shung's new title."

Achan slapped Shung's back. "As well she should." But would her father find enough honor to give up his youngest daughter?

"You hungry, Pacey?" Kurtz asked. "I can get you some stew, I can. Sir Gavin won't allow us anything but watered-down wine whilst we're on the verge of battle." Kurtz leaned close. "Though I've a bit of my own I could share if you need a nip, eh?"

Achan's gaze locked with Toros Ianjo. The priest sat with a soldier on the back of one of the wagons that edged the perimeter. Achan started to cross toward Toros, but a soldier bowed before him and held out a steaming drumstick.

"Like something to eat, Your Highness? We've also got stew, if you'd rather."

"Thank you, no. I've eaten already."

Three more soldiers bowed, which sent a ripple of movement through the crowd. Positive emotions swelled over the negative ones. Men hailed him, some cheered, and all seemed to stare. He should probably say something.

He swallowed and spoke as loudly as he could. "That you've all joined me on this journey honors me more than I can express. I pray each night would be spent like this, reveling in each other's good company. But at some point we will take up swords against this enemy that has controlled Er'Rets for far too long. When that day comes, may Arman shield each of you so that we may all join together in a victory celebration in Armonguard."

The men cheered. Achan tried to move in Toros's direction again, but soldiers closed in to greet him. Shung and Kurtz kept the men back to a certain degree. For the first time in his life, Achan understood why powerful men summoned people to come to them. They would never get anything done if they always went out in public like this.

Achan shook many hands, remembered no names, and wondered how many of these men would die before their objective was completed.

A man with the lute played a song called, "The Pawn Our King," which told the tale of Achan growing up in Sitna under the thumb of Lord Nathak. That anyone had written a song about him seemed more unreal than his being prince.

Then Lady Gali stepped before him and curtsied awkwardly. The woman who held Shung's heart stood a few inches taller than Achan. Her features were sharp as if Sir Gavin had chiseled her out of wood. She wore a sleeveless tunic of short fur and black trousers. As always, bone bangles circled her bare arms and neck, which made her seem even taller somehow.

Achan bowed to her. "Lady Gali. You honor me with your presence and the pledge of your sword."

"And you honor all of Berland by knighting one of our own." Her dark gaze flicked to Shung, and she pushed one of her dark braids over her shoulder.

Achan held out his hand before them. "Would you join us? I'm sure Shung had left many details out as to how he helped me defeat the mighty cham."

So Achan boasted of Shung's prowess as he worked his way across the clearing. Shung seemed a bit embarrassed at Achan's version of the event, but from the wide-eyed glances Lady Gali was sending Shung's way, the man would thank Achan later.

By the time Achan reached the wagon, Toros was on his feet. "How can I serve you this evening, Highness?"

"Are you busy?"

"Just visiting with old friends. This is Rosef. He and I fought together at the Battle of Gadow Wall."

Achan searched his memory. "I don't recall that battle."

"Happened over a decade before you were born, Highness," Toros said. "Another Zona Fight."

"A Zona Fight?"

"Zona was the woman King Justos took from Sar Orind during the Great War. The reason for the continued strife between Magos and Cherem. You should learn the history, as it will soon become a part of your daily life."

"I'm sure Sir Caleb would love to teach it to me."

"Well, the Battle of Gadow Wall started when one soldier bet another he could rekindle the war between Cherem and Magos. He started a rumor in Cherem. Claimed one of Zona's descendants was King Axel's mistress and that a child had been born. Cherem saw such a child as an heir to the throne and a chance to take control of Er'Rets."

"That's pretty bold, isn't it?" Achan asked. "To start a war based on rumor?"

"It was. Though several servants concurred that a babe had been in the palace."

"Bah," Kurtz said. "Could've been any servant's babe."

Achan doubted his father had taken any mistress, for Sir Gavin had spoken of how much his father had loved his mother. "Could it have been me?"

"No, Highness. This was the year 551."

According to Sir Caleb, Achan's true day of birth happened on spring second of the year 569. So this mythical child would have been eighteen years Achan's senior.

Toros continued. "Cherem attacked Gadowl Wall with plans to take Armonguard. But they never made it past the wall. King Axel could command an army better than anyone I've ever known. It was over in a few hours. Anyway, did you need my service, Highness?"

The question caught Achan off guard until he remembered that he had asked Toros if he were busy. "Yes, I had some questions. Might you be willing to come to my tent sometime to discuss them?"

"I shall come with you now."

"Thank you," Achan said.

It seemed to take hours to weave their way back through the men. Inside Achan's tent, he bid Toros sit across from him at the round table.

"What's on your mind, Highness?" Toros asked.

"The Veil."

Toros watched him closely. "What about it?"

"If Arman created everything, and everything He created is good, how is it that the Veil exists and that a person can get lost in it?"

"You imply that the Veil is not good."

"It doesn't seem to be."

"Why not?" His tone insinuated that Achan was wrong.

"I don't know. It's scary there. People die."

"It's scary in Er'Rets too. People die here." Toros grinned. "The Veil was not designed for man to roam. It is a road that takes a man to his eternal home."

"But it isn't a road at all. It's Er'Rets but not Er'Rets."

Toros raised an eyebrow. "You've entered the Veil?"

Achan nodded. "And I felt the pull—of Shamayim, I hope. Why would Arman allow someone to be lost before their time?"

"I do not believe He would."

"What do you mean?"

"Many have entered the Veil as a result of man's will. A bloodvoicer's force. But I don't believe Arman would accept them home if it was not His will at that time."

"So you think Arman wants those people to die?"

Toros chuckled. "I will not speak for Arman. But He is good. He is in control. And His plans are always best, even though it may not seem that way to you or me."

"If someone kills a man, you believe it's Arman's will?"

"Again, Your Highness, I'll not speak for Arman. But if Arman had purpose for the man to live, the man would live." Toros leaned forward, propping his elbows on the table. "Most people focus too much on things that are of no real concern. The real question is, do you trust Arman or not? If you trust Him, none of this matters."

"But my friend is lost in the Veil. I want to know—"

"Do you trust Arman, Highness?"

"Yes, but—"

"No buts. Either you trust Him or you don't."

Achan shifted on his chair. "Maybe I don't, then."

"I agree. You don't trust Him fully or you'd know you did. Arman wants your trust, Highness. When He asks something of you, He's seeking your heart. Your attitude, your disposition, your fears, your strengths, your obedience, your allegiance. All of you.

When you trust Arman with your life, you run the risk of exposing your real fears. You run the risk of Arman having total authority and say in your life. Most men don't like that. They like to be in control."

"What's so bad about being in control?"

"Nothing, if you want to make a mess of your life. You think you can run your life better without Arman?"

"I know I can't. But how can I learn to trust Him more?"

Toros smiled. "Learning is not the easiest way, Highness. It's easiest simply to do it, even when it's hard. Simply trust Him."

"How is doing easier than learning?"

"Have you heard the saying, 'Don't pray for patience or Arman will bestow trials so you may practice patience'? I believe the same is true of trust. Don't pray for trust if you're not ready to face the trials that'll force you to trust Him, to lean on Arman for strength. A life of continual trials isn't pleasant. But it's one way to learn to trust Arman."

Odd way of looking at it.

"Arman held nothing back from you when He gave you His Son. Hold nothing back from Him. Trust Him. His will is always perfect, Highness, even when it doesn't make sense."

When Achan lay in bed that night, he asked Shung to sit with his body so he could enter the Veil. He went back to the room where Sparrow lay and was surprised to find a noblewoman asleep in a chair beside the bed.

Sparrow? Achan focused on Sparrow's face, wishing he could nudge her shoulder. *You've closed your mind. Are you back in your body?*

A long moment passed with no answer. Achan could sense Sparrow's shields around her mind, but he had no way of breaking through without being able to locate them.

Sparrow, please. You have to lower your shields to talk to me. At least say something so I know you are well. I promise to leave you be after that, but I must know that you're not hurt.

At least she looked more comfortable now. Someone had repositioned her arms and combed back her hair. The noblewoman, perhaps?

Achan sent a knock the formal way, in case Sparrow expected him to use his manners. *Achan Cham.*

Still no response. He hovered, calling to Sparrow on and off until he felt himself growing weak with fatigue. He returned to his body. He would do Sparrow no good if he were lost himself, and he did not want to discover what happened if a man fell asleep while his mind was in the Veil.

The next morning Achan woke to find Matthias watching him. The boy had put his bedroll on the floor beside Achan's bed. They had fallen into a morning ritual, and being on the road would apparently not deter Matthias from it. Each day Achan woke to find the boy waiting. Matthias chose one of Achan's scars, and Achan would tell the tale. Then they would wake Shung in the most amusing way possible.

Achan spotted Shung's bedroll across the linen drape of the door, but remembered Sparrow was lost in the Veil. "Not today, Matthias. I must search for Sparrow."

The boy's expression sagged.

And Achan could not bear to see Matthias frown. "All right. Quickly, though."

Matthias's dark eyes roamed Achan's chest, then flitted to his face. He pointed a black finger at Achan's cheek.

"Esek cut me." Achan turned his head to show Matthias the cut on his other cheek. "Both sides. With Ôwr, my father's sword. But I have it back now. Ôwr's blade will never harm me again. Now, run fetch us some breakfast and tell Cole I will not be riding again today."

Matthias had to step over Shung to leave the tent.

Some shield when a small boy could pass unharmed. "Shung, watch for me while I look for Sparrow?"

The man grunted and rolled over, pulling a hairy arm over his head.

Achan threw his pillow at the man. "Wake up, Shung! Sparrow is lost, and I need you!"

Shung opened his eyes and pushed up onto one elbow. "The little fox would not like your manners."

"We'll never know if we don't find her."

Shung sat up and yawned. "Aye, Shung is ready."

But when Achan appeared in the room in Sitna manor, Sparrow's body was gone.

Sparrow? Where are you? He reached out and found her shields stronger than ever. He tried to focus on them, to no avail. He floated out of the chamber in Sitna and back to the dungeons, checking each cell. *Sparrow, please. I must know if you're safe. We're all very worried. You've been stormed. Please answer me.*

No sign of Sparrow in the dungeons.

Achan pulled back from the Veil and sat up. *Sir Caleb!*

Sir Caleb burst through the drape on Achan's tent and stumbled over the edge of Shung's bedroll. "What? What's happened?"

"Sparrow's body is gone."

"Oh." Sir Caleb relaxed. "Can you sense her?"

"Aye, but her mind is still shielded, and she won't answer. I should have stayed in her room all night. Sir Eagan and I could have taken turns guarding her."

"Perhaps she came back into her body and escaped."

Achan contemplated this. "Then why won't she answer? Could she still be angry enough to ignore my questioning her well-being?" Why wouldn't she believe him about the mistress thing? That it had only been a stray thought.

"Hard to guess what makes a woman angry. But they never forget the things you say."

Wonderful. "What about the things I think?"

Sir Caleb put his hands on his hips. "What do you mean? I thought she has not been answering. You've not been carrying on conversations with Vrell in your mind, have you? That would be most inappropriate now that you are betrothed to Lady Averella."

Achan gritted his teeth. "Sir Caleb, I am merely trying to help Sparrow back from the Veil. If her body is gone and she is not answering, how can I know for sure she is safe?"

"I know not. Sir Eagan would be of better assistance."

"Fine. Fetch him for me. Please?"

Sir Caleb bowed and exited the tent.

Achan glanced at Shung. "She would answer if she could, don't you think?"

"Without a doubt. The little fox does not joke of serious matters. Should Shung message her?"

"No. Duchess Amal said too many voices might frighten her if she had lost her memory. And I think she has, for she didn't seem to know me." He lay back down. "I'm going to look around Sitna Manor again. See if I can learn anything."

So Achan searched all of Sitna Manor. Things were different. Lord Levy's family had moved into the rooms in the keep where Lord Nathak and Esek had once dwelled. Poril was no longer the cook. A portly woman had taken over the kitchens. Stranger still, Noam was not in the stables.

What in all Er'Rets was happening?

When Achan returned to his body, his tent and most of the camp had been packed around him. The morning air chilled his arms. Sir Eagan and Sir Caleb were standing at his bedside, Cole just behind them with Matthias. Soldiers bustled about, mounting their horses and filling carts with rolled-up tents. Many heads turned toward the half-dressed Prince, who was still in bed.

Achan met Sir Eagan's cool gaze. "I can't find her."

Sir Caleb and Sir Eagan helped Achan to his feet. Two soldiers immediately began collapsing his bed.

Matthias approached, holding a set of clothes. "Time to dress, sir."

"We can talk more in the wagon," Sir Eagan said.

Achan's thoughts scattered. "But the rescue party is still going out, right? We can't just leave her."

"We can't send a rescue party to Sitna without knowing where her body is," Sir Caleb said. "It would be futile, a waste of manpower."

Achan glared at Sir Caleb. "Would you leave Esper?"

Sir Caleb's eyes lit like a fire, but his expression remained neutral.

Achan tried another tactic by appealing to Sir Eagan. "I sense her shields. She's not dead."

Sir Caleb took the pile of clothing Matthias had been holding and handed it to Achan. "Continue the search from your wagon, Your Highness, but we must get moving."

Shung, Kurtz, Cole, and the knights escorted Achan through the soldiers to his wagon where Achan dressed himself. Then he flopped down on one of the sofas. *Shung?*

The wagon lurched as Shung climbed inside. Sir Eagan lifted Matthias through the doorway then entered himself.

"I'm going to keep looking," Achan said.

Shung nodded. "Shung will keep watch."

All day Achan searched Sitna Manor from the Veil, but he found no sign of Vrell Sparrow. He did discover that Poril had gone south with Lord Nathak. So he looked through Poril's eyes.

The old cook sat beside the driver on a cart that followed a few dozen horses and a litter at night. A lantern swung from a post on the wagon seat, dangling behind the driver's head. Achan counted four more lanterns ahead that seemed to float through the dark night.

No, it couldn't be night already, could it?

Achan left Poril's mind and searched each face in the party. He found Lord Nathak and his wife in the litter, and a wooden box in the back of Poril's wagon.

A coffin.

After a long moment to raise his courage, Achan peeked inside, but the wooden lid blocked all light and he could not see anything within. If Sparrow had died, though, he would not be able to sense her. And he could.

Sparrow, please speak to me. Tell me you are not in that coffin. Please?

After a long wait with no answer, he came back to himself. Shung met his gaze briefly. Matthias sat on the floor with his back against Shung's legs, dozing. Sir Eagan sat at the table reading a scroll. Achan remained silent, knowing they'd pass by Sitna at some point this day—maybe already had. His old home, the place where Sparrow had to be.

It made him nauseated.

He glanced back to Shung and froze. For where Matthias had been sitting, there was Sparrow, her silky black hair spilling into Shung's lap. The man combed it with his thick, burned fingers, a half smile on his hairy face.

Achan's breath quickened. "What are you doing?"

Shung raised a bushy eyebrow and grunted a question.

Achan stood up so fast his head scraped the ceiling. Shung had no right to touch Sparrow. Achan bent down and lifted her into his arms. She was lighter than he remembered. He tucked her head under his chin and breathed in the smell of roses. "Sir Eagan, we must get Sparrow something to eat. I fear she's half starved."

The wagon rolled through a rut and Achan lurched. Rather than try to keep his balance, he fell back onto his sofa, cradling Sparrow in his arms.

The movement woke her. She locked her cat-like eyes onto his. "Are you all right, sir?"

Achan frowned. For the voice did not belong to Sparrow but to Matthias. He was holding the boy on his lap. He swallowed, feeling like a fool, and set the boy beside him on the sofa. He looked at Shung, and then to Sir Eagan.

Sir Eagan regarded him warily. "Are you well, Your Highness?"

Achan opened his mouth to answer, then lunged for the drape and pulled it open.

A starless black sky hung overhead as if it were the middle of the night, though Achan knew it could only be late morning. Pig snout. That explained the waking dream.

They had entered Darkness again.

14

Noam steered the cart off the dirt road, through a field of waist-high grass along two trampled wheel tracks.

A road seldom traveled. Averella was thankful to be gone from Sitna Manor. She still did not understand what had happened to her, but these people meant her no harm.

She floated alongside Kopay, one hand resting on his back, though she could not feel him and knew her hand would pass through him if she lowered it. Noam had hitched Kopay and another horse to this cart and filled it with supplies. It also carried Averella's body, covered in blankets as if she were merely asleep. Gren sat in the cart beside her body. Harnu sat up on the driver's seat with Noam.

Since dawn they had traveled west, toward the dark horizon. Averella hoped they would not meet a storm.

Noam had apparently fixed his gaze on the same thing, for he asked, "Is it my wandering mind or does Darkness look nearer than before?"

Averella stopped, and the cart rattled away from her. Surely they were not going into Darkness? Averella had never been there and had no intention of changing that fact.

"How could Darkness be closer?" Gren asked. "It's been in the same place all my life."

"It just looks closer, that's all," Noam said.

Their voices had grown faint, so Averella drifted after the cart until she caught up.

"How close to the Evenwall is this cabin, anyway?" Noam asked.

"Never wanted to know." Harnu scooted to the edge of the bench and squinted ahead. "Any moment a stream will enter the south side of the Sideros. We'll cross just past the fork and follow the stream into the forest. It's not far then."

It happened just as Harnu had predicted. The fork came, then a rocky ford. Averella floated right over the gurgling water. After crossing the river, they followed the creek into a thick forest. A bird squawked. Not a pleasant chirp or birdsong, but a caw, like a bird of prey circling a carcass.

Averella looked up. A black bird stared down from a wiry poplar branch, its dark eyes fixed on her. How could a gowzal see her when nothing else could?

When she looked back, two more birds had joined the first. One cawed again. Averella floated to the other side of the cart, keeping it between her and the eerie birds.

Sparrow? Where are you? a man said.

Averella's ears itched suddenly, as if mosquitoes were biting her. She tried to run her hands over her head, but they only passed through. Her skull suddenly squeezed, as if someone were pressing against both sides with their hands. *Sparrow, please. I must know if you're safe. We're all very worried. You've been stormed. Please answer me.*

Master Cham again. *I am here, Master Cham. Though I doubt you can hear me.*

Sure enough, he did not reply. Averella fought back tears. If only she could understand what it meant to have been stormed. She had some knowledge of herbs and healing, but she had never heard of such an ailment.

The sun vanished behind a cloud, and a chill clapped onto her arms. The forest was so thick here, it seemed like dusk. A branch snapped on her right. Or perhaps it had been a pinecone or acorn falling from a tree.

Thick fog grew around her ankles. Beads of perspiration hung from Master Poe's chin. Kopay sniffed, ears pointed high, eyes peeled wide. Something concerned him. There were no snakes in this forest. Perhaps a cham bear or wolf? Or perhaps he didn't like the gowzal either. Averella drew closer to the cart and scanned the forest.

Noam snapped the reins. "Come on, boys. Not far now."

The horses trudged on, though their hooves danced as if eager to turn and run.

"What's wrong with them?" Gren asked.

Noam struggled with the reins. "Something's spooked them."

Harnu reached back into the cart and lifted a sword. "This won't do much against a cham, so we'd better pray to Cetheria it's something smaller."

Then, as if Arman had closed a lid on the land, everything went black.

Gren screamed. The horses whinnied. Averella groped for Kopay, useless when she could not feel or see anything.

"The gods have cursed us!" Harnu cried. "We should've left Lady Averella with Lord Nathak."

"Don't be a fool!" Noam said. "It's only Darkness. I told you it looked closer."

"How do you know it's Darkness?" Harnu asked.

"Think, man. What else would it be?"

Silence stretched on until a bird screeched. Something in the trees above clicked like two sticks of wood striking one another.

"Grenny, there should be a lantern back there," Noam said. "Can you find it?"

The wagon creaked. Metal clanked against wood. "I've got it. Just a moment."

A firesteel sparked. Once. Twice. Three times. On the fourth try, the lantern glowed. The cart swelled into Averella's view, right where it had been. She still hovered beside Kopay, though her hand had passed into his middle. She pulled it back and folded her arms.

"What should we do?" Gren asked.

"We can't go back," Noam said. "Not with Lady Averella in the cart."

"We could take her to Carmine," Harnu said.

"No!" Gren's urgent tone suggested some secret knowledge. "She does not want to go back there. She wants to follow Achan."

Averella frowned. It seemed very unlike her to follow a man anywhere. Especially a man she did not know. Although hadn't Gren told the old man that Averella was betrothed to this Master Cham? None of this made any sense.

"The cabin is close," Harnu said. "I say we stick to our plan."

"You mean stay in Darkness?" Gren said. "Harnu, do you know what people say about this place?"

"I've met people who lived here," Noam said. "They train themselves to stay calm. Not let it get to them."

"It's already getting to me," Gren said.

"Well, I can't think of anything else," Harnu said. "At least let's go to the cabin to talk about it. This forest is unnerving."

"Agreed." Noam cracked the reins and the horses lurched forward.

The horses moved faster than Averella would have liked. Perhaps they could see better than she could. The lantern cast so little light. But the idea of losing sight of it kept her moving.

"There!" Harnu shouted.

A dark structure built of logs loomed into sight. It was bigger than the cottages in Sitna Manor. Lantern light glinted off the iron hinges on the shuttered windows on either side of the front door.

Noam stopped the cart in front of the cabin and climbed down. "I'll take care of the horses if you and Gren will unload the cart."

Harnu jumped down. "There's a shed 'round to the left. You can put the horses there."

Noam unhooked Kopay first and led him away. Averella loathed to see Kopay go, but she did not want to leave the lantern. Harnu hung it on a post outside the door. He and Gren began to carry things into the cabin. Averella wanted to go in but stayed with the wagon until Harnu carried her body inside.

The musty smell grabbed her as she followed Harnu through the door. Inside, Gren had lit another lantern, which hung on a hook over a square table in the middle of a timber room. Gren stood there, taking things out of a crate and piling them on the table.

Harnu carried Averella's body to a small room. He settled her on a pallet and left. Averella could see nothing in the darkness except the end of a sideboard lit dimly by the light from the lantern coming through the door. The air felt damp, as if Darkness carried moisture. She stood with her body for a long while, then explored the small cottage and wandered out to where Noam had stabled Kopay. When she returned, Harnu and Gren were engaged in a heated discussion.

Harnu stood halfway between the entrance and the table. "It would solve everything. Why can't you see that?"

"Because I don't think of you like that," Gren said, standing at the table, her voice thick with tears. "I can't. The things you did."

Averella drifted inside the cottage.

"You forgave me." Harnu's voice held a tinge of exasperation. "Said it didn't matter."

Gren twirled a bundle of linen in her hands. "It doesn't matter because there's no future for us."

"But you came back."

"Only for help. I'm not going to live in Sitna."

"You plan to stay in Armonguard for good?"

"Perhaps. It depends."

"On what?"

Gren set down the bundle and met Harnu's gaze. "On who."

"Achan? You think he still wants you?"

Gren clicked her tongue. "Achan loves Lady Averella, Harnu. He and I will only ever be good friends."

"You worry for Lady Averella, then," Harnu said. "Gren, I'm sure she'll wake soon and then—"

"His name is Bran Rennan." Gren lifted her chin. "He's a squire, due to be knighted any day. I think he means to marry me. After the war, of course."

Averella gasped and drifted toward the table, examining Gren anew. Bran Rennan marry Gren? Merciful heart! Of all the ridiculous notions. For Master Rennan was secretly engaged to Averella. Wasn't he?

Harnu's eyes swelled. "A knight? Marry *you?*"

"And why not?"

"Because he is betrothed to me," Averella said, though no one heard her.

"I—" Harnu closed his mouth. A smart move, for Averella was certain nothing he could say would please Gren. He sighed. "I'm going to go catch us some dinner." The walls trembled with his footsteps as he crossed the room and stepped outdoors. He slammed the door behind him, one last bang followed by a blanket of silence.

Gren fell into the chair and buried her face in her arms.

Averella watched Gren a moment, but it only made her angry, so she returned to her body, staring into the surrounding darkness, pondering what Gren meant about Bran. A long time passed until another yell pulled her back to the moment. Averella moved to the doorway of her room.

"I thought we might want to eat something warm and fresh." Harnu again stood in the middle of the room. His trousers were wet from the thighs down. He held a fat trout under the gills with his fingers.

Gren stood at the front of the table, glaring. "That smell!" She clamped a hand over her mouth. Her shoulders heaved.

Noam stepped into the cottage carrying the lantern that had hung outside. "What's the matter?"

"Gren?" Harnu inched closer, staring as if he thought she might be dying. "Are you well?"

She ran past him, bumping his arm so that he twisted around to watch her run out the door. Sounds of retching reached back inside the house.

"Think she's ill?" Harnu asked Noam.

"She's with child," Noam said. "Weird things happen, or so I've been told."

With child? Averella's thoughts jumbled together.

Harnu took the lantern from Noam and carried the fish toward the door, then started back the other way. "I'll take this out the back."

"Smart plan." Noam walked to the cluttered table. "You truly care for her?"

Harnu paused before a door at the opposite end of the room. "For as long as I can remember."

Noam grunted. "Probably shouldn't have beat her friends on a regular basis, then. Achan especially."

"Think I don't know I was a scoundrel? A fool to follow Riga like a dog? I've begged her forgiveness a dozen times over. She says it doesn't matter. What else can I do?"

"Nothing, if she won't have you."

"There must be something."

Noam sat at the table and stretched out his legs. "You've kept her house. Now you're going to feed her. You've helped her with her friend's body. Be patient. Maybe she'll come around."

"But what of this knight she speaks of? Has she lost her head? Could a knight have pledged to marry a widowed peasant? One already with child? It's madness."

Averella had to agree. Unless the child were Bran's. The thought made her knees weak. Bran would never . . .

"Nothing would surprise me these days," Noam said.

But Harnu shook his head. "Despite what happened with Achan, Gren's no lost princess. I don't believe a knight would woo her with pure motives."

"Why not? If you were a knight, you would."

"That is not the— Enough of this!" Harnu wrenched open the back door and took his fish out into the Darkness.

Averella's head spun. It was simply impossible. Bran would never take advantage of a woman. He had the purest heart of any man she had ever known.

Gren inched back in the open front entrance, her posture sheepish.

"He took the fish out back," Noam said. "Make an effort to eat it. There's nothing else."

"But it smells horrible!"

"Gren, can *you* hunt for us? Because I know nothing about killing animals or fish. Without Harnu, we starve. Think of your child. It needs the food as much as you."

"I'm not saying I won't eat it. I just don't like the smell."

"And I am simply suggesting you try to be a little kinder to our provider, lest you drive him away. I know the situation is awkward, but . . ."

"I'll try, Noam. For you."

"Thank you, Grenny."

Gren brought in a lantern and pulled a fresh blanket over Averella's body, as if she were merely napping and not infected with a storm. Averella hovered by the sideboard, staring at a pitcher of water, suddenly extremely thirsty. How many days had passed for her without food or drink? Would her body die without nourishment?

A shadow fell over the bed. Averella turned to see Harnu standing in the doorway like a sentry guard.

"We should talk of what to do if she never wakes," Harnu said.

"Don't say that!" Gren said. "What if she can hear you?"

Harnu shrugged. "How could she possibly hear me?"

"She's only sleeping, you know. If she hears she's dying she might give up the fight."

Harnu looked like he was making an effort to stay calm. "Gren, we can't stay here forever. My father needs me."

"*Your* father. Everything is always about you. What about me?"

"Gren, I've done everything I can for you. I finished your cottage. Stood by while you married my friend. Stole this lady from Lord Nathak's wagon. Unless you agree to be my wife, my responsibility is to my father."

"So if I marry you, you'll help me. That's what you're saying?"

"I'm helping you already. What more do you want?"

"I want you to leave me alone, Harnu. Go away." She turned her back to Harnu and straightened the blanket around Averella's chin.

Harnu stared at the back of Gren's head until he finally said, "Good night, Grendolyn."

The following morning, Averella, restless with boredom, followed Gren and Noam outside. Noam went around to the stable. Gren knelt at the water's edge and washed her face. Noam appeared a moment later with Kopay and led the horse to the stream.

A bird squawked, drawing Averella's attention to a tree across the creek. A gowzal perched in the branches, facing her, its eyes black and hypnotic. *You have lost your way, my lady. Come with me and I will take you home.*

Averella stared at the creature. Had it just spoken to her?

Do not fear, my lady, it said in a familiar humming voice. *I have been sent to help you. Lady Nitsa awaits your company.* The bird flapped its wings, quickly at first, hovering in the air above Averella, then it flapped slowly and rose above the roof of the cabin.

Averella floated up over the cabin and after the gowzal, eager to see Mother. The creature led her through a black void. How could it see in the dark? For that matter, how could she? By the time the questions occurred to her, she could no longer see the lantern glow at the cabin.

She hardly had time to panic for fear of losing sight of her guide. They flew a long time, occasionally passing over pricks of light below.

Suddenly, hundreds of sparks came into view like a swarm of fireflies. A city loomed ahead. As they neared, the sparks grew into torches perched along mismatched stone sentry walls, reflecting on oily water below. This was not Carmine, but Mahanaim. Averella had been here before with her mother. It must be time for another Council meeting. For that was the only reason Mother would be here.

The creature flew up to the central watchtower and entered an open window.

Averella slowed as she approached the window. She ducked her head, though her legs passed through the stone wall beneath the windowsill.

The bird soared into the open door of a birdcage and perched inside. It nipped at a dead mouse.

Averella stood in a circular room at the top of the watchtower. The room was empty but for an elderly man wearing a black hooded robe, asleep on a small cot, and the birdcage on a marble pillar. A lone candle on the floor flickered, burned down to a stump of wax.

The man groaned, a long, keening sound. Averella backed against the window. Why had the creature brought her here? She did not want to meet this man. She wanted her mother.

The man lowered his feet to the floor and sat up. "Good, you are still here." His droning voice was the same one that had come from the bird.

He stood, shuffled to the birdcage, and closed the door, latching the creature inside. The hood of his cloak covered his head, but she could see his face clearly. His skin had the color and leathery texture of oyster mushrooms. His eyes were grey, but stared at her in the same knowing manner the bird had.

"The problem, my dear, is simple. You have died."

No. That could not be. For she had just left her body in the cottage, and, last she saw, it had been breathing.

"There is nothing you can do to put things back the way they were."

Why, then, did you bring me here? Averella asked.

"We can help one another." His voice was like the lowest string on a harp. "I have the power to reunite you with your body."

What do you want in return?

"Your eyes." His eyes drilled into hers, pale and moist. She wanted to look away, so horrible was the chill his gaze inflicted. "Join with this gowzal. Fly where I need you to. Report to me what you see. When I am satisfied, I will put your mind back in your body."

It wasn't until he replied again that she realized he could hear her! Still, she didn't like his look. *How can I know you will fulfill your side of this bargain?*

"You cannot, my dear. But you have no other choice. Do not worry. I shall be more than fair."

Averella stared at the caged creature and saw it had a fuzzy black beard. *It is a male bird?*

The old man chuckled. "That does not matter. Simply concentrate on the creature. Look out through its eyes."

Averella wrinkled her nose. The bird was so hideous that looking at it twisted her stomach. How could she bear to share its mind? What if it bit that mouse again?

But she so wanted to return to her body. Could this truly be the only way? She focused on the creature, felt herself draw nearer. Something dark gripped at her heart.

Sparrow, please speak to me. Tell me you are not in that coffin. Please?

Master Cham's voice pulled Averella away from the bird. *Master Cham! Can you hear me?*

She waited, glanced from the old man to the bird and back to the old man. Master Cham had mentioned a coffin. Had he followed her trail from Sitna? Come upon Lord Nathak's procession? He seemed intent on finding her. The idea of such devotion filled her with familiar warmth.

Arman! She had forgotten her Creator.

Forgive me, Arman. I am lost, separated from my body, and, I fear, my memories. Is this man and his bird the only way back? Why can Master Cham not hear my words? What should I do? Help me, please.

A musical scream came from outside. "Kee-eeeee-arr." The majestic sound lasted several seconds. Averella turned to see a great speckled hawk light on the windowsill. It screamed again. "Kee-eeeee-arr."

Heat filled Averella from the inside. She could not keep from smiling.

The old man lifted a gnarled hand. "No, my lady! Do not trust it."

But Averella already trusted it with all her heart. She threw her arms around the hawk's neck, and it took off out the window and into the dark land.

Either the hawk flew faster or Averella was too filled with joy to notice the passing time. For moments later the hawk soared through the roof of a round pavilion, setting Averella's transparent feet onto a woven straw mat.

With one last, "Kee-eeeee-arr," the hawk flew away, leaving Averella inside the warm tent.

15

Achan lay on the bed in his tent. He'd been awake for hours, burrowing under his blankets like a mole, not wanting to get up yet. Today would hold much that he would rather not live through. A battle? A negotiation? Peace? Death?

He doubted peace would be the conclusion.

Sparrow would have said something sarcastic. She was able to make light of the heaviest circumstance. He hated the hole she'd left in his life. He wanted to bloodvoice her again, to spend the day searching, but the idea of failing . . . It was too much. Still, like a man who couldn't stop drinking, Achan reached for her, clutching the cord around his neck.

Sparrow? Please answer me.

Why do you call me Sparrow, Master Cham? Do I look like a bird to you?

Achan sat up so quickly he started to choke. *Sparrow!*

You can hear me now, Master Cham?

Aye. Where are you? Describe your surroundings.

I am in a tent. A hawk left me here moments ago.

A hawk? Describe this tent. Do you see Esek?

Who is this Esek everyone speaks of? And why have you ignored me these past days? I heard your calls and answered, but you never seem to hear me. How can this be?

You closed your mind. You forgot how to bloodvoice.

Me bloodvoice? I have no such skill. I only wish to go—

You can *bloodvoice, you've only forgotten. Part of bloodvoicing is placing shields around your mind. You likely did this to protect yourself. That's good, but when you hear the voice of someone you want to speak to, you must lower your shields so that person can hear you.*

She sighed as if he were the most exasperating man in all Er'Rets. *Can you tell me how to get back into my body?*

Aye. Are you with your body now? Can you see it?

No. The black bird took me from it. Then the brown bird brought me here.

Achan paused, frustrated, yet desperate to control his temper so he would not frighten Sparrow away. *Tell me about this tent. Are there any people in it?*

Yes. There are two men.

What do they look like?

One looks to be a guardsman, asleep in a chair by the entrance. Drooling too, I believe, which is rather disturbing for a guardsman. The other man is shirtless, sitting up in a bed, looking around with the most puzzled expression.

Achan jumped off the bed. *What is he doing now?*

Oh, he just stood up. Praise Arman he is wearing pants.

Indeed. "Sparrow, you're here!" Achan said aloud. "You're with me right now!"

Sparrow gasped. You *are Master Cham?*

You don't recognize me?

Should I?

Aye, you should. Achan wheeled around and grabbed his Shield's shoulder. "Shung! Wake up, man. Sparrow is here!"

Shung moaned and glanced around the tent. "The little vixen has returned?"

"Yes! Yes! In this very tent."

He squinted past Achan. "Shung sees no woman."

"She's in the Veil. Watch my body. I'm going after her."

"Aye, Shung will watch."

"Good." *Sparrow, I'm coming. Stay where you are. Uh . . . where are you?*

I am by the center pole, over the straw mat.

Achan stared into the empty air surrounding the pole and exhaled. Amazing. He fell back onto the bed and closed his eyes. Concentrating, he sat up, this time leaving his body where it lay. He looked directly toward the center pole.

Sparrow hovered above the mat like a ghost. Almost before he thought to move, Achan was at her side.

She shrieked. *How can you move so quickly?*

You just have to concentrate.

Why call me Sparrow, Master Cham? Is that a code?

It's your surname, silly girl. Vrell Sparrow.

Sparrow's eyebrows puckered. *Are we friends? For only my sisters and close friends call me Vrell.*

You have sisters?

Four.

Really. Sparrow once told him she had no one in all Er'Rets. Since then he'd learned she had a mother and now four sisters. *Where do they live?*

Sparrow pursed her lips. *If we are such close friends, you and I, how is it that you do not know I have sisters? Or where they live? Why should I trust you, Master Cham? You could be a scoundrel.*

He laughed at her formality. *I am* not *a scoundrel.*

She lifted her chin so that her nose tilted upward. *So you say. But how am I to know that for certain?*

He grinned, struck again by her regal behavior. Always the odd duck, Sparrow was. *You just have to trust me.*

Little Cham. Shung's voice roared in his head.

Achan spun around. Sir Eagan, Sir Caleb, and Matthias stood inside the doorway to his tent.

"Tell the prince to come back," Sir Caleb said.

Sir Caleb says come back, Shung said.

I heard him. Achan turned back to Sparrow. She had drifted to the wall of the tent. Her eyes were wide like a deer when it hears a branch snap in the forest.

Sparrow, what's wrong?

You are the prince? Prince Gidon? You look different.

I'm not Esek, Sparrow, blazes. Let me explain what—

Your Highness, please, Sir Caleb said. *New Kingsguard soldiers approach carrying a white flag.*

Sir Caleb's words captured Achan's full attention. *They surrender?*

Doubtful, Your Highness. They wish to parley, more likely. We must ride out to hear their terms.

Terms? He looked back to Sparrow. *Promise you won't leave, Sparrow? I can help you get back to your body. Say you'll wait.*

She gave a sharp nod of her head.

Nothing Achan felt confident about, but what else could he do? *I'll return shortly. Much has happened that you have forgotten. I'd like the opportunity to explain. Will you wait?*

Yes.

Thank you. He bowed to her, a formal act for Sparrow, but it felt right somehow. Achan blinked and found himself back in his body. He sat up and stared at the place he last saw her. Sir Caleb gripped his arm to help him stand. Achan continued to stare into the empty space at the wall of his tent. *Please keep your word, Sparrow,* he bloodvoiced.

She did not answer.

Sir Caleb and Matthias began dressing Achan in layers of padding and armor. Achan could hardly speak he was so overcome with having found Sparrow and not being able to help her. He had to force himself to spare a thought for the coming meeting.

Too soon he found himself atop Dove, riding out of camp, flanked by guardsmen carrying torches through the gloom. A hundred horsemen at his back were armed with bows.

They crested a small hill, and hundreds of torchlights came into view. Five horsemen stood abreast in the middle of a field. The men on each end held a torch. Far behind them, a wall of soldiers stood like a parapet, their torches reflecting off shiny black armor. Black knights. Many of which appeared to hold bows, arrows knocked.

Achan gripped Dove's reins and straightened, coming back to his calling. *Be with us, Arman. Give me Your strength. Your words.*

Terms. He didn't even know who approached. The Hadad? Lord Nathak. Or perhaps Lord Falkson of Barth?

As they narrowed the distance between them, Achan soon had his answer. Sir Kenton Garesh's curtain of black hair was like no other, a sharp contrast to the white flag he held in one hand. And Esek Nathak, unless he was a ghost, sat alive and well on a black steed, both arms intact.

How could that be?

A chill rolled down Achan's spine. He found it difficult to look anywhere but at Esek's arms. He *had* cut one off, hadn't he? The right arm. He had relived the moment again and again in his nightmares.

Your Highness? Sir Caleb spoke to his mind. *Keep your wits about you.*

But his arm.

Is likely a wooden one.

Achan's posture relaxed. Of course. Esek would want to appear whole to his followers.

"Heir of Axel Hadar, we meet again as equals."

Achan stiffened. Esek's voice was the same, yet different. A thick undertone drew out every word a breath longer than need be. Dove shifted beneath Achan, swished his tail. Achan stroked the horse's neck. *I know boy, I feel it too.*

Esek spoke again. "You have nothing to say?"

Sir Kenton and Esek wore marks on their foreheads. Three bars like those on the foreheads of the Eben giants who had attacked Achan outside Mirrorstone months ago.

"I say we are anything but equals, Esek," Achan said, his words bolder than his courage. "When I left you last, you were not even whole. Now you bear the mark of madmen and carry a white flag. You surrender so soon?"

Esek lifted both hands, stretched them out toward Achan.

Sir Gavin drew his sword. "None of that, now."

Esek chuckled. "I wield no magic in these hands, Sir Gavin. I am not a black knight." He wiggled his fingers. "I merely wish to show your prince that I am indeed whole."

Achan did not understand. "How?"

"One does not share secrets with the enemy, Your Highness."

Why does he show me respect? Achan asked Sir Gavin. *What's his game?*

I know not, Your Highness. Remain on guard.

"Your man carries the white flag, Esek. What do you want?" Achan asked.

Sir Caleb glared in Achan's direction. Apparently this was not the proper way to negotiate terms. Well, hang the proper way. Achan wanted to get back to Sparrow. Her face came to his mind now, lifting his mood considerably.

"Why, I want peace, of course," Esek said.

Achan huffed. "*You* want peace?"

"Who wants to rule a warring nation? Too much work."

"You still plan to rule?" Achan's voice came out flat.

"Of course."

"And how do you plan to do that peaceably?"

"By giving you what you want. Have Lady Averella and her inheritance. Rule Carmine—rule all of Carm, if you wish. Call yourself a king. I no longer care. But leave Armonguard and the south to me."

Achan shook his head. "You think that's what I want?"

"What is it *you* want, then?"

"I want a cottage in the woods. Vrell Sparrow as my wife. No throne under my control. Perhaps some goats."

Esek shifted on his horse. "Then *you* surrender?"

Achan's dry laugh sounded loud in the surrounding silence. "Aye, that I did, but not to you. Arman is my master now. And He wants me to rule all Er'Rets. Not just Carm. So, I thank you for your . . . gift, was it? But I do not accept. We ride for Armonguard. Prince Oren holds the castle for us. If you stand in our way, you will become part of the road."

Esek snorted. "Prince Oren may reside within Castle Armonguard, but he does not *hold* anything. We will take the fortress before you ever have a chance to see its splendor."

"Permission to speak, Your Majesty," Sir Gavin said.

"Granted," Achan and Esek said together.

Esek chuckled, clearly pleased with himself.

Sir Gavin's horse walked forward a few steps. "Esek Nathak, do not be a fool. I counseled you on the subject of dark magic. I sense you've already aligned yourself with its power. There is still time to rebuke it. I can help you."

"Why would I do that?" Esek said. "My master gave me a new arm, Sir Gavin. He is one hundred times more powerful than this One God you serve. If you and your princeling insist on war, then you will have it, and you will lose. For my master communes with all the gods of Er'Rets."

"There is no other God but Arman," Sir Gavin said. "Your gods are a trick of Gâzar. Serving them will bring you nothing but death."

"This meeting has been a waste of time." Esek straightened in his saddle. "Reconsider my offer before you reach Mahanaim, for you and your followers will not pass through the city alive." Esek reined his horse around, and the horse took off at a gallop.

Three of Esek's men followed, leaving only Sir Kenton, Esek's Shield, behind. "You would be wise to reconsider, Gavin," Sir Kenton said. "Never have I seen such power."

"You speak of the Hadad," Sir Gavin said.

"Aye. The Hadad will rule this nation."

Sir Gavin answered, his voice soft but forceful. "For years I wondered if your master was truly Lord Nathak, but now I see the truth. Killing King Axel and Queen Dara was the Hadad's plan. You both serve the same master."

"As will you, if you live through the next few days."

"Do not be a fool, Kenton," Sir Eagan said. "We taught you better than this."

Sir Kenton tossed the white flag to the ground and turned his horse. "No one taught me better than the Hadad. We shall see who is stronger." He rode away.

Achan sat on Dove, watching the horses merge with the Darkness.

"It's war then." Sir Gavin sighed. "Figured as much."

A chill coursed over Achan's arms. "War."

"Sparrow?" Achan entered his room and pulled off his helm. Sir Caleb, Shung, and Sir Eagan followed him inside.

Sir Caleb took Achan's helm from his hands. "Your Highness, we must go to the meeting tent. Gavin is gathering the generals to share Esek's demands."

"I must do something first." Achan turned to the men. "Sparrow is here. In this tent."

Sir Eagan's gaze roamed the tent. "Why did you not say something?"

"Sir Caleb said we had to leave for the—"

"Esek could have waited," Sir Eagan said.

"Really, Eagan?" Sir Caleb said. "Vrell and her problems are more important than all of Er'Rets?"

"We trained to the same code, Caleb. Always rescue the lady first." Sir Eagan fumbled at the points of Achan's breastplate and quickly pulled it free.

"Yes, but Vrell is always in some sort of mischief." Sir Caleb took the breastplate and set it on the armoire. "Why is she our responsibility?"

"Because I love her," Achan said.

"You love her." Sir Caleb threw up his hands. "Well that's just fine. What will Duchess Amal say to that?"

Sir Eagan shoved Achan's backplate into Sir Caleb's arms. "Sit, sit, Your Highness. You must bring her back right away."

Achan sat onto the end of his bed.

Shung sat beside him. "Shung will be watching."

Achan nodded. Feet on the floor, he fell onto his back and entered the Veil. *Sparrow?* He did not see her. He sought her mind and found it blocked.

No! Why had she left? *Arman, why?*

He sent a knock the proper way, but when she did not respond, he barged ahead with his message, knowing now that she could hear him. *Sparrow, you've raised the shields around your mind again. I can't help you this way. Let me in.*

He opened his eyes and stared at the brown ceiling of the tent. *Why did you leave? You said you would wait.*

"Found her?" Shung asked.

"She's gone." Achan held his hands in front of his face. They were trembling. He sat up and looked from Sir Eagan, who sat on the end of his bed, to Sir Caleb, who stood by the armoire. "What can I do? Is there nothing I can do?"

"Can you guess where she went?" Sir Eagan asked.

"No. She doesn't know me. I frighten her. She thinks I'm Esek or something."

"Esek?" Sir Caleb asked. "Why?"

"You think I know? The whole thing is maddening!"

Sir Eagan's calm voice urged him along. "Keep messaging her. Do not give up."

"What's the point? Even if I can reach her, how can I convince her of the truth? She doesn't remember me."

Sir Eagan gripped Achan's shoulder. Warmth and calm flooded through the connection. "When someone has forgotten, it helps to bring them to a familiar place. Familiar scents and sounds can also kindle memories."

"I thought *I* would be familiar."

"Pray harder. Ask Arman to help you," Sir Eagan said.

Of course. Why did Achan always forget to pray first? He slid off the bed to his knees, which were still draped in layers of chain and leather armor. He put his hands on the straw mat and lowered himself to his stomach. *Arman? Please, show me where Sparrow is. Take me to her. Let her remember. Give me the words to convince her to return. Show me where—*

A breeze stroked Achan's back. Talons scratched his shoulder blades. His body lifted off the floor. His mind, actually, for his body lay still as a dead man on the straw mat. Shung sat on Achan's bed. Sir Eagan and Sir Caleb stood together in the doorway. None seemed to see Achan rising through the tent, legs flailing.

He twisted around and saw a great speckled brown bird holding him, gripping the back of his surcoat with its claws. A brown wing flapped across his view. When it lifted for another stroke, the bird had carried him through the roof and into the black sky.

Achan wanted to scream. He should at least message Shung and inform his Shield that a bird of prey had taken his soul. But a great calm washed away every concern.

This bird was Arman's answer to his prayer.

It carried him from the torchlights of camp. Each flap of its massive wings brought a warm gust of air on Achan's neck and ears. In the darkness, Achan had no way of tracking which direction the bird flew. But Darkness quickly faded to a charcoal fog, then a grey haze, then a white cloud. Bits of blue peeked between fluffy white clouds. Achan could hear nothing but the occasional flap of wings and his own breath.

The bird dove into a leafy forest, soaring between trees. There was something grand about this place. The trees appeared greener. Or bigger. Maybe both. And the smell . . . Achan inhaled long and deep. Such sweetness had never entered his nostrils.

In the distance, a golden light shone between flaky bronze tree trunks, as if he were approaching a bonfire through a forest at night. The bird swooped between two massive redpines and entered a vast meadow. Thick grass stretched in every direction, hedged by the forest on all sides. Flowers in every color Arman had made filled the air with nectar.

Something white gleamed in the distance. As they neared, it took shape. A fence. As tall as any sentry wall. Made of white stone . . . or was that pearl? Whatever the substance, it was carved in scallops and scrolls and towered above the flowers clustered at its base.

Achan's heart swelled. A full, giddy joy consumed his senses. Oh, to go inside such a place. If only the bird would carry him over the fence.

But the bird slowed and descended. Achan could see the blades of grass through his transparent boots. His gaze settled on a woman who was standing before the gate, her back to him. Her body was dwarfed in size by the splendor of the looming structure. She stared through the white bars as if hoping to go inside.

Sparrow.

The bird dropped Achan in the soft grass ten paces from the woman, then settled atop the pearly gate without a sound.

Achan stumbled forward.

Sparrow turned, and her wide eyes narrowed. "You!" She perched her hands on her hips. "Stop following me!"

Achan started to run, then remembered he wasn't in his body, so he materialized at her side instead.

She screamed. "Do not do that."

Over a head shorter than him, dressed in a scraggly brown peasant dress, one frizzy braid still intact, the other side, tangled and loose . . . she looked lovelier than ever.

But the expression on her face was more suited to Jaira Hamartano. Hard eyes, as if everything behind them mistrusted him. Lips drawn into a thin line. Cheeks flushed with accusation.

Achan gripped Sparrow's arms, and though touching her did not feel the same as flesh on flesh, energy raced through him. "Step back from the gate, Sparrow. It's dangerous."

Her eyes widened at his touch, but, amazingly, she did not pull away. "How do you . . . ? I have touched nothing for days. Yet this gate is solid. I am tired, Master Cham. This is not natural, is it, to be out of my body? Am I dead?"

"No. If it were your time, the gates would open."

Her eyes flickered to meet his, so much greener in this place. "Really?"

He didn't know. But it had sounded wise, so he nodded.

She scowled and tugged on Lady Averella's sleeve that was still tied to his arm. "Where did you get this token?"

Heat filled his face. "Sparrow, I can explain."

"*Who* gave it to you?"

He sighed. "Duchess Amal presented it to me in a missive offering her eldest daughter, Lady Averella, to be my bride. Sir Caleb and the others thought it was the best match."

Sparrow shook her head. "That is impossible."

"I'll give it back. Sparrow, it's *you* I want."

She coughed out a dry laugh. "Nothing makes sense here. It must be a dream." She turned back to the gate, gripped the bars, and shook them. "Arman! Open the gate. I beg You. I want to come home. Or wake up." Sparrow stepped up onto the lowest hinge and heaved her body up. Grinning, she raised her foot to the next hinge.

Achan gazed up at her profile, at her lips set in a determined twist. "This is not your home, Sparrow. Not yet, anyway."

"How do *you* know?"

"I feel it. We have much to do, you and I. We must help Arman push back Darkness. We must bring His light to all people, or at least to those who will believe."

Sparrow's brow furrowed. "You believe?"

"I do. I pledged my heart to Arman and accepted His Son's sacrifice." He sifted through his memories, seeking something she might find familiar. "Remember how we used to wrestle? When I thought you were a boy?"

Sparrow's head turned, her eyes so wide that every bit of white showed. "I never!"

He breathed a silent laugh at her expression. How proper she was without her memory. "Remember the first time you knocked me down with a leg sweep? I loved you in that moment, though I didn't understand it until later."

Now her eyebrows sank. "You love me yet you wear *that* without my knowledge or consent?" She gestured toward the sleeve, then lost her balance and gripped the bars again, pulling her body tight against the gate.

"You left. You would not even speak to me. I didn't know what else to do."

"Best wishes to you, Master Cham. Now if you will excuse me." She heaved herself up another step. Then another. She was halfway up the gate. If she fell, would she float? Come to think of it, why didn't she simply float up over the gate? Had she tried? Achan kept that thought to himself in fear she might attempt it and be lost forever.

But what else could he do? Something familiar, Sir Eagan had suggested. A smell or sound. An idea seized him that warmed his cheeks. He never considered himself a strong singer, but he could think of nothing else. At least no one but Sparrow was here to witness it. He cleared his throat and squinted up at her.

View not my face, I'm undone beside you.
The beating of my heart won't cease.
While I'm near you, while I'm near you.

She stopped climbing and looked down. "What is that? What you are singing?"

He sounded like a fool, but if it would bring Sparrow back . . . He took a deep breath.

Pity on my heart from the day I first saw you.
Your pleasing face burns my memories.
Whenever we're apart—

She shook her hand at him. "Stop that!"

Whenever we're apart.
Though I'm nothing to you, I love you.
How can I make it known that I love you?

She gazed down, blinking as if something was in her eyes, then climbed down a step. "I know that song."

"Yes," Achan said. "We learned it in Berland."

She climbed down another step. "I have never been to Berland."

He held out a hand. "Oh, but you have." He gripped her hand and helped her down to the grass. "A young woman named Yumikak sang this song to us." He waggled his eyebrows. "She even danced with you."

"There is nothing strange about women dancing together. I dance with my cousins all the time."

He threaded his fingers in hers. "I suppose not. But this was strange, for you were pretending to be a boy."

Sparrow's eyes narrowed again, and she pulled out of his hold. "Of all the— Why would I do such a thing?"

"To protect yourself. To keep from becoming someone's mistress."

She gasped. "How dare you insinuate—"

Achan grabbed her shoulders and kissed her. Her energy poured into him, fresh and pure like water, quenching his thirst. She squirmed free and slapped him. It did not hurt, but the force caused him to sail sideways a few steps.

Then she squeaked, and her lips pursed as if she were blowing on something hot. "I have struck you before."

Achan grinned and glided back to her. "Aye, you have."

"Why?"

"Because I've kissed you before."

She folded her arms. "Then you deserved it both times."

Achan shrugged. "If you say so."

She glanced back at the gates. "If I am not to enter Shamayim this day, what shall I do, Master Cham? For I can no longer bear wandering Er'Rets like a zephyr."

"Go back to your body. Do you know where it is?"

"In a cabin in the Sideros Forest, for that is where Master Poe said his father's cabin was."

"Harnu? Why would he take your body?"

"Lord Nathak put my body in a casket. But before he left, Master Poe and Gren replaced my body with potatoes. It was all very exciting to watch. Master Poe suggested we stay in his father's cabin until I wake. He was worried Lord Nathak would search Sitna once he found me gone."

"I'm sure he was right." Though Achan hated to concede anything to Harnu Poe. "How did you come to be in Sitna in the first place?"

"I do not remember, but from what Gren says, she and I were going to Armonguard."

"What? Sparrow, Armonguard is no place for you. And how could you allow Gren to come with you?"

"I beg your pardon? You think I have some control over what Gren does? She is not my maid."

"Your maid? What are you talking about? I can't keep chasing after all you women. If you would stay put—stay where you're supposed to be—"

"And where might that be, in your *humble* opinion?"

Achan narrowed his eyes. "I don't know. You never told me where you lived."

Sparrow propped her hands on her hips. "You claim to love me yet know not where I live? This I cannot fathom."

"Just . . . never mind." Achan seethed. The audacity of Sparrow to take Gren from Carmine. He simply could not comprehend what she had been thinking, nor could he—

SEEK PEACE AND PURSUE IT.

The heat of Arman's voice knocked Achan senseless. Sparrow had turned her back to him, arms folded, gazing through the bars to Shamayim. He had no idea why she had made the choices she had, but his anger would not change them. He closed his eyes.

Arman, forgive my temper. Nothing matters but reuniting Sparrow with her body. Please, show me the way to this cabin. Help me to—

Sparrow squealed.

Achan opened his eyes to find the speckled hawk flapping overhead. Achan held out his hand. "The bird will take us to your body."

Sparrow gripped his hand. The great speckled hawk lifted them by the backs of their clothes, Sparrow in one foot, Achan in the other. They twisted this way and that, so Achan put his arm around Sparrow's waist to keep her steady. The bird flew away from the Pearly Gate, soared over the meadow, through the forest, and into the clouds.

"It moves quickly, does it not?" Sparrow said.

The clouds were already greying. "Aye, it does."

"Can you really put me back together?" Sparrow's pale face faded as the grey mist turned to charcoal.

"No. But you can."

Within moments, they were descending into blackness. The bird dropped them outside the door of a small cabin. Cracks of light spilled through gaps in the shutters.

This time Sparrow dragged Achan by the hand. She led him through the thick door, past where Gren and Noam sat at a table, and into a small room. Achan craned his neck to see Gren through the open doorway, but Sparrow's voice pulled him away.

"See? Here lies my body. Tell me how to claim it."

Achan turned to the bed. Sparrow's body lay under a thin brown blanket. Though she looked no different from the spirit form beside him, something in his gut quickened at the sight of her pale skin and thick eyelashes. He knelt at the bedside and let his hand fall through her real one.

"None of that, Master Cham. We have no chaperone."

He grinned, liking the conflicted look on her face. "Come here and listen. Once you return to your body, you will not see me, for I will still be in the Veil."

"Will I remember you if I see you again?"

"*When* you see me again. There will be no *if* about it. I'm guessing that your memory will return in full when you reenter your body. I will pray for it every day until I hear you say it is true."

"Such passion you have for my memories."

"Aye, for they include me." He blew out a short breath. "Listen. Gren and Noam can be trusted. Harnu, I'm not so sure. My army is not far from here. Should you wish it, I'll send men for you and Gren."

"And what will two women do in a war?"

He laughed. "I know not. The moment you remember, please tell me what you had in mind by setting out for Armonguard with—as you like to put it—no chaperone."

Sparrow coughed out an indignant gasp. "Surely we were not alone. There must be another explanation."

"You are an odd duck, Sparrow. I've never met anyone quite like you. You never act the way I expect."

"Just how would you expect me to act, Master Cham? I am separated from my body and I—"

"Enough." Achan grabbed her Veil hand and tugged her close. "Listen to me. Simply concentrate. Focus on looking out of your own eyes. That should put you back where you belong."

She glanced at her limp body, her brow furrowed. "That is all I must do? But how do I—"

And she vanished. Sparrow's hand, which had been limp, moved. Achan turned back to the bed to find her already propped up on one elbow. She stared through him, her free hand groping for his. "Are you still there?" she whispered.

You can't feel me when I'm in the Veil. But now I'll leave you. Until we meet again, my beloved flower.

Achan went back to his own body and opened his eyes.

He lay prostrate on the floor of his tent. He rolled to his side. "Sparrow is in a cabin in the Sideros Forest."

Sir Eagan crouched to help him stand. "You found her?"

"Her soul and body are reunited, Sir Eagan." Achan couldn't help the grin that spread across his face.

Sir Eagan beamed. "Well done, lad! I shall inform Nitsa at once."

Achan faced Sir Caleb. "Help me change for the war council, Sir Caleb. We must discuss Esek and his threats."

"We are not terribly outnumbered," Sir Caleb said, "though all my tallies are speculation. Who can make a fair estimate in Darkness?"

Achan and the generals sat around a long table in the meeting tent. "Where is Esek's army exactly?" he asked. "Allowntown? Mahanaim? Somewhere in between?"

"My bloodvoice scouts sense the largest number outside Mahanaim," Sir Gavin said. "There is also a vast army between Xulon and Armonguard."

Achan's thoughts drifted to his uncle. "Has Prince Oren been warned?"

Sir Gavin nodded. "He has."

"How will we be getting our army to Armonguard, then?" Inko asked. "Will we be riding on the boats?"

"Captain Chantry's ships have not yet reached the isle of Nesos," Sir Eagan said.

"And we cannot afford to tarry," Sir Gavin said. "We'll travel east of the king's road, stay in Light as long as possible. We can move faster that way and avoid the bulk of Esek's army. Perhaps we may even pass over the eastern Reshon Gate before they realize what we've done."

"Won't we be seen?" Achan asked. "Does not Esek also have bloodvoice scouts?"

"He likely does," Sir Gavin said. "But at least this way they won't sneak up on us in the dark."

"I am thinking it is being safer to be waiting for the boats," Inko said.

For once Achan agreed with Inko, but for a different reason. "Why don't we just fight and be done with it?"

"Because Armonguard is the prize, not Mahanaim," Sir Eagan said. "If we engage Esek now, we could lose too many men to stand up against Esek's southern army. But if we can slip past at the eastern Reshon Gate while he awaits us in Mahanaim . . ."

"We stand a chance of beating his northern army to Armonguard," Sir Gavin said. "Even things up a bit. Do you approve, Your Highness?"

"I do." As if there were any other options. "We draw aim toward the eastern Reshon Gate. If there's nothing else . . . ?" No one spoke, so Achan said, "Meeting adjourned."

Sir Caleb waved Achan to follow him. "Sir Shung is a worthy Shield, but he is not as useful if he never eats or sleeps. I'm sure you've noticed how tired he's been of late?"

Shung always wanted to sleep, but Achan hadn't considered the reason might be because of his position as Shield.

Sir Caleb held open the tent flap for Achan to exit. He ducked outside and found two guardsmen waiting.

Sir Caleb stopped before the men. *With your permission, Your Highness, Sir Gavin has assigned these men. They'll work in pairs with Sir Shung and Kurtz, alternating schedules so you'll have two Shields at all times.*

Achan considered the soldiers. Both were in their early twenties. One was tall and thin with blond hair slicked back into a tail. The other had light brown skin, shaggy dark hair, and a flat nose. *If Sir Gavin trusts them, then of course I give permission. Thank you.*

Sir Caleb set a hand on the blond man's shoulder. "This is Cortland Agros, my nephew. He escaped Allowntown's siege because he was in Mitspah on an errand."

Cortland bowed his head. "An honor, Your Highness."

Achan took in the resemblance between Sir Caleb and his nephew, smiling at how Cortland had tamed his hair.

Sir Caleb motioned to the brown-skinned man. "And Manu Pitney came to us from Nesos. He is, in fact, your cousin, as your mother and his father were siblings."

"Your father is Lord Pitney?" Achan asked.

"No, Your Highness." Manu's voice was a lower pitch even than Shung's. "Lord Pitney is my uncle. My father was the youngest of the family."

"Pleased to know you," Achan said. "I should like to meet all your family someday."

Manu bowed. "That would be an honor, Your Highness."

Clearly Manu had been taught every shred of decorum Achan lacked. Perhaps in time his cousin would become more friendly, like Shung.

The idea of friends made Achan think of Sparrow. He hoped that time would loosen Sparrow's knots as well. That she would not only remember, but that things might go back to the way they were before.

PART 4

THE WAYS OF WAR

16

"But why would I run from the man I love?" The reason seemed obvious to Averella. "Perhaps I do not care for him as much as you say I do."

Gren shook her head. "Oh, no. On our trip from Carmine, you cried yourself to sleep each night thinking about him."

Averella sat up in the bed where she had awakened. Gren sat on the edge beside her. Though Averella's mind and body had reunited, her memory had not returned. Gren told her that she had spent nearly a year dressed as a stray boy, that she did indeed love the man called Achan Cham, who was the real Gidon Hadar, Crown Prince of all Er'Rets, and that—for some reason—she had run away from him.

And apparently cried herself to sleep over it. None of this made sense. "After having been away from home for so long, I would have been heartbroken to leave again."

Gren cocked one eyebrow. "I saw you in his chambers after he'd been hurt. You held his hand. Sang to him."

The very idea tickled Averella. "There, you see? My voice is not equipped for song."

But Gren went on. "Something about pity for your heart from the day you saw his face. I can't remember the tune."

Averella stiffened at the words. It was the song Master Cham had sung at the Pearly Gate. "Regardless, until my memory returns, I must do what is best for my reputation, which is to return to Carmine. According to Lady Fallina, I have disgraced myself."

"But what of Achan?" Gren asked.

Averella could not imagine loving anyone but Bran. "You say that Master Cham does not know that I am me." She shrugged. "Let things be. If at some point he courts me the proper way, perhaps our relationship will . . . change."

"But you want to serve Prince Oren's army as a healer. You can't do that from Carmine."

"Gren, I know a great deal about plants, but not enough to be a healer. And an army is no place for a lady."

Gren frowned as if Averella was a child who misunderstood her. "I beg your pardon, my lady, but you simply don't remember. Just last week you set a broken arm, removed arrows, bandaged severe cuts. I was amazed at your skill. To be a healer in the war—this is what you wanted."

"Well, I want it no longer. We should set off for Carmine as soon as possible."

"No!" Gren jumped up. "I must go to Armonguard. Noam and Harnu agreed to see me safely there."

"And why must *you* go to Armonguard?"

Gren's cheeks flushed. "In light of the circumstances with your memory, my lady, I'd rather not say."

"Do not be difficult. Tell me the truth."

Gren swallowed. "I wish to be near Master Rennan once the war is ended."

"*Bran* Rennan?" Averella struggled to keep the emotion from her voice, but she recalled Gren telling Harnu about this. She glanced at Gren's stomach, recalling also that the girl was with child. "I am trying to be patient . . ." She took a deep breath and her voice quavered. "But in my mind, Master Rennan is betrothed to me."

Gren patted her hand. "You were away so long. Both of you . . . changed. Your parting was mutual."

Mutual? Averella could not imagine such a thing. "Did not Harnu's father say Achan once loved you?"

"He did."

"So we have exchanged suitors?"

"I suppose we have."

Averella rubbed her temples. "This discussion wearies me. Please go. I must attempt to bloodvoice my mother. She will advise me on what is best."

Tears pooled in Gren's eyes. "Very well, my lady. I'll go." She curtsied and left the room.

Remorse welled up inside Averella. She had not meant to be rude, but Gren was a peasant. Society dictated that Averella's conversations with Gren were already far too personal. They both needed to remember their place. And she was Lady Averella Amal, heir to Carm, *not* Vrell Sparrow, some ridiculous stray girl in hiding.

She concentrated on her mother's face, uncertain how she knew bloodvoicing was done this way. *Mother? Can you hear me? This is Averella. I am attempting to message you by means of bloodvoicing, though I feel slightly mad to even attempt it. How does one know if they have succeeded in making contact or are merely talking to themselves?*

Averella! Praise Arman you are back!

Tears stung Averella's eyes. *Mother! What a relief to finally speak with you. Yet praise is debatable.*

What do you mean? Have you returned to your body?

I have, though it seems that part of my memory is gone.

Mother's voice softened. *How much have you forgotten?*

How could one know what one has forgotten, Mother? Last I recall it was early winter. Master Rennan and I had approached you about our engagement.

Oh, dearest! That was over a year ago! So much has happened since then.

Averella sighed. *So people have been telling me. Is it true? Have Master Rennan and I broken our engagement?*

I am afraid so.

The words caused Averella's heart to crack. *And I am in love with this mystery prince? And he whom we both believed to be Prince Gidon was an imposter all these years? How could any of this have possibly come to pass?*

Mother explained what she knew of the past year, but Averella could scarcely believe it, for it sounded like a long tale penned by a minstrel. She did not realize she had been weeping until her nose dripped liquid onto her lap.

She sniffled and looked for a handkerchief. *To think I have become so deceitful. I hardly know what to do.*

Dearest, I do believe you kept the truth from the prince too long, but you have grown in many ways since you left for Walden's Watch. I am very proud of you.

But I have forgotten all of this growth. Gren tells me I am a healer. Master Cham tells me he loves none but me, that he is to be king and wishes me to be his queen, yet he knows me only as a stray named Vrell Sparrow. You tell me my father is not Duke Amal but a prisoner from Ice Island. And no one is here to tell me how I feel about any of this, so I must discover it all again, if such is even possible.

It will take time, my dear, but most people's memories return eventually. Come home, and I will help you.

I would like to, but it seems I promised to take Gren to Armonguard. She hopes to be there for Master Rennan once the war is over. She thinks they are to be . . . married.

Really, Averella. How do you expect to make such a journey? Especially now that Darkness has spread so far? Besides, Master Rennan is imprisoned in Allowntown with Sir Rigil and Sir Jax. You told me yourself.

I did? Averella must not have mentioned this to Gren. *I need time to think this over. I will let you know when I have determined my next course of action.*

My thoughts and prayers are with you, dearest.

Averella did want to go home, but she doubted being there would help her memory return. She must have had good reason for going to Armonguard, no matter how awkward the idea of Gren and Bran being together made her feel. She could not trust her emotions for Bran. They were based on a past reality, apparently. Mother had confirmed it. But if Bran were imprisoned in Allowntown, going to Armonguard would not help him.

Averella bit her bottom lip. She needed to look through his eyes and see for herself where he was.

How did she know to do such a thing? Yet, instinctually, she closed her eyes and concentrated on Bran's face. A line of men appeared before her. Dozens, perhaps hundreds. Distant torchlight made them look like an army of shadows. Chains rattled and clanked.

She gasped in a breath of rancid air. This was a prisoner escort. Such parties had come through Carmine many times during her life, transporting men to Ice Island.

Bran's feelings pressed in on her. Fatigue. The tightness of shackles on his wrists and ankles. Soreness in his feet. *Master Rennan. This is Lady Averella. Can you hear me?*

Bran's familiar voice squeezed her chest. *I can, my lady. Are you well?*

She forced her words to sound calm. *Your well-being is the concern at the moment. Where are you being taken?*

They are moving us to Mahanaim, though it seems a waste. Please tell me you are still in Carmine?

I wish I could, Master Rennan. I am, instead, in a cottage outside Sitna.

Averella could feel annoyance rush through Bran's body. *I should have known you would refuse reason.*

There is no cause to be rude, Master Rennan. Much has happened in the past days.

I have time, should you wish to tell the tale, my lady, but know in advance I will speak my mind.

Speak his mind? Mercy! What an icy attitude he held toward her already. *Very well. Days ago, I lost my memory whilst in the Veil. Mother tells me horrors of how I have spent this past year. But none have distressed me as much as what a peasant woman named Gren has said. Master Rennan, please tell me it is false. Tell me we are still in love and that you have not deserted me for this peasant girl.*

Heat swirled inside Bran's chest. *Averella, you go too far. I can no longer stomach your manipulation.*

How dare you accuse me of manipulation! All I have confessed is truth. Ask my Mother if you do not believe.

I have no method of speaking to your Mother at present.

Well . . . ask the real Prince Gidon, then. For he is the one who rescued me from the Veil.

I have no method of speaking with the prince, either. I cannot bloodvoice, Averella.

Forgive me, Master Rennan. I did not know that I could bloodvoice until hours ago.

Why is Madam Hoff with you?

The name snagged in Averella's mind. *Madam Hoff?*

Gren. The "peasant woman." What are you doing together?

Madam? *Gren is married?*

Averella, please. You know fully well the details of Riga Hoff's death and how his widow came to be in Carmine.

I do? She suddenly recalled that Harnu had called Gren a widow. She squeezed her hands in frustration. *According to Gren, we left Carmine together. We went to Sitna to meet up with some of her old friends. That is where I was caught. Reggio Levy had me thrown in the dungeon, so Gren says. And Mother says I was stormed, which is to have the soul parted from the body. Lord Nathak planned to take my body to Mahanaim in a coffin. And Lady Fallina made horrible accusations of me. Prince Gidon was finally able to bring me back to myself. Yet they tell me that I—* No. She could not bear to tell Bran that she supposedly loved Prince Gidon.

The heat in Bran's chest melted. *Averella, I am sorry I spoke harshly. You have gone through a terrible ordeal. And if you have truly lost your memory, I had no cause to speak to you so. But you must turn back. A war is brewing in the south. It is not a safe place for two women to travel.*

There are four in our party, Master Rennan. Gren's friends from Sitna. A blacksmith named Harnu Poe and a stableman named Noam Fox.

I know these men from my time in Sitna. They are not soldiers.

Bran's voice soothed her. She found it familiar and comfortable, no matter what he said. *Is there no chance of you and I reconciling?*

She could feel Bran's stomach tighten. *If I believed you loved me . . . Yes, I would try again. But, Averella, give it time. Your memory will return, and when it does, you'll know that the prince is the man for you. I only hope, for your sake, that he is a more patient man than I.*

"We must help them, naturally," Gren said. "Achan needs men of such quality. Sir Jax, Sir Rigil, and Bran can do him no good in prison."

Averella and Gren now sat on one side of the table, across from Noam and Harnu, in the main room of the cabin.

"I do not doubt Sir Rigil or Master Rennan's experience with a sword," Averella said, "nor their loyalty to the rightful king. I do not know Sir Jax. Which house does he serve?"

Gren put a hand on Averella's back. "You know Sir Jax well, my lady. He escorted you from Walden's Watch to Mahanaim. He's a dear friend to you, so you said."

Averella wished she could remember. Not knowing the past was giving her a headache. Her left side ached, as well. And her dress had so little structure she felt indecent before these men. If only she had changed into her own dress before leaving her room. "We must do what we can. Perhaps someone loyal to Prince Oren's cause could assist us."

"Achan's cause," Gren said. "For Prince Oren swore fealty to him. Achan showed me Prince Oren's ring."

My, how much had happened in so short a time.

Harnu crossed his arms across his chest. "If we can't find anyone to help, how will we get to the dungeon?"

"In all the times I have visited, I have never seen the dungeons," Averella said.

Gren took Averella's hand and squeezed. "But you have, my lady! It's where you nursed Achan back to life."

Of course. Averella had forgotten that part of the story. "Well, I remember nothing of that time."

"Servants might talk," Harnu suggested. "I bet they don't like what's happening with the change of leadership."

"We'd have to be careful," Noam said. "Asking the wrong servant could get us arrested."

"Master Poe, you are a forbidding fellow," Averella said, taking in his muscular arms. "And my green travel dress is plain enough to allow me to pass as a merchant's wife. Let us pose as man and wife. Master Fox, you and Gren can be our servants. We shall claim to be fleeing Darkness and offer our services to the New Council Mother told me about. That should be enough to get us inside the city. Have you any fabric, Gren? Perhaps you could make Master Poe a merchant's tunic."

"The bedspread might work." Gren got up and entered the bedroom.

Averella smiled at the men. "We ride for Mahanaim in the morning. Pray that Arman will guide our steps."

• • •

Averella's decision made Mother unhappy. This did not deter Averella in her promise to Gren, however, which puzzled her. Though she often disagreed with her mother, she had never been bold enough to disobey. Perhaps this was some of Vrell Sparrow's persona coming to light.

Whether Vrell Sparrow was inside her or not, the next morning Averella unpacked her green travel gown, thankful to have something proper to wear.

When she unlaced the peasant dress and slipped it off her shoulders, three things startled her. First—and she had suspected this since she awoke yesterday—she was wearing no corset. Second, a man's ring hung on a gold chain around her neck. And third, linen bound her waist. No wonder she had been feeling sore.

No one had mentioned her being wounded in their tales of Vrell Sparrow. But this explained why she wore no corset, for it would aggravate a wound in such a location.

Averella clutched the bodice to her chest and stepped up to the candle to inspect the ring.

The wide gold band was topped with the crest of Armonguard—a castle—and engraved with the letters AEH. A ruby glimmered in the castle's entrance. Three smaller rubies decorated each tower on the castle.

Merciful heart! This was King Axel's signet ring.

It was all true. And even if Mother had pledged Averella to this mysterious Crown Prince, Averella would never wear such a token around her neck unless she cared for the man.

Achan Cham. Prince Gidon Hadar.

Not the Gidon Hadar she had always known and loathed. For all this time he had been an impostor.

She must truly care for the real Prince Gidon, then.

She set the ring on the sideboard and unwrapped the linen bandage. An ugly pink gash marred her smooth skin. A crusty brown scab held the wound together like wax. She could not be sure, but it looked like she had been stabbed.

She reeled over this. What kind of danger had she gone through? Hoping her travel pack held some answers, she searched it and found a satchel filled with herbs, jars of salves, linen strips, a lock of dark hair, a man's red sleeve, and a small sword she somehow knew was called Firefox.

But no corset. Even with her wound, why would she travel so far and not bring one for when she was healed? The very idea was scandalous. Perhaps Gren had it in her things.

She pulled the bodice back over her arms and cracked open the door. "Gren? Could you come here a moment?"

A shadow passed between the distant lantern and where Averella stood. The floor creaked. The shadow stopped before the door and the faint light from Averella's candle illuminated Harnu Poe's face.

"Gren went out with Noam to check on the horses."

Averella gasped and pushed the door closed. "Thank you, Master Poe. I shall wait until she returns."

She remained beside the door until the heavy footfalls faded away. Merciful heart! How awkward to have such a man under the same roof. She couldn't very well prance around in front of him without a corset. The very idea!

She could not wait until Gren returned. She pictured Gren's face in her mind. *Gren? Can you hear me?*

My lady? Gren's voice squeaked. *Where are you?*

In my chamber, of course. Has no one spoken to you with bloodvoices before?

I did not think I was capable of such magic.

It is my magic, not yours. This fact seemed obvious to Averella, though she could not guess why. *I need my corset. Do you have it?*

No, my lady. You told me you disliked how tight they were. You said the boning in your gown was corset enough.

I would never!

Gren sighed as if exasperated with Averella. *Maybe not before, but that is what you told me on our journey. Something about having to wear a disguise for so long.*

Heat flushed up Averella's spine and burned her cheeks. *Thank you, Gren. Forgive my tone. I am not myself.*

Not that she had any idea who she was anymore. That she would ride a horse with no corset shocked her to no end, wounded or not. She dug the strips of linen out from her satchel and wrapped her chest as best she could.

She draped the peasant dress over the end of the bed and pulled on her own gown. The soft cotton kissed her skin, a relief from the scratchy wool of the peasant's dress. She could not fasten it herself, as the laces were on the back.

She reached out for Gren again. *Gren? Could you come and help me lace my dress?*

Right away, my lady.

Averella caught sight of the ring on the sideboard. She quickly put the chain back around her neck and dropped the ring inside her bodice. It hung between her gown and bindings, creating an awkward lump over her stomach. She reached into her neckline and tucked the ring and chain inside the linen bindings.

"My lady?" A knock followed Gren's voice.

She jumped and spun around so that her bare back faced away from the door. "Come in."

Once Averella was properly dressed, she went out to the main room of the cottage and sat at the table across from Noam, who was greasing horse tack. Gren sat beside her. Master Poe remained where he was across the room, leaning against the wall, arms folded.

"Are we ready to depart?" Averella asked.

"Should be, my lady," Noam said. "We only need to fill all our water jugs."

"I must warn you," she said. "My mother said that Darkness will play tricks on our minds, cause us to hallucinate. We must keep up conversation to prevent this."

"Told you there wasn't a snake," Noam said to Gren.

She smirked. "Nor were the horses talking to you."

Noam shifted his gaze to Averella. "But, my lady, we only have two horses. Will we travel with the cart?"

"I think that is best. That way we will look like a homeless merchant and his household." Averella looked from face to face. "Master Fox will drive, Master Poe will ride with him on top. Gren and I will sit in the back."

"What if someone stops us?" Noam asked. "What if they check me for the mark of the stray?"

"Do not fear, Master Fox. If we are truly at war, there are more important things for soldiers to worry about than a missing stray."

"Will you tell Achan of our plans?" Gren asked.

The room became very silent. "I see no reason to. My mother is aware."

"He would want to know," Gren said.

Averella searched for some excuse. Any excuse. "I am not certain I can message the prince."

Gren shot her a daring look. "You're not willing to try?"

"Not until my memory returns. And if it does not, well, too much communication would only complicate matters."

Gren huffed a sigh. "Achan is the best of men."

"I am sure he is honorable and just and good in every way. But I have no memory of him, Gren, except of our time spent in the Veil. I simply need more time."

The wagon creaked over the dirt road, south, through Darkness, toward Mahanaim. Gren and Noam sang a song.

Hear the pretty maiden sing,
    Hair and ribbons all flowing.
She can take my heart away,
    By her side I long to stay.

Averella did not know why, but this song made her uncomfortable. She tried to block out the words by focusing on their destination. If they could get inside Mahanaim . . .

A sour smell grew. An animal must have died nearby. She covered her nose with her hand and stared into the black surroundings. Mahanaim sat on a maze of stagnant canals, she knew, but it would be days before they reached the city.

Water lapped at the sides of the wagon. How could there be water beside the wagon when she could not hear the horses wading through it?

The wagon jolted underneath her. She gripped the side. A deafening howl penetrated the night. Something rammed the side of the wagon. Water splashed into the wagon bed, drenching Averella in cold, slimy water.

She yelped and drew back from the edge of the wagon. "What is happening, Master Fox?"

But Noam was not there. No one was. In fact, Averella no longer sat in the wagon at all. She lay alone on the bottom of a small animal-skin boat.

The keening howl ripped through the Darkness again. Averella pressed her hands over her ears. The boat rocked, hit something solid. A creature jumped on her.

She screamed and slapped the creature. It was wet and furry and—

"My lady, please! Ah!"

Averella stilled at the sound of Harnu's voice. Pale torchlight illuminated the wagon. No boat.

Harnu held Averella on his lap, cradling her like a child, rocking back and forth. His dark eyebrows sank low over his eyes. "Are you well, my lady?"

Averella squirmed off his lap and onto the wood floor of the wagon. Her heart was still beating so fast that it thudded in her ears. "I am fine, Master Poe. I—" She took a deep breath to clear her thoughts. "I had not experienced a vision of Darkness yet. It surprised me. I believed we were being attacked by a water beast."

Harnu pushed to his feet and climbed back onto the driver's seat. "Choose a song we all know, Noam."

Averella shivered, her heart still beating faster than normal. "What songs do *you* know, Master Poe?"

He grunted. "I rarely went to the Corner."

"Look! Lights!" Gren pointed to the right where a dozen torchlights glittered to the southwest. "Let's see who it is."

"No," Averella said. "We should steer clear. If they are unfriendly, we would not know until it was too late to flee."

"But what if they are friendly?" Gren asked.

"We cannot take that risk. We should stay on the road. The road we can trust."

"Whatever you say, my lady," Noam said.

Averella slouched against the side of the wagon. What did she know about anything? Why should she be in charge? She could be wrong about the lights. Maybe they were friendly people. People who could help them free Bran.

More bizarre thoughts assailed Averella throughout the day—or was it night?—but she was able to stop them before they went too far. She lay down in the back of the wagon, eyes drooping heavily. She should message Mother and inquire as to what would happen when she fell asleep. But before she could form the connection, her mind drifted.

Pain shot through her skull. She cowered in a briarberry bush, clutching her temples. The soldier was close, debilitating her with the pressure of his untamed bloodvoice.

She concentrated on closing her mind, something she had never needed to do simply to keep from experiencing pain. The pressure eased some, and she crawled to the top of the ridge and peeked over.

Shrouded in fog, a Kingsguard soldier fought two Poroo in a small clearing, his movements quick but careful.

She had been right. The gifted one was a soldier. Younger than she had expected, but no mere boy. He was tall, strong, and wounded. Plum bruises covered his handsome face. His dark, wet hair and soggy Kingsguard cape whipped about as he swung his sword. Studded jewels on the ivory crossguard caught her eye. He must be a noble to wield such a weapon, yet she had never seen him at court.

Movement to the far left turned her head. Prince Gidon! The heir to the throne of Er'Rets leaned against an allown tree, watching the soldier fight.

Where were his distinguished guards? The mighty Shield? And why was His Highness just standing there? He was quite gifted with the sword, or so his reputation said. He could be helping the soldier fight off the Poroo.

She snorted. Our new and noble, lazy king.

A third Poroo charged up behind the soldier.

Look out! *She yelled to his mind.*

Scratch? *The soldier spun around just in time to parry the jab of a spear. He scurried back in the pine needles, holding his sword up to his attackers. "If you're not going to help, Your Highness," the soldier said to the prince, "at least climb the tree. I'd hate for you to be killed. Your death would secure my own."*

Her brows shot up at his snide tone. Prince Gidon only smirked. One of the Poroo charged. The soldier waited until the last moment before dodging and swinging his blade into the creature's side. The soldier stiffened and the Poroo fell at his feet.

She felt his horror of having killed. He swallowed and exhaled before wrenching his blade free with a growl. His grey eyes flashed to the other two Poroo. He steeled himself and stepped forward.

He could do this.

Averella awoke, chilled by the sweat soaking her skin. She sat up, simply breathing until her heart fell into a steady rhythm. Dreams of Darkness felt so real, yet she had a feeling this last one had been more than a dream. A memory. Of how she came to meet the man known as Achan Cham. He had served the false Prince Gidon, the man everyone now called Esek, who had been a pretender to the throne for thirteen years. And Esek had left the real prince to die.

But Vrell Sparrow had saved him, removed arrows from his flesh, packed his wounds with spider's webs and yarrow.

Averella frowned. What in all Er'Rets was yarrow?

Her mind tumbled through the scenes again. The real prince bore the mark of the stray on his shoulder, and his back carried more scars than she could ever imagine.

According to Gren, Averella had transported him to Mahanaim, tended his wounds and sat with him in his dungeon cell, nursing him back to health. Until the Great Whitewolf and his men had freed him. She had been torn over his departure from prison, missed his company.

And that was all Averella could remember.

She shook her head. Missing his company was not love. She pitied him for what Lord Nathak had done and for the horrible life he'd been forced to live. But pity and compassion were not love. Not romantic love, anyway.

Averella's ears itched. She now knew this was a sign that someone was about to message with their bloodvoice.

Achan Cham.

Oh dear. Averella had hoped a few days might pass before he spoke to her again. If only she remembered more.

Yes, Your Highness?

Sparrow! How do you fare? Has your memory returned? I have been praying that Arman would restore it.

I am well, thank you. I have remembered only a small flash.

That's a good sign, then, don't you think? If you've remembered some, surely you'll remember more.

Perhaps, though I do not expect it to happen soon. I have nearly a year's-worth of memories to restore.

They'll come. Have you decided what to do? Shall I send someone for you?

We are going to Mahanaim to free Master Rennan, Sir Rigil, and Sir Jax. We travel south along the King's Road.

Mahanaim! It's not safe. Esek's soldiers patrol all of the King's Road. Allow me to send men to escort you here.

Do not worry, Your Highness. Master Poe and Master Fox are with us. We travel under the guise of a merchant and his wife and their two servants fleeing Darkness.

Silence stretched on for a long moment before the prince said, *Who is married to whom?*

I am posing as Master Poe's wife. Gren is—

Why him?

Master Poe is much more confident to pose as a merchant. And I am the logical choice over Gren.

I don't like this, Sparrow. It sounds dangerous and involves Harnu. I should come for you myself.

Gren told me of your unpleasant history with Master Poe. I am sorry for that. But I assure you, Master Poe is no longer a brute. And without him we would surely—

Fine, Sparrow. Just take care. I'll feel better once you are in camp with me again.

Averella winced. *Your Highness, forgive me if I sound presumptive, but I must make myself clear. I have gleaned much from those around me about what transpired between us. I understand we did not part on good terms.*

That was my fault. I—

Please allow me to finish. Without my memories of our time together, I think it would be best, for now, if we officially parted ways. You have plenty to concern yourself with, upcoming war and all. And I am responsible for Gren. Perhaps later, should my memory return, we might discuss how to proceed. I do not wish to be cruel, but my reputation has already been tainted due to my falsehoods. For that I apologize. Let us have no more communication for now. We shall each do our duty to Arman and Er'Rets. And later, should Arman will it, we can speak again. What say you?

What say I? Sparrow, I cannot stomach your formal tirades. And now you no longer wish to communicate? Am I really that horrible of a conversationalist?

Of course not, Your Highness. Bother. He had taken her words more harshly than she had meant them. *But in light of our past . . . it would be wise to tread carefully. I cannot pretend to care for you when I do not recall ever doing so, especially since you do not know who I really am. And I do not wish to mislead you in hoping my feelings may rekindle. For at the moment, I have no feelings for you at all.*

I see. Very well, then, Miss Sparrow. Forgive me for trying to save your life. From now on, you are on your own.

Your Highness, please do not be cross. I am simply trying to exp—

But Prince Gidon had closed the connection.

Averella did not know why, but his silence brought tears to her eyes.

17

Arman, help Sparrow remember everything. Now.

Achan should be paying attention to Sir Gavin explain the plan to seize the eastern Reshon Gate, but Sparrow's rejection still throbbed like a hornet's sting.

He sat at the table in the meeting tent with the generals and his advisors. They had stopped on a coastal prairie just west of the Lebab Inlet. The smell of the sea reminded him of home. Sitna, anyway. And it felt good to be in Light again, no matter what his mood.

How foolish to dwell on Sparrow. If she had forgotten their entire friendship, perhaps that was best. Full recollection would only remind her why she had rejected him the first time, and she'd probably feel the need to reject him again. He didn't think he could take that a second time.

Do what you must, Arman. Still, I pray for what I want. And I want Sparrow to remember.

"I need to scout out the gate, see if Esek has men there and how many," Sir Gavin said. "Inko, Sir Eagan, and Captain Demry will accompany me."

"And me?" Achan asked.

"You remain here," Sir Gavin said. "I'll message you if there's something you need to see."

Figured. The moment Achan needed to keep his mind busy, he had nothing to do. "Why ride to the gate, Sir Gavin? Scouting the location through the Veil would save time."

"It's no longer safe for this old man to enter the Veil," Sir Gavin said. "Shamayim's pull is too great for my bloodvoice to resist. I could send Sir Eagan, but I'm the general of this army and must see for myself what we're up against."

The meeting ended and the men filed outdoors. Only Achan and Sir Eagan remained at the table. Achan had no intention of moving. There was no place to go, anyway, but to be mobbed by soldiers wishing to greet him.

"Your Highness, may I speak with you a moment?"

Achan regarded Sir Eagan's pale face. "Of course."

Sir Eagan cleared his throat. "There is a situation with your betrothal to Lady Averella Amal."

An invisible wave rushed into Achan's stomach and tossed it around. "Oh?"

"Duchess Amal messaged me. She felt the matter could not wait for a messenger who might be intercepted." Sir Eagan shifted in his chair. Achan had never seen him so uncomfortable. "First and foremost, a confession. Lady Averella was unaware until recently that I am her father."

The room seemed suddenly ten times smaller. Achan choked on a breath, yet felt a strange, thrilling calm. Before he could speak, Sir Eagan continued.

"I never expected to leave Ice Island, so I figured she was better off not knowing. But when I returned to Carmine and saw Lady Nitsa, well, things changed. Lady Averella has now learned the truth."

Sir Eagan pounded his fist into his palm. "She was understandably shocked and angry. But she has taken it further. As a result of this news, she has renounced her inheritance and her claim to Carm. Which brings me to the part that concerns you, Your Highness."

Achan already understood. If Lady Averella had renounced her inheritance . . . "It's Duchess Amal's business to appoint her heir. The details of Lady Averella's birth don't matter to me. You must know that."

"That is very generous, Your Highness, but only part of the problem. Lady Averella . . . well . . . she refuses to marry you."

Achan could only stare, numb.

"Naturally, Duchess Amal is extremely apologetic. On one hand, this means I might, someday, claim my daughter publicly. On the other hand . . ."

"The duchess can no longer fulfill her side of our bargain."

"Correct. To compensate for this mishap, she offers you Lady Gypsum, who is now heir to Carm Duchy."

"*Lady Gypsum?*" That little girl?

"Yes. But the duchess wishes you to know that she in no way expects you to accept this offer. She makes the offer freely, with Lady Gyspum's consent, but understands if you would like to make other plans."

"Me?" Achan could hardly dare think it.

"Should you decide to choose your own bride, you still have Carm Duchy's full support in your campaign."

"I see." Achan sat very still, though inside he danced.

"Forgive me for deceiving you, Your Highness. All Er'Rets believed Lady Averella to be Duke Amal's daughter. It was not my place to speak until Nitsa chose to." Sir Eagan blew out a long breath. "Now you know why I said I would not change my past. Nitsa and I suffered great consequences for our choices. Yet a lovely young woman breathes because of it. Only Arman can reverse such sorrow. My one regret now is how Lady Averella's anger may affect you."

"Oh." Achan tried to sound sorry to be set free. "Don't burden yourself, Sir Eagan. And please inform Duchess Amal that I am not angry, or saddened, even. I never met Lady Averella, so I feel no great loss toward her."

Sir Eagan lowered his gaze to the table. "You are very kind, Your Highness."

"What will Sir Caleb say about all this? Will he insist I marry Lady Gypsum?"

"I have already spoken to him and the others."

Achan could read nothing from Sir Eagan's impassive expression. "Please, Sir Eagan, what did they say?"

Sir Eagan chuckled. "The point of your betrothal to Lady Averella was to secure an army. You have that army. We think it wise that you continue to wear Lady Averella's sleeve until the throne is won. But we leave the choice of your bride up to you. No matter her station. You need only message Duchess Amal to officially break the betrothal. After that, you are free. We only ask that you wait until after the war to take your bride. Is that acceptable to you, Your Highness?"

Achan wanted to laugh. "Indeed. Very acceptable."

Sir Eagan smiled, his round cheeks balled up. "I suspected as much."

• • •

When Achan exited the meeting tent, the waves surging inside his gut threatened to knock him down. Sir Eagan must have been manipulating his emotions to keep him calm. Achan hadn't even realized the situation had upset him until now.

He was free. Truly free.

So why should he care about Lady Averella? A sting to his ego, perhaps? To be rejected . . . again. Aw, who cared? He needed to tell Sparrow! He almost barged right in to her mind to tell her the news until he remembered their last conversation. Best wait a bit.

Movement behind him caused him to turn. Cortland and Achan's dark-skinned cousin followed close behind. Achan searched his memory but forgot his cousin's name. Shung must be off duty. Perhaps Lady Gali was as well?

Achan nodded to the men and started for his tent, stopping to return greetings to a few dozen soldiers along the way. The sun had nearly set. Seagulls circled overhead, dipping down to swipe food, no doubt. Achan was surprised Matthias hadn't brought his dinner to the meeting.

He found the boy waiting inside Achan's tent. "Are you hungry, sir?"

"Very." Achan unlaced his doublet while Matthias laid out his meal at the table.

Achan shrugged out of his doublet and tossed it on the bed. He untucked the waist of his tunic and shook it out, letting a cool draft of night air up his shirt. Much better.

While Matthias filled a plate, Achan sat on the edge of his bed to remove his boots. But when he leaned over, his necklace swung into his view, which brought Sparrow to mind again. Though he knew better, he sent her a knock.

Yes, Your Highness? Her cold tone did not bode well.

He suddenly felt like a fool, but pressed on, giddy with his newfound freedom. *I thought you should know I'm no longer betrothed to Lady Averella.*

Is that so? Her voice somehow grew colder.

Achan sent his next words with a bit of sarcasm, the way he and Sparrow used to joke. *Turns out she's not actually Duke Amal's daughter. What do you think of that?*

Shocking.

It is, isn't it? When no answer came, he said, *What's wrong, Sparrow?*

Why are you telling me this?

I thought that . . . well . . . I just thought—

That it would change things between us? Your Highness, to my mind, you are nothing more than a man I met in the Veil. I tried to make it clear that—

I only wanted to say that now we can—

—I cannot continue in this manner. I do not wish to be cruel, but if you insist on messaging me for intimate conversations, I will be forced to ignore you entirely.

A stone grew in the place where Achan's heart had recently stopped bleeding. *Very well, Miss Sparrow. Good evening.* Achan broke the connection.

Matthias stood beside the table, a dinner of fish and potatoes laid out. "It's ready, sir."

Achan was no longer hungry. *Shung, where are you?*

A long moment passed before Shung answered. *Visiting Lady Gali at the bonfire. Should Shung return?*

Pig snout. *No, Shung. I just wondered where you were, that's all. I'll see you later. Have fun.*

Achan's stomach clenched, jealous of Shung's joy. Why did things happen this way? If only the knights had given him leave to choose his own bride before Mitspah.

Everything had started going badly in Mitspah.

Achan stood, walked to the table, glared at his meal. Perhaps if he wandered by the bonfire he could strike up a conversation with Shung and Lady Gali.

"I'll be back in a moment, Matthias." Achan strode from the tent. Cortland and Achan's cousin jogged to keep up. Achan ignored the occasional well-wishing soldier, each step increasing his anger. Typical of Sparrow to hide from the unknown. Finally, here was his chance to mend things—to make promises she thought he could never make—and she believed him a stranger.

The bonfire raged in a clearing inside the wagon circle. He spotted Shung and Lady Gali right away, dancing merrily, black braids whipping the air, oblivious to everything around them.

Soldiers stood in clusters, most holding mugs of mead. Achan narrowed his gaze to a wagon on the other side of the bonfire where Kurtz sat with a group of women. Cole sat crosslegged on the ground, his boyish freckled face gazing at Kurtz as if the man were Moul Rog the Great.

Achan crossed to the wagon and gripped Kurtz by the shoulder. "Did not Sir Gavin give orders against spirits while we are engaged in war?"

"Oh, hello, Pacey. How are you this fine evening, eh?"

Achan glanced at Cole, then to his guards, and back to Kurtz. "Do not change the subject. Spirits? Sir Gavin? War?"

"Worked that out, we have. No more than a hundred can drink each night, which leaves most the men on guard, eh?"

Achan frowned. "Yet *you* seem to be indulging every night. Do you never take a turn on guard?"

Kurtz grinned. "Someone has to organize it all, he does. Besides, I'm on your personal guard."

Typical Kurtz. "I see. Still, it seems dangerous, don't you think? If we were to be attacked . . ."

"Bah! The bottle *calms* you, Pacey. I'll likely fight better than anyone, if it comes to that, eh? Besides, many aren't drinking. Cole, here, is afraid of it. And Sir Shung won't touch the drink. Just wants to dance with his lass. That's all most the men want. A little friendly company. Plus, Sir Gavin's not here tonight. Rode off with his scouts to see about something or other. Tonight's the night, Pacey." Kurtz passed him a bottle. "Think about it, eh?"

Achan accepted the bottle from Kurtz, muddled by the man's reasoning. It was true: all Achan wanted was a little company. To cross swords with Shung or wrestle out his anger.

Instead he walked toward the sea, flanked by Cortland and Achan's cousin from Nesos. The sunset dusted the prairie grasses in gold. The air smelled salty and cool in his nose and mouth. He swung the bottle by the neck, whipping the tall grass aside as he made his way to the beach.

The prairie grass gave way to sand, sloping down a small hill to the surf. Achan sat in the dry sand, staring at the glassy sea, the sun sinking into the water like a yolk into a simmering pot.

His gut festered. He wanted to rant at Arman about his misfortune, but he knew what Arman would say, *if* He bothered to answer. Achan didn't want to hear it. He wanted things to go his way for once. It was selfish, sure, but he didn't care.

He ripped Averella's sleeve off his arm and threw it. The lightweight fabric landed at his feet, the maroon glistening in the setting sun.

He brought the bottle to his mouth, worked the cork free with his teeth, and spat it on the ground. He smelled the contents, expecting the briny smell of mead, but the tangy combination of currants and cedar filled his nostrils.

Had Kurtz meant to give him wine? Achan had wine with dinner most nights, so it wouldn't matter to drink some now. He took a sip. Robust sweetness filled his mouth. He swished his tongue around, tasting the flavor as long as it would linger. Blazes, that was good. Much better than what Lord Eli had served in Mirrorstone.

Yet when the taste faded, the wine left his mouth dryer than before. So he took a longer drink and wished he had some food. The wine seemed to point out just how hungry he was. He should go back to his tent and eat.

Instead he took another drink.

The waves lapped against the shore, simmering like butter in a skillet. He dug the heels of his boots into the sand, extending his legs and making two deep trenches. He took another drink then stood and walked onto the smooth, wet sand. The tide slid in again, and he let it wash over his boots. As the water drew away, it pulled the sand from under his heels. He stopped and watched it erode, amazed at the power water had over dirt.

Arman had that kind of power over men. The power to give and take away. Dying for any cause of Arman's would be worth it. Achan recalled the intense pleasure the pull of Shamayim had brought. He would not be unhappy to return to that place. That much he knew.

Yet it seemed Arman wanted him here for now. So here, in Er'Rets, Achan must stay.

Now Sparrow, she had that same water-over-sand pull on Achan. He did not know how or when it had happened, but she affected him. Too much. The things she said. How she said them. The way she looked at him. The way she smelled. He tried to stop thinking about her, but that decision only made her ever more present in his mind. Sparrow and her stubborn ways. Even without her memory.

He took a long swallow.

He'd had enough of this weakness, this power Sparrow had over him. Was he man or boy? He was a man—a prince. Soon to be king. He needed to forget about Vrell Sparrow. There were plenty of women who would covet his attention. And now he was free to choose any of them. He could have his pick of the most beautiful women in the world.

His stomach clenched at that idea, for that was why Sparrow had claimed to be afraid to love him—back when she'd had her memory. That as king he would be surrounded by women seeking his attentions. He laughed to himself, alone on the beach but for his two Kingsguard shadows.

"Yes, Sparrow, I can hardly keep the women away."

He snorted, then flubbed out a long breath through his lips. The idea of throngs of women trying to turn his head. He laughed, then sobered when he caught sight of his guardsmen standing where the grassy prairie met the sand.

Achan suddenly wanted to see Sparrow's thoughts. Plant memories, perhaps? Make her remember him. The desire only made him take another drink.

The tide swept out, and Achan stumbled as the sand melted under his heels. He trudged up the hill. Dry sand stuck to his boots. He stomped to shake it free.

A burst of laughter pulled his attention back to the orange glow of the bonfire. Shadows of dancers circled over the tops of the tents. The fiddle hummed, voices chorused, and the clapping and laughter tugged at his heart.

He wanted to laugh too. So he did. Long and hard, like a madman. His guards followed a few paces behind. Achan glanced back every few steps, wondering what they thought of the laughing prince. The question made him snicker.

Well, why couldn't the Crown Prince have fun? Why must he always be alone in his tent or alone on the beach or alone with his advisors or shadows or servants?

"Bah." He smiled at the sound of his voice imitating Kurtz's favorite word. He said it again, louder this time, "Bah!" and laughed. His smile lingered. Head tingling, he set off for the reveling.

He stopped between two tents at the edge of the clearing. Over three dozen couples danced around the bonfire now. And the women were not all Berlanders. There were peasants in the throng. How had they gotten into camp? Was that safe? What if they were working for Esek? Wasn't someone going to check?

Achan furrowed his brow, wondering how anyone might prove such a thing about a woman.

A couple whirled past him. The woman's flowery smell brought Sparrow's face to mind. He smiled at the pleasing aroma, then spotted Shung and Lady Gali swaying in the crowd. Lady Gali laughed at something Shung said and tugged on one of Shung's fat braids.

Achan's smile faded. He squeezed the neck of the wine bottle. Why was it everyone could do as they pleased but him? Why could he not have fun? Forget the fear of the pending battle? Wash his cares away with a bottle of mead? Many men lost their sanity from the bottle. And he was safe here, was he not? He had two guards at his back, making sure of it, and an entire army of his own around him. He could think of no better time for such an experience. He tipped the wine bottle up to his lips.

Only a sip dribbled out.

Could he have drunk the whole thing? Impossible. Kurtz must have given him a half-empty bottle.

He dropped it and threaded his way through the dancers toward where Kurtz sat on the end of the wagon with a peasant girl on his lap. If anyone had a fresh bottle of wine, it would be Kurtz.

"Your Highness!" someone said.

"It's the prince!"

A chorus of greetings rang out. The music segued into "The Pawn Our King." Another man spoke to Achan, but Achan ignored him and pushed through the crowd.

He bumped into a pair of dancers. "Sorry."

"Not at all, Your Highness."

Another couple plowed by, knocking into Achan's sore shoulder. It hardly hurt anymore, but the contact aggravated the wound and threw him off balance. He spun halfway around, lost his footing, and fell onto the trampled grass. His shoulder stung, yet he couldn't keep from laughing. His guardsmen rushed up on either side and helped him stand.

"I'm so sorry!" someone said. "Is he all right?"

Cortland tugged Achan away from the crowd. "Your Highness, let's get you back to your tent."

Achan pulled his arm from Cortland's grip and rolled his shoulder, easing away the soreness. "I'm fine."

Sir Gavin Lukos.

Achan cocked his head and listened. A woman's high-pitched giggle turned his gaze back to the wagon. Kurtz whispered in the peasant woman's ear. She giggled again, drawing out her laugh as if she were tired of laughing yet couldn't get enough of it. Kurtz kissed her neck, her lips.

The woman's eyes met Achan's. He stared, heart thudding in his ears. She whispered to Kurtz.

"Eh?" Kurtz pushed the woman off his lap and jumped off the wagon. "Heh-hay! Pacey! You came back!" He waved Achan over. "How's my favorite oarsman?"

Achan's ears tickled. *Sir Gavin Lukos.*

Achan grinned, remembering the time he and Kurtz had visited a tavern in Tsaftown. See? Kurtz knew how to have fun. "Your favorite oarsman is thirsty."

Kurtz's eyes lit up. "Ahh . . ." He threw an arm over Achan's shoulders and steered him back to the wagon. "The question is, thirsty for what?"

Achan's gaze roamed the wagon, searching the bottles for more wine, but his sights snagged on a set of dark brown eyes.

Sir Gavin Lukos.

Achan shook away the buzzing in his head. He blinked at the girl sitting in the back of Kurtz's wagon. She was Lady Tara, yet she was not, for Tara's eyes were blue. But this maiden had the same golden ringlets and sly smile that had weakened Achan's knees.

"Challa, would you like to dance with the prince?" Kurtz lowered his voice. "And if you don't mind my saying so, Your Highness, you look like you could use a dance."

Achan stared at the girl. "Yes, I think so too."

Challa crawled to the end of the wagon, an unladylike thing to do, for the position bared more flesh of her neckline than Sparrow would ever find appropriate.

Achan averted his eyes, then cursed himself for thinking of Sparrow again. Would she haunt him forever?

"Help me down, Yer Highness?"

The uncultured edge to Challa's voice curled Achan's lips into a small smile. She sat on the end of the wagon, kicking her bare feet and holding out both hands. He took them and tugged her forward. She jumped off the wagon and into his arms.

She did that on purpose.

Sparrow again. The words she'd said when Lady Jaira had fallen against Achan back in Mirrorstone.

Get out of my head, Sparrow, Achan told himself.

He stepped back from Challa and bowed.

She tipped her head back and laughed. "Such a gentleman, yeh are. No one's ever bowed to me before."

"A crime, my lady, for you look like a noblewoman I know."

Challa giggled. "A noblewoman? Me?"

"Aye." Achan bowed again, delighted by her laughter. "My lady Challa, may I request the honor of a dance?"

"Well, I already said I'd dance, didn't I?"

Achan grabbed her hand and waist, and they joined the crowd of dancers. They danced a long while, stopped for a drink, and danced some more. The crowd seemed delighted by Achan's presence, and he reveled in their unabashed attention. Then somehow—though Achan could not remember when it happened or whose idea it had been—he and Challa ended up lying on their stomachs underneath Kurtz's wagon, watching the dancers from the waist down and trying to guess who was who.

"That's Shung and Lady Gali, for I'd recognize those charmice tails anywhere," Achan said. "And there is Kurtz."

"No, Yer Highness, Kurtz has brown boots, not black. He's there." Challa pointed to the other side of the clearing.

Achan squinted. Everything blurred together. "The torches must be burning low, Lady Challa, for I can hardly see your hand let alone where you're pointing."

She waved her hand in front of his face.

He laughed. "Now *that* I see."

Challa set her hand against his cheek and turned his face away from the dancers. The torchlight reflected in her eyes like sparks from a firesteel. And suddenly she was kissing him, hungrily, like he was food and she hadn't eaten in days.

He gasped for breaths between kisses, surprised by her affection, wondering if he should say something, but not wanting her to stop. She slid her hand up his tunic and clawed at his back like a baby cham bear.

Achan heard himself whimper, sensed the barrage of words Sir Caleb might say, but kept all rational thought at bay, remaining firmly in the fog thrilling his senses.

Challa pushed him to his back and crawled on top, nearly bumping her head on the bottom of the wagon. Dried grass pricked the back of his neck, but she kissed him again, and he forgot the irritation. Her kisses grew more intense.

A distant song broke through the fog. A woman's voice, growing nearer. Familiar tune. Familiar lyrics. Achan held his breath, frozen like a rabbit that sensed a predator. Challa moved her kisses to his neck.

" . . . apart. Whenever we're apart. Though I am nothing to you, I love—"

"Fool song knows nothing." Shung's voice was a low growl. "Gali is Shung's moon, stars. Shung's everything."

"Aww. But still . . ." And Lady Gali finished the song. "I love you. How can I make it known, that I love you?"

Her voice . . . It raked over Achan like an icy wind.

He recalled Sir Eagan's words from his manhood ceremony. *"It is a man's duty to protect a lady's honor."*

And Sir Caleb's said during one of many lectures, *"It's the very things a man never intends to do that sneak up and ensnare him."*

Achan gripped Challa's shoulders and pushed her off him. "Forgive me, Challa. You are worth more than this."

"You want to pay me more?"

Achan blinked, squinting to see her face in the darkness under the wagon. "Pay you?"

"Well, Kurtz, he already paid me plenty of—"

Achan sat up and bashed his head against the bottom of the wagon. He groaned through the pain and crawled out from under the wagon's edge on his knees and one hand, the other hand clutching his head. He stood, and his vision swam in a blurry haze. He grabbed the wagon box to steady himself. When the dizzy spell passed, he crouched down and found Challa giggling.

"Are yeh all right, Yer Highness?"

Achan spoke softly, hoping to ease the pressure in his head. "I mean to say . . . that I am drunk on wine and pain. It was wrong of me to take advantage of you."

"Oh, I don't mind, Yer Highness."

She didn't mind? "You should, Challa." Shouldn't she?

Not his problem. He stumbled away. Movement behind him caused him to turn, ready to apologize to Challa again if need be, but it was only his Kingsguard shadows. Both men averted their eyes when Achan looked their way. They had been standing nearby the whole night, he had no doubt.

He turned, cheeks blazing, and trudged out of the clearing. The path ahead blurred the tents together. He tripped over a guy line and barely caught his balance before his shadows swooped in to coddle him again.

"I'm fine!" He held out his hands to prove it and give his balance time to return. He stepped slowly along the path. Every movement sent pangs of nausea through his stomach.

"Your Highness! Wait!" Kurtz's voice, behind him.

Achan gritted his teeth, angry at Kurtz, angrier still at himself.

Kurtz wrapped an arm around Achan and pulled his head into the crook of his arm. "What happened, Pacey? Of all the women I've met tonight, Challa is by far the most beautiful. Did she do something wrong?"

"You paid her to dance with me."

Kurtz rubbed his hand in Achan's hair. "Aww, don't take it that way, eh? We paid the lot of them to come. And Challa would have danced with you on her own, she would. Don't you go doubting that, eh? Why not take her with us as your concubine? She can travel with you in your wagon. Sleep in your tent. And once you reside in the palace at Armonguard, you can give her a room in a different part of the castle from your wife." Kurtz slapped the flat of his hand against Achan's stomach and lowered his voice. "It's always best to keep them apart from one another, it is."

Concubine? Achan's head throbbed. "I would never destroy her life by doing such a thing."

Kurtz raised both eyebrows. "She's a prostitute, Your Highness. If she became your concubine you'd be *improving* her life, eh?"

The breath rushed from Achan's lungs. "How old is she? Surely no more than sixteen years?"

"I know better than to ask a woman her age." Kurtz clapped him on the back. "You'd be doing her a favor to take her from here. Imagine, a peasant prostitute moves into the Armonguard palace. Minstrels would write songs about her."

"I—" Unwelcome thoughts of Challa's smile filled Achan's mind. "No, Kurtz. That is not how Arman would have me live—or Challa—or my queen."

Whoever she may be.

"Bah! Foolhardy nonsense. Your father had many concubines, he did."

Achan wrinkled his nose. "No." King Axel had loved his queen ever since he knew boys and girls were different. Sir Gavin had said so.

"Eh . . . forgive me, Your Highness, but the king had dozens, he did. Mistresses too. Saw it with my own eyes more times than I can count. There's no harm in it, eh? All men of power have the right, they do."

A wave of nausea peaked in Achan's stomach. He took a deep breath and pulled away. "Good evening, Kurtz." He trudged through the camp, head pounding as if something inside were trying to push its way out.

Achan had painted a vivid history of his parents' relationship in his mind. But it was based on songs sung by minstrels and snippets of stories from the knights. He pawed through his memories, seeking some hint he may have forgotten. Surely Kurtz was mistaken.

Achan ducked into his tent, got tangled in the drape under the valance, and beat it away. His shoulder struck the edge of the doorway, shaking the entire structure. He stumbled inside. A lone candle burned. Achan squinted in the low light, trying to make out the best path to his bed.

"Your Highness." Sir Caleb's voice came from somewhere nearby. "I was just about to message you."

Achan wanted—no, needed—to lie down. He spotted a large patch of blue to his left and stumbled toward it. His feet carried him slightly askew. He focused on the blue blankets and his course veered true.

"Where have you been?" Sir Caleb's voice spun around him, coming from everywhere at once. "Have you been drinking?"

Achan turned toward the candlelight. His eyes stung. He could barely make out Sir Caleb, sitting at the table. "A bit."

Sir Caleb stood and snapped his fingers. "Dismissed."

Achan's heart leapt at the sound. "Dismissed from what?" Footsteps scraped over dirt behind Achan. He turned to see his guardsmen trudge away. "Oh, them." He scowled. "What *is* my cousin's name? I can't remember."

"Manu Pitney." Sir Caleb motioned Achan toward him.

Achan walked that direction and banged his shin against something solid. "Pig snout." He cowered and rubbed his leg. In front of him, the chaise lounge came into view.

"Sit," Sir Caleb said.

Achan lowered himself down slowly, careful not to jar his aching head. He closed his eyes, bracing himself for Sir Caleb's lecture.

"You smell . . . pretty."

And there it was. A hint of chastisement in tone. Achan sighed, not unhappy to have the subject broached. For he wanted answers of his own. "Kurtz said . . ." Achan lowered his voice. "He said my father kept concubines." He opened his eyes, concentrating to focus on Sir Caleb's expression.

Sir Caleb pursed his lips then sighed. "If King Axel had been present the night of your manhood ceremony, I've no doubt he would have confessed that very thing."

Achan wilted. "But I thought . . . He and my mother . . ."

"He loved your mother very much."

"Then why—?"

"Certain things snare a man. Women. Power. The pipe. Anger. Wine." He raised an eyebrow. "Don't judge your father on his mistakes alone. For Arman conquered his snares. From the moment of your birth your father never paid mind to any woman but your mother. Arman changed him."

What did *that* mean? For Achan knew Arman, and he had nearly lost himself in Challa's embrace. Was he not changed? "There was a girl. Kurtz introduced us. I didn't know she was a prostitute."

Sir Caleb nodded as if he'd been expecting this confession. "Would you have brought her back here?"

Achan's face flamed, but he could only stare. His lips felt dry, his tongue and throat too. His stomach roiled.

Sir Caleb chuckled. "I would have made it a merry trio. We could have played dice."

"Do not jest. I . . . I don't . . . I'm afraid."

"Of?"

"Toros said, what mastered the father will tempt the son. I never realized . . ."

"So you have been tempted. Did you fall to it?"

"No." Achan ran his hands over his head. "No. I apologized. I didn't know that Kurtz had paid— I'm sorry, Sir Caleb. I know you said to treat women with—"

"Shh. You are forgiven." A long moment of silence passed. "Is there something else?"

"I never felt like that. So lost in . . . I wanted so bad to just . . ." He let his head fall back against the chaise lounge. There was no other way to put it. "I had no intention of stopping her."

"Why did you?"

"Sparrow." He shrugged. "Or maybe it was Arman. Or the things you told me. Or all of it together." Achan sighed. "I cannot say, exactly. But I don't trust myself." For what if Kurtz threw another pretty woman into his arms?

"Nor should you."

"Will you always be sitting in my bedchamber?"

Sir Caleb laughed. "Once we are at Armonguard, I will likely never be sitting in your bedchamber. In times of war, however . . ." He crouched before the long chair and slapped a hand on Achan's shoulder.

"Listen well," he said. "If you wish to break your vows to Arman and your wife, you will do it. But it takes more than wishing to keep those vows. It takes strength and character and determination, all qualities you have in great measure. Do not despair, Achan. You are not a weak man. But temptation will always be there. And when you are tempted, resist, flee from it, refocus your thoughts. Find your strength in Arman. Only by Arman's strength can you prevail."

Achan released a long, cleansing breath. It felt like he hadn't breathed since he had talked to Sparrow.

Please, Arman. Help her to remember me. I need her.

YOU NEED ME.

Achan closed his eyes. *Aye, Arman. I need You.*

Achan woke to blinding pain.

He must be dying. Esek must've hidden in his tent, stabbed a blade through his skull while he'd been sleeping.

The gorbellied coward.

Achan opened his eyes, which made the pain worse. He ran his hands over the sides of his head and found no knife.

A sound made him turn to the other side. Matthias stood at his bed, eyes wide.

"Morning, Matthias," Achan mumbled.

"You've got new wounds, sir."

Achan lifted his head and winced. "What?"

"On your back." Matthias pointed. "Cat scratches."

Achan's mind swirled. A cat? He sat up and twisted around, trying to see what Matthias was on about. He could barely see the end of a pink welt that curled around his side halfway between his arm pit and his waist.

What in all Er'Rets?

"That *cat* got you pretty good, Your Highness. Best be careful around them in the future." Sir Caleb was sitting at the table, poring over scrolls.

Achan rubbed his eyes and squinted at Sir Caleb. "Have you been sitting there all night?"

"No. For night has gone, as has the new morning and most of the new day."

Scenes from the previous night flashed through Achan's memory. Challa. She had scratched him. He wilted under the force of his own stupidity. Praise Arman for new mornings.

Matthias still stood at Achan's bedside, awestruck. "Was it a chatul cat, sir? Did you kill it?"

"Huh?" Achan's tongue felt like a wood chip. He needed water.

"The cat, Your Highness," Sir Caleb said. "The boy would like to know if you killed it."

Blood rushed to Achan's face. Pain spiked in his temples. His stomach seized. Fluid rose up his throat and nose. He pressed his lips together, clamped a hand over his mouth, and lunged out of bed toward the chamber pot.

After retching for what seemed like an eternity, Achan fell onto his rear and lay on the floor, arms and legs spread out like the destination on a map. His nose and throat stung. He panted short, deep breaths to calm his angry stomach.

A shadow passed over him. Sir Caleb looked down, shaggy blond mane framing his face. He held out Averella's dress sleeve and a dark wine bottle. He smelled the bottle's opening and set it down beside Achan's waist. "Smells like it was good."

Achan groaned through another intense pang in his head.

"I learned long ago, as you likely have from your experience last night, that one should not drink more than one glass of any Carmine red in one sitting. And never on an empty stomach." Sir Caleb dropped Averella's sleeve, which fluttered in the air over Achan until it settled on his bare chest. "Best not to lose that until after we are safe in Armonguard."

Sir Caleb walked away, and Matthias's small face reappeared at Achan's side. The boy crouched and sniffed the bottle then folded his arms and stared at Achan.

Without moving his head, Achan shifted his eyes to meet the boy's. "The cat got away, Matthias. She nearly killed me, though."

Matthias smiled, as if this concession made the whole ordeal worthwhile.

18

"Head for the main gate, Master Fox."

"Aye, m'lady."

Noam steered the wagon through the outskirts of Mahanaim. The road was deserted. In the Darkness, Averella could not guess the hour.

"I shall bloodvoice Master Rennan to see if I can learn his precise whereabouts." Averella closed her eyes and focused. *Master Rennan? May I speak with you, please?*

Bran sounded tired. *My lady, are you well?*

We are, thank you. We approach the gate. Can you tell me the way to the dungeon? Will the front entrance—

Averella, do not attempt this.

We stand a much better chance of success with your guidance, Master Rennan.

Prisoners are being executed daily. Fed to the great tanniyn. I would never forgive myself if you were captured.

Perhaps Bran still cared. *We shall not stand by while innocent men are slaughtered. The location of the dungeon would help us greatly.*

Bran's tone rose. *Do not be a fool! There is nothing two women can do. Go home. Tell Gren I said the same.*

Averella bristled. *Women are not so completely useless as you believe, Master Rennan. And as I mentioned before, we have two able men with us. Abandoning you would break Gren's heart, for she seems intent on being near you.*

It's far too dangerous for Gren. Bran's voice softened. *She could be hurt—or lose her child.*

Is this the real reason we have parted ways, Master Rennan? Is this child yours?

Averella sensed Bran's anger flare. *You know me better than that.* Even in his mind, he sighed with frustration. *Fine. If you insist on this madness, the dungeons are in the lowest levels of the stronghold. Any descending staircase will lead you there eventually. Arman be with you.*

Averella opened her eyes. The scene blurred before her. Behind the jagged parapet of the sentry wall, the city of Mahanaim peaked like a mountain of stone. Hundreds of torchlights lit the structure, but the colors of the stone were dull under the shadow of Darkness. The overwhelming smell was like a privy filled with rotted fish.

Before Master Fox could slow the wagon at the gate, two soldiers approached. They wore black armor and black capes with the gold symbol of Mahanaim on them.

One of the men spoke. "State yer name and business."

"I'm Harnu Poe. We come seeking sanctuary from Darkness and to offer our service to the New Council."

"What do you know of the New Council?"

"Just that things are changing in Er'Rets. I aim to serve however I can."

"Who you got with you?"

"My wife and two servants."

"How do you plan to serve the New Council?"

"My man and I mean to fight. If you're in need of seamstresses, the women can sew."

"You'll need coin to rent a room. Ask the stablemaster about trading that wagon for a boat."

"I will. Thank you."

"Come on down and let us search yer wagon."

The four of them climbed out and watched the soldiers ransack their supplies. They made a mess, tossing everything about, but took nothing but a mouthful of dried fish.

Then they searched Harnu and Noam.

The man searching Harnu took his coin purse—which was really Averella's. "We'll be taking a fee for entry and an offering for Dâthos. And you'll have to hand over that blade."

"I'll do no such thing," Harnu said, forbidding as ever. "If I'm to join the soldiers, I'll do best with my own blade."

The soldier glanced at his partner, who shrugged. "Let him keep it. It's in sad shape, if you ask me." He pocketed a few coins and tossed the coin purse back to Harnu.

The soldiers approached the women next. Averella clutched Gren's arm. "You will not touch us!"

The soldier laughed. "Oh, but we will, Madam. Plenty have tried to sneak trouble past our gate by hiding it on their women. Put your arms out, real nice like."

Averella shot a glance to Harnu, who shrugged. "We've nothing to hide. Search 'em if you must."

Typical male response. Harnu had acclimated to his role all too well. Averella closed her eyes as the guard ran his hands over her.

A tickle at her neck. "What have we here?"

She opened her eyes to see the guard pulling the gold chain that held the king's signet ring. Her heart fluttered. She grabbed the chain.

"None of that now," the guard said. "We can't allow you to wear such a trinket in times like these. It's not safe. Plus, such an offering would please Dâthos."

Averella and the guard both held tight until the chain snapped. The guard pulled the chain through Averella's fist until he had it all. She gasped when the ring did not appear. She could feel it still nestled inside her makeshift corset.

The guard sneered and pocketed the chain. He didn't know there had been anything else attached! "Yer free to enter. Make any mischief and we'll feed you to the tanniyn."

As the guards raised the gate, Noam helped Averella and Gren into the wagon bed. Once everyone was seated, Noam steered the horses inside the stronghold.

"Sorry 'bout your necklace, my lady," Harnu said. "I didn't think we should pick a fight just then."

"You were wise, Master Poe, though it would not hurt you to be more protective of your wife." She reached into her neckline and pulled out the ring. "Fortunately I am not as shapely as Gren." Averella blushed, shocked at her words. Since when did she say such forward things?

Gren's lips parted. "Achan's ring? They almost took it?"

"Arman did not let them. Gren, do you have some twine that I might use to put it back around my neck?"

"Of course."

As Gren busied herself looking for twine, Averella took in their surroundings. The courtyard—which had been filled with merchants and animals the last time she was here—was deserted. The horses' hooves and wagon wheels clacked over the cobblestone. "It must be a late hour."

"Which way to the stables, my lady?" Noam asked.

"To the right of the fountain, past the temple."

The wagon turned sharply. Averella gripped the side and stared at the fountain. What once had been a beautiful cascade of water over the sculpture of the Mahanaim justice scales now oozed dark slime. She wrinkled her nose and turned toward the temple of Dâthos.

The circular colonnade filled the northeastern corner of the courtyard. The black and white banners hung limp, moist from the stale air of Darkness.

Noam stopped the wagon at the stables. Harnu got down and quickly bartered a trade with the stablemaster.

"Any of them boats down there'll do." The stablemaster gestured toward narrow stone steps that led down to the canals. "You want to put up your horses, it will cost you extra."

Noam unharnessed the horses, but Harnu said, "Leave 'em to me. You and the women carry the supplies to the boat. I'll meet you there." He and the stablemaster each led a horse inside the stables.

Noam stood staring after them.

Averella set her hand against his arm. "He is taking his role to heart, is he not, Master Fox? Come, I am sure all will be well. Can you carry the larger pack?"

The stairs leading down to the water were lit so poorly they could hardly see. They moved slowly down them until they reached a stone pier that stretched along a murky canal under the courtyard above. Dozens of small wooden boats were tethered along the pier. The occasional torch reflected off the dark water. On the end of the pier, to the far right of the stronghold, the canal turned and snaked between a city of buildings.

They loaded their gear into the nearest boat and stood beside it, waiting for Harnu to return.

"What about the horses?" Noam asked.

"They will be fine in the stables," Averella said. "We will do as the guards suggested: we will rent a room and plan what to do next." Her words were more confident than she felt. *Arman, show us the way.*

Gren paced along the waterfront. Noam stood at the foot of the stairs, staring up. Averella sat in the boat, rocking gently in the canal.

A man yelled in the distance. A burst of orange flame arched overhead and landed on the thatched roof of a three-story high building. A woman screamed.

Another cluster of arrows, tips ablaze, passed over the sentry wall and hissed as they sank into the canal. Armor jangled above as guards ran to duty. Voices split the silent night.

"From the east."

"It's the Pawn King!"

"Guard your thoughts, for he can enter your mind faster than Darkness."

Averella smiled, amused at this embellishment of Achan's gifts. But her amusement changed her smile to a frown. For what did she truly know of Prince Gidon's gifts? And since when did she feel comfortable calling him Achan? It was as if her heart knew something her mind hadn't yet learned. Or remembered.

Another sprinkling of fiery arrows fell from the sky.

"He should be back by now!" Gren said.

Averella reached for Harnu's mind. *Master Poe, are you well?*

My lady! The stronghold's under attack. Soldiers have set up a siege engine in front of the stairs. I cannot reach you. I'll find you later.

Very well, Master Poe. Fare you well.

An arrow landed in the boat. Gren screamed. Noam clambered into the tiny craft and tossed his pack on the arrow, snuffing the flame.

"Into the boat." Averella stood to help Gren into the craft.

Gren looked over her shoulder at the staircase. "What about Harnu?"

"He is trapped at the moment, as will we be if we do not move now. Come, Master Poe will find us later."

Averella pulled Gren into the boat.

Noam helped her sit, then loosed the tether and pushed the boat away from the wall. He sat in the middle, facing the women, and started to row. "Where shall I take us?"

Averella took in their surroundings again. Now that they were on the water, something about this canal felt familiar. "Out into the city."

An explosion of rock cracked overhead. Averella hunched down moments before a massive splash surged their boat forward. Pebbles and water rained over her head.

Noam rowed faster. The canal twisted and turned around buildings, some burning, some dark as if their residents were still asleep.

"My lady!" Noam said. "'Tis a fork. Which way?"

Averella studied the paths before them. "Left."

Noam paddled the boat down the left canal. Averella's heart thudded. Torchlight was scarce now. Darkness fell heavily upon them. She nudged Gren. "The lantern. Quickly."

Gren fiddled with the lantern. A rotting yellowstone building loomed ahead. The lantern burst aflame, spilling golden light over the boat.

"Straight ahead, Master Fox. Through that hole in the wall."

"My lady, are you certain?"

"Yes, though perhaps we should duck."

Averella tucked her head between her knees. Gren screamed. The temperature dropped suddenly and all was black but the light in their boat. Averella picked up the lantern and held it over her head. "Slow down, Master Fox. There will be some turns ahead. I just cannot remember . . . There!" Averella pointed to a narrow crack in another wall. "Through that opening."

Noam steered the craft through. The left side of the boat scraped against the stone wall.

Averella's skin crawled at the sound. She quickly scanned the walls. "Slightly right, through the gap that looks like the letter M."

Noam mumbled, "I don't know my letters, my lady."

"Never mind that." Averella set her hand on his shoulder and pointed. "It looks like the flapping wings of a bird."

"I see it." Noam rowed them through the opening.

"How do you know where we are going?" Gren asked.

"I have been here before. This path leads to the dungeons. There!" She pointed to a stony ledge that ran along a wall to their distant left. "Stop the boat there."

Noam obeyed. He found a peg to anchor the boat to, and the three of them got out. It was silent, as if all was well above the castle.

Averella took the lantern from Gren and made her way along the wall until her fingers found a gaping crack in the stone.

She slipped inside and followed a narrow tunnel. Rock and minerals drowned the bitter smell as they moved away from the water and up a jagged stairwell carved from rock.

An orange glow lit a narrow crack ahead. Averella set the lantern down. "We shall leave this for our return." She inched between two wall-sized rocks. Voices came to her mind. Flashes from a different time, spoken here, in this same cave.

"What did the letter say?" Achan asked.

"You never read it?" Averella's voice, raspy and strange in her memory.

"I meant to, but I didn't want Gidon to catch me."

"I cannot remember it word for word, but—"

"She can't spell."

"I noticed."

Achan sucked in a deep breath. "Tell me."

"Well, she said you were her true Kingsguard knight. She wanted you to run away from the prince. She wanted to marry you and not . . . Riga, was it? She loves you."

He blew out a sigh. "Figured it was something like that."

"Why did you throw it away?"

Achan's feet shuffled. "Because it didn't matter what she wrote. It changes nothing."

Averella's stomach tightened. "How can you say that? It must have broken her heart to write those words. You should have cherished it."

He scoffed. "So I can read it again and again, dragging myself through the memories? That would be torture. Sparrow, you should have been born a woman."

Averella bit her lip, then shoved Achan, figuring that was what a boy would do when called a woman. She chose her next words carefully. "What's wrong with remembering?"

"It hurts, that's what. And I want to forget. That's why I tossed it."

"My lady!" someone whispered, angry, like a hushed yell.

She blinked away from the past and met Noam's brown-eyed gaze. "Forgive me, Master Fox." She pointed out the crack. "This corridor passes between two half flights of stairs that separate the first and second dungeon levels. We are already past the gate. We must watch for guards who might be patrolling. Are you ready?"

"Suppose I'll have to be," Noam said.

"Gren, wait here. If anything should happen, go back for Master Poe."

"As if I could find my way out of that maze. I'm coming with you. I'll pretend to be Sir Rigil's sister."

Averella choked back a laugh. The very idea of this peasant girl being mistaken for Lady Viola . . .

"That's a good idea," Noam said. "But Lady Averella would be more convincing, don't you think? Do you know whether Sir Rigil has siblings, my lady?"

"Well, yes. His elder sister is married to my cousin. She is not much older than I am. I suppose I might pass as her. Sir Rigil also has a half-brother, my fath . . ." A gust of knowledge rushed through Averella. Her father was Sir Rigil's half-brother. When had she learned this?

"Think I could pretend to be the brother?" Noam asked. "What is his name?"

"Sir Eagan Elk. I don't think it would be wise to claim to be him, Master Fox. He is in his late forties and is a famous knight from King Axel's reign." Averella took a deep breath. These sudden memories made her feel like a woman in the Veil, floating between two realities. "I shall be Lady Viola. And since you are dressed as such, you both will be my servants. First let me call to Master Rennan. Perhaps he can help us find his cell sooner."

Master Rennan? We are in the dungeons of Mahanaim, past the guard. Can you tell me where your cell is?

How in all Er'Rets did you get past the guard?

Never mind that. We must make haste.

Of course. Well, once you are past the guard, turn left at the foot of the stairs. Follow that corridor to the corner, turn right, and go to the end of the next corridor. Our cell is on the right. I shall watch for you.

Averella squeezed through the crack. Her skirt scratched against the rough rock. She walked along the corridor as if she had done so all her life. She descended the steps, her skirt dragging behind her. The stench of urine and body odor assaulted her senses.

At the foot of the stairs, she turned and continued down to the third and final level. When she reached the floor, she picked up her skirt to keep it from dragging on the filthy floor and turned left. Their footsteps scuffed along. She reached the end and turned right. At the end of the corridor, a guard turned the corner and walked straight toward them.

Arman, help us!

19

Achan's head still throbbed two hours later as he sat in yet another meeting of the war council that Sir Gavin had called to discuss his discoveries from his scouting mission. Only this time, Sir Eagan and Captain Demry were absent.

The coin Sir Gavin had given him at his coming-of-age ceremony sat on the edge of the table in front of him. Achan sipped his tea, staring at his father's profile on the gold, numb at the knowledge he now possessed.

Had Sparrow's accusations been right? Would Achan go the way of the other kings of Er'Rets and indulge in whatever pleased him? Or would he find the strength to flee, as Sir Caleb suggested he could? Would he even remember Arman when such enticements turned his head?

He took another sip. The morning air was cool so near the coast, and Matthias's tea kept him warm and would hopefully soothe his headache. "What did you discover on your scouting mission, Sir Gavin?"

The old knight leaned forward until he met Achan's gaze. "Four hundred soldiers, ten black knights, four cham riders, and two tanniyn."

Achan choked on his tea at the mention of sea beasts. "Tanniyn are real?"

"Aye. They almost never come near shore. The only one I've ever seen—until last night—was when I sailed from Tsaftown to Armonguard aboard one of Lord Livna's ships."

Achan could only stare. "You saw one last night?"

"Two of them, between the Reshon Gates. The mere fact that the gates still stand is proof enough that the beasts are being controlled.

Without careful instruction from a man, they would easily knock down the gates. I messaged you to look through me to see them, but you didn't respond."

Achan lowered his gaze back to the coin, ashamed of his behavior the previous night. Sir Gavin had needed him, and he had been caught up in Kurtz's games. His father's games. Yet he was almost grateful he had missed the opportunity to see the sea beasts. The cham bear still gave him nightmares.

"And we mustn't be forgetting the gods," Inko said. "The Hadad will be conjuring every idol he can. Barthos, Dendron, Dalakesh, Thalassa, Zitheos—"

"Unless Sir Eagan succeeds in his mission to kill the Hadad. Besides, you know how to fight the idols now, right, Your Highness?" Sir Gavin asked.

Achan nodded. He only hoped the Hadad would not call them all together at once.

"I will lead my men to the eastern Reshon Gate," Sir Gavin said. "The remaining soldiers will pack up camp and be ready to move on my command. Your Highness, you will enter the Veil with Duchess Amal and deal with the black knights and beasts by means of storming. Captain Demry and his fighting five hundred are already nearing Mahanaim."

"He's five hundred now instead of fifteen?" Achan asked.

"Aye. Captain Demry has claimed the Ice Island men and a portion of the Tsaftown army for his own. Their purpose is to distract the Hadad, make him think we're attacking Mahanaim. While the five hundred attack, Sir Eagan will find and assassinate the Hadad."

An insane mission. "He volunteered, didn't he?" Achan asked.

Sir Gavin nodded. "Aye, he did."

The same man who had told him that vengeance belonged to Arman. Achan took another drink of tea. "How will he find the Hadad with all the fighting?"

"We know he hides in his tower, issuing commands and using his mind to influence others. If we can take him out now, the next battle will be smoother."

"When do you ride out?"

"As soon as we're done here."

"Where will I go to meet the duchess?"

"You will go to your wagon. Your guards will stay with you. Sir Shung will watch over your body as you work with Duchess Amal. Should the army move while you are in the Veil, you will be ready for travel. If all goes well, you'll awake on the southern shore of the Lebab Inlet."

It all seemed so easy.

After the meeting, Sir Gavin and his army rode off. Achan returned to his wagon with Shung, Cortland, Kurtz, and Manu at his heels. As he made himself comfortable on one of the sofas and waited for Duchess Amal to contact him, he thought of Sparrow. He hoped she would be out of harm's way when Captain Demry attacked.

Arman, keep Sparrow safe. Help her to remember and to change her mind about me. I know that's a selfish prayer, but I offer it with the faith that You can do anything. If it's not Your will, let the pain pass quickly, for I have much to focus on. May it be as You decree.

He grabbed an apple and bit into it. If Darkness claimed the rest of Er'Rets, no more fruit would grow. What would they eat? Gowzals? He took another juicy bite. *I do not understand what You want of me, Arman. Why You've chosen me. What can I do that others cannot? I am just one man.*

He lay back, humming Yumikak's song in hopes the tune would comfort his fears. The wagon rocked. Achan glanced at the entrance to see Shung climb inside.

He walked to where Achan lay on the sofa and scowled. "Where did Little Cham learn that song?"

Achan pushed up onto one elbow. "In Berland. Yumikak sang—"

"Yumikak had no right. It is tradition."

Achan recalled Sir Caleb's explanation. "That a woman sing it to her betrothed?"

Shung nodded. "Song not to be sung carelessly."

Achan lay back. "I'm sorry, Shung. I'll try not to hum it anymore, but it's a catchy tune, and Sparrow sang it often. It reminds me of her." Achan sat up, suddenly and swung his feet to the floor. "Wait a minute. Lady Gali sang that song to you, Shung. Did you ask her to marry you?"

"Must ask her father first, but . . ." Shung grinned, exposing his yellow teeth. "Too strong, I guess, Shung's pull on women."

Achan laughed. "Of that I have no doubt."

Shung fell onto the sofa on the other end of the wagon. "Little Fox sang song to Little Cham?"

"Aye, she did." Achan sighed. "But she doesn't remember, Shung. She's forgotten me."

Shung frowned. "But how can—"

Duchess Amal.

Achan held up a hand. "It's the duchess. You ready?"

Shung nodded.

"Good." Achan lay back on the sofa. "Because I'm not sure I am."

"The little cham is a warrior. Will defeat many before taking the throne."

"Thanks, Shung." If only he had as much confidence in himself. He opened his mind to the duchess. *Hello, my lady.*

Your Highness, we have quite a task ahead. Are you feeling well-rested?

Achan winced, scolding himself yet again for his overindulgence of wine the previous evening. *I'll do my best, my lady.*

Then come to me, for I sit at your side.

At his side? Achan's stomach sprung. How much had she heard him say about Sparrow? Then he remembered it did not matter, for Lady Averella had broken their agreement. "I'm off, Shung."

He banged a fist against his chest. "Shung will not leave your side."

Achan closed his eyes. When he rose up into the Veil, he found Duchess Amal on the couch beside him. Achan blew out a quick breath and offered his arm. *Shall we?*

She smiled, sending a small jolt through his stomach. There was something about her smile that got him every time. He could not place the reason. She took his hand, and before he could ask where they might go, she pulled him through the roof of his wagon and into the bright sky.

He held tight, knowing he was safe with her, but still unsettled by the sensation of flying. Especially when Shamayim's pull tugged at his heart. The speed at which they traveled blew their hair flat as if they were drenched from rain. The land spread out below like a map. Achan could see his camp, his wagon a small dot below his feet. The prairie grasses covered the ground in a soft green blanket, edged with a sandy coastline. Straight ahead, in the distance, the Lebab Inlet narrowed between the two Reshon Gates. The southern coast consisted of rocky cliffs. To the left, Darkness painted the horizon like a layer of black ash.

My lady, if we can see where Sir Gavin rides, won't the Hadad see him as well?

Certainly. But we hope Captain Demry's diversion will distract the Hadad enough so that Sir Gavin can take the gate and lower the bridge. Our job is to deal with the tanniyn.

Achan's stomach tumbled. *How will we do that?*

Storm the one who controls it and send it back to sea.

Will the tanniyn listen to us?

Tanniyns are peaceful creatures when left alone. It will be happy to leave. If not, we can influence it.

But I thought we weren't to control anything?

It is not advised, but we are not doing so to use the creature for harm. We are trying to help it. Arman has given us dominion over all the creatures of this land. He will not fault us for returning them to the sea.

Achan could see the gate clearly now. Two pillars of stone towered on either side of the water. An iron portcullis stretched across the sea between them. A small garrison sat beside the northern pillar. Behind it, a massive drawbridge stood erect like a door without walls. That was what needed to be lowered if the army were to cross here.

From the air, it was easy to see both armies. Before the entrance to the drawbridge, Esek's soldiers sat atop horses, side by side in rows of fifty or more, five rows deep. At the end of each line were two chams, saddled and each carrying a rider. The front row was made up of archers. Directly in front of the gate, at the back of the line, ten black knights stood conjuring orbs of green light that hovered overhead. A jousting field's distance out from the gate, another three rows of black knights—or so it appeared—stood in a line across the prairie.

How many of the black knights were flesh and blood, and how many were illusion? And since when could chams be trained to carry men?

Another jousting field away, Sir Gavin's army approached. They too moved in formation. Two long rows of men in red cloaks on horseback. Archers in front followed by men with lances. Then, fifty feet beyond, came three groups of soldiers in square formations, six across and six deep.

The duchess and Achan approached the water. Across the inlet, the coast was a cliff of craggy orange rock. A yellow dirt road extended from the southern pillar into a thick forest and on to Armonguard.

To the west, Darkness hid the second Reshon Gate and the city of Mahanaim. Achan knew it was there, though. Had Sparrow arrived? Or was she still on the road?

Do you see the tanniyn? the duchess asked.

Achan turned back toward the gate and searched the grey waves. At first he saw nothing. The waves seemed rougher here than on the coast of Sitna. Then, like a thread pulling through fabric, a dark loop ran through the water until the tip of a tentacle sank beneath the waves.

Is it like a big fish? Achan stared at the place he'd seen it, then scanned the surrounding water for where it might appear next. He had seen drawings of tanniyns, but no two were the same. Some resembled chams with the body of a fish. Some looked like fish. Some water snakes.

Duchess Amal tugged him closer. *I will take you to it.*

They soared over the sea. The sunlight shone on the glassy surface, reflecting the clouds above. Achan and the duchess were invisible and produced not even a shadow.

There! Duchess Amal pulled Achan to the right.

This time he saw a greenish-grey body spin through the waves. Keeled scales roughened the skin and darkened its appearance until smoothing out into three separate tails.

It has three tails?

Duchess Amal smiled, her ivory skin greyed by the water behind her misty form. *Do not panic. It cannot see us or hurt us while we are in the Veil.*

She dove into the water, dragging Achan along. The water instantly cooled him, though that was probably an illusion provided by his mind. Everything darkened.

See there? Duchess Amal's hair and gown floated up around her. She pointed behind Achan.

He spun around just as a dark shadow swam toward him, a maw flashing four large fangs with dozens of spiked teeth between them.

The tanniyn swam past. Its head and long neck resembled a snake attached to the body of a massive lizard. Instead of legs or a tail, it had five long tentacles. Its head was brown, but its skin was spotted brown and white. It was ten times as large as the cham bear that had attacked Achan.

Had Achan been in his physical body, he would have blacked out from forgetting to breathe.

I sense the presence of a bloodvoicer, the duchess said.

Achan concentrated on the beast, detecting the faint pressure of a wall around its mind. *I sense shields. How can you tell they are from a man?*

An animal is incapable of shielding its mind.

Right. *Shall we storm the influencer now?*

We wait for Sir Gavin's order. He is expecting my report. Duchess Amal gripped Achan's arm, and they floated out of the sea and back to shore.

Sir Gavin Lukos.

As they flew over Esek's army, Achan opened his mind to Sir Gavin. Duchess Amal was relaying what they saw from their positions, the numbers of the enemy, and the location of the tanniyn.

Your assistance is most appreciated, my lady, Sir Gavin said. *Are you there, Your Highness?*

Aye.

You and Duchess Amal will storm the mages who are conjuring spells. Once you take them down, we'll know how many we're really dealing with. Prince Oren will help.

Achan glanced at the gate. His uncle was in the Veil? *But what about the tanniyn?*

Leave it until it becomes a problem, Sir Gavin said. *The mages are the bigger threat at the moment.*

Didn't you say there were two tanniyn?

Aye, there were. If you didn't see a second, perhaps they moved it closer to Mahanaim.

Come, Your Highness, Duchess Amal said. *Let us have another lesson in storming, shall we?*

Achan followed Duchess Amal back over the enemy ranks. The black knights were evenly spaced along the back line. They wore their black painted wooden masks over their faces, so Achan had no guess who they might be.

A knock came to Achan. *Prince Oren Hadar.*

Achan opened his mind. *Where are you, Uncle?*

Floating atop the end of the drawbridge.

Achan flew that way, and soon could make out his uncle's shimmering form just where he said he'd be. Achan had his uncle's height, blue eyes, and dark hair, though Prince Oren's had some grey in it.

Prince Oren smiled. *You look well, my boy. I see Caleb is dressing you in the latest fashions.*

Aye, Arman forbid I wear a red cloak like everyone else.

Prince Oren chuckled. *I understand how you feel.*

Duchess Amal floated up beside Achan. *Good day to you, Prince Oren. How would you like to proceed?*

What say I start on the far left, you start on the right, and Achan takes the middle? Do not let the green light touch you, Nephew. It can harm your physical body.

How can their magic touch me in the Veil?

Because they wield dark magic, Prince Oren said. *Sir Gavin is ready for us. On my command.* He floated off the end of the drawbridge and down the left of the enemy line.

Duchess Amal also floated away. Achan let himself drift down over the center of the line of black knights. He sought out Silvo Hamartano's slicked-back hair but didn't see it.

The sight of all those black knights and soldiers twisted Achan's stomach. He recalled Duchess Amal's words about storming. Combine your push with the element of surprise. Combine your push with the element of—

Now! Prince Oren yelled.

Achan dove toward the nearest black knight, focused on the shields around his mind, and pushed. His hands made contact as he soared past. He twisted around to see the black knight's physical body crumple to the dirt road. The vague image of the black knight's mind soared back and vanished through the drawbridge.

Achan glanced down at the end of the line in time to see Prince Oren—without even moving—send the mind from a black knight up into the sky as if tossing a pebble.

Pig snout. Achan had forgotten to throw his man. Should he chase him down and fling him as Prince Oren had done? And how did Prince Oren do such a thing without even making contact? This man was a true Veil warrior.

A green fireball shot past Achan's shoulder. He glanced down in time to see a black knight staring up at him.

How does he see me?

Move, Your Highness, Duchess Amal yelled. *Now!*

Achan zipped toward the drawbridge, hoping to pass through it and hide, but the moment he did, he came face to face with his first foe, hovering over the water.

The black knight punched Achan, sending him right back through the drawbridge. He flew backwards, passed through a person's body, and slowed just above the ground right in front of the physical black knight who could see him.

Râbah yârad! The knight opened his mouth. A green spear shot out like an arrow and grazed Achan's right ear. Fire blazed on the side of his head, and he cried out.

Your Highness? Prince Oren called. *What is happening?*

Achan fled. He flew through the stone walls of the garrison house. Light vanished as he entered the musty interior, until another green ball of fire shot over his head. He zipped through the building and out the other side. *The green fire burned my ear. Now he is chasing me somehow.*

Wake, Your Highness, the duchess said. *It is the fastest way to escape. Return in another location and try again.*

Achan tensed. Wake? But he had failed to—

Another green ball of fire shot toward his torso. Just before it hit, a shake of his arm brought him back to his body. He opened his eyes to see Shung standing over him. The right side of Achan's head smarted. Something stank. Bitter, like burned wool.

"Little Cham listens too slow to please Shung. Duchess Amal said wake. Yet Little Cham waits to be killed."

"Thank you for keeping close watch." Achan touched his tender ear. His hair felt crusty and short. His fingers came away bloody. He sat up and swung his legs to the ground in one motion. "Is my ear bad?"

Shung grunted. "Part gone. Hair too."

Achan stared at his bloody fingers. "Gone?"

Shung walked to the end of the wagon and withdrew a length of linen from a basket. "Green fire ate it, no doubt. Let's wrap head before Little Cham returns to battle."

"Hurry." Achan gritted his teeth as Shung worked. His ear throbbed, and pressing it against his head didn't ease the discomfort. When Shung finished, Achan lay back and returned to the Veil.

He found himself in the spot where Sir Gavin had been. Only Sir Gavin was no longer in the same location.

Achan shot into the sky to get a better view. Black and red capes swirled below in a mêlée. Achan was pleased to see a great deal more red moving than black. Maybe some had been apparitions conjured by the black knights. He floated slowly toward the gate, taking in the scene. Two orbs still hovered in the sky. His connection to the others was still open. *Duchess Amal? Prince Oren?*

Your Highness! Are you well? Duchess Amal's voice had never sounded so rushed and intense.

My ear was damaged, but I can hear fine.

Praise Arman, Prince Oren said. *Come. Sir Gavin's men have reached the drawbridge. Two black knights remain, and we must keep the chams at bay.*

Achan floated toward the battle. *What should I do?*

Storm the chams on the east. Duchess Amal will stop the chams on the west. I will finish the black knights.

Achan slowed until he was ten paces from the nearest cham. He clutched the claw at his neck and simply stared at the beast, never having seen one in daylight. It was twice the size of any full-grown bear. A tendril of smoke rose up from its nostrils. Its mouth of fangs made Achan's shoulder ache where a different cham's teeth had once bit down.

The wall around the bear's mind sent a chill over him. Achan pushed against it. His force paused, as if the man influencing the cham had placed all his shield power in one location. Achan pulled back, then darted forward in a new location. The shields caught him again. So he focused all his strength in one place as well and pushed through. The man's shields tore like a tapestry that suddenly gave way.

Now that Achan had breached the shields, he threw the influencer's mind from the cham as easily as knocking a child from a haystack in a game of mountain king. The cham shook its head like a wet dog, then sank on its forearms and brushed a paw at the bridle on its face. It turned its head and roared, sending a burst of flame that just missed the rider.

The rider tightened the reins, but the cham roared again and rolled. Achan winced. When the cham came back to all fours, the rider lay limp on the ground. The cham loped off, tossing its head and smoldering.

Achan turned his focus to the second cham. Its rider wielded a longsword, fighting one of Achan's soldiers on the ground. The cham spat a stream of flames at another of Achan's men. The soldier cowered behind his shield, then dropped it when the wood caught fire.

Achan looked into the bear's mind and found the influencer. He easily pushed past the shields this time, but as he prepared to storm, the influencer lunged out of the cham, straight toward Achan. Just before impact, Achan recognized the man's face. It was Khai Mageia, one of Esek's guards.

Khai struck Achan, and the two tumbled head over heels through the air.

Didn't you die? Achan asked. *For I saw Vrell Sparrow stab you in the back.*

Typical of that woman. Khai gripped Achan's throat and squeezed. *She betrays you as well, but you cannot see past her pretty face long enough to figure it out.*

Achan pushed against Khai's chin and dug at Khai's fingers with his other hand. *What are you talking about?*

Your mind may be stronger, orphan prince, but I know how to use mine better.

An invisible force shot Achan into the sky like an arrow. He passed through a cluster of clouds and did not slow. What if he couldn't stop? He felt Shamayim's pull and flailed his arms and legs, trying to control his movement, doing all he could to reduce his speed. He was being pulled in!

BE STILL.

The heat from Arman's voice calmed him instantly. He shuddered, wanting to obey Arman, yet still needing to try and stop himself from moving. At this speed he would fly right over the Pearly Gate. *A little help?*

CONCENTRATE.

Achan closed his eyes. He could feel himself still flying, but he pictured the drawbridge and opened his eyes.

He hovered at the foot of the drawbridge.

Praise You, Arman! Thank You! Thank You!

But when he looked up, a black knight stood before him, a ball of green flame raised in one hand.

Achan barely had time to widen his eyes before the black knight hurled the ball. The thought to wake occurred to him, but before he could connect idea to action, Prince Oren appeared between him and the black knight.

The fireball struck Prince Oren, and he vanished.

20

The dungeon guard slowed, hand on the sword at his waist. "What's this?"

Averella's pulse throbbed, but she was determined to seize the moment and play her role. She lifted her chin. "Guard, I require your assistance."

The guard stopped. "What yeh doin' down here, woman?"

Averella continued to walk as if this were her home. "I have come to see my brother. I am Lady Viola Livna, sister to Sir Rigil Barak of Zerah Rock. The man at the gate sent me down, told me to find a guard to let me in. I suppose you shall have to do."

The guard's eyebrows curved into two arcs. "Forgive me, m'lady. Course I'll let yeh see yer brother." He turned back the way he came. "I was just fixin' to choose another prisoner t'execute. Good thing yeh caught me a-fore I did. Might-a picked yer brother to feed to the tanniyn." He chuckled, as if executing a man were all good fun. At the end of the corridor, he banged on a door. "Back up, yeh roaches. Back, I say!"

Shuffling carried out into the corridor. Grumbling.

The guard peeked through the bars on the door. "Ser Rye-jewel? Come forward."

Averella glanced at Noam and Gren, who both had turned as pale as milk.

"Lady Averella?" Sir Rigil's voice.

But when she raised onto her tiptoes and peeked through the barred window, she met a stranger's face. Scruffy cheeks, oily hair, filthy clothes. "Sir Rigil! Is that you?"

"Unfortunately, yes. Why are you here? Master Rennan said you were coming, but I could not believe it."

Averella motioned to the guard. "Open this door."

The guard snorted. "Woman, yer a loon if yeh think I'm gonna do that. Most those men are knights. And I thought yeh said yer name was Lady Viola. Why'd he just call yeh Lady Ava-whatever?"

"Only a nickname." Averella batted her eyes and stepped up to the guard. "Is there no way I could persuade you?"

The guard scowled, though his ears turned pink. "None of that, now. Yeh can't dally yer way past me."

"My lady, please!" Sir Rigil called through the window.

Averella ran her fingers along the guard's arm then tugged at the neckline of his tunic.

He stared down on her, his expression befuddled. "Now, I'd be glad to spend time with yeh, m'lady, but not so—"

In one motion, Averella executed a perfect leg sweep. Eyes bulging, the guard hit the floor hard. She stomped on his face, and he rolled away, groaning.

She picked up his sword and snagged the keys off his belt. Her voice was calm, though her fingers trembled. "Noam, see that he stays down."

Noam regarded her as if she had just spoken Barthian. "Yes, my lady."

"The black key!" Sir Rigil yelled through the bars. "The one with three prongs."

Averella found the key and managed to twist it in the lock. The door swung open. Sir Rigil rushed out with Bran and two other men at his heels. Bran pushed Noam aside and dragged the dazed guard into the cell. Six more prisoners exited, including a giant with long braided hair, who had to hunch over to keep his head from hitting the ceiling.

The giant's big brown eyes stared down like overripe plums. He smiled, revealing two rotten bottom teeth. "How are you, Vrell?"

A flood of memories burst through her mind at the sound of his voice. Him standing in Lord Orthrop's study. Riding a horse behind his festrier. Averella perched in a tree while the giant wielded axes and fought off Eben giants. Him fastening a sword around her waist.

"Jax! Your name is Jax! I remember!" She threw her arm around his waist in a side hug but gagged at his strong body odor. No baths in prison.

"Well, I should hope so, my lady. I'd hate to hear you'd forgotten me so soon."

She pulled back from their embrace. "Oh, I've forgotten everything. Though some has come back in flashes."

Sir Rigil took the keys from Averella and locked the cell door. "My lady, we must go. Now. It will not be long before another guard patrols this corridor." He handed the keys to another prisoner. "Boten, free as many as you can. Take care."

Bran glanced at Averella, then Gren, his face as red as ever. Averella knew it was not from sunburn this time.

She cleared her throat and turned her focus to the other soldiers. "Prince Gidon's army attacks even now, weakening the stronghold from the outside. If you can get weapons, you can cripple it from the inside. Arman be with you all."

Boten pulled keys off the ring and passed them to other soldiers. "Let's do this as quickly and quietly as possible."

Averella handed the sword to Sir Rigil, whom she believed was the highest ranking soldier present. He accepted the weapon and grinned. "After you, my lady."

She lifted her skirt and ran back to the stairs. Halfway up, she met two guards coming down. Sir Rigil, Bran, and Jax surprised them and were able to take their weapons. They dragged the guards back to the third level and locked them in a cell. They took the stairs again, this time making it to the crack into the wall.

Averella found her lantern where she left it. She moved slowly, for Jax had a difficult time squeezing through the tunnel. She reached the boat and waited, holding the lantern up so that everyone could see as well as possible.

Gren reached her first, then Sir Rigil, who nodded to Gren. "Madam Hoff. Fancy meeting you in such a place."

She curtsied. "Good day, Sir Rigil."

Sir Rigil turned his gaze to Averella. "Master Rennan said you had two men with you. Where are they?"

"Master Fox is there," she nodded to Noam, "and the battle separated us from Master Poe."

"These are peasant men from Sitna, is that correct?"

"We were forced to be creative with our recruitment process, were we not, Gren?"

Gren mumbled, "Yes, my lady."

Jax finally ducked out of the tunnel. He walked to the boat and inspected it.

"What I want to know," Sir Rigil said, "is where in all Er'Rets you learned that move, my lady? When you took down that guard? It was very well done."

A thrill coursed through her veins at Sir Rigil's praise. "I cannot be certain, but I believe the real Prince Gidon taught me."

Bran chuckled, his tone icy. "Well, that explains it. You always were an independent one. I'm not surprised you fell for a man who taught you to fight."

"Master Rennan!" Sir Rigil scolded.

Fire kindled in Averella's chest. "I do not know for certain that Prince Gidon taught me. I merely suspect he did. I cannot remember him, really. So I certainly have not *fallen for him*, as you accuse, Master Rennan."

"I'm sorry you don't remember, my lady," Bran said. "But it's true."

She sputtered, angry that he was angry, but Sir Rigil took her arm and led her to the boat. "Lady Averella, you say the castle is under attack?"

"It had only just started before we came underground." She set the lantern on the ground and stepped into the boat, gripping Sir Rigil's hand to keep steady. "Once we are on our way, I will see where Master Poe is."

"And where are we going?" Bran's voice sent a chill over Averella as she settled onto the back bench. The familiarity of his tone both elated and angered her. She could not explain why.

Her only defense was to give Sir Rigil her answer. "We had planned to travel to Armonguard. We have two horses in the stables but traded our wagon for the boat. I covet your wise council, Sir Rigil, as to what our next move should be."

"We're better off in the boat," Sir Rigil said, climbing into the craft. "Prince Oren says the road south is blocked."

"I did not know you could bloodvoice, Sir Rigil."

Sir Rigil sat on the bench beside Averella. "I cannot. But Prince Oren speaks with me when he has opportunity."

"But your brother has the gift," Averella said, thinking of Sir Eagan.

"Aye, but it came from Sir Eagan's mother, Princess Alondria. My mother, Lady Zora, was from Jaelport."

Averella wrinkled her nose.

Sir Rigil laughed. "I quite agree, my lady. But Lady Zora does not ascribe to the teachings of her mother and aunts. Since Lady Zora had no affinity for magic, her mother sent her to Nesos when she was a small girl. She was one of Queen Dara's childhood companions."

"Was she?" Averella said, guessing she probably knew this already but had forgotten. "How interesting."

Bran helped Gren sit beside Averella, then climbed in himself and sat next to Noam on the center seat.

Only Jax remained on the ledge. "If you will navigate, Master Fox, I will row. My arms are aching for exercise."

Noam nodded, and he and Bran moved to the front bench. Jax nearly capsized the craft when he climbed in, but soon had them sailing through the dark cavern with surprising speed.

"Is there a way south by water?" Averella asked.

"Aye," Jax said. "Just get me out to the canals."

While Noam gave Jax directions, Averella bloodvoiced Harnu. *Where are you now, Master Poe? Are you well?*

My lady, I'm fine. What of Gren?

We are all well, Master Poe. Our only concern is you.

I'm fighting with your sword, my lady. All my life I've created them, but never have I used one.

It is a sad specimen. Tell me what is happening.

The battle rages. Many have fallen. Old Kingsguards somehow got inside. I found a man who was killed and took his red cape so I wouldn't get stabbed by the good side. And now I'm keeping pace with the Old Kingsguards. We're trying to kill as many as we can, but there are beasts and sorcerers who shoot green fire. It's like living a long tale.

Averella's heart smiled at Harnu's excitement. *We have freed the knights and are coming back toward the stables. I will let you know when we arrive.*

Thank you, my lady.

Averella opened her eyes. Torchlight lit the surrounding canals and buildings in a dull glow. They were back in the canals. A squawk turned her gaze up. A black bird soared along the path of the canal.

She tracked its progress. It joined three other birds and passed over a building, out of sight.

Jax turned the boat at the keep but paddled along the pier platform that ran under the courtyard above as if he had no intention of stopping.

"We should dock here. The stables are up that staircase." Averella pointed to the narrow steps that led to the courtyard.

But Jax continued to row. "As Sir Rigil said, we're safer in the boat. I won't stop until we're out of Mahanaim."

"But we have a man in the bailey," Averella said.

Sir Rigil took Averella's elbow. "My lady, we must do what we can to see you safely out of—"

"Master Poe risked his life for us, Sir Rigil. How dare you suggest I leave him behind? You feel his life is worth less than mine?"

"That is not what I meant, my lady. I simply—"

"And Kopay? My horse is in the stable. My horse!"

"A fine animal," Sir Rigil said, "but there will be other horses. And perhaps, after the war, he will still be there."

"You cannot possibly believe that, Sir Rigil. I know enough of pillaging to know that, with no lord ruling Mahanaim, there will be little left of— Wait." Averella's gaze tracked two more black birds. A memory flashed. A gowzal. A man in a tower. A dark voice. "Dock the boat, Jax. This instant! Stop, Jax!" Averella stood up. "I shall swim if I must."

Sir Rigil sighed. "Jax, do as she says." He gripped her hand. "But sit, my lady, please. For I am told that swimming in the Mahanaim canal is a fate worse than death."

Since Jax was coasting to a stop along the platform, Averella sat. "I survived such a swim, did I not, Jax?" Her statement surprised her. But she *had* fallen into the canal. Jax had been there, but he had not rescued her. Achan had. She blushed at the instinctive way she was now thinking of the prince by his first name alone—and not even his given name, Gidon, but his familiar name.

Mercy. Did she truly know him *that* well?

Jax chuckled as he looped a rope over a peg to secure the boat. "That you did, my lady. Swam off with the prince."

Averella met Bran's eyes across the boat.

"Regardless, my lady, it's best you do not swim again. Let me help you out." Sir Rigil stood and offered his hand. "Now, where will we find this man of yours?"

"We will find Harnu later. First we must kill a man." Averella reached for Sir Rigil's hand.

"But you just said . . ." Sir Rigil withdrew his hand. "Kill who?"

"I know not his name, but he is godless. His heart resembles that of his master, Gâzar. He is the one who controls those gowzals overhead. His goal is to take and kill and destroy. It is he who seeks to kill the real Prince Gidon and take control of Er'Rets."

"Averella, please," Bran said from the back of the boat. "For once, simply let go of your plotting."

She scowled at Bran, searching for something witty and cutting to say. All that came out was, "I am not plotting."

"You know for certain he is here?" Sir Rigil asked.

She poured her full attention on Sir Rigil. "Oh, yes. He is in the watchtower. Please. We must try."

He nodded. "Of course we will. Try and succeed."

"Sir Rigil. May I speak?" Bran asked.

"Of course."

"We cannot take Lady Averella's word alone on this matter or any other. Her personal agenda clouds her reason."

Averella sucked a breath between her clenched teeth. "My personal agenda was to find you, Master Rennan. And so I have done."

"Master Rennan," Sir Rigil said. "I have known Lady Averella all her life. She is not a deceiver."

Bran barked out a coarse laugh. "Forgive me. But if you believe that, then you do not know her at all, sir."

"That is most unfair," Averella said, tears choking her words. She glanced at Jax, who was staring into the sky, his eyes wide and glassy. "I know about the man in the tower because when I was stormed, a gowzal took me there. Only four days ago. The man wanted me to join with the bird and spy on Prince Gidon."

"Perhaps you were dreaming."

"I was *not* dreaming," Averella yelled.

"Hold!" Jax said, himself again. "Vrell speaks truth. Not only do I sense it, I have just now looked into the watchtower and have seen this man. He must be stopped."

"Very well." Sir Rigil stepped over Jax's bench and pushed down on Averella's shoulder. "My lady, you and Madam Hoff stay here with . . ." He motioned back to Noam.

"Absolutely not! We will not stay here." Averella turned to climb out of the boat. It rocked under her feet.

Sir Rigil gripped her arm. "You will, or we will forget the entire thing and paddle your scowling face out of here."

"How dare you speak to—"

"You will not win this battle with sharp words. Sit, and let us take care of it, or we will leave. Your choice, my lady."

Averella's cheeks burned. As if Sir Rigil had the right to scold her. As if she were a child. As if he had not just praised her for taking out the guard. She sat and folded her arms, frustrated she could not think of a thing to say.

Sir Rigil climbed out of the boat, then Jax and Bran. The three men ran down the stone platform to the stairs.

"We'll return soon," Sir Rigil called. "Stay put."

Averella propped her elbows on her knees and set her cheeks against her fists. Insufferable men!

An idea came over her suddenly. She could watch them. She closed her eyes and peeked into Sir Rigil's mind. He was at the top of the stairs. He turned and followed Jax into the courtyard. A battle raged before them.

"This will take a while to get through," Bran said.

Averella's head spun, and she returned to her own eyes. Watching made her weak. She had forgotten. She took a moment to catch her breath. Then she hung her satchel over her head and shoulder and climbed out of the boat.

"My lady, what are you doing?" Noam asked.

"We must follow the knights. Come."

"But Sir Rigil asked us to wait," Noam said.

"There is no time. Sir Rigil, Jax, and Bran are caught in a battle. We must kill the man in the tower ourselves."

Gren's face tinged green. "I don't want to kill anyone."

"You may wait here then." Averella stared down along the pier platform.

"Wait!" Noam stepped out of the boat and turned to Gren. "I'm going with her."

"Fine! I'll come too." Gren climbed out, and she and Noam caught up.

Averella took them the opposite direction the men had gone, to a flight of stairs that led to the gatehouse, which was now abandoned. She gazed at the oversized red front doors to the Mahanaim stronghold. Between the entrance and the gatehouse burning wagons and vendor stalls lit the courtyard. What had been deserted a short time ago was now filled with fighting men. Prince Gidon's army had infiltrated. Red-cloaked men dotted the darkness like flower petals spinning in a pool of oil.

She caught sight of Jax's thick braids two heads above everyone else. He fought near the Temple Dâthos, which was nowhere near the castle's entrance.

"Come," Averella linked arms with Gren. "You and I will run for those red doors. These men are so caught up in their battles they will not bother two women. Master Fox, stay close behind. Hopefully no one will see you. Once we are inside, we must climb to the roof before we can enter the watchtower."

But Averella had barely made five steps before a soft cry stole her attention. A set of watery blue eyes watched her from under a wagon. She crouched beside it, and when her eyes adjusted to the dimness, she saw a small girl looking back. Rivers of tears streaked the girl's dirty cheeks.

"Are you hurt, small one?" Averella asked.

"Paw." The girl glanced behind her.

A man lay on the cobblestone, clutching his arm, eyelids fluttering. He was wounded! Averella waved the girl aside and crawled under.

"My lady, what are you doing?" Gren's voice followed Averella into the darkness of the wagon's underbelly.

What was she doing? She blinked at the blood oozing between the man's fingers. She could not explain how, but she could help this man. More of Vrell Sparrow working her way back? She had just opened her satchel when Gren crawled under the wagon and knelt beside her. "I have to help him. He is cut." Averella motioned to the blood that had seeped into the mortar cracks in the cobblestones. "To the bone, I suspect."

She bandaged the man's arm as quickly as she could, in awe of her own ability and speed. When she finished, she cupped the child's cheek. "Stay here until the fighting ends. Then be sure he drinks plenty of water. Change the bandage once a day with clean linen."

"I will." The girl closed her eyes and bowed. "Thank you, Iamos."

Gren giggled. Averella rolled her eyes, wanting to correct the child. Iamos was the pagan goddess of healing. Averella did not believe in such things, but it did seem as though Arman had risen up inside her and performed a miracle, restoring this part of her memory.

An explosion of rock distracted her thoughts. Averella peeked out from under the wagon to see part of the northeastern parapet crumble. Huge chunks of rock crashed on the cobblestone.

"Come, my lady." Noam extended a hand and helped Averella to her feet. He darted around two fallen men who lay head to toe and ran toward the keep. But Averella stopped at the men. The first man lay at her feet, his black cape draped over his face. Beside him, a red cape twisted around the torso of the second man.

Averella knelt at the side of the man in black.

"Please, my lady." Noam ran back. "We do not have time to help the wounded. And that man is clearly dead."

"You didn't bother to help the enemy before," Gren said.

Still Averella unlatched his black breastplate and lifted the top half off. Despite Noam's pronouncement, the man's chest moved. She found the wound in his chest, far too deep for her to be of any use.

The man beside him in the red cape groaned. Averella looked him over and found him without a thumb. Blood glubbed from the laceration onto the cobblestone like a bottle of wine tipped on its side.

Averella ran around to his side and pressed her palm over the other man's wound, holding his hand in both of hers. "Some linen, quickly, and some water."

Noam and Gren scrambled to obey.

"Noam, when I release him, pour water over the wound. Gren, be ready with the linen."

Averella removed her hand. Noam poured the water. Averella wiped her palm off on the man's cloak, then took the end of the strip of linen Gren held out. "Stop, Noam."

Noam pulled the jug away. Averella quickly wrapped the man's hand until it resembled a snowball. She set it atop his chest, thumb side up, and used another piece of linen to tie it there and keep it higher than the rest of his body.

An arrow struck the cobblestone a breath from Gren's knees and skittered over the man's body.

"Gren, here, put this on." Noam held out the front of the black knight's breastplate."

"I don't know how to wear that."

"You need the backplate," Averella said. "Help her, Noam. It will protect her baby."

Averella darted toward another man with an arrow in his thigh. She worked on him until Noam and Gren approached. Noam was carrying a sword and a shield bearing the Mahanaim crest. Gren wore the black knight's breastplate and helm, and she held a sword of her own. Averella grinned. "But take off the helm for now, Gren, so you do not look like a target."

Gren obeyed.

Just as Averella finished the man's leg, someone yelled, "Iamos! Help me next!"

Averella met Gren's amused gaze and smiled.

"Not until you put this on," Noam said.

Averella turned to see Noam holding up a bronze breastplate and helm. "Where did you find that, Master Fox? It is lovely."

"On a dead man."

Averella winced. "Then I suppose he will not mind."

She allowed Noam to fasten the breastplate over her shoulders and under her arms. As the battle raged around them, no one seemed concerned about the women and the man who moved from body to body, helping those who stood a chance at life and leaving those who did not.

A squawk pulled her gaze upward. Gowzals circled the Mahanaim watchtower. Averella pulled on her helm and ran inside the double doors, stopping to pick up a discarded sword on her way.

Averella crossed the vast foyer of the Mahanaim stronghold, darting around drum pillars on her way to the grand staircase, Gren and Noam at her heels.

They had climbed to the sixth level when Gren collapsed on the landing, gasping and clutching her side. She let her sword clatter to the marble landing and pulled off her helm.

"I'm sorry," she said, panting. "I need to stop. Just a moment, please?"

"Of course." This was far too strenuous activity for a woman in Gren's condition. "You should wait here, Gren. Your baby . . ."

"I will be fine . . . in a moment."

Noam stepped up to Averella. "Might you take this opportunity to inquire as to Sir Rigil's whereabouts?"

"An excellent suggestion, Master Fox. Thank you." Averella removed her helm and sat on the top step beside Gren. She closed her eyes. *Sir Rigil? Where are you?*

We are outside the front doors, my lady. A battle has waylaid us. Please have patience.

Averella opened her eyes. "They are still in the battle."

Gren had already put her helm back on. "I am ready."

Noam helped Gren stand. Averella put her own helm back on, and they continued up the stairs, at a slower pace this time, for Gren's sake. Averella urged herself to be patient, but she felt like a horse before the jousting flag lifted.

The experience brought a memory to mind. Climbing these very stairs behind an old man named Carlani as he led her to Macoun Hadar's chambers on the eighth floor.

She paused on the eighth floor landing and peered down a dark corridor. Macoun Hadar lived down there. The second door on the right. How could she know such a thing?

Memories flooded her suddenly. A wrinkled old man touching her face. Great pain. Being tied up. Jax. A lecherous man named Khai. A basketfull of trinkets, fabric, and hair. His coarse fingers on her neck, his words, a humming threat.

. . . tell me what you know of the prince's plans . . .

"My lady?"

She glanced up, for Noam's voice had come from above. He and Gren stood on the landing between the eighth and ninth floors.

A chill gripped her as the understanding set in. The man in the tower was Macoun Hadar. Had to be. The man she must kill. Her old master. She released a shaky breath and continued climbing. "Coming."

They made their way to the tenth floor, then down the corridors to the tower stairs. Two guards lay slain at the foot of the stairwell.

Noam stretched out his arms to stop the ladies. "Perhaps someone has already come to deal with this man, my lady."

"Perhaps." Averella stepped around him. "But I will not rest until I know for certain." She lifted a torch from a sconce on the wall, pinched her skirt in the same hand, lifted her sword in the other, and started up the stairs. Her thighs ached from the ten levels she had climbed. This flight of stairs would likely take them up another three or four levels.

Dizzy from circling, she paused at an arrow loop to give her legs a chance to rest. She could see nothing but swirling darkness from the window. Noam and Gren's footsteps clattered behind her. They would not be sneaking up on anyone, that much was certain.

Averella continued on. Her temples tickled. Could Prince Gidon be trying to see her thoughts? Someone must be, for the pressure increased. Oddly, however, her fear diminished. In fact, she felt quite calm, as if she were merely going to tea with Gypsum and not off to kill a man. Perhaps Arman had given her this peace. She would need it to be able to do this deed, for she had never killed a man before.

She set her sword hand on the wall to catch her breath, somehow knowing she was mistaken. She *had* killed before.

Whom had she killed?

Movement above drew her attention. A shadow fell over her. A hooded man knocked the torch from her grip and clamped his hand around her neck. He pushed her against the tower wall and held a knife through the crack in the plates of her breastplate. The steel pricked her waist.

"All of you!" he said. "Drop your swords, or she dies."

21

Achan hovered, staring at the place where Prince Oren had disappeared. A gust of air tore his gaze to the black knight, who had conjured a new ball of green fire.

Hatred and anger coiled inside Achan until he folded in on himself and exerted his mind. He didn't understand how, but he suddenly looked out from the black knight's mind. Achan saw the battle from the ground. He stood inside the black knight's body, before the raised drawbridge, holding a ball of green fire in his hand. Achan forced the knight to lob the fireball at another black knight. The man screamed and disintegrated into dust.

A thick tendril of power sizzled in this man's mind. Achan seized it and shuddered as it coursed through his body. Green sparks danced along the knight's gloved palms. Achan could feel the man pushing against him with no more force than when Matthias tried to tackle him.

Your Highness? Duchess Amal's voice spoke to his mind. *Where are you?*

Inside the last black knight.

Achan stormed the man's mind away and sensed it soar into the sky above.

Come out at once, Your Highness. You must not do that.

In a moment. The power dancing through this body was exhilarating. Achan focused on the man's hands, on those green sparks, mesmerized by the brightness, the light. An orb grew between the man's palms, small at first, then to the size of a human head.

Your Highness, Duchess Amal called, *please leave that man's body. It is not—*

A humming voice cut her off. *Arman is light. In him is no darkness. Seize the light, Your Highness. Use it.*

Achan frowned, for that thought sounded logical. Here Achan stood, holding light itself. He could use it. The power.

But this light was not Arman's.

Oh, but it is! Arman is in you, fool boy. Use your power to serve him. Use your power to do his will.

Achan took in the activity on the battlefield. The bridge had been lowered. Achan's army had started to cross over. The line of soldiers and carts ran all the way to the horizon.

They had won.

Achan, Duchess Amal said in a firm voice. *Please.*

She had never called him "Achan." He relaxed, intending to obey her, but a screech pulled his gaze to the water. The tanniyn raised its head up out of the water, over the drawbridge.

Those on the bridge ran, some forward, some back. The tanniyn rammed into the crowd, knocking a knight from his mount. The tanniyn's jaw snapped onto the horse's hindquarters and rose higher, its neck slithering, rolling to a height almost as tall as the pillars, the horse dangling upside down, whinnying, flailing its head and front legs.

The tanniyn tossed the horse and took the entire thing into its mouth.

Use the light, boy, the man's voice said. *Destroy the beast!*

Of course. Achan glanced at the black knight's hands. The green light flickered over the black leather, invigorating Achan like a gulp of Carmine red wine.

The tanniyn swallowed the horse. Then, like a coil of rope suddenly dropped, it fell in one motion and hovered just above the bridge, hissing at the knights still trying to back off the bridge. The procession had pressed against itself. Knights were trying to herd the people back, but many couldn't see what was taking place out over the water.

The tanniyn screeched again, its very breath blowing a knight off his mount.

Strike it, boy! Use the power. Kill the beast!

Yes. Achan could destroy it with the green fire. His anger boiled. The orb in his hands grew to the size of a wagon wheel. He hurled it at the tanniyn. The green fire sailed through the air as if weightless. It struck the tanniyn's snake-like throat halfway between its body and head. Green fire engulfed the beast until the entire thing turned to black ash that floated down to the surface of the water and landed in a long, curling, black stripe.

No, Your Highness! Duchess Amal said.

Now those soldiers on the bridge, the man said. *They are Esek's men sent to kill your generals in their beds tonight if you do not stop them now.*

Traitors!

But before Achan could react, something slammed against his mind. His soul flew out of the black knight and into the sky. Cold panic gripped him. He was being stormed. He could not even move his limbs. They were stuck to his sides. *Arman!*

Achan lay on his back on his couch. The wagon shifted under him. Moving. About to cross the bridge, or maybe it already had.

Shung sat beside him, looking down. "The little cham was in trouble."

Relief washed over Achan like a warm breeze. "Thank you, Shung."

Your Highness? Duchess Amal asked. *Are you well?*

Shung woke me. I'm in my wagon. What happened?

The fire had possessed you. I had no choice but to take you from that black knight by force.

No, my lady. I was not possessed. Though even as he said this he knew it was a lie. That green light, that fire, that power. It had gripped him entirely, more so than any of Challa's kisses. He had wanted it, yet there had been a hint of wrongness. Some small thing that had nagged at him.

—you hear me?

I'm sorry? Did you say something, my lady?

You must focus to break free from its hold.

The power is gone. I was only remembering it.

Look into the Veil. Now. I am in your wagon.

Achan met Shung's eyes. Shung nodded, and Achan pushed himself up to sitting in the Veil.

Duchess Amal was standing beside his couch. She took hold of his chin. *Remembering it is a way to bring it back. Promise me you will guard yourself against such temptation.*

I promise. The words came too easily, though. They felt hollow somehow.

Look at me, Your Highness. Look into my eyes and promise me.

He obeyed. Her eyes were green, like Sparrow's. The thought brought a gasp to his lips, as if she could read his mind. *Forgive me, my lady. You spoke wisdom, and I did not heed it. I promise you, I shall flee from that kind of power if ever I feel its presence again.*

And you will never again possess any man.

I possessed a man? The black knight. When he'd entered that black knight's mind, he'd been filled with anger because of—*Prince Oren! What happened to him?*

Promise me, Your Highness.

I promise, my lady. Never again will I possess another.

She released him. *Prince Oren stepped in front of the blow meant for you. I did not see where the orb struck him. We can only pray he survived.*

Blood drained from Achan's face so fast his head lolled backward. *How will we know? Who stood guard over his body while he went into the Veil?*

I did not ask. I suspect Sir Gavin will know. Now, Your Highness, stop and—

A sudden impact jerked the wagon up on two wheels. Achan fell back into his mind just as his head slid against the wall. Shung set his hand on the wall to keep from falling on Achan. The wagon slammed back to all four wheels, and Achan slid off the couch to the floor. Outside, horses squealed and men shouted. Smoke drifted on the air.

Stay in the wagon, Your Highness, Duchess Amal said. *You and Shung must exit when I say. Armed to fight.*

A softer blow rattled the wall. A gust of green light blew the door drape inward and set it aflame. Achan crawled to where his belt and sword had fallen off the table. He drew Ôwr from its scabbard and picked up his shield. Smoke curled down from the ceiling. "Get your sword and shield, Shung. We await Duchess Amal's word."

Shung crouched and retrieved his weapons. "Black knights?"

Now, Your Highness, Duchess Amal said.

"Now, Shung! Go!

Shung held the smoldering curtain aside and ducked out the doorway. Achan hefted his shield over his head and followed.

They had stopped in a forest with trees so high Achan couldn't see the tops. The wagon's tongue had been severed, and the horses were gone. The driver lay on the ground, dead. Gowzals circled overhead.

Black knights were spaced around the wagon. Achan could hear their low chanting of *râbab yârad* and so on. Three wielded a wall of apparitions to the north that held off Achan's soldiers. Three looked south doing the same. The green glows of fake knights arched into the trees, creating a boundary around the wagon's side. The last two black knights faced the wagon. One was locked in a swordfight with Kurtz. The other stood behind Kurtz, lobbing balls of fire at an invisible foe.

Duchess Amal, no doubt.

"Shung, take those three." Achan gestured north with his sword, then ran south. The three flesh-and-blood enemies had their backs to Achan, focused on their magic. The nearest one had a puff of grey hair that betrayed his identity. Sir Nongo. Did that mean Silvo was here too?

Beyond the wielders and their puppets, Achan could see Sir Caleb and Toros at the front of the line fighting apparitions as if they were real men. Achan kicked Sir Nongo in the back of the knees. The man stumbled and lost his wooden mask, and his apparitions faded. Toros darted through the gap, but one of the other wielders produced a new foe that pushed the warrior priest back again.

Sir Nongo turned and drew his sword, holding it two-handed.

"Come to try and sacrifice me to Barthos again?" Achan hefted his shield into place and set Ôwr's flat against the edge. "Didn't you learn anything the last time?"

"I learned to be killing you quickly this time." Sir Nongo's black blade snapped forward like a whip. Achan parried it with his shield, caught off guard by the strength of Sir Nongo's arm. Achan had forgotten. But he'd learned much since that night in Esek's camp, and he sent a strong cut back to Sir Nongo's waist.

Sir Nongo caught the cut with his flat and threw off Ôwr's blade. He stepped in close and followed with a series of one-handed blows that didn't give Achan a chance to counter, as if he were trying to cleave Achan's shield in two.

Achan twisted Ôwr out, wrapping the blade around Sir Nongo to strike the back of his shoulder. Sir Nongo's steps faltered long enough for Achan to throw out his shield against Sir Nongo's empty arm. The shield's edge rooted Sir Nongo in place, and they sparred in a one-handed duel, their blades clashing a rapid tempo.

Sir Nongo's speed kept all coherent thought at bay. Dozens of swords clanked around them. Men uttered battle cries. Boots shuffled over the dirt road. The wagon fire crackled.

Kurtz had pushed his opponent near Shung and the mages facing north. A rock struck Achan's shoulder. The mage Duchess Amal had been fighting was now free, using his magic to throw rocks.

Duchess? Are you well?

I fight Macoun Hadar in the Veil.

Pig snout.

Sir Nongo cleaved one last strike and darted back, freeing himself from Achan's shield. Something popped in the wagon fire, sending a splash of sparks over Sir Nongo's head. Sir Nongo circled away from the fire. Achan moved with him. Heat seared his side. The wagon was blazing now.

Sir Nongo stabbed. Achan deflected with his shield and cut from side guard. To Achan's left, Shung fell beside a rock the size of a head of cabbage. Shung's opponent raised his blade to finish Shung off.

"No!" Achan deflected a cut from Sir Nongo, unable to do anything for his friend. But Kurtz stepped in and cut the man down.

Praise Arma—

Achan's sword flew out of his hand. He returned his full focus to Sir Nongo, but it was a moment too late. The black knight swept Achan's legs out from under him.

Achan fell on his backside. Sir Nongo's black gauntlet gripped the top of Achan's shield and pulled. Achan grabbed the straps with both hands, fighting to keep hold.

A figure leapt over Achan and bashed against Sir Nongo like a battering ram, knocking the man into the wagon, which was now a raging bonfire. Sir Nongo screamed. His hair caught fire, making him look like a living torch.

Kurtz finished Sir Nongo with a quick stab, then turned to offer Achan a hand up. Before Achan could reach out, Kurtz turned to deflect a blow from the rock-wielding mage who had let down his magic and raised a sword.

Achan pushed to his feet and scanned the ground for Ôwr.

"Looking for this?" a lofty voice said from behind Achan.

He turned to see Silvo Hamartano holding Ôwr in one hand and his own blade in the other. The man was no older than Achan, thin with oily black hair.

Oh, horror.

Achan gripped his shield in both hands and held it in front of him. Silvo wasted no time in his attack. He swung both swords at Achan as if they were hammers.

It crossed Achan's mind to simply turn and run, but just as he contemplated it, he tripped over Shung's body. His elbows hit the ground first. The force stunned him long enough for Silvo to kick his shield aside and pounce on Achan's chest.

Silvo's weight stole Achan's breath. He put a hand on the ground to push himself into a roll, but the edge of Silvo's sword pressed against his throat like a taut, cold thread.

Silvo's thin lips parted in a smile. "This is the happiest day of my life."

"Your Highness!" Sir Caleb ran toward them, sword in hand, Toros at his side.

"Stay back!" Silvo said, throwing Ôwr down and gripping his hilt with two hands. "I'll kill him!"

Sir Caleb stopped beside the wagon driver's body. "If you do, you'll die."

Achan reached out for Duchess Amal. *My lady, where are you?*

He is keeping me from you, Your Highness. Is it over?

Achan glanced into Silvo's dark eyes. *Not quite.*

"My master will resurrect me," Silvo said with as much confidence as Sir Gavin had shown when he'd spoken before the Council of Seven months ago. But the blade quivered against Achan's neck. Silvo was scared.

"Are you certain?" Sir Caleb asked.

"Even if he doesn't, I will die a hero."

Arman? Achan called. *You want to come and help me out of—*

"Hear me!" Silvo yelled. "You are all traitors to this land. The Council voted that Esek Nathak rule Er'Rets. The Hadar line ends here." Silvo's oration seemed to bolster his courage. He pressed the blade firmly against Achan's throat.

The sword's edge was so thin and sharp, Achan could almost convince himself that something so fine could do no real damage. He searched the ground for a rock, a branch, anything he might use to strike Silvo.

Your Highness, don't do anything rash, Sir Caleb said.

Do you have a better plan?

Arman wouldn't have brought you this far only to let you be killed by Silvo Hamartano.

A nice thought, Sir Caleb, but Arman is not the one with the sword against His throat.

"Goodbye, stray."

Achan held his breath and swung his elbow around the blade to push it off. Better to lose an arm than his head.

22

Averella dropped her sword. Noam's and Gren's blades clanged against the stone steps as well.

Gren began to cry. "Don't hurt her, please."

The hooded man gestured to Gren with his head. "You in the black armor, take off your helm."

Gren wrenched off the helmet. Her hair frizzed out. Her eyes were red and puffy.

The man released Averella and pulled off her helm. He lowered his knife. "My stars! I could have killed you! Why are you here, Averella? Explain."

Averella trembled in the realization that she had not been killed. She snapped her eyes to the man's face. "Who *are* you?"

"Your father." He shrugged off his hood revealing thin black hair and blue eyes, but it was his round cheeks that made Averella pause.

"You are Sir Eagan Elk?"

The man picked up her smoldering torch and circled to the top of the stairs. Averella followed. On the landing before the tower door, two guards lay dead. Sir Eagan tucked the torch in with the one burning beside the door. "Still have not regained your memory?"

"Only a few flashes," Averella said. "Why did you attack us?"

"I sensed you coming, but did not know you were you. Why are you here, my lady?"

"We must destroy the man in this watchtower. His name is Macoun Hadar, and he is responsible for great evil."

Sir Eagan's eyebrows arched high on his forehead.

Averella frowned. "You already know that?"

"I do and have come to do the job."

Praise Arman! She would not have to kill again.

"You need not look so relieved, my dear. The door is locked, and I have no way inside."

Noam made his way up the stairs. "Can we remove the door, my lord?"

"I am afraid not. The door opens inward, so the hinges are on the inside. Perhaps you could help me break it down? I have tried already, but with two of us, we might prevail."

Averella recalled the way the tower looked the day the gowzal had carried her here. A stone ledge circled the outside, just under the window.

BANG!

Averella slapped her hand to her breastplate and looked up to the locked door. Sir Rigil and Noam reared back and bashed their shoulders against the door again.

BANG!

Averella leaned out the window. She could not see the roof, ten levels below, or any signs of the battle, only blackness. The torchlight on the sentry walk and several distant house fires were all that lit Mahanaim.

The stone ledge that circled the tower was almost as wide as her foot. She twisted her body to look up and could barely see the shadow of the crenellations from the torchlight at the top of the stairs. She set her helm on the floor and hoisted herself onto the windowsill. She pulled up until her feet were on the ledge and her body was outside. A fleeting breeze swept her skirt out, tugging her waist back. Her stomach clenched, and her fingers gripped the window ledge so tightly it hurt. What had she been think—

BANG!

She clutched the side of the window, trembling. Once she calmed down, she gathered the back of her dress over her shoulder. Then, reaching up to grab the side of a stone merlon on the battlement, she shifted her feet. Once she had a firm grip with her other hand, she moved her feet again.

Gren screamed. "My lady! What are you doing?"

Averella squeezed the merlon tightly, heart pounding.

"Noam! Help me pull her in before she falls!" Gren said.

"Do not touch her." Sir Eagan's smooth voice soothed Averella's pounding heart. "Averella? What is your plan?"

Averella turned her head so she could see Sir Eagan's head looking out. "There is a window in the chamber. I am going to open the door from inside."

"I wish you would have let me do this," Sir Eagan said.

That would have been nice. "I did not think it through. I have always liked climbing trees, but this is different."

"You do not remember how brave you have become over this last year," Sir Eagan said. "There is much you would do now that you never would have before."

"Going without a corset?" Averella's face flushed. Mercy. She could not believe she had said such a thing aloud.

Sir Eagan laughed. "Perhaps."

"Pray I do not fall." With that, Averella inched her toes around the ledge and moved her hands to the next merlon. The torchlight from the window reached its limit and she could no longer see the battlement. "Could you hold a torch out the window?"

Moments later golden light shone on the crenellation. "Thank you!" A gowzal landed in the crenel above and hissed. "Shoo!" She waved her hand. The bird simply watched her with its onyx eyes.

"Are you well, my dear?" Sir Eagan asked.

"A gowzal." She glanced the other way and saw three more birds on the crenellation. "I dislike them."

"Move quickly." Her father's voice was confident.

She took a deep breath and shifted her feet. She brought her right hand to where her left held on, then lunged with a step and reached out with her left hand. The gowzal hopped back a step, and she grabbed on.

Tiptoeing left again, she repeated the process. The gowzal's eyes followed her as she passed by. She moved quickly. The creature hopped after her. A gust of wind pushed her sideways. She clung to the battlement, waiting for it to cease. Once the air had calmed, she kept moving.

The torchlight faded, but she could see a pale glow from the tower room window now. Three more merlons and she would be there. As she slid her left foot out, a sharp pain stabbed her right hand. She turned back to see the gowzal's teeth barred.

She swatted at it and shuffled her feet until she was able to shift her hands again. A gowzal flapped in the air behind her, blowing puffs of stale wind over her face. She waved a hand at the creature. Her foot slipped and she fell.

Heat flashed over her body. She screamed, clutching the merlon with both hands. Pain spiked in her left hand. She knew a gowzal had bitten her again, but she held tight and pulled herself up until both feet were firmly planted.

Gritting her teeth, she inched around the tower, sliding her hands one at a time, establishing a firm grip with one before letting go with the other. She finally reached the window, grabbed on to the sides, and dove inside.

She landed on her side. A bird squawked. The one in the cage on the pillar. Across the room, Macoun Hadar lay motionless on the cot. Apparently, his mind was out of his body at the moment.

She should kill him now. But she had left her sword out in the stairwell. She glanced around the tiny room but did not see anything she could use as a weapon. Could she strangle him?

Averella pushed up and ran to the door. She lifted the lowest bar first. It was heavy and the left end was wedged tightly into the slot. She banged up on the bar with her fist to loosen it. It rose enough that she was able to lift it free.

Something pinched her ankle. A gowzal on the floor hissed. She kicked it. "Go away!"

It fluttered back a step and watched her.

Averella set the bar against the wall. The second bar, level with her waist, came out easily. She set it with the first. She felt another pinch on her leg. There were three birds at her feet now. She shook her skirt. "Leave me be!"

"Averella?" Sir Eagan's voice was muffled by the thick door. "What is happening?"

"Gowzals," she cried.

She could not reach the third bar. She raised onto her tiptoes and pushed up with her fingertips. The right side shifted a bit. She bounced on her toes again and shoved. This time, the left side lifted.

A gowzal nipped her shoulder. Another her leg. Her hand. They were everywhere now. Where had they all come from? She screamed and grabbed one of the bars she had removed. She swung it at the birds.

"*Yârad!*" a man said.

The birds scattered to perch around the room. Averella spun around to see Macoun Hadar sitting up on his cot.

"What brings you back to my tower, my lady?"

"I . . . How did you know I was here?"

He nodded to the gowzal in the cage. "My eyes called me back. Besides, you weren't exactly quiet."

Averella stared at the caged gowzal. "You found someone to enter the bird after all."

"I would rather have had you."

Averella spun back and pounded the board in her hands up against the bottom of the last bar. The bar jumped out of its slots and fell onto her arms. The door pushed in and struck her foot.

Sir Eagan stuck his nose inside. "Step back, my lady."

Averella obeyed, and the door swung in. "He's awake."

Sir Eagan entered the tower room, sword in hand. "Wait in the stairwell, Averella."

But the door slammed shut. "My eyes tell me you worked hard to get into this room, my lady," Macoun Hadar said. "You must not leave in such a hurry."

Sir Eagan twirled his sword and stepped between Averella and Macoun. "Her efforts were to let me inside. Neither of us have come for a pleasure visit."

"If you have come to kill me, you must know that you will fail." Macoun lifted his palm to Sir Eagan. A tendril of light flew from his hand and coiled around her father, binding his arms against his sides. His sword clattered to the floor.

Macoun held up his other hand to Averella. "And now, my lady, you will experience one of those things I spoke of during your training. Things that some consider immoral."

The gowzals began to squawk. Green fog billowed from Macoun's palm, drifting toward Averella.

Averella, get out of here! Sir Eagan said to her mind.

She ran to the door and pulled at the handle. It did not open. She banged on it with her fists. "Noam! Open the door!"

The door rattled. "I can't, my lady! Is it locked?"

A chill crept up Averella's legs. She whirled around to see the green fog clouding her feet. The blood in her toes turned to ice, and the feeling crept up her legs and torso. She gasped at the cold, wondering why she had stopped trying to run.

"Pick up your father's sword, my lady."

Averella's body moved, though she had not wanted it to. What madness was this? Her lips would not part to utter the question aloud.

Averella! Sir Eagan said. *You must refuse his tricks. Call on Arman!*

Yes, she must. But instead, she crouched at her father's feet and took hold of Eagan's Elk, the blade Achan had wielded when she had first seen him. The blade her father called Rhomphaia. The leather-wrapped grip felt odd, worn down by hands larger than hers.

"Averella, please!" Sir Eagan yelled over the screeching birds.

"Now, kill your father."

No, she wanted to say. She stared at Eagan's Elk's copper and ivory crossguard, the carved ivory dagfish, the symbol of Tsaftown. Years ago, Sir Eagan had won this sword from her cousin Sir Eric. Now it would take his life.

What defeatist thoughts were these? She could not allow this evil man to manipulate her. She glanced at her father's eyes, so blue and bright. *Arman, help me!*

Heat melted over the top of her head, dripped down her spine and legs until she burned. Not at all painful. And yet the overwhelming, fiery euphoria stole her breath.

THE ONE WHO WAS BORN OF GOD KEEPS HIS BELIEVERS SAFE, AND THE EVIL ONE CANNOT HARM THEM. GREATER IS HE THAT IS IN YOU THAN HE THAT IS IN THE LAND.

Averella trembled. Tears wended their way down her cheeks. *Thank You, Arman. I love You!*

AND I YOU, CHILD.

Vrell gripped the sword's hilt in two hands. Macoun was still holding out his hands, expelling his misty magic, but it had no effect on her.

I am free, Sir Eagan, she said. *Arman freed me.*

Wonderful! He has not released my bonds, though. You must be the one to stop Macoun. Can you do it?

She stared into her father's eyes. *I can.*

She stepped back, crouching into position and holding Eagan's Elk at middle guard. Macoun's laughter and the gowzals' cries fueled her resolve. She recalled Achan's lesson that this was a cutting blade. No use trying to stab Macoun, which would be harder, anyway. She raised Eagan's Elk to side guard, stepped back a bit farther, and swung at Macoun's head with all her strength and—by the fire still flowing in her veins—Arman's strength, as well.

She barely heard a sound. She completed her swing and stared at him, ready to take another slice. Had she missed him? She'd thought her aim was—

Like a toy toppling off a shelf, Macoun's head tipped off his neck and fell to the floor. His body collapsed as well, leaving black ash drifting on the air where he had stood.

The gowzals shrieked all at once. Several flew out the window, raising a dust of feathers and ash. Two flew to Macoun's body and began pecking.

Averella intended to look away, but movement caught her gaze. A near-naked man stood in Macoun's place, though she could barely see him. His milky white skin was a coating of gossamer over hard muscles. He had black horns on his head and a mouth full of jagged teeth. The creature hissed at Averella like an angry cat, and leapt through the wall.

Averella turned to her father. "Did you see—?"

"I did." His wide-eyed stare refocused on her face. He smiled and swept her up in a tight embrace.

She wilted there, never having felt so safe and secure in her life.

"Well done, Averella," her father said. "Well done, indeed."

23

Achan's elbow struck the side of Silvo's blade.

A gust of heat sizzled over Achan's head, and Silvo vanished with a squeak. The sword fell. The flat slid over Achan's chest and off his side. Sand rained down. He held his arm over his eyes and pushed himself to sitting with his other hand.

"I come in peace!" a familiar voice said.

Achan lowered his arm to see Lord Nathak dismount a horse that was slick with sweat and breathing hard. Toros and another soldier trained their blades on Lord Nathak.

As always, Nathak wore a molded brown leather mask over half his face to hide his ruined skin. His hair was white on the right side and black on the left, as if a young man and an old one had been sliced down the middle and stuck together. It reminded him of the tree in Allowntown that had been both dead and alive. It reminded him of all of Er'Rets. Lord Nathak's short, pointed beard was split and had been twisted so the black and white spiraled together like the snail shells that washed up on the beach east of Sitna Manor.

Shung and Sir Caleb crouched to help Achan stand. His legs were shaking so hard he kept hold of the men for fear he would fall over. "You are well, Shung?"

"Cheating black knights and their rocks." Shung spat on the road. "I am well."

Achan grinned and patted Shung's shoulder. "I am glad to hear it." He turned to look on Silvo but saw nothing but charcoal smoke pouring off the remains of the wagon like water in a rocky stream. "Silvo?"

Sir Caleb motioned to a drift of black ash on the dirt road. "Gone."

Achan looked back to where Lord Nathak stood beside his horse, arms lifted in surrender to Toros's sword. "And Lord Nathak?"

"Saved your life." Sir Caleb pointed to the remaining black knights and Lord Nathak, then addressed Toros. "Bind these men and put them with the captives."

"Don't take me away. Not yet!" Ragged desperation choked Lord Nathak's voice. "I must speak with the prince first. Please!"

Achan brushed the ash of Silvo Hamartano off his chest. "Say what you must, Lord Nathak. You have my attention."

Lord Nathak swallowed, his gaze shifting over the surrounding soldiers. "I am tired, boy. Tired of living. Everything I've worked for is out of my hands. Always has been, I suspect. My son betrayed me. He answers to a new master now."

"The Hadad?"

Lord Nathak groaned. "Macoun is a liar, as was Jibhal. But so am I, and so is my son. When you keep company with liars, at some point you will be deceived."

Seemed obvious to Achan. "And the Hadad deceived you?"

"Oh, yes. They all did. Jibhal played on my weaknesses from the start. Knew too much about me. Used that."

Achan narrowed his eyes. "What did he know?"

"Everything."

"Did you really find me in the fields near Sitna?"

"No. I pried you from your dead mother's arms."

The words jerked the ground out from beneath Achan's feet. "You were there when the Hadad killed them?"

Another wheezy chuckle. "Jibhal lied, you see. Promised I'd be free if they were dead. Free from the anger and pain. Free to take my rightful place as king . . ." Lord Nathak coughed. "I was never free. And it nearly killed me."

Achan could only stare. He could barely comprehend what he was hearing.

"I've explained this to my son time and again, but he never listens. He doesn't understand the consequences." Lord Nathak tugged a finger at the ties under his mask. They came loose, and he pulled off the mask and tossed it on the ground. The skin on the right side of his face was withered and smooth, like a dried apricot. A saggy eyelid hung over his empty socket.

A murmur tore through the crowd. Achan shrank back.

Lord Nathak fixed his good eye on Achan. "My son has let his obsession with you overtake him, as I once let my obsession with my father overtake me. It has been my ruin, just as you shall be Esek's. You have the gods' protection." He removed his glove and held out his hand. "I'd like to show you my memories. It's the best way for you to see the truth."

Achan glanced at Sir Caleb. *What do you think?*

I don't like it. What does Duchess Amal say?

Achan reached for the duchess again. *My lady? Are you here?*

I am, Your Highness. Macoun left me suddenly.

Can this request of Lord Nathak's be a trap?

It could. But if Shung stands with you to give you strength to close your mind quickly, you should be safe.

It's worth the risk, Sir Caleb. Achan gripped Shung's wrist, then held out his other hand to Lord Nathak, who gripped it tightly.

Images flooded his mind. Flashes of memory. Lord Nathak's memories.

Sitting on the knee of a young King Axel.

The scowling face of Queen Dara.

A boy riding in a wagon, looking back at a castle on a lake.

Macoun Hadar, mid-age, coaching a young man in a bloodvoicing exercise.

A young, unscarred Lord Nathak kneeling before a man shrouded in black. Being knighted by the same man. Training alongside black knights.

Slitting Queen Dara's throat. Stabbing King Axel and staring into his shocked, yet loving eyes as he died.

No! Lord Nathak had killed Achan's parents? Achan tried to pull away, but Lord Nathak's other hand clapped on top of Achan's and held him there.

Dragging a toddling boy out from under an allown tree. Raising the bloody knife. Stabbing down. Lightning striking the tree, striking Lord Nathak. Falling.

Watching two small boys play together in a field.

Watching a young Myet brand one of the boys. Watching him brand *Achan.*

Giving the child to Poril.

Standing before Lord Levy and the Council of Seven, masked, holding the other boy in his arms.

Lord Nathak released Achan then.

Achan pulled his hand away and met the eye of the man who'd taken his childhood, enslaved him, killed his mother and father. He lunged to pick up Ôwr and thrust it at Lord Nathak.

The man jumped aside, elbowed a soldier in the jaw, and stole the man's sword. Achan took Ôwr in both hands and stepped to the middle of the dirt road. Lord Nathak crouched, ready to fight.

"You're my own . . . brother?" Achan recalled Toros's story of the Battle of Gadowl Wall. The rumor of an illegitimate child born to King Axel. Eighteen years before Achan had been born. Nathak was about that much older than Achan.

And the way Lord Nathak had just shared his memories. The chill that came whenever he was around. "And you can bloodvoice."

Lord Nathak smiled. "It was best if no one knew."

"Then my mother—Queen Dara—was not your mother." Achan knew this now, but wanted to hear Lord Nathak explain, for none of it seemed possible.

"The inability to produce a child shames any woman. But Queen Dara, pressured by the crown on her head, felt it more than most, I suppose. Especially when one of King Axel's mistresses conceived before she did. The young woman gave birth to a boy, whom the king named Luas."

Nausea shook Achan like a violent sea. He faked for Lord Nathak's legs and cut for his head.

The blades clanked as Lord Nathak parried the blow. "It was covered up, half-brother. Swept away. Only the king, queen, my mother, and Macoun Hadar knew the truth of my lineage. My healthy birth only magnified the queen's failure. She begged King Axel to send my mother and me away. And he did. Father banished us with a large sum of money to what became Sitna. And I became a stray. Scandalous, is it not?"

Achan could think of nothing to say. From what Kurtz and Sir Caleb had said of his father's philandering ways, he didn't doubt that it could be true.

Lord Nathak was his brother? His brother? Half-brother. Who killed his parents.

Achan stabbed. Lord Nathak knocked it aside. Achan swung under Lord Nathak's blade and backslashed across his front. Ôwr's tip scratched Lord Nathak's leather jerkin.

Achan's soldiers circled around, but no one tried to stop him from fighting Lord Nathak. They were likely as dumbstruck as he was.

"I was given âleh to stifle any possible bloodvoicing, so no one would discover me," Lord Nathak said. "That was my—*our*—father's idea. Macoun, being a stray himself, took pity on me. He ordered my mother to stop feeding me the drink and taught me to use my gift. He first taught me to block, so no one would know I'd learned to bloodvoice. Macoun mentored me for years. But he was taking orders from the Hadad, even then.

"And one day Macoun introduced me to Jibhal Hamartano, who was training an army of black knights. His abilities enthralled me, so I became his apprentice. Together, he and I plotted the king's death and my ascension. I was the heir to Er'Rets, after all."

And he was, in Achan's opinion. First born son of King Axel. But killing the king had lost him any birthright he may have claimed.

The good half of Lord Nathak's mouth curved up with his smile. "The shock in Father's eyes when I stabbed him was bittersweet. He refused to accuse me, even when bloodvoicing Sir Gavin with his dying words. He loved me, you see, even as his assassin. He would have raised me as his heir if not for his controlling wife. Now, Queen Dara . . . Never in all my life have I taken such pleasure in killing someone."

Achan swung Ôwr so hard he knocked Lord Nathak's block back enough to nick his shoulder. Lord Nathak sucked air between his teeth and shrank back into the wildflowers edging the road.

"You defend a mother you never knew?" Lord Nathak shook his head. "She doesn't deserve such loyalty. She tried to bloodvoice my identity but only managed the word 'stray' before I silenced her forever. Bless her for that. It made hiding you so much easier all these years. I had intended to kill you next. But then Darkness came like a storm cloud from the west."

Lord Nathak reached up and stroked the ruined flesh on his face. "It struck my face, crawled up my legs, and stopped only when I moved my blade away from your pudgy throat. The allown tree withered before my eyes. I knew Sir Gavin would be coming, so I took you and fled to Sitna."

Achan's thoughts clouded. His chest heaved. A stray *had* killed his parents. Lord Nathak—Luas Hadar—his father's unclaimed child. "But why? Why not confront the king with bloodvoice mediators and make your claim? Why kill him?"

Lord Nathak growled a laugh. "One did not confront the king. Besides, the queen would never have allowed it. No, it was far too late for reconciliation. My father betrayed me. He deserved to die. And with his signet ring in my hand, the Council had no reason to doubt my story."

"But Arman had not chosen you."

Lord Nathak teetered in the thick moss. "Arman. The father god never favored me. I am Arman's stray. Discarded, left to die."

Pity pooled in Achan's gut. He wanted to hate this man, not understand him. "That's a lie. Arman has a plan for your life. But you hardened your heart because His plans did not match your own. I understand that. But one cannot rebel against Arman and succeed. And who would want to?"

Lord Nathak snorted. "Been listening to Sir Gavin, have you? Well, Arman took everything from me." He gestured to his scarred face. "Still does."

Achan squeezed Ôwr's grip. "Why have you told me all this? Do you want me to kill you? Is that why you've come? Do you wish to die?"

"No! I want my son to live. I want Esek to let go of his vengeance before Arman ruins him too."

"So you believe in Arman."

"He is powerful. He destroys those who kill His anointed. If I had killed you that day, I would have died, I have no doubt. If Esek kills you, he will die. Unless you've sired an heir already."

Achan shook his head. "Sorry to disappoint you."

"We are family—you, Esek, and I. We must work together. You can appreciate that, can't you? You've always been a noble sort. Let Esek rule. Spare his life."

Achan blew out a long breath. He could not deny that these men were his family. As much as Prince Oren was. "Arman wants me to be king, and that I cannot refuse."

Lord Nathak snorted again. "Arman is the reason I don't rule already. His wretched curses have nearly destroyed me."

"It was not His curses but your choices that have undone you, Lord Nathak. You chose to defy Arman and ally with servants of evil. Your own choices have brought Darkness on your soul and all Er'Rets."

Achan cut Ôwr hard toward Lord Nathak's neck. Lord Nathak darted back, and Achan stabbed for the man's chest. He pushed Lord Nathak back off the side of the road and past the bushes, stepping over spongy moss.

Lord Nathak would only parry—would not take an offensive strike. In no time Achan had worked him up against a tree and pressed Ôwr's tip against his chest.

"Justice has come to you this day, Lord Nathak. You have killed enough in your selfish quest. Take this moment to embrace Arman's forgiveness before I send you to the foot of his throne for judgment."

"I will never crawl to your Arman for anything." The normal side of Lord Nathak's face contorted, angry, wrinkling up to match the disfigurement on the other side of his face.

Then a look of surprise overtook him. His chest jerked up as if he'd been stabbed from behind. He moaned, breathless, and seemed to swell before Achan's eyes. The ruined skin bubbled, smoothed out.

Dumbstruck, Achan lowered his sword and stepped back. What was happening?

An eye materialized in Lord Nathak's empty socket. Before Achan's eyes, Lord Nathak's skin continued to heal until it was fresh and smooth. White hair turned black. Even his wrinkles vanished until he looked Sir Rigil's age.

Two sparks of green lit his eyes then traveled down his shoulders and arms like a fiery green thread. Lord Nathak gasped, shook his head as if trying to throw something off.

Then he calmed, and his glowing gaze came to rest on Achan. A wicked smile twisted his now flawless mouth. "Macoun Hadar is dead, my brother. I have been . . . joined. It seems I no longer require your assistance."

24

They were all back in the boat now, having met Sir Rigil, Jax, and Bran on their way down the tower. Averella felt crowded with seven people in the small boat. She sat with her father and Gren on the bench in the bow. Jax took up the center row, and Noam, Sir Rigil, and Bran were cramped into the stern. Water lapped against the sides of the craft as Jax navigated it down the dark canals. There were no more sounds of battle, yet the rotten stench of Darkness remained.

Averella called out to Harnu to check his location. *Where are you, Master Poe?*

I've been forced to retreat with Prince Gidon's men. The enemy pushed us back. I tried to wait for you, but these soldiers refused to leave me. I took your horse. Hope you don't mind, but I thought in case none of you got back . . . .

Tears stung Averella's eyes. *Oh, bless you! We were forced to leave by boat. I hated to abandon Kopay.*

The men are saying Iamos, Mikreh, and Marpay healed many, scaled the watchtower, and killed the sorcerer. It's most amusing, for I know it was you, Noam, and Gren.

Averella remembered the child who had called her Iamos after she had helped the girl's father. How silly that word had spread so quickly. The people must believe Noam was Mikreh, god of fate and fortune and elder brother to Iamos. And that Gren was Marpay, Iamos's maidservant, a minor goddess gifted in herbs and healing. Averella gave all the credit to Arman. It still seemed unreal that she could do such things. That she had forgotten so much. That it was all coming back. How much more would she suddenly remember?

We are in a boat and have nearly exited the city on the southern side. Can we meet you somewhere?

Don't risk yourselves for me. The knights will be better protection for you, anyway. I'll remain with the army. I'm . . . enjoying being a soldier, I think. Perhaps we'll meet again in Armonguard.

Arman be with you, Harnu Poe. You are a brave man.

Thank you, my lady. Take care of Grendolyn for me.

I shall. Averella relayed Harnu's news to Sir Eagan.

He chuckled. "You are Iamos, are you? Well, I am proud of *you*, Averella. And your mother shall be, as well. How do you feel? Those gowzals wanted you for dinner."

The memory of killing Macoun flashed in her mind, but she pushed it away. "I am sore, but I imagine being stabbed feels worse."

Sir Eagan hummed. "Remembered that, did you?"

"No. But Mother says that is how I got the wound in my side." A deep breath filled Averella's nostrils with body odor and the stench of the canals. She sat on the center bench. A few distant torches glowed in the blackness, but their boat carried no light as it passed out of the city.

"I am sorry we lost Harnu, but glad for Kopay. That is silly, is it not?"

"We've no further need of Harnu," Gren said.

Angry thoughts surfaced in Averella's mind. "Gren, Harnu left his father for us. Risked his life. Fought in a battle. Mainly because of his affection for you. Have you so small a heart that you would leave him to die?"

"Harnu is tough. And now he can go back to his father."

"You must know that he will not. He will do all he can to keep you safe. He said he will see us in Armonguard."

Gren snorted a laugh. "As if Harnu could offer more protection than these knights."

Averella scowled. "Of all the self-absorbed things to say. These men have more important matters at hand than escorting two women around. I blame myself. Why I ever agreed to leave Carmine, I shall never understand."

"To serve Prince Oren as a healer," Gren said.

"Then why not travel with the soldiers?"

Her father answered. "Because Prince Oren, Sir Jax, Master Rennan, and your mother forbade you to come."

Averella's eyes widened. "Really?"

"You have become quite stubborn, my lady." Bran's voice floated up to the bow and startled her.

His tone brought more angry thoughts to mind, but she did not let her pride overtake her. She twisted around and addressed everyone in the boat. "Forgive me then, for I have caused you all much grief." Averella paused, confused, and looked to Gren. "But why did you come, Gren?"

The water lapped. Silence. "I will tell you later."

Sir Rigil leaned around Jax. "Tell us now, Madam Hoff, for—"

A horrible screech silenced Sir Rigil's demand. The boat drifted past an intersecting canal, giving Averella a glimpse of a distant platform at the western Reshon Gate. A half dozen enemy soldiers stood on the platform, pulling ropes that were attached to a massive snake that had raised up from the water. The creature screeched again, then swerved from the platform and dove under the water, causing two black knights to fall off the platform.

Sir Rigil whistled low. "I must confess, Lady Averella, regardless of how or why you came to Mahanaim, I am glad you did. For you have saved dozens from such a fate."

The boat passed into a deep canal and they lost sight of the platform. Darkness closed in again. "What supplies did you take from the keep?" Averella asked her father. "For I am hungry."

Sir Eagan reached for a pack on the floor between his boots. "I have dried fish, flatbread, an apple . . ."

Averella took the apple and held the fruit under her nose. Its faint smell was sweet. She inhaled deeply, wishing Darkness smelled of fresh apples rather than spoiled ones. She bit down and the sound brought a memory to mind.

Achan's voice. *"And some apples. Crunchy ones!"*

Followed by a thrill in her heart and the remembered knowledge that she would find Achan an apple no matter what.

The memory warmed her cheeks. Merciful heart! She did not understand why these memories brought on such reactions. And in them he was always *Achan*, not Your Highness nor Prince Gidon nor even Master Cham. Mother said no one knew he was the real

Prince Gidon Hadar when Averella had first met him. And since she had been dressed as a stray, she would have had no reason to speak formally.

See? There was nothing scandalous to these memories.

Water splashed over the side of the boat, bringing Averella back to reality.

They were approaching the end of the canal. Though it was too dark to see, she knew that Arok Lake lay to the right and that going left would take them to the inner Reshon Gate. "How will we pass the gate with the soldiers there?"

"We will not pass through the Reshon Gate," Jax said. "Even if we managed to get through the gate, there will be too many of Esek's men on the King's Road. There is an underground river not far from here that comes out in one of the Nahar caves. From there we'll go on foot to Xulon, get supplies and horses, then decide how to continue on to Armonguard."

It sounded like a wise plan. They soon exited the canal and swept into the dark waters of the eastern end of Arok Lake. Stone houses edged the southern shore, their windows flecks of light in the Darkness. Jax steered the boat toward two cottages built into the low cliff. A narrow canal separated them. Jax propelled the boat inside, and Sir Rigil ignited a green torchlight.

The green light cast an eerie glow. Moss-covered beams stretched between the buildings above, perhaps to help support the walls on either side. Or perhaps to support the floor inside each home.

Jax pulled the paddles inside and reached up to slow the boat by slapping a beam. He kept his hand in the air and used the next two beams to slow the boat to a stop before an iron door coated in rust and moss. A stone wall encased the door and matched the masonry of the cottage on their right. Anyone who traveled this canal might assume this a back entrance to the cottage.

Jax reached around to the backside of the beam overhead and pried out a knot of wood. He reached inside and handed an iron key to Sir Eagan.

Sir Eagan took the key. The boat bobbed under his weight as he stood and reached for the door. Waves smacked the sides of the boat and the stone walls, and Sir Rigil's green torchlight swayed over their faces.

Sir Eagan fiddled with the key until a soft click sounded. He handed the key to Averella. "Pass that to Jax, please."

Averella did, and the giant put the key and the wooden knot back in place. Sir Eagan pushed the door inward. It moved slowly in the water, creating a small whirlpool. Sir Eagan pulled on the door frame, drawing the boat into the dark chasm. Jax helped by pushing on the beam.

"Bran, close the door?" Jax said.

The door clanged shut. Gren whimpered. The torchlight lit up the canal walls. They were smooth stone with patches of slimy lime coating. Bushy green moss covered sections of the roof like sheepskins.

Wood scraped behind her. Jax picked up the paddles. They splooshed into the water and the boat surged forward.

The tunnel walls raced by, their contours rippling in the torchlight. Averella felt as if they were being poured down a long stone chute.

"Noam, help me take this armor off," Gren said.

"Leave it on," Noam said. "It'll keep you safe."

"But it's too heavy. I can't bear the weight anymore, nor can I breathe. And if I fell overboard, I'd go straight to the bottom. Master Rennan, would you like to wear it?"

"Sir Rigil is the better warrior."

"Which is why you should wear the armor, Master Rennan," Sir Rigil said.

Averella was just as tired of the stiffness of her own armor. "Sir Rigil, you may wear my armor, if you like."

Still holding the torchlight, Sir Rigil stretched his arm out over the edge of the boat. "As long as you can bear the weight, my lady, I beg you keep yours on."

The boat rocked as Averella and Sir Eagan removed the armor from Gren and Noam and Sir Rigil fastened it onto Bran. Averella passed the time by fishing her old rope belt out of her pack and tying it around her waist. She sheathed the new sword she had acquired in the Mahanaim courtyard, hoping her old sword, Firefox, would serve Harnu well. She put her helm and satchel in her pack to make everything easier to carry, and she felt for Prince Gidon's ring. It was still hanging on the twine around her neck. Good.

Hours passed before Jax said, "Here we are."

The tunnel came to an end in a circular cave. The ceiling was covered in pale dripstones that resembled dirty icicles, some of them furry with what looked like frost but was likely some type of lichen. Perhaps Jax could reach a sample so Averella could take a closer look. A small cave in the back must be the way out. The idea of standing on solid ground again lightened the weight of Averella's armor some.

Jax jumped out of the boat. Sir Rigil handed the torch to Bran, then got out on the other side. The men ran the boat aground, splashing through the water. A cluster of black on the ceiling shifted. The torchlight reflected dozens of tiny pricks of light. Eyes?

"Sir Jax, are those bats?" Averella pointed toward the blackness on the ceiling.

"Gowzals, I fear." Jax helped Gren out of the boat. "It's best we move quickly. They can be savage in a bunch."

They certainly could. Again Averella pushed thoughts of the Mahanaim watchtower away. She put on her pack. Jax helped her stand, then grabbed her waist, lifted her out of the boat, and set her feet on pebbled sand before the mouth of the cave.

"Ooh, look how pretty the rocks are!" Gren crouched and scooped up two handfuls. "Could they be obsidian?"

Averella's breath caught, frozen by a distant memory she could not quite grasp. "No, Gren. Do not touch—"

Gren screamed. She dropped the rocks and jumped up and down, shaking her arms and hands.

Sir Rigil ran over. "What is it?"

Black spots wriggled on Gren's skirt. She screamed again. "Get them off!" She shook her skirt, but the black things remained. "Get them away! I don't want them to—"

"Shh!" Jax said.

Sir Rigil batted at the beetles on Gren's skirt.

Gren continued to shriek. "There's another one there!"

A shriek of a different kind chilled Averella's blood. Gren quieted. Everyone's head turned in unison toward the cluster of black on the ceiling. The gowzals rustled and chirped, a sweet sound like a hundred hungry baby chicks.

"Out." Jax waved at the cave. "Quietly as you can."

Averella took Gren's hand and walked over the crunchy ground to the cave. Gren's hand trembled. Averella pulled her along, trying not to think about the beetles underfoot. Sir Rigil lit a second torchlight and handed it to Gren.

The green light revealed a bare tunnel. No beetles in sight or gowzals on the ceiling. The sound of rustling wings behind Averella caused her to increase her speed. Then the gowzals cried out, high-pitched screeches that seemed to shake the tunnel walls. Steel scraped against wood. A sword drawn.

Averella and Gren passed through the dark, winding cave, stumbling over rocky terrain. She glanced over her shoulder to see Sir Rigil run around the corner holding his torchlight above his head, followed by Jax and Bran, who moved backward, shuffling their feet, swords drawn.

The gowzals came in a cluster, the way a herd of cattle might stampede. Hundreds of eyes glinted in the torchlight.

"Run!" Jax shouted.

Averella's memory of the gowzals in Macoun's tower made her legs move faster. Gren stumbled. Sir Rigil grabbed her arm and pulled her along.

A hole in the ground swallowed Averella's right foot. She fell, breastplate and sword clanking on the stone floor. Her hands, knees, and her left cheek slammed against the ground. Jax lumbered past, but Bran tripped over her. His sword clattered to the ground, and their armor scraped against each another.

"Averella! What are you doing?" Bran said.

"I fell. There's a hole." She pushed her raw palms against the ground to lift herself, but Bran threw himself over her, pressing her back against the cool stone.

Wings flapped above like the trill of a tabor drum, fanning what little bit of her arm that was not shielded by armor or Bran's body. Averella held her breath, praying the creatures would not notice them, praying the panic and excitement would keep the flock together.

Sudden silence but for Bran's heavy breathing in her ear.

He shifted, and his weight left her back. "It's all right now. They've gone."

"I do not hear Gren screaming. Think they are well?"

"They must be," Bran said.

"Unfortunate that they have taken both lights with them." Averella pushed up with the sides of her hands, avoiding the stings of her ravaged palms. She put down a knee, but it hurt as well. She grunted and pushed up anyway.

A sword scraped against wood. Bran sheathing his weapon. “Are you well?”

“I skinned my hands and knees. I shall live.”

Bran wrapped an arm around the armor protecting her waist. “Need me to carry you?”

She laughed. “If I can breathe, I can walk. How can we know which way is forward?”

Bran’s hand found hers. “Let me worry about that.”

His touch sent a thrill through her. She held tight as they proceeded forward slowly. Averella’s free hand found the right wall and used it as a guide. She relaxed when torchlight gleamed around the curve of the cave. But then it went out, and the blackness returned. Her temples itched.

Jax mi Katt.

We are well, Jax. I fell in a hole and skinned my—

Ebens at the mouth of the cave, Vrell. Keep quiet!

25

Lord Nathak thrust his hands out. Green fire sizzled from his palms like a bolt of lightning. Achan threw himself to his stomach on the mossy ground to avoid the hit. The firebolt struck the already burning wagon, causing it to leap off the ground and come smashing down in a pile of shredded wood.

Lord Nathak cackled like a madman and let fly two more streams of green fire, one to Achan's men to the north and one to the south. Men screamed. Some fell to the road, on fire, rolling in the dirt.

Achan pushed himself up, standing between Lord Nathak and his men. He lifted Ôwr, breathing through his nose like a bull, terrified but unwilling to watch more of his men be slaughtered. "You came here for me. So deal with me."

Another ball of fire formed on Lord Nathak's palm. He flung his hand backward as if to throw it, but the green fire flew off his hand and struck a tree behind him.

His eyes widened. Achan looked up.

High above their heads, the tree trunk severed. The top cracked as it broke away and fell. Lord Nathak leaped back just before the tree trunk stabbed into the mossy ground.

Achan stumbled back over the squishy terrain. The leafy treetop tipped toward him. He dived out of the way just as the branches slapped against the road, leaves rustling. A few whipped his back.

When Achan got back to his feet, the fire had jumped from the wagon to the tree, but the leaves and branches sizzled and smoked, too green to burn well.

"This isn't over, brother!" Lord Nathak yelled.

Achan peered through branches. Lord Nathak had mounted his horse. "Now that I am the Hadad, you would be wise to give up your claim to the throne and serve me."

As if Achan would give up now. "That's never going to happen!"

"Then I suppose I'll have to kill yet another family member." He turned his horse and rode off through the forest.

Achan backed out of the branches and sat down on the fat end of the tree trunk. It smelled fresh and sharp, a pleasant change from the thick smoke of the fire. A misty green cloud swarmed with the black smoke and hung over the wreckage. Orange flames licked the sky over the remains of his wagon. He wiped the sweat off his face, then wiped his hands on his trousers. His arms were trembling.

"Are you well, Your Highness?" Sir Caleb stepped off the road. He sank in the moss, nearly up to his knees.

"I dropped Ôwr under the tree."

"I'll get someone to look for it."

"I don't understand it," Achan said, shaking his head. "What came over him? He got so powerful all of a sudden. And then that last green magic ball . . . it looked like it fell off his hand, like he meant to hit me with it but dropped it."

Sir Caleb stood. "The ways of sorcerers are beyond me. Perhaps they make mistakes as well." He looked around at the carnage, then back at Achan. "Why don't you rest here while I fetch another wagon? It may be a while. I'll have Shung and Kurtz come sit with you."

"See to those burned men." Achan wanted nothing more than rest at the moment. His mind was too full to think or logically discuss matters.

A knock rattled the shields around Achan's mind, mincing his already sore head. *Duchess Amal.*

Achan didn't know when he'd closed his mind to the duchess. *Yes, my lady?*

How do you fare?

As if he could put such a thing into words. Lord Nathak had just admitted to having killed his parents. The keliy had come to him, healed him before Achan's eyes. His men had been burned alive. And Prince Oren had been stormed. *I am yet living, my lady.*

Do not be glum. Look around you. We have done what we set out to do. Your army has crossed over into southern Er'Rets. Tonight, you and your men will rejoice in a job well done.

If I had been better trained I would not have made such terrible mistakes, and Prince Oren might still be here. I am no Veil warrior.

None of that now. Prince Oren knew the risks. We all did. Any one of us could have perished.

But only Prince Oren had.

Achan cried out to Arman. *Let it not be so, I beg You, Arman. Spare his life. Spare my family.* But that prayer only made him think of Lord Nathak—another member of Achan's family. *You know who I mean, Arman. Spare Prince Oren.*

Achan's ear smarted like a dozen bees had stung it. He reached a hand up and found his head bandaged. Right. The green fire had struck him. Barely.

What, then, had it done to Prince Oren?

That evening, Achan sat at the head of the table in the meeting tent. Also present were Sir Gavin, Sir Caleb, Captain Demry, Toros, and Shung, who stood just inside the entrance.

Sir Caleb unwound the linen from Achan's head, while Achan held his breath at the way the flesh burned. How had Shung ever survived the horrible burn to his hand and arm?

"This should not have been bandaged," Sir Caleb said.

"Shung said it was bleeding," Achan said. "And I had to go back to the Veil."

"But it's a burn," Sir Caleb said. "I'm not as good a healer as Eagan, but I do know that burns should be left to air out."

The last of the linen fell away. The cool air soothed Achan's ear, but the men's stares made him feel uncomfortable. "What? Is it that bad?"

Sir Caleb's fingers brushed the hair above Achan's ear. It sounded coarse, like a beard. "You'll need a haircut."

Achan tugged out the thong holding his hair in a tail. A handful of hair came with it. Long strands. A lot of them. He groaned and set his forehead against the table.

"Has Sir Eagan still not returned?" Captain Demry asked. "I can call one of the other healers."

"Sir Shung can send Matthias," Sir Caleb said.

Achan lifted his head to see Shung dart out the door.

"Sir Eagan has not returned," Sir Gavin said. "Esek's northern army blocks the King's Road, so Sir Eagan is taking an alternate route. He has killed the Hadad, who was Macoun Hadar. When that happened, the keliy must have passed to Lord Nathak."

This statement made Achan shiver as he recalled Lord Nathak's transformation. He rubbed his arms. "We'll have to face him at some point, right?"

"I fear that's always been the case, Achan. Not that you face Lord Nathak, necessarily, or even Esek, but that you face the keliy."

Achan winced at a throb in his head. "But how can I stand against such power? Such evil?"

"You can't. But Arman can and will."

Achan swallowed an angry retort. People threw that phase around as if it were nothing more than a greeting. Arman will do this. Arman will do that. Trust Arman. But Achan was the one prophesied to push back Darkness. He did not doubt Arman would help him, but he still felt overwhelmed, insignificant, and clueless as to what he would need to do.

Just don't forget to let me in on the plan, Arman.

"What will you do with the black knights who survived the attack?" Captain Demry asked.

Sir Gavin tugged on his beard braid. "Keep them bound and full of âleh as long as we can. Then throw them in the dungeon at Armonguard. Maybe execute them. That will be your choice, Your Highness."

His choice. A shudder coursed through him. Lord Nathak's story . . . his whole life. What a waste. How could Queen Dara have been so cruel? And why had the king done such a thing in the first place? Sir Gavin had said King Axel loved his wife. What had gone wrong? The question brought his thoughts back to his own blunder with Challa.

"And what about Kurtz?" Toros Ianjo, the warrior-priest of Arman, directed his question to Sir Gavin. "Will you arrest him as well?"

Achan perked up. "Arrest Kurtz? For what? He saved my life and Shung's. I should knight him."

"I'm afraid there is more to it than that, Your Highness." Sir Caleb swallowed, as if he'd rather not admit what he had to say. "When I went to claim a new wagon for you to travel in, I found them all at the back of the procession. The prostitutes Kurtz hired were living in them. Kurtz and his comrades had shifted the supplies to carts and such to make room.

"The women have been traveling at the back of the procession so that the officers would not notice them. But the wagons were designed specifically to hide you. That's why they all looked alike. And they were to be spaced evenly throughout the procession. Kurtz's decision made it obvious to the black knights which wagon was yours. One of the black knights confessed as much. I don't know what in flames Kurtz was thinking."

"Kurtz has a tendency to disregard rules. It's the primary reason he was never knighted." Sir Gavin sniffed in a long, thoughtful breath. "I feel I owe you all an explanation about Kurtz Chazir." He turned to Achan, wincing as if remembering something painful. "If you would like to know why I put up with him, Your Highness."

What did *that* mean? "Of course."

"My mother had a baby sister she cared for along with me. That girl—my aunt—was named Melena. She was but four years old when my mother died. I was eleven. Melena was like a sister to me. When she grew up, she wanted her own family more than anything. Went through men like a loaf of bread. Miscarried six times that I know of. I didn't know what to do with the woman.

"When I was promoted to the Kingsguard, she ran off with a trader from Berland. I didn't hear from her for almost twenty years. Then one day I got a message from her husband—a Berland soldier. She had died in childbirth, and her husband said she'd wanted me to know her son.

"Kurtz is her son?"

"Aye. I visited him over the years. He only ever wanted to be a soldier like his father. Grew up in the barracks like I did. Had no woman around to teach him manners or compassion. All that to say, if he wasn't my cousin, I'd have discharged him long ago."

Achan couldn't help but think if it weren't for Gren, he might have turned out the same as Kurtz.

"It's just that he thinks himself invincible," Sir Caleb said. "That his actions have no consequences."

"Probably my fault as well for cleaning up so many of his messes. Likely he expects I will again." Sir Gavin pounded a fist on the table. "But not this time."

"What shall we do with the women?" Sir Caleb asked. "They're nothing but a distraction to our men. They must be sent back."

"Not without an escort," Toros said. "And they know too much about us, enough to hurt us if they wanted to. The prince, especially."

"Hurt me how?" Achan asked.

Sir Gavin's mustache twitched. "Do not fret. I see no way for the women to do you harm."

"It was only a kiss," Sir Caleb said to everyone at the table, as if clarifying a highly disputed fact. "If any of the men ask, make that clear."

Achan stared at a knot in the wood of the table, wanting to change the subject. Wanting to sleep a very long time.

"A kiss and a scratch," Captain Demry said with a wink. "Your boy is bragging about how his master was attacked by a chatul cat and has the wound to prove it."

The men laughed.

Pig snout. Now Achan would have to speak to Matthias. Come to think of it, he should speak with Cole as well, for the lad spent far too much time in Kurtz's company. Achan tapped his finger on the tabletop. What to do about Kurtz?

"Enough talk of this," Sir Gavin said. "So the women will come along? What do you suggest, Toros?"

Toros leaned back in his chair, revealing the embroidered interlocking red circles on the front of his dingy white surcoat. "Choose a guard of trusted, honorable men, and put the women to work. Laundry, mending, cooking. Perhaps some can make arrows. Reformation at its best."

"That will not make Challa happy," Achan said.

"We do not exist to make Challa happy, Your Highness, nor do you."

Her happiness hadn't been Achan's concern. "I simply meant that she will likely be difficult."

Captain Demry scanned the table, his brow furrowed into a thick line. "What is our next move then? Have the scouts reported anything?"

"We ride south as fast as we can," Sir Gavin said. "Esek's southern army has almost reached Armonguard. With Prince Oren missing, I don't doubt it will fall."

A silence gripped the tent. If Armonguard fell before Achan and his army reached it, it would be all the more difficult to take it back.

"But tonight we celebrate," Sir Gavin said. "We lost many today. Our men deserve to hear from us both." He sent a pointed look at Achan. "So, Captain Demry, select a trusted guard for the women. Sir Caleb, figure out how they'll travel so we can redistribute the wagons as should be. And, Toros, will you offer some sort of benediction for the men we lost today?"

Toros jerked his head in a quick nod. "Absolutely, Sir Gavin."

"That's all I have, then." Sir Gavin turned to Achan, eyebrows raised.

"Dismissed," Achan said, as if he had been leading this meeting.

When only Achan and Sir Gavin remained, the old knight turned his mismatched eyes to Achan and said, "I'm sorry none of us spoke to you about spirits, Your Highness. I assumed a man your age knew better than to indulge, but I don't suppose you've had much drink in your life."

"I've seen enough fuddled men to know better, Sir Gavin. I just didn't expect it to happen so quickly."

"Well, it's a poison the king's personal guard swears to abstain from. I gave it up years ago when I began working for King Paxton. Now, as for the girl—"

Achan thought of his father's face on the gold coin in his pants pocket. "You needn't fear. I'll not make *that* mistake again."

"Aye, that's well and good, but Caleb said you were concerned about what Kurtz said about your father."

The reality of it threatened to choke Achan all over again, like someone dunking his head underwater. "I was surprised. Angry, even. And then to learn that Lord Nathak had killed him and that . . ." Achan took a deep breath. "Did you know Lord Nathak was—"

"You father's son? Your half-brother? Nay. There were rumors of other children. But there are rumors with any king."

Children, Sir Gavin had said. Achan shook that thought away. "And such rumors are there because all the Hadar kings—my father, my grandfather, my great grandfather, and so on—they all kept mistresses?"

Sir Gavin met Achan's eyes and nodded. "Aye, though not Paxton, as far as I know, and I knew him well. But Paxton saw firsthand what Macoun went through, living in that castle as a baseborn son of a king. Paxton took care of Macoun for years, not that Macoun ever appreciated it. Paxton was fifteen when Johan was killed. Married a month later. Crowned on his sixteenth year of birth."

Achan had not known that. "Who did he marry?"

"Fasina Levy, who later became Lord Levy's aunt when her brother had children." Sir Gavin chuckled. "Now there was a match. Fasina was but thirteen, a shy little thing. I don't know that she and Paxton said three words to each other the first year of their marriage. But they worked things out eventually."

Eventually. Would that be Achan's lot? Three words said to Lady Gypsum in the course of a year? "Well, I'm glad to know the truth." To know what he needed to guard against for himself, for he would not betray his wife, whoever she may be.

But Sir Gavin mistook Achan's meaning. "As am I, lad. After thirteen years, it explains what bothered me most about your father's death. Not who had killed him so much as why Axel would not tell me who'd done it."

"He wanted to protect his son."

"That he did. Even as he and his queen lay dying by his son's hand." Sir Gavin gripped Achan's shoulder. There were tears in his eyes. "That is who I want you to remember, lad. The man so filled with Arman's love that he could forgive his son for taking his life and the life of his bride. *That* is the man I knew. The king I served. Just you remember it."

"But a man with many mistresses. A man who wouldn't have had that problem if he'd—"

"Aye, he was no porcelain saint. He was mixed, torn, pulled by light and darkness, as is every follower of Arman. That is what it is to love Arman and yet still live in this world. Pity those who do not know Arman, because in them there is nothing at all pulling them toward light."

Achan felt some of his anger at his father recede. That Sir Gavin could know about King Axel's failings and yet still admire him as a follower of Arman gave Achan courage as he examined his own mistakes. "I will."

After Toros's brief service for the dead, and after Achan and Sir Gavin had encouraged the soldiers, Achan went to the tent where Sir Caleb had confined Kurtz. It was a narrow brown tent with two cots inside. He found Kurtz lying on one with his hands tucked behind his head. Cole was sitting cross-legged on the other.

When Cole saw Achan he jumped up. "Good evening, Your Highness."

Achan frowned at the boy. "Have you been in here the whole time, Cole?"

"No, Your Highness. I just came from the reveling. Didn't feel much like celebrating, though."

"Would you give me a moment to talk with Kurtz?"

"Sure I will." Cole almost ran out the door.

Achan watched Cole dart between Shung and Manu and bit back his laughter. When he turned back to Kurtz he found the man standing, gaze trained on the grassy floor of the tent.

Achan took a quick breath, then said what he needed to say. "I was prepared to knight you after the recent battle. You saved my life. And Shung's. But in light of what Sir Caleb has brought to my attention . . . I cannot."

Kurtz's eyes shifted, looking at everything but Achan. "Understood, Your Highness. I don't need to be knighted, I don't. Fancy titles don't matter none to me, eh?"

"They matter to me, Kurtz. And I think you are worthy of such a title. It can still be in your future. Don't sabotage your worth to my army by putting a wagon-full of wine and prostitutes higher than our cause."

Kurtz said nothing, would not meet Achan's eyes.

"Sir Caleb wants you arrested, and Sir Gavin is done bailing you out. But I am a man of second chances. I set the men in the Prodotez free from their crimes. I do the same for you. But as I told them, 'Just know, if you go back to your old ways, I'll not be so forgiving next time.' Is that clear?"

Kurtz's face flushed, but he smiled. "Aye, Your Highness. Clear as sugar wine, it is."

26

Is anyone hurt, Jax? Averella asked.

No. The Ebens have not seen us. They are moving on. Put out your torch and come quietly.

We don't have a torch. Averella squeezed Bran's hand and whispered, "Jax says to come quietly."

"What is it?" he whispered back.

"Ebens. They're moving on, though."

Bran drew his sword silently and inched forward. Averella followed.

The mouth of the cave came into view, dimly lit from outside. Distant torches illuminated a thick forest. Over two dozen giants walked away from the cave in a line, threading through the trees. Jax, Sir Rigil, Noam, and Gren were standing along the wall of the cave, their own torches out.

What were they doing? Averella asked Jax.

Hunting. I suspect the flock of gowzals drew their attention. Two came up to investigate, but turned back before they came inside.

What will we do?

I know not. Ebens have camps all over this area now. I heard them talking about it. I can't lead us into the unknown. We'd be better off going back through the tunnel to Mahanaim, though that could be suicide also with Esek's men in the city.

The word "tunnel" brought a man's face to Averella's mind. *Peripaso, Jax. Could you message him? He knows this area better than anyone. Maybe he could help us.*

A wise idea, Vrell. I'll message him right away.

The Eben torchlight had faded entirely now.

"Set up camp in the cave," Vrell whispered. "Back from the mouth. Sir Rigil, you stay here with Jax and keep watch. Bran and I will relieve you in a few hours."

"Very well, my lady."

Averella took Gren's hand and reached for the tunnel wall. "Master Rennan and Noam, come with us. Master Rennan, once we turn the corner, would you light your torch?"

"Absolutely."

Averella inched along until Bran's torchlight lit their way. She found an area of ground that was somewhat smooth and claimed it for the camp. She set out her bedroll beside Gren's and encouraged Noam to sit on it. They ate a meal of dried fish and apples and whispered to one another when they had to speak. But mostly they remained silent. Jax messaged her that Peripaso was on his way to help them.

Praise Arman.

After that the hours passed slowly. Eventually she and Bran took their watch at the mouth of the cave. It was very dark. Unless an animal snuck up on them, Averella figured they would see light from miles away. She could barely see Bran's outline from the dim torchlight of the camp.

"I'm still hungry," Bran said. "Or maybe I'm just bored."

Averella dug into her satchel and gave Bran some mentha leaves to chew on. "At least your mind will feel like it is getting something."

"Thank you, Averella."

She put her hands down and pushed back against some roots that wound in through the mouth of the cave. Here the ground was covered in dried grass and pine needles. She could smell the faint scent of pine over the rancid smell of Darkness. Darkness had not been here long enough to kill everything. She lay back, but no position was comfortable in plate armor.

She closed her eyes and tried to still her mind, but the clicking in the trees above magnified. She pictured a peaceful place, and into her mind came an image of a narrow castle built into the side of a cliff. It was covered in moss. A waterfall spilled down each side like flowing hair. The water pooled at the bottom of the falls and ran out across the bailey in a river that vanished through an iron grate in the sentry wall. Thick trees edged the far side of the pool and reflected on the water's surface.

The scene shifted. Averella stood in the water behind a waterfall, shivering. Everything around her was white frothing liquid. Water trickled down her face and arms. She shifted and rubbed the tickle away, but found something firm there. She tried to flick it away, but it clung to her skin. She twisted her body to see it.

A leech.

She shuddered and pried the creature off with her fingernails, but there were more on her now. She was naked and the leeches covered her body like a slimy black gown. She screamed and dug at them.

Strong arms grabbed her. She tried to scream, but a hand clamped over her mouth. She squirmed, wanting nothing more than to get the leeches off her skin. She scratched her captor's face and squealed.

"Vrella, please!" a soft voice whispered. "You must not make noise!"

She twisted her head and freed her mouth. "The leeches!"

His hand found her mouth again. "You are dreaming. There are no leeches here."

She stilled, for that was Bran's voice. She could see nothing, yet knew that he was the one holding her. Her head was cradled in his arm, his free hand cupped over her mouth.

"Just a dream," he said.

She sucked in long breaths through her nose. Darkness smelled sour.

"Are you with me, Vrella? If I let go, you'll be silent and not scratch me anymore?"

She nodded, hoping he could discern her answer from the motion of her head.

Bran lifted his hand. "I'm sorry. You were screaming so loud I don't doubt all Nahar Duchy heard you. And you scratched my face good."

Vrell? Jax bloodvoiced. *Are you well?*

A dream, Jax. Forgive me. I did not mean to fall asleep.

Would you like me to relieve you?

No. I'm awake now. "I'm sorry, Master Rennan." She opened her satchel and felt for her jar of salve. "Let me put something on that scratch."

"It's not that bad, I'm sure."

"Do not argue." She dipped her fingers into the cold salve and rubbed it on his cheek where she thought she saw discoloration. "I do not like Darkness, Master Rennan. I never have."

"Nor do I, Vrella."

Something in that name gave Averella pause. "It's been a long time since you called me *Vrella,* has it not?"

"Aye. Much is different now."

"Can we not go back to how it used to be?"

His chest rose and fell with a deep breath. "I will always care for you. But both our hearts have changed."

"Completely? Surely not."

He did not speak for a moment, as if considering it fully. "He loves you. And you him."

Her chest tightened at the mention of "he." She pushed herself up and twisted around to face Bran. "That is not what I asked, Bran."

"Ahh." There was a laugh to his sigh. "So, you are calling me *Bran* again, are you?"

"Do you love me?"

The soft glint of his eyes met hers. His breath was shaky. "Aye, Vrella. I do . . ."

Averella's heart leapt within her plate armor. She knew it! Merciful heart, there was still hope.

" . . . but I will not take you from him," Bran said. "He needs you more than I do."

"I do not want to talk about Prince Gidon's needs. What about Gren? Do you love her, as well?"

"I-I don't know, Vrella. I care for Gren, but it's not the same. And she does not believe Arman's truth, so . . ."

"*I* still love *you.*"

Another dry laugh. "No. You only think you do because you cannot remember that you don't."

"Sounds somewhat silly when you say it like that."

Bran's tone went sour. "The whole ordeal is maddening."

"Mother says we quarreled."

"I was angry. You left me without a word. Told me nothing of Esek, of dressing as a boy. And you never once spoke to me with your bloodvoice, though you were more than capable. I begged your mother for an explanation, and she finally told me some of it. But not where you were or when you would return. And then . . . when you did come back . . . you had changed. I came to understand that you did not love me as much as you loved the idea of me."

She pushed up onto her knees and brushed her lips over his.

He gripped her shoulders and turned his head. "Vrella, please."

She grabbed his face in both hands and kissed him again. It was like kissing a post.

Then Bran's posture relaxed. He slid his hands into her hair and moved his mouth against hers, tasting of mentha. He slid his hands down to her throat. One finger tangled in the cord at her neck. Achan's ring.

She pulled away. "I am sorry!"

Silence descended but for Bran's heavy breathing. He finally growled. "Why must we always kiss to test our love?"

"I . . ." Had they done that before?

"Were you able to figure things out this time?"

Averella swallowed her shame. "Not really."

He grunted. "Here." He patted the ground beside him. "Sit and I'll tell you what I know of the prince. Perhaps it will help you remember."

Averella did as Bran asked, not wanting to hear about Prince Gidon, but feeling too guilty to protest. He told her how Achan had beaten Silvo Hamartano at a tournament, long before he'd known he was of royal blood, and how he was brave enough to insult Lady Jaira back after she'd insulted him for being a stray.

After a long while, Bran's voice faded. Averella lay awake, trying not to think of all Bran had told her. But visions of Darkness came then, so she focused on herbs, picturing them in her mind and thinking about their medicinal uses, wondering how she knew so much about them all. When she finally did sleep, it was restless.

Dreams came again. Ebens. Esek. Prince Gidon. A man named Khai Mageia. Macoun Hadar. Sir Gavin. And Bran. In her dreams, she walked along a stone corridor, exiting the Mahanaim dungeons, wondering where might she find the best apples.

Mags would know.

"I don't put 'em here, I just keep 'em here," a man's voice snapped from up ahead. "Take it up with Lord Levy if you like."

Averella rounded the corner to see the back of a guard standing at the dungeon gate. The man he was talking to sidestepped as if preparing to leave.

Bran.

It felt strange to see him after so long. He looked different, but the same. Maybe even taller. She wanted him to recognize her, sweep her off her feet, and take her home. At the same time, she hesitated. If she revealed herself in front of this guard, he would report it. She might be taken prisoner.

As she approached the gate, she struggled to know what to do. She wanted to go home, did she not?

Of course she did, but first she had to help Achan.

Her surroundings shifted. She stood in a dungeon cell. The smell of mildew and human waste made her gag. Across the cell, Achan hung from his wrists, shackled face-first against the stone wall. Deep red welts crisscrossed his back. A guard raised his arm and whipped him again. Averella jumped and looked away, hands covering her face. But nothing could mask the sound of the leather against flesh and Achan's grunts as he fought the pain.

She awoke, panting. Her chest burned as if coals were smoldering inside. It had been a dream. Simply another vision from Darkness. She lay on her side on the hard ground. She clutched the blanket to her chest, wanting to burrow under it. The blanket did not give.

She propped herself onto one elbow to see what the problem was. Master Rennan lay on his side, facing her. She had been pulling at his sleeve.

Reality came rushing back. They were in Darkness. Achan was far away, likely engaged in battle.

She shook her head. Why did it matter where Achan was? She lay back down, putting space between her and Master Rennan.

She suddenly knew that those last scenes had been memories. She had seen Bran in the Mahanaim dungeon. He had brought Achan's bag. But Vrell had not confessed her identity. She could not fathom why she had kept silent.

But she already knew. She had not confided the truth to Bran that day because she had been too concerned for Achan's welfare. More concerned about this mysterious young man than her betrothed.

She turned around and stared into the darkness where Bran lay sleeping. He had not been to blame for their parting.

She had been the one to go astray.

27

Achan and his army moved south toward Armonguard and the eventual battle—now only eight thousand strong, having lost a thousand in the battle of Reshon Gate. Desperate to be outdoors in the sun, Achan rode Scout behind Shung and Manu. Sir Caleb had insisted he wear his armor if he were going to ride, though he couldn't wear his helm due to the burn on his ear. His new haircut garnered more stares than ever. The fireball had singed so much hair that Achan's short haircut made him look like a little boy.

The army moved in one seemingly endless line, stretching in both directions as far as he could see, which wasn't far considering the thickness of this massive forest. Achan rode beside his wagon, which moved at the back of the vanguard and at the head of the center of their procession. He could see the archers before Shung and Manu, bows strapped to their backs or saddlebags. Scouts moved through the forest, keeping watch for any who might come at them from the sides.

Since Achan had ridden Dove yesterday, he rode Scout now. Scout tended to get jealous of Dove. Bart, the piebald packhorse Cole was riding, didn't seem to care who he belonged to. Though he likely believed Cole his owner, if anyone, since Cole rode and cared for him.

Achan steered Scout up to Bart's side. "How are you today, Cole?"

"I'm well, Your Highness. Thank you for asking." Cole always spoke to Achan with more decorum than a noblewoman would use.

"Have you thought any more about training as a squire?" Achan asked.

Cole shook his choppy brown hair out of his eyes. "I'm but a stray, Your Highness."

"So am I, in case you forgot. Both my parents are dead."

Cole merely stared.

"Do you want to train as a squire or not, Cole? Let your rank have nothing to do with it and answer the question."

Cole flushed so that his face blended in with his hundreds of freckles. He combed his fingers through Bart's mane. "Suppose I'd like to try, Your Highness."

"Then try you shall. Come to my tent after dinner tonight."

Cole looked up with wide eyes. "I'm to be *your* squire?"

"Why not? I don't have one. Only four shadows and a valet-page."

"But you should have a trained squire, one who can serve you well. I could squire for someone else. Kurtz, maybe."

Achan glanced behind him to where Kurtz and Cortland rode side by side. Sir Caleb had freed Kurtz at Achan's request. "You're *not* squiring for Kurtz."

"But I bunk in the same tent as him. It makes good sense," Cole said. "Then you could pick someone better."

The last thing the lad needed was Kurtz teaching him the ways of the world. "Only knights and royalty take on squires. Since Kurtz is neither, he's not an option. I'd prefer to train my own squire, Cole, and have chosen you. What say you?"

"I'm . . . I'm honored, Your Highness. Thank you!"

Achan chuckled. The boy was honored whenever Achan looked at him. "You're welcome, Cole. Until tonight." Achan rode up beside Shung's mount. "I'm going to ride down the line."

Shung nodded and turned his horse. "Kurtz, Cortland, ride ahead. Manu and Shung will follow the prince."

Achan stifled a grin. Shung only ever referred to him as "the prince" when he spoke to others as the head of Achan's guard. Otherwise, Achan was always Little Cham.

Achan followed Kurtz and Cortland down the line, greeting the men, especially those who bore injuries. Thanking them for their service. Most seemed happy to talk with him. Only two glared openly. Perhaps they'd been deeply affected by the segregation of Kurtz's lady friends.

The soldiers' horses parted for him like cream in water. Achan rode along merrily, until he spotted a face so familiar and so out of place as to almost unhorse him.

Harnu Poe? Riding a stunning white and black courser.

"Whoa, boy." What was Harnu doing here? Anger flooded him as he looked at Harnu's pockmarked face. Achan swallowed, torn by how to address the bully who'd tormented him all his childhood. Politeness would be best, so long as they had an audience. "Harnu. I'm glad to see you well. When did you join our army? Is Noam with you?"

"No . . ." Harnu glanced at Shung, then bowed his head. "Y-Your Highness. We were separated in Mahanaim."

"Separated? How?"

"I was trading my wagon for a boat when your men attacked the city. I was unable to get to the boat, so I joined the battle and just . . . decided to stay on."

"Your Highness," Cortland said. "Why not bring this man to the side of the road so the others can keep moving."

"Of course." Achan steered Scout into the grass on the side of the King's Road. Harnu followed, his horse flicking its tail. The army trudged on, horses' hooves scraping over the dirt, men talking, wagon wheels creaking. "Tell me, Harnu. What became of Gren, Noam, and Sparrow?"

Harnu's dark eyebrows sank over his eyes. "Sparrow?"

"Vrell Sparrow. She was traveling with Gren. She told me you and Noam rescued her from Sitna Manor."

"Oh." Harnu's forehead wrinkled. "They're together, the women and Noam. The lady, er, *Vrell*, she spoke to my mind. I told her to leave me behind since Captain Demry allowed me to join the ranks." He bowed again. "Your Highness."

Sparrow must be safe if she'd left Mahanaim. "If Captain Demry asked you to join his men, you must have fought well." Achan felt some of his anger leaking away. Harnu now served in *his* army. And served nobly, at that.

Harnu lowered his gaze. "I did my best. I have no formal training with a sword. As you know."

"If only Captain Demry had some pitchforks on hand."

A mixture of expressions fought for purchase on Harnu's face, but he settled on a smile that looked painful.

Achan continued before Harnu said something he'd regret. "But you've likely created enough swords to know a weapon's strength. Did you find that knowledge useful?"

"I did."

"Well, I thank you, Harnu, for assisting Sparrow. Vrell, that is. For helping Gren rescue her from Lord Nathak's wagon, for getting her safely to your father's cabin, and for watching over her until she returned to her body."

"How do you know all that?"

Achan glanced at Shung. "We bloodvoicers talk."

Harnu's gaze darted between Achan's guards, his face suddenly pale. "Uh . . . Your Highness, since I took care of your lady friend, might I ask a similar favor?"

Achan frowned. Don't push it, swine. "You may *ask*."

"Help me convince Grendolyn to marry me?"

A moment passed before Achan realized that his mouth was hanging open. He barked out a laugh. "Uh . . . I think Gren may have her heart set on . . . someone else. Furthermore, I won't force Gren to marry anyone she does not wish to marry."

Harnu scowled. "Didn't stop you before."

Achan straightened in his saddle. "What do you mean?"

"Riga. Gren didn't want to marry Riga."

"Well, I know that. She wanted to marry me, but her father would not hear of it."

"But you set the marriage in motion. Riga told me so."

"I had to!" Some of the passing soldiers stared at Achan, so he lowered his voice. "To *save* her."

"No," Harnu said. "I'd been trying to talk Riga into marrying Kelmae Samsol. I'd nearly convinced him too, 'til you came barging in with your accusations."

"It was no mere accusation. Esek wanted to take Gren as a mistress."

"Only to spite *you*."

Achan's stomach boiled. But Harnu had more to say.

"Where were you on her wedding night?"

The question shocked Achan. He glanced to the passing army, to a cart stacked with rolled-up tents. "I was in bed under the ale casks." Grieving. The brief memory brought a weight over Achan. He was done speaking to Harnu Poe. He wanted to go back to his wagon, but Harnu's next words snared him.

"You caused her misery and left. But I had to stand outside their bedroom door and pretend I didn't care what was taking place within. I had to stand guard, indifferent to the sound of her crying while—"

Achan shook his head. "Don't."

"—Riga took what—"

"I said don't!"

Harnu gave him a pointed look, his dark eyes like arrows trained on his head. "You need to hear this."

"I do not!"

Cortland nosed his mount between Achan and Harnu's. "Your Highness, perhaps it's time to move on?"

Harnu's face hardened. "You're just like him, now, aren't you? Esek? Ruining lives. Barking orders. Running off to hide in the comfort of your private chambers."

"Your Highness?" Kurtz rode up on Achan's other side. "Shall I cuff this drudge for you?"

Achan held up a finger, but did not look away from Harnu. "I helped Gren the only way I could. The wedding would have happened anyway. It—"

Harnu shook his head.

"—would have! And you're a fool to believe otherwise. Nothing you or I could have done would have changed it."

"She loved you," Harnu said. "Loved you. Despised Riga. But me . . . I was invisible. And I was the only one who didn't break her heart. And she can't see that, even now."

This was madness. "You broke her heart every time you broke my face, or some other poor sap's." Achan grimaced. "If you have loved Gren always, tell me why. What about her is so grand?"

Harnu's disposition softened at this question. He ran his fingers through his horse's mane. "She's kind to everyone, no matter their station. She's loyal, truthful, and honorable. She's a hard worker and can do as much with fabric as I can with iron. Her voice makes me calm when I hear it. And I only have to look on her face to know peace in my heart. I've no joy without her in my life."

Blazes, the fool did love Gren. "Have you told her? What you just told me?"

"She never gives me opportunity. And I can't write."

Scout flicked his ear at a fly. "Where would you live and how?"

"I maintained Riga's cabin. Added a second room for the child. If she allowed it, I'd live there with her. Or we could live with my father. His age has altered him greatly. The armory will pass to me when he dies, so I'll be able to provide for her and the child. If the child is male, he'll inherit Master Hoff's trade. If the child's a girl, Gren will teach her to make clothing. I'll keep the child safe and see she makes a good match in marriage—one of her own choosing as much as possible."

Achan stared at Harnu, enthralled by the dreamy look in the man's eyes and weighted down by his own guilt. The idea of caring for Gren had crossed his mind only once since he'd heard of Riga's death. Was Harnu a better man than he was? What had happened to Achan's nobility?

He knew the answer without even thinking her name. Vrell Sparrow. She had stolen his heart from Gren. When this war ended, he would find her and do all he could to mend what was broken.

"Harnu, I cannot promise such a thing without speaking to Gren. I will speak to her, though. That much I can do."

Harnu's grin looked foreign on his pockmarked face. Achan didn't think he had ever seen the man offer a genuine smile until this moment. "Thank you, Your Highness. That's all I ask."

Achan nodded. "Go on then. Catch up with your men."

Harnu spurred his horse into a canter along the grassy edge of the trail. Achan watched him go, thoughts drifting like pollen in the wind.

"No one could doubt his love is true," Cortland said. "He could be a minstrel, the way he talks about his girl."

His girl. Achan glanced at Cortland, a man who knew nothing of the knotted past Achan shared with Gren and Harnu. And Riga.

Gren, Harnu's girl?

Only Arman knew the answer to that.

28

"My lady, it's time to wake."

Averella opened her eyes expecting to see Bran. Instead, she saw the faint outline of an old bald man. She blinked and sat up to find that it was not an old man at all, but Peripaso, the man who lived in the tunnels under Nahar Forest. His thin, bony body, though young, was hunched from years of scuttling through tunnels like a beetle. His skin was wrinkled like a raisin from living in the constant moisture of the underground hot springs.

Before, he had worn nothing but blackened undershorts. Today he was wearing a brown tunic and trousers—filthy in the knees—and shabby leather shoes. He held a coil of rope looped over one shoulder.

"Well, now," he said, his voice twangy. "Who'd of thought that all this time you were a lady?"

She grinned. "Hello, Peripaso."

Bran stepped beside Peripaso and extended his hand. "We are ready to depart. You might want to eat something first."

Averella accepted his help to stand. She straightened the bottom of her skirt that had twisted under her bronze breastplate. "Peripaso, what is our plan?"

He patted the rope. "I'm goin' to lead everyone out, Lady Vrell. There's a tunnel not too far from here. It's larger than most and goes straight up. It'll be hard climbin', but once we reach the top, we'll slide down the other side. Lets out a day's walk from Noiz."

Noiz was the king's sanctuary. "We are going to Noiz?" Averella asked.

"Jax thinks it wise," Bran said.

"Ebens are camped all over Nahar Forest," Peripaso said. "We'd never make it to Xulon. And Noiz isn't far from Armonguard."

Averella recalled the slide in Peripaso's cave. But slide down an entire mountain? "I thought you caved in all the tunnels that let out into Darkness and Eben territory."

"I did, Lady Vrell, but that was 'fore Darkness shifted. Now plenty let out in Darkness. Ebens set up camp by most of 'em. Lazy hunters. Waiting for critters to take shelter. Ebens haven't bothered with this one, though. Guess they figure no creature would shelter somewhere so steep."

Gren had already packed up Averella's things, so she quickly ate the dried dates Bran had given her to break her fast.

Peripaso held up his rope. "Can't use a torch in our flight. It'll be a beacon for anyone to follow. You all hold tight to this rope, and you'll not be left behind."

"But how can you know where you're taking us if you can't see?" Gren asked.

"Peri knows this forest like his own hand," Jax said. "He can lead us out of here."

Peripaso handed the looped end of his rope to Sir Eagan, then unrolled it as he handed it off to Bran, Sir Rigil, Gren, Jax, Noam, and Vrell, issuing warnings as he went. "Hold tight or you'll be left behind. Must not let go, no matter what. When we reach the tunnel, go slow. It's real steep."

Peripaso went up to the front of the line, took the looped front end of the rope from Sir Eagan, and threaded it over his shoulder. Averella twisted the course rope in her hands, not liking her place in line at all.

Bran walked back and pulled Gren and Noam out from the middle. He also took Averella from her place at the end. "I want you three towards the front."

"Thank you," Averella said.

"Yes, well thought out, Master Rennan," Sir Rigil said. "Jax and I will bring up the rear."

Gren clutched Bran's arm. "I'm so frightened, Bran. Do you think we'll meet any Ebens?"

"Shh. We'll talk later." Bran patted her hand, then glanced up and met Averella's gaze. "Averella, stay here, right behind Sir Eagan.

Gren, you stay behind Lady Averella. Noam, stay behind Gren. Jax, Sir Rigil, and I will be at the end of the line to watch for Ebens and stragglers."

Averella ducked under the rope and gripped it with her left hand. Gren did the same.

Bran squeezed Averella's shoulder. "Do not let go of this rope, Vrella, please." His eyes burned into hers.

She blinked, hoping to break the intensity of his stare. "I will not. I promise."

The corner of his mouth twisted, as if her promises meant little, but he released her shoulder. He nodded to Gren, then took his place at the end of the line.

"He doesn't seem too happy to see *me,*" Gren whispered.

"There is much on his mind at present." Averella smiled, hoping to cheer Gren, but feeling guilty knowing what Bran had shared with her last night. *Arman, please help me. Everything is so complicated. I know not how to set it right.*

"Ready to go?" Sir Eagan asked.

She nodded, again comparing his features to hers. They had the same mouth, it seemed. And cheeks. And hair. She frowned. *Why not give me Mother's hair, Arman?*

Peripaso tugged the line, drawing Averella's gaze his way. He whispered, "Hold tight now, Lady Vrell." He made his way to the mouth of the cave.

She doubted they could outrun anything traveling in this manner.

Once outside the cave, Peripaso took a sharp right and walked into the darkness. How he knew where he was going, Averella would never know. She stumbled along, clutching the rope as if it were the only thing keeping her from plummeting to her death.

"There's a slope here," Sir Eagan said. "Pass it back."

"Pass it where?"

"Tell the person behind you."

Averella's next step landed before she expected it to. The ground was sloping upward. Oh. She stopped and turned her head. "We are starting up a hill. Tell the person behind you."

"Keep moving, though, Averella," Sir Eagan said.

She faced forward and took a tentative step up the dark slope. The tread of footsteps over rock muted the whispers of the message she had passed down the line. Clicking rang out all around, like someone shaking walnuts on a string. A gowzal screeched in the distance. It still sent a chill through her that made her gowzal bites throb.

Averella had no choice but to stumble along through the darkness. There was no way to monitor time, no sun or stars or moon to look to for guidance. All she could do was hold tight to the rope and trust that Peripaso knew what he was doing.

They walked over rock for hours—indeed, for what seemed like a full day—until the sound of their footsteps changed, suddenly echoing around them. Had they entered a cave?

Peripaso stopped. Metal scraped against metal, loud and hollow. A spark bloomed a few feet before her and struggled into a powerful flame. Peripaso lifted a torch high.

They stood in a shallow cave of golden rock. Just behind Peripaso, a dark hole pierced the rock. Averella knew from her experience with Peripaso that they would be going inside that hole.

"Come close, ever'one." Peripaso waved them forward. "Don't let go of the rope, jest crowd 'round. Like I said 'fore, the tunnel's a steep climb. If the person in front of you struggles, best way to help is to make a step out of your hand and give a boost. And stay calm. Panickin' will cause trouble for ever'one. That clear?"

Sir Rigil responded with a "Yes," though the rest merely nodded.

"Now, I can't climb with a flame, so I have to put the torch out. Tunnel's pretty jagged on top, so watch your head. There'll be plenty of hand and footholds."

The freckles on Gren's face looked golden in the torchlight. "How far up is it?"

"Never thought to measure. It'll take a good two days to get to the top."

"Two days of climbing!" Gren said. "What will we eat?"

"I brought enough for ever'one. It's no feast, but it'll do."

"What about water?" Bran asked.

"There's plenty of water in the tunnels. Won't go thirsty. Now, it'll be blazin' today up in there as we near the hot springs, but don't go tossin' off layers of clothes. You'll need 'em when it gets cold."

"How will it get cold if there are hot springs?" Averella asked.

"The hot springs are under Nahar. Once we pass into Cela Duchy, we'll be so far up the mountain, you'll be shiverin'."

With that, Peripaso put out the torch, and the rope tugged Averella forward again.

29

Achan sat at the table in his tent. It was long past dinner. The sun had set, giving him the eerie feeling of being in Darkness again. Cole sat across from him, squirming like a man who'd just removed two dozen leeches. Shung and Manu stood inside the door.

"There's much to learn in becoming a squire," Achan said. "You'll be taught to read and write. You'll learn the history, customs, and etiquette for each city of Er'Rets. You must memorize wisdom from the Book of Life and try to please Arman in all things. Do you think you can do all this?"

Cole shook the hair out of his eyes. "Sure seems a lot, Your Highness. But I'll try."

Achan folded his arms. "I'm most concerned at present with your learning to use a sword, at least to some degree."

Cole's eyes popped wide. "You think I'm strong enough?"

"Of course, lad! Fine spirit like yours. And practice will make you stronger."

Sir Gavin and Sir Caleb entered the tent. Achan had barely begun with Cole, but Sir Gavin came to Achan's tent these days only when he had important news.

"Manu, would you take Cole to Captain Demry and see that he is given a sword and shield?" Achan asked. "Come back when you've got it, Cole, and we'll continue."

Manu bowed and held the drape aside. Cole jumped up and scurried out of the tent. Cortland followed.

Then Cole poked his head back past the drape on the door. "Thank you, Your Highness. I'll be back later."

Achan smiled. "You are welcome, Cole."

Cole vanished.

Sir Gavin chuckled. "He's an eager one to learn."

"More eager to flee your presence, I'd guess," Achan said. "You're always frightening the children, Sir Gavin."

"It's the eyes, no doubt," Sir Gavin said, groaning as he fell into the chair Cole had abandoned. "Though I'm sure you're not eager to discuss my attractiveness or lack thereof." Sir Gavin pulled out the chair beside his with a glance at Sir Caleb and a nod of his head. Sir Caleb sat as well.

"I've spoken with Sir Eagan and Sir Jax," Sir Gavin said. "They're together. Currently traveling south through Darkness with Sir Rigil and Bran and a few others they've gathered along the way. They're headed for Noiz now. Since they're all on foot, it'll take them some time to reach Armonguard."

"All are well?"

"Aye, all are well."

It pleased Achan to know this. For these were all good men, and he did not want to lose any of them, though he would have liked to have fought beside them in whatever battles were coming.

Achan's mornings continued to run with a consistent ceremony. Once Matthias was satisfied with a tale of one of Achan's scars, the boy would go fetch them breakfast. Achan wondered what would happen if he ever ran out of new scars to talk about. For better or worse, though, that was not likely to happen for a long time yet.

Then Achan would dress himself in whatever clothing Matthias had laid out, an arrangement Achan liked better than having a child dress him. Matthias would return with breakfast. And, at some time while Achan was eating, Toros Ianjo would come with spiritual counsel.

Today was no different. Toros entered Achan's tent just as he finished off his bread.

"Good day, Your Highness. I trust you slept well?"

"I did. Knowing my friends are alive and well gives me great comfort."

"Ah, well. Comfort comes easiest when our soul is content. Alas, our soul is rarely content for long." Toros pulled out the chair across from Achan and sat down.

"Why is that?" Achan asked. "Why does nothing in Er'Rets bring complete satisfaction?"

"Perhaps it is a gift from Arman."

Achan met Toros's gaze, drawn in by the dark brown depths of the priest's eyes. "What do you mean? Why would that be a gift?"

The warrior-priest swept his hand around in the air. "Would you really want this broken, hurtful land to be the fulfillment of your every wish? Doesn't it please you to know that something far superior awaits you?"

"Shamayim?"

"You will never want for anything once you are in Arman's presence."

Achan chuckled. "That's the truth. When Arman speaks, I barely remember my name. Though he no longer speaks to me as much as he once did. Why do you suppose that is?"

"Do you speak to him?"

"Well, yes. To pray."

"For what?"

Achan paused while Matthias took his trencher away. "You want to know my prayers?"

Toros urged Achan with a nod.

"Very well. I pray for help. For the war. For guidance." For Sparrow to remember him, and to love him. To be safe.

"You pray for you." Toros cocked his head. "Arman does long to hear your prayers, but He also deserves your praise and worship. Your allegiance."

"I know. Why is it so difficult to remember that?"

"We are selfish creatures, even those of us who know Arman. We're also creatures of habit. But we can be retrained. I suggest you try to form new habits."

Toros's visits never had the same effect on him. Some days, Toros would leave Achan feeling like Arman's best friend. And some days, like today, Achan felt as though he fell short of Arman's expectations.

Sir Caleb strode into Achan's tent, cheeks flushed. "Your Highness. Sir Gavin just got word from Sundergow. Armonguard is taken! Esek's black knights attacked the fortress at dawn. The road south is blocked by black knights. And the remaining enemy troops from Mahanaim followed us from the north. We are trapped."

Trapped. Achan pushed back from the table. "How is this possible? Prince Oren had his own army *and* the Mârad. And who is Sundergow?"

"Prince Oren's advisor."

"Did he speak of Prince Oren's state?"

"Stormed."

"Stormed!" Achan jumped up and circled the table. Toros stood as well. "That can't be. He was struck with the green fire. The same fire that took the top of my ear. How can he be stormed?"

"Sundergow seems to think Prince Oren stormed himself to escape the coming impact of the fire."

Achan paced beside the table. "Stormed himself? Is that even possible?"

"It is, Your Highness. Prince Oren's body is with Sundergow in the dungeon."

Achan recalled finding Sparrow's lifeless body in the Sitna keep. At least Prince Oren was trained in the Veil. Still, should Achan go looking for him? Could Duchess Amal? "What will we do?"

"Sir Gavin has called the generals. We are to go to the meeting tent right away."

Achan bowed to Toros. "Forgive me, Toros. I must go."

Toros returned the bow. "My prayers go with you, Highness."

When Sir Caleb and Achan arrived in Sir Gavin's tent, several conversations were taking place at once. Achan quickly took his seat and called for quiet. He asked Sir Gavin to share the details of the situation, which offered no more information than what Sir Caleb had already shared.

"I see we have but two options," Sir Gavin said, referring to his massive leather map that again covered the table. "One, we go east and await Captain Chantry's fleet from Tsaftown. We board the ships and attack Armonguard from the sea."

"Are the ships close enough?" Captain Demry asked.

"Can they hold all our men?" Sir Eric asked.

Captain Demry's muscular build and dark eyes were a stark contrast to Sir Eric's wiry form and blue eyes. The two sat side by side.

"They can hold us all, but they've only passed Walden's Watch," Sir Gavin said.

"Then they're still several days from us," Captain Demry said.

"But it'll take us several days to reach the coast." Sir Gavin drew his finger along the path they might take. "We'd likely get there around the same time."

Altair, the captain of the contingent from Zerah Rock, grunted. "'Likely' isn't good enough when we're trapped on all sides by the enemy."

"I agree," Captain Loam said.

"What's your other option, Sir Gavin?" Sir Eric asked.

Sir Gavin ran his finger the opposite direction off the King's Road. "We head west through the game trails, making our way to Edom Gate. What's left of the Mârad army retreated there to wait for our instructions. They are five thousand strong. We'd have to leave the wagons behind, for the trail is narrow and quite steep once we reach the mountains. Captain Demry and most of the men—maybe two thirds—could set up camp inside Edom Gate, while the rest of us travel another day to Noïz to plan our attack."

"Couldn't Esek's men be trapping us in Noiz easier than they already have been doing here?" Inko asked. "There is only being one way coming in and going out of Noiz."

"That's not entirely true," Sir Caleb said. "There's only one road in and out of Noiz, but there are other ways to get there. Rivers. Mountain trails."

"Now, wait," Achan said. "They intend to fight us here? On the King's Road? Why?"

Sir Gavin tapped the burned image of Castle Armonguard. "To keep us from reaching our goal. The more of us they kill before we reach Armonguard, the easier time Esek's men will have defending her."

"Yes," Captain Loam said, "and then they get to dictate to us where the battle should be fought."

"So we will not let them," Achan said. "There are mountains and hills to the west. We have been in their shadow for days. In fact, isn't Noiz high in the mountains? Edom Gate as well?"

His generals nodded.

"Why not fight them there?" Achan asked. "We have to fight them sometime. Why don't we claim the high ground of our choosing and let them come if they dare? And if they don't come, then we'll go to them, still with the advantage of high ground. And with an extra five thousand men."

"The prince speaks wisely," Captain Loam said. "Armon-guard is nearly impenetrable from the ground, what with the way it sits on Lake Arman like an island. It would be well to have this battle away from there, now that the enemy holds it. We should take out as many of the enemy as we can before attempting to breach the castle itself."

"I disagree," Altair said. "The longer we wait to attack, the more time Esek has to set up defense in Armonguard. We should attack now, before too much time passes and he becomes deeply entrenched."

"If we attack now, we lose men before we even reach Armonguard," Sir Eric said. "The ships will give us safety."

"Why don't we do both?" Altair said. "Esek traps us from north and south. So we do the same. Send some to the boats and some to Noiz."

Sir Gavin shook his head. "It would be unwise to split our forces. United and in a strong position, we could repel any assault. But divided, both parts could be easily overwhelmed, and then we would have nothing."

"Noiz is being the safest place for the prince," Inko said.

"But Noiz is in Darkness," Sir Eric said. "The ships will keep us in Light longer."

"That won't matter for long," Sir Gavin said. "Darkness overtook Armonguard yesterday, so Sundergow said."

The men reacted to this with stunned silence.

"Armonguard in Darkness?" Sir Eric said. "Have we lost already?"

Another silence.

Achan rubbed his eyes. Everything was drawing to a close, he could feel it. "Why does that matter?" Achan asked, fighting the fear he felt gripping all of them. "I've always known the last battle would be in Darkness. This is not a surprise."

"Still," Sir Caleb said, "if we risk everything now by marching quickly to Armonguard, we risk our chance of even getting you there—to do what you must do."

"Which is what, by the way?" Achan felt every head turn toward him, but it was long past time to broach this subject. "I've been praying, but Arman has not answered."

"You will face Lord Nathak," Sir Gavin said. "Maybe Esek, as well. But I feel you must destroy the keliy."

"How?"

Sir Gavin shook his head. "You and I will work that out before we send you in. For now I say we get you to Noiz, and work out our plan of attack once we get to safety."

After the meeting, Achan returned to his tent to help Matthias pack. Matthias put all Achan's clothing into saddlebags, and Cole carried them to Bart.

With so many people working together, camp was disassembled within minutes. The army rode west into the dark woods. Toward Darkness. The sun shone through cracks in the trees, and Achan savored every last glimpse of warmth. He suspected he would not see the sun again until this war was over.

Or until he entered Shamayim.

Arman, help us all find the way. Help me know what to do. The procession upset a flock of sparrows. Achan watched them fly through the trees. *And help Sparrow to remember.*

Thoughts of Sparrow suddenly consumed him, and his heart twisted into a knot. He wanted to speak to her, if only to know she was well. But he could not stomach her anger or disdain. What would she say if she saw him face to face? If she came to Armonguard, would she come to see him? She had better, or he would send for her.

He grinned. Sparrow would not like that at all.

30

Averella's arms and legs ached from the awkward position of crawling up, up, up the steep tunnel. Every once in a while the tunnel leveled out enough for everyone to take a break—they slept twice in such places. Both times, as soon as they moved on, the tunnel grew steep again.

They all had taken a short spill at least once. Most skidded a few paces, clinging tightly to the rope. But Noam had slipped and nearly vanished. Jax had only just managed to catch the wisp of a man before he shot between Jax's legs. If only Gren would stop retelling the tale of his near demise, Averella's heartbeat might return to normal.

Water springs ran down the tunnel walls in numerous places, both hot and cool. Every time Peripaso passed a cool one, he pointed it out and told everyone to drink their fill.

Averella raised her foot to find the next foothold and pushed herself up. Her head slammed against something sharp overhead, blinding her with circles of white light. How had both Peripaso and Sir Eagan missed that one?

The rope tugged at her hand. Her father's voice drifted down from above, echoing softly in the stone cavern. "Averella? Are you well?"

"I struck my head." She twisted her neck and raised her voice. "There's a sharp rock hanging down. Go carefully!"

Not long after Peripaso stopped for their third night, he lit a torch. The light illuminated a round cavern and the dirty faces of their party. A trail of blood trickled down Gren's forehead from a scrape on the tunnel's roof. Averella opened her satchel and did what she could to stop the bleeding. She had used most of her supplies on the injured in Mahanaim.

Peripaso rationed out another meal of dried reekat. The greasy meat took Averella back to the underground river outside Xulon where a reekat had overturned their boat. It had been one of the most terrifying ordeals of Averella's life.

She gasped at the sudden memory. No wonder she had forgotten this past year. So much of it had been horrible!

Gren's soft voice drew Averella's attention. "Is it much farther?"

"We'll reach the top tomorrow," Peripaso said.

Gren sighed. "My legs will fall off before then."

Peripaso chuckled as he bedded down in the dark cavern. "Never you fear, Madam. All this hard work will pay off. For what goes up must go down, and going down will be much faster, much more fun, and no work at all, I promise you."

Averella wanted to believe him, but the aches in her body disagreed. She lay on the hard stone floor beside Gren.

"At least there are no beetles in this place," Gren said. "I hate any kind of pest."

Achan had once called Averella a pest. He had been teaching her to swordfight. He'd named her sword Firefox, she remembered now. Told her she was a hero with her bag of herbs.

Memories assaulted her then, all at once, glimpses of her forgotten days.

Achan wrestling her to the ground, calling her a weakling, teaching her to pin someone, to punch someone, to sweep out their leg. Achan knocking the breath from her time and again, forcing her face into a mound of snow.

And Mother claimed Averella loved this man? She fingered the ring around her neck and frowned. How could she have possibly endured being treated in such a way? And yet that leg sweep *had* proved useful only a few days ago.

More memories came.

Averella stealing Achan's food, pouncing and knocking him off a bench, slapping honey bread against his face. Knocking him down with a leg sweep. Swimming underwater and yanking his ankles so that he fell in. And back on dry land, drawing her dripping sword and poking him in the stomach.

The memories gave way to dreams laced with fear. She woke twice from someone else's screaming. Gren, both times. It seemed that Darkness haunted them, even in sleep.

The temperature in the tunnel dropped, and when Averella woke, the ground was frosty. Once they got moving again, the frost melted under their hands. But when they stopped for lunch, they were sitting on icy stone.

As Averella gnawed on her reekat meat, Peripaso approached. "We'll reach the ice soon, Lady Vrell. You mind helpin' me wrap ever'one's hands? It'll keep 'em warm, and from stickin' to the ice."

"I do not have enough linen to wrap everyone's hands."

"Oh, I'm prepared." His grin shifted the wrinkles on his face. "I got bits of reekat skin for the hands and creepers for our boots. Jest need some help gettin' 'em on."

Averella helped Peripaso tie the soft suede skins around everyone's hands. She had never heard of creepers, but they were short strips of carved bone, smooth and flat on one side and jagged like teeth on the other. Thongs of leather cord were looped through holes on each end so they could be tied under the sole of a boot to give traction on a slippery surface.

"Why you have so many?" Gren asked.

"I get bored, and they tend to break. I got a whole bucket full back home."

"Where is your home, sir?" Noam asked.

"You're standin' in it!" Peripaso laughed. "But I got a cave I spend most my time in, just north of Xulon. That's where I keep my things."

"Why aren't we going to your cave?" Gren asked.

"My cave is no place for all you fine folk."

Averella waved Gren over. "Give me your foot so I can tie this creeper on."

Averella and Peripaso finished tying the creepers in silence. Then Peripaso put out the torch and led them back into the tunnel. Sure enough, in a very short time, Averella's suede-wrapped hands slipped over a patch of ice. Frustrated voices rose behind her.

"Dig your foot in before you step!" Peripaso yelled.

Where it had been difficult to hold onto the rope and climb before, it was nearly impossible now. Averella concentrated on her feet. She stomped one foot into place, straightened that leg, dug the next foot in, and stood. It was like climbing a slippery ladder.

The ice got thicker, and the air cooled around her until each breath chilled her lungs. Her cheeks burned, her nose watered, and her fingers and toes went numb. The tunnel leveled off some, and

Averella was grateful for the reprieve. She moved to her hands and knees, giving her toes a break.

But Peripaso did not stop to rest. He usually did this whenever the incline leveled off, at least long enough so everyone could catch their breath.

Perhaps Jax had not messaged Sir Eagan yet. Jax, who was at the end of the line, always bloodvoiced Sir Eagan when he reached level ground. That way Peripaso would not stop to rest with anyone still on an incline.

"Sir Eagan?"

He panted and breathed out a "Yes, Averella?"

"Has Jax messaged yet?"

"He has."

"Might Peripaso be persuaded to take a brief rest?"

Peripaso answered, "We'll rest soon enough, Lady Vrell. Have patience a bit longer."

Averella did not know if she could make it. Her arms and legs trembled with each step, weary from exercise and cold. She hummed a tune to occupy her mind. The song Achan had sung outside the gates of Shamayim.

As she pondered this, her head smacked Sir Eagan's leg.

"Forgive me, Averella, but your wish is granted. Peripaso has stopped."

Averella rolled to her side and tucked her fingertips between her knees, shivering.

"We have reached the summit of this tunnel," Peripaso said. "I'm on the edge of a sharp decline. It's very icy. We'll slide down on our backsides, feet first. You'll be tempted to put out your arms to grab hold of somethin'. Don't. That's a good way to lose a limb. Keep your arms over your chest. Hold your own hand if that's what it takes to keep your arms in."

Peripaso cleared his throat, and Averella could hear him shifting on the icy rock. "At the end of this first leg, you'll fall into a pool of water. If I can keep it dry when I go in, my torch will be lit. Sir Eagan and I will pull you out of the water. We'll gather there 'til we're all accounted for, then take on the second tunnel. Understand? Madam Hoff?"

Gren's voice wavered. "I-I think so, y-yes."

"Good. It's real important ever'one wait their turn. Once the person ahead of you goes down, count to twenty, slowly. Then go on down. Jax, will you come last and bring the rope down?"

Jax's deep voice sounded closer then she expected. "I will."

"'Right, then." Peripaso lowered his voice. "Lady Vrell? You wait longer before you go. Give Sir Eagan and me some time to light the torch and get into position. Can you count to one hundred?"

Averella scoffed and pushed herself back to her knees. "Of course I can."

"Do that, then, after Sir Eagan pushes off."

"I can just bloodvoice her when we're ready for them," her father said.

"Even better," Peripaso said. "In fact, can you bloodvoice everyone? It would be a bit safer than havin' 'em all count."

"Will do," Sir Eagan said.

"I'm off, then." And Peripaso whooped a joyful laugh that faded as the tunnel swept him away.

"Well, he makes that sound like a grand adventure," Sir Rigil said.

Gren's voice came from right behind Averella. "I don't want any grand adventures. Especially through an icy tunnel."

Something slid past Averella's knee. She jumped, then realized it was the rope. Jax was gathering it up. She tucked her fingers under her arms and tried not to think about it being her turn soon. The action helped her fingers, but her breastplate felt frosty against her arms.

A hand patted her head, her shoulder. "Averella?" Sir Eagan's voice lacked its usual calm. She reached up and clasped her suede-covered hand to his. He squeezed. "All will be well. I love you, Averella."

His words sent heat through her body. She felt a deep connection with this man. But love? "I remember so little, but thank you for loving me."

He squeezed her hand again and released it. "You are most welcome, dear child. I am going down now."

"But what about Peripaso?"

"He's reached the bottom. Listen for my voice."

"I will."

Sir Eagan did not cry out when he launched himself down the tunnel, but Averella could hear the whir of his body sliding away over the ice.

"Did he go?" Gren asked.

"Yes."

Gren exhaled a long sigh. "He's a brave one."

Averella moved her pack to her front, so she would not lie on it. Her stomach wrung within her. Her teeth chattered. How fast would she slide over the ice? How deep was the water? How cold was it? She had never been the strongest swimmer. If there was a current, would it sweep her away before Peripaso and Sir Eagan could catch her?

What if the men didn't catch her at all? What if they were not there? What if a cham dwelled in this cavern with the convenient water source? What if it shot fire at her and ate her for dinner? What if it had already eaten Peripaso and her father? The thought tempted her to look through their eyes, but she was worried the act would weaken her. And she wanted to be strong for whatever she might face at the end of the—

Sir Eagan Elk.

She opened her mind. *Yes?*

Come on down, Averella. We are waiting.

He did not sound worried or hurt, but it was easy to control the tone of your voice while bloodvoicing. *I am coming, Sir Eagan.*

Averella scooted to the ledge, feeling with her hands until she felt the side dip down. "I'm going, Gren."

Gren's voice trembled. "Oh, be careful!"

"Feet first, my lady," Sir Rigil added.

"And keep your arms in." This from Bran.

"I shall." Averella straightened her legs and scooted to the edge. Her heart beat like a tabor drum inside her head. She could not help but be grateful for the dark. It was better not to see where she was headed.

"Wait!" Gren screamed. "Who is going to tell me when to go?"

"Sir Eagan will. See you at the bottom." Averella pushed off. She slid slowly over the lip, hugged her arms over her breastplate, laid back as best she could, then wiggled to make herself go.

And go she did.

She shot down the tunnel like an arrow in flight. Her heart, stomach, lungs—everything seemed to fly out, leaving her insides hollow and ringing. She hugged herself tight, wanting to scream, but no sound came. One of her internal organs lodged itself at the base of her throat, balled up, gnawing at her insides.

Before she was ready, golden light consumed her. The ground beneath her vanished. She could not help but release her arms as she flailed about for anything solid.

The pool of water was not solid.

It drenched her suddenly like a gown of icicles, pricking deep into her nerves and shocking her. Her feet hit a cold surface under the water. She kicked off it, splashed, and gasped. Strong hands grabbed her, pulled her up, lifted her out of the water.

The icy air burned her skin. She squirmed against the men's hold. "Put me back! Let me get back in!"

Peripaso chuckled. "Oh, no, Lady Vrell. Your body only thinks the water's warm compared to the air. It's a lie the water tells you so it can keep devouring you."

The men set her on a stone floor. She straightened her soggy skirt around her legs and hugged her knees to her armored chest. Sir Eagan draped a warm fur around her shoulders. She took in her surroundings.

A mushroom-like cavern arched above, the ceiling and walls covered in icy dripstones, icicles, or a combination. The torchlight reflected off the pool of water that still had waves from Averella's swim. A thin layer of ice circled the pool as if it had tried to freeze over but could not manage to. She saw the tunnel now. It ended at half her height above the water's surface. Icicles hung off the ledge like a goat's beard.

The men jumped back into the water and positioned themselves to catch Gren.

"Tell her to come on down," Peripaso said to Sir Eagan.

"But do not tell Gren that thing about the water wanting to eat you," Averella said. "In fact, do not tell anyone that. It is a horrible thing to say. We shall all have nightmares."

"As you wish, Lady Vrell." Then Peripaso said to Sir Eagan, "She was less bossy as a lad, you know."

"I rather like her bossy," Sir Eagan said. "And she makes a good point about not frightening Madam Hoff."

Sir Eagan's reply kindled a warmth in Averella's chest. Hoping to keep it in, she drew the fur around her shoulders, wondering how Peripaso had managed to keep it dry. Her stiff, cold fingers felt for the twine around her neck. Achan's ring was still there.

A distant whistle pulled Averella's attention to the tunnel. The whistle increased in volume until it became a high-pitched scream. Gren flew off the ledge, arms circling. Her brown skirt flew up to her knees, revealing her bare legs.

Averella hoped Sir Eagan and Peripaso had not seen *her* legs bared. Her gown was heavier than Gren's. Still, her cheeks burned at the very idea.

Going underwater silenced Gren. But when her face broke the surface of the water, she went on screaming. The men closed in and grabbed her.

They carried her to the stone ledge and sat her beside Averella. Sir Eagan wrapped a second fur cloak around Gren's shaking form, then went back into the water.

She and Gren sat a long while. As each newcomer joined them on the wet stone, they had to trade off the furs, for Peripaso had brought along only two. Averella shivered long and hard. By the time Jax splashed into the water, her body ached from shivering.

"We can't stay here without dry clothing," Gren said, "we'll f-freeze."

"We're not staying here." Peripaso walked to a dark opening in the wall. "The tunnel continues on—"

"Ohh, no!" Gren wailed. "I don't want to go again."

Averella put her arm around Gren's shoulders and pulled her close. "It will be all right. Let us at least hear the plan before we refuse."

Gren frowned and laid her head on Averella's shoulder.

"The tunnel's only coated with ice about halfway," Peripaso said. "There's a river overhead. We'll slide down, as we did before, and meet the stream, which will carry us the rest of the way. We'll pass through several sprays of water, until at last, we come out at Mowtsa Falls and into the plunge pool."

"Is it snowmelt?" Sir Rigil's usually perfect hair looked painted over his scalp. His lips were blue.

Peripaso's tunic clung to his skeletal, hunched form. "Some is. But some is from the Mowtsa River, which wends its way from Mount Bamah. And some is from the hot springs. So it'll feel warmer."

"Is it deep?" Gren asked.

"Aye, but we'll be there to catch you again. In fact, Jax, why don't you go after Sir Eagan so there'll be three of us to tow people to shore."

"I can do that," Jax said.

"And I think those of you wearing armor should take it off and hold it, just so it won't pull you to the bottom. The plunge pool is a ways deeper than this one."

"How did you keep the furs dry?" Averella asked. "And the torch?"

"I bundled them around the torch before sliding down and held them above my head."

Averella turned to Gren. "Help me untie my armor. You can hold the back half over you to keep the water off as you go down."

"Thank you." Gren and Averella worked at the points until the armor separated. Bran did the same with his armor and gave the backplate to Noam.

"Let us not tarry then." Peripaso took the furs from Jax and Sir Rigil. He laid the first one out, fur side up, then spread the other on top. "All of you line up against the wall. Sir Rigil, you go last this time and make sure everyone comes down. And everyone, wait for Sir Eagan's word before you slide."

When everyone had lined up along the wall, Peripaso picked up the torch and smothered it with his bundle.

Darkness clamped upon them once more.

When Averella's turn came again, she resituated her pack in front and gripped the breastplate over it. She shivered and scooted toward the edge, not as frightened this time, though she would still rather be elsewhere. When Sir Eagan messaged her, she merely said, "I am going, Gren. See you at the bottom."

She pushed off and lay back, clutching the front section of the breastplate over herself and her pack. She flew down the chute. Her heart, lungs, and stomach ran wild again. The mysterious organ lodged itself back at the base of her throat. But after a few twists and turns, she calmed. In summer, such an experience might be fun. If she could see.

A spray of icy water hit her face. She gasped and twisted her head to the side, pulling the breastplate higher. The next time she passed under water, it drummed against the bronze armor. A small victory.

This tunnel ran longer than the previous one. She suddenly realized there was no more ice beneath her. She was moving slower, washing along on a few inches of cold water.

The floor gave way in the same moment as fists of water pounded on her breastplate and face. She screamed this time, for she could see nothing as she fell. Just as she wondered if this fall might not end, she splashed into water. It seemed every bit as cold as before. A hand grabbed at her shoulder and missed. She kicked and held tight to the breastplate, not wanting to lose it. Her head burst through the water's surface.

"There she is!" Sir Eagan yelled.

Jax's voice came from behind. "How'd she get over there?"

Averella twisted around in the water. A burning torch had been driven into the dirt on the shore. It lit the surrounding cove like a yellow moon and reflected off the water like flakes of gold. Thick trees and a mossy ledge edged both sides of the plunge pool. The Mowtsa River cut a line through the forest, heading south. Overhead, the waterfall splashed from at least three levels high. The sparkling cascade stole her breath.

"How beautiful!"

Jax swam toward her, a shadowy form on the glistening water. When he reached her, he took the breastplate and pitched it onto the shore. He grabbed her arm.

"Oh, I can swim fine, Jax. Go wait for Gren."

"Fine. But do not tarry, Vrell."

Averella slowly made her way to the shore. The water did not stab like the water in the frozen cavern had. She felt as if it were thawing her very bones. Was that another trick of the water?

A scream rang out. Averella looked up in time to see Gren shoot out of the middle of the waterfall. The other half of Averella's breastplate went spinning off to the side. Averella swam after it. Thankfully it floated a moment like the hull of a boat before being pulled under by its weight and the water pouring into it. She marked its shiny surface reflecting the torchlight as it sank below the water. She dove after it, then swam to shore.

She used some low tree branches to heave herself onto the mossy bank. The air gripped her wet body, but felt warmer than expected. Her soggy boots squished as she walked over the spongy moss. She fetched the front of her breastplate and propped them both against a birch tree, pausing to marvel that the tree that was not slimy and black yet.

How long until Darkness changed it?

Gren slogged up to her. "I'm so glad that's over."

"It was not so bad, looking back."

"Are you mad? It was the worst thing I've ever experienced."

Averella wanted to ask if it were truly worse than marrying that Riga fellow, but she held her tongue.

She and Gren found a space between four trees and started to set up a camp. They shook out Peripaso's bundle and hung the furs in the tree to air. No one seemed to want them once they were fished out of the plunge pool.

Jax hoisted Bran onto the shore. He rolled on the moss and got to his feet, clutching his forearm, which was coated in blood.

Averella ran toward him, opening her satchel on the way. "What happened?"

Bran sucked a breath between his teeth. "My breastplate caught on something in that last tunnel. It twisted, hit the wall, and sliced into my arm. Perhaps it would have been better to nearly drown."

Averella sank to her knees on the mossy ground. "It's deep." She rinsed the wound, added some salve, and bandaged it. Then she strapped his arm across his chest in a sling so that his hand rested over his heart. "Make sure your hand stays up here. You need to keep your arm elevated until the wound stops bleeding."

Bran paid her with a wide smile. "Thank you, Vrella. I'm sure it will heal."

When everyone was accounted for, Averella led Gren into the trees to a place lit enough to see in the torchlight but concealed enough from the men to remove their clothing. They stripped out of their heavy dresses, wrung them out, and reluctantly put them back on. Then they returned to the shore and sat with the men, nibbling reekat meat.

Gren rocked back and forth, holding her knees. "Are we safe now?"

But before anyone could answer, a wolf's howl rang out from the north. Distant, but close enough to raise the hairs on Averella's arms.

A second wolf answered, this one from the south and very close. Averella twisted around to see a black shadow standing on the opposite bank of the plunge pool, watching them with glittering eyes.

31

Achan lay on his bedroll that night in his tent, humming Yumikak's song. He could hear the men singing in the distance, a chorus of voices attempting to block the tricks of Darkness. The familiar clicking of wood over his tent sent a chill up his arms. Darkness called to his worst imaginings.

One more day of travel, and they would reach Edom Gate. Then another day to Noiz and the high ground there. But how many days until the battle would begin?

A man screamed. The side of Achan's tent shook. Achan sat up, and Shung scrambled to his side, dagger drawn. Manu ran out the door.

Moments later, Sir Caleb entered with a lantern. "It's all right. Manu got him under control."

"Got who?" Achan asked.

"Just a soldier who thought Esek slept in here. I suspect Darkness is taking its toll on the men."

Which was why Achan had been keeping his mind filled with Sparrow's song.

The next day, if a black sky could be called *day,* they rode through the trees until Achan lost the feeling in his backside. They came upon Edom Gate suddenly. One moment Achan was slapped in the face by another scratchy branch, the next Dove had carried him into a clearing. The torchlight from the procession lit up their path. They traveled a road that twisted along a narrow gorge. Mountain cliffs rose on both sides like the walls of an outdoor corridor.

Ahead, an iron gate stood ten levels high and was built into the cliffs on both sides. The soldiers in front of Achan trickled through a smaller gate within the massive one. Soldiers stood at the gate, watching with bored eyes. They wore grey and black uniforms with a crest emblazoned on their chests: a wall before a setting sun.

Inside, the procession led Achan into a clearing, a pass between the mountain cliffs on either side. Hundreds of tents were already set up. Men and giants stood along the road, cheering their arrival. The Mârad army, no doubt. Achan nodded to the men and glanced up to the steep mountain walls enclosing the clearing. He could see that about two dozen stone structures had been built into the rock wall. No fortress at all. Achan followed his guards to a place where some men were erecting his tent.

Sir Caleb was there already. "One more day, Your Highness, and you will have the comfort of a bed again."

"I have the comfort of a bed each night, Sir Caleb."

"Well, a roof overhead, then. And not a canvas one."

"I expected more here. I thought your wife—"

"She is at Noiz with Bodwin and his family. This is only Edom's Gate. Bodwin is Inko's son and the warden of Edom's Gate, though he resides at Noiz. The men at the gate are his men."

"And they were expecting us."

"Aye. Inko's son can bloodvoice and informed them of our arrival."

"How many men work this gate? It seems so small."

"About a hundred. They bunk in the cave dwellings. As you can see, the gate is formidable. There's no way to breach it without having someone on the inside. That's why it was built. To be a sanctuary for the king."

"Noiz, you mean?"

"Noiz is the sanctuary. Edom's Gate is the door. A door that is always kept locked. Tomorrow, you and the generals will march on up to Noiz and plan our next move. The rest of the army will camp here with the Mârad until we give further orders."

That day and night passed slowly, as did the next day. The gorge road snaked along the Darkness through the hazy glow of a thick fog lit from the soldiers' torches. The narrow road forced the army to travel two horses abreast. Achan stayed beside Shung.

A stale wind blasted Achan, nearly knocking him from Dove's back. He hunkered down, thankful for the fur cape Shung had made from the cham Achan had killed. He squinted up at the rock walls and found he could no longer see them through the smoky glow the torchlight gave to the fog. Was the fog hiding the cliffs or had the gorge widened? He faced forward and found the land ahead a gleam of fog as well. He patted Dove and kept his eyes on the tail of Manu's horse before him, hoping Manu was doing the same.

The trail grew steep and narrow, forcing Shung to move behind Achan. Dove's hooves clattered over rocky terrain, joining the sound of the hooves from the other horses and creating a rain-like clatter. The sound suddenly increased, sounding louder and hollow, like they had moved underground. Then the sound returned to normal. A tunnel, perhaps?

The army passed through three more such tunnels, wound around steep corners, zigzagging up an incline. The fog came and went, as if they were walking among actual clouds at night—and if they were truly climbing a mountain, perhaps they were.

The trail widened again and the ground became soft.

Shung rode up beside Achan. "Shung sees nothing."

Cortland's voice came from behind them. "Keep your eyes on the horse in front of you."

Achan glanced over his shoulder. "Have you been here before, Cortland?"

"Aye, with my father. Many noblemen make the trek to Noiz to visit the tombs of the kings."

Achan frowned. "Are there many?"

"Aye. Most of the kings are buried here."

A shiver crawled over Achan's arms. Most of the kings. Most of his ancestors. Buried here. Perhaps he would be buried here someday as well.

The thought did not bother him as much as it should. But he had seen the gate to Shamayim. That was where he would someday reside, even if his body remained in this dreary land of fog. He wondered how many of his ancestors dwelled inside Shamayim's pearly gates.

"Lead the way, then, Cortland." Achan led Dove aside enough to let Cortland pass. "Dove is so tall I cannot see the ground through this fog."

"They are clouds, Your Highness." Cortland's voice moved with his torch as he rode his horse before them. "It is a shame that Darkness has shrouded the view, for Noiz is a breathtaking site. We stand in a small valley with mountains on all sides but the west, where the Gadowl Wall begins. There are two waterfalls to the north. Their waters run together in the center of this valley and form a small lake before branching out into various streams that take different courses down the mountains. The fortress hangs on the mountain cliffs above the village of Noiz."

"Like Mitspah?"

"Somewhat, though the waterfalls are not near the fortress. On most days, the villagers look up to find the fortress hidden by clouds. We will take another steep trail up the rocky mountain before we arrive. Are you ready?"

"Aye. Lead on, Cortland."

Achan, Shung, and Manu followed Cortland through the village and up another rocky trail. The smell of pine was thick here. Darkness might now cover this land, but it had not yet sucked out all its life.

Achan's backside was sore from riding. He longed for days spent in a home with a kitchen and chairs. Would Armonguard truly become that home? Or would Esek ruin it before giving it up?

After several hours, Cortland eventually stopped on rocky ground. "We have arrived, Your Highness. You may dismount."

Achan slid off Dove's back. His boots smacked against cobblestone, and the balls of his feet smarted.

Cole appeared out of the fog, took Dove's reins, and tugged the animal away, new sword swinging at his side.

Achan called after his squire, "Thank you, Cole."

Cole turned and bowed. "You're welcome, Your Highness."

Achan looked around, but could still see nothing but golden fog lit from invisible torches. He followed Cortland into the unknown.

"Watch your step, Your Highness," Cortland said. "We're going up."

Achan slowed until he saw a wide set of stairs carved into rock. He moved slowly, one arm outstretched before him, hoping he would not collide with anyone or anything.

Achan's thighs ached from the climb. On and on they went. Just when he began hoping Cortland would suggest a brief rest, the rocky ground flattened and an entrance materialized out of the fog.

Two brick red doors were propped open. The walls around them were white, trimmed in wood painted red to match the doors. Achan passed inside, and the fog vanished.

He stood in a long corridor at the foot of yet another staircase. This one was grand, however. A red carpet tucked along the center of a wide staircase that stretched the length of the room. An iron banister ran along both sides of the red carpet, dividing the stairs into three rows. There must have been another thirty steps to the top. A high ceiling vaulted over the foyer, stairs, and whatever was at the top.

"The great hall is up there," Cortland said. "Come on."

Achan took a deep breath, squeezed his thigh muscles in a brief stretch, and started up the red carpet. Being able to see made time move faster. As soon as Achan's line of sight rose above the top stair, he could see the great hall.

It was not so great. In size, anyway. The room was as wide as the stairs and only as deep as two tables and the benches around them. To the far left, a short head table on a dais ran the opposite direction. On the far right, a narrow stairs ran up the wall and passed through a dark archway. Halfway up the stairs, a man and woman were tangled in an embrace, kissing as if it were the only way to breathe.

Achan's gaze stopped on the couple and he grinned. *Sir Caleb, is it proper to kiss a woman in such a way in public? What will people think?*

Whatever pleases them. I've not seen my wife in over a year. Go bother someone else, Your Highness.

Achan laughed and pointed out Sir Caleb to Shung, who raised a dark eyebrow.

Inko stood in a cluster of people at the foot of the stairs. He squatted and lifted a small girl into his arms. She kissed his cheek. "Your Highness!" Inko waved them over. "Be coming and meeting my family!"

Achan and Shung made their way to the stairs. Inko introduced them to his son, Bodwin, a tall Barthian man with a shaved head and a cropped grey beard. Bodwin's wife, Zoral, was a plump woman wearing a blue dress with a wimple that bared only her grey-skinned face. A skinny boy stood beside her, his curly grey hair sitting like a cloud on his head. The girl in Inko's arms had grey hair too, only hers was braided along her head in dozens of tiny braids.

Sir Caleb and his wife made their way downstairs, hand in hand. Esper looked younger than Sir Caleb by at least ten years. She had grey skin as well, but her hair was black and hung down her back in a long, silky drape.

"Esper, this is Prince Gidon Hadar, also known as Prince Achan."

She curtsied and spoke in a low voice. "How do you fare, Your Majesty?"

"I am well, my lady, and pleased to know you."

She chuckled. "You are too polite, Your Majesty. I hope my husband has not made himself a nuisance."

Achan smiled. "Only a little, my lady."

She shot Sir Caleb a knowing look.

Sir Caleb looked surprised. "The king must have manners, my dear."

"Are you hungry?" Esper asked Achan.

"Very much. It has been days of eating dried food. I long for something different."

"Then you shall have it."

"It's being in the middle of the night, Your Highness," Bodwin said. "But I'm having wakened enough servants to be seeing that you're being fed."

"Oh. I thank you, but I can make do until breakfast."

"Be thinking nothing of it, Your Highness. My servants were being here long before I. They have been waiting many years to be serving their king again. It's being an honor they have been waiting years for."

"I see. I hope I will meet their expectations, then."

Bodwin bowed. "I'm being sure you shall."

"Has Sir Eagan arrived?" Achan asked. "I was told he was on his way here with his own party."

"We've not been hearing a word from him. No one was telling us he was coming, either."

Achan would have to bloodvoice him the moment he sat down. "He's expected any moment, I am sure. I hope he'll have no trouble at the gate."

"I'll be letting my men know to be watching for him."

Bodwin led Achan and the others up the narrow staircase. They exited onto an outdoor path that passed several structures built into the wall of the mountain. The exterior walls were rock and masonry. Stone pathways branched off here and there, leading up to other dwellings.

Achan followed Bodwin up another stairway, this one chiseled out of the rock. At the top they turned left, wove around another rocky corridor, then walked up another short flight of stairs to a red door in a wall of masonry that curved outward in a half circle.

"This is being your chambers, Your Highness. And a very lucky place to be laying your head. For on a clear day, one can be seeing Mount Bamah."

"I am sure once Darkness is vanquished, the view will be immaculate."

Bodwin shifted his feet. "Yes, well . . . I'll be having some food brought up right away."

"Thank you, Bodwin."

Inside, the circular room was made from masonry on one side and carved rock on the other. A large bed sat in the center of the room, covered in white furs. It had no headboard or canopy. There seemed no way to know which side was the head.

Matthias was already present and had hung several of Achan's shirts up on a rack.

"I see you've wasted no time, Matthias."

"Your clothing got wrinkled in the saddlebags, sir. The trunks kept everything nicer."

"Why bring all the clothing, then? One or two outfits would be plenty."

"Oh, Sir Caleb insisted I not leave any behind, sir."

"That's not surprising. Come help me out of this armor."

Matthias came running. Shung still needed to assist with the points, but Matthias was becoming quite adept at his job. When all the armor was removed, Achan felt light and free.

Matthias went to lay out the chain hauberk, so Achan pulled off the gambeson, tossed it aside, and fell back onto the bed with his feet still flat on the floor. The furs felt soft against his bare skin. Matthias returned and tugged off Achan's boots. Achan sent a knock to Sir Eagan.

Sir Eagan replied right away. *Yes, Your Highness? How do you fare?*

We have arrived in Noiz. Sir Gavin told me you were coming here. Are you close?

We are but a day away.

Excellent. I look forward to seeing you all.

Thank you, Your Highness.

Achan closed his eyes, starting to drift off almost instantly. He distinctly remembered someone grabbing his legs and twisting the rest of his body up onto the bed. But he didn't wake. He willingly let sleep take him captive.

32

"I need to stop." Gren stumbled in front of Averella and lowered her pack to the ground. "I can't carry this anymore."

"We mustn't stop," Peripaso said. "That'll give the wolves a chance to surround us."

As if in answer, a wolf howled somewhere ahead. Trees towered above both sides of the trail like sentry walls, though they were not solid. Wolves could easily dart between their narrow trunks and onto the path.

"Jax and I are taking turns watching for them," Sir Eagan said, "though animals were never my strength. Sir Gavin is the Great Whitewolf, not I."

"I sense there are two ahead on the trail," Jax said.

"Can you storm them?" Averella asked, thinking of her mother.

Jax shook his head. "I'm not trained to storm."

"I could try, but not until we stop somewhere safe," Sir Eagan said. "I cannot see, and it will take some time for me to locate them in the forest."

Noam stopped on the trail beside Gren. "If the wolf is ahead of us, should we leave the trail?"

"That would seal our deaths," Peripaso said. "Wolves like to send their prey in circles until they tire."

"But we're already tired!" Gren said.

"That's why we must press on," Peripaso said. "The sooner we reach Noiz, the better."

Noam put his arm around Gren and gave her a side hug. "What is Noiz, anyway? I've never heard of it."

"Noiz is a sanctuary for the royal family," Sir Eagan said. "The king retreats there for leisure or refuge."

"Won't the wolves follow us there?" Gren asked.

"Wolves avoid crowds," Peripaso said. "Once we reach the settlement, we'll be safe."

"But can't we rest a bit?" Gren asked.

"Allow me, Madam." Bran stepped forward and hoisted Gren's pack over his good arm.

Gren wilted with relief. "Oh, thank you, Bran."

Averella's heart warmed to see Bran step in to help Gren. Her gaze met Gren's, and Gren looked away. Averella knew not how to behave around Gren in light of Bran Rennan's presence, knowing his true feelings for them both.

They continued on. Wolves howled around them. Some-times far away. Sometimes so close the hair on Averella's arms bristled. The forest path became rocky and mountainous. Sir Rigil took Gren's pack from Bran. Not even Jax could keep up Peripaso's pace.

They came upon a deep cave in a rocky cliff. After a thorough search, Jax pronounced it safe, and they made camp inside. Though all were exhausted, the men devised a schedule for watch, and everyone else went to sleep.

Averella woke from a nightmare of Esek striking her. Had that been dream or memory? It was difficult to tell with the tricks of Darkness and the horrors she had apparently been through this last year. She lay awake, sorting recent thoughts.

Achan *had* rescued her from drowning in the Mahanaim canals. Jax had confirmed that. She also recalled Achan carrying her on his back to keep her out of the dark waters of Arok Lake. There had been leeches in the water. Horrible little slugs that drank blood.

She shivered. Maybe that had been a nightmare.

Mother told her that some man had discovered she was a woman and had attacked her. So her dream of the man called Polk must have been true. Or was that the attack by the man called Khai? In any case, Achan had used his mind to control some man and stop him from going too far.

And Achan had also rescued her from Esek's tent. Mother confirmed the truth of this. But Averella had also dreamed about Achan carrying her, lifting her onto Dove's back.

Dove? Oh, it was a horse. Who did Dove belong to?

That mattered little. The point was that Achan had rescued Averella again and again. Put himself in danger for her sake. Why had she run from such loyalty? Who would not want to marry such a man—especially since he was to be king?

She rolled over. Jax, Bran, and Sir Eagan lay sleeping around the fire pit. Two moths fluttered above the campfire, casting their shadows on the rocky ceiling of the cavern.

Sir Rigil sat staring into the flames, arms propped on his knees. For being one of the best groomed knights in Er'Rets, he was a mess, even after a swim in the plunge pool. A smudge of dirt darkened one cheek. His bangs hung in greasy strands, curling around his ears. He had grown a short beard too. It made him look older. Tired.

"Why so glum, Sir Rigil?" Averella whispered, propping her head on one hand. "We are almost to our destination."

He turned his blue-eyed gaze to her and held up the sword Averella had taken from the Mahanaim guard. "My sword. It is lost. I've had it since my manhood ceremony. It was taken in Allowntown."

"I am sorry."

He winced. "I know it's only a hunk of steel and wood. Still . . . Keseel felt like a friend."

"I can imagine the bond a man must have with his weapon, especially when it has served faithfully for so long."

He smiled, still handsome even in filth. "That's it exactly, my lady. You don't think me petty?"

"Of course not. I had to leave Kopay, my horse. It is natural to cling to what is familiar."

"Which is why so many marry a friend." He gazed into the flames again. "Ah, if only I could wed my sword. Keseel and I would make a fierce pair. No one could cross us."

Gren giggled, startling Averella, for she thought only she and Sir Rigil had been awake.

Sir Rigil groaned. "Now you too will think I'm petty, Madam Hoff. Or odd, at least."

Gren lay just behind Averella. "Do you mind my asking, sir? Bran and I have not been friends long. Do you think that would make us a poor match?"

A crooked grin stretched across his grubby face. "Not because of your friendship or lack thereof. I've other reasons for thinking you and Master Rennan are a poor match."

"Because I'm a peasant and a widow and pregnant with another man's child, and he—"

"No." Sir Rigil raised an eyebrow. "Because you're the most argumentative woman I've ever known. More so than even Lady Averella, and you see what happened with her and Master Rennan."

Gren frowned at Averella. "What's wrong with a woman who speaks her mind? That's not argumentative. Just honest."

Sir Rigil merely raised an eyebrow.

"And I didn't see what happened with Lady Averella and Master Rennan."

Averella sighed, glancing to where Bran lay sleeping on the other side of the campfire, his bandaged arm resting on his chest. "I hardly know that myself, and I supposedly lived it."

Sir Rigil cocked his eyebrow Averella's way. "I'll tell you what happened, my lady. The two of you fought yourselves right out of love with one another. Both so bossy the other couldn't stand it."

Averella clicked her tongue. "Really, Sir Rigil."

He batted a moth away from his face. "'Tis true. I swear it upon my good name."

Gren sat up, scowling at Sir Rigil. "Master Rennan has never bossed *me*."

Sir Rigil laughed. "Only because the two of you have done nothing but walk in circles. He was on duty, Madam Hoff. To keep you safe, not to debate life, not to court you."

"But he said he cares for me."

"I'm sure he does. But Rennan is too wise to pledge his heart to a woman he barely knows."

Gren turned red and opened her mouth to retort.

But Sir Rigil held up his hands, which the campfire shadowed on the cave wall behind him. "Peace! I will tell you what you must know. When his betrothal to Lady Averella ended, he asked me about you, Madam Hoff. To see if I thought you a wise choice to pursue. So take heart that he does have interest to see whether you and he are compatible. *After* the war. That is not a proposal, Madam, so do not mistake it as such. It is merely a statement that a good man wishes to know you better."

"And you told him I'm a poor choice?"

Sir Rigil sighed, met Averella's gaze, and grinned. "Madam Hoff, I have already given my answer. You need a man you can have charge of. A man with little will of his own. And take it from me as Bran Rennan's master these past seventeen years, he does not like to be yoked."

For reasons Averella could not explain, this brought a smile to her lips.

Not so with Gren. "How dare you say such things! That I would yoke my husband to my side like a mule. Even if you are highborn, and I'm only a—"

"Shh, woman!" Sir Rigil waved. "You will wake the whole camp and call the wolves with your wailing."

Averella met Gren's scowling expression. "Do not let Sir Rigil bore under your skin, Gren. He thinks himself a shrewd elder, though he is only thirty-two years."

Sir Rigil faked a wounded gasp. "Wicked lady! Leave it to you to proclaim my age to all who may hear. If only that were part of what you had forgotten."

"Oh, yes." Averella smiled. "The wolves are taking note of your age, I am certain. The real question, Sir Rigil, is whether or not *you* like to be yoked."

Sir Rigil raised a finger. "To a cart, never, but if the lady were pretty enough—and sincere, mind you—I would climb Mount Bamah for lava rock, fetch a snowball from the roof of Ice Island, and swim around the Shelosh Islands—despite the tanniyn that live there—all because she asked me to."

"To prove your love?" Averella asked, amused.

"Nay. My word is enough to prove my love. I would do these things just to please her."

Averella laughed and rolled onto her stomach. She crossed her arms on the ground and set her chin on them. "I have never seen any woman pretty enough to keep your head turned, Sir Rigil. I do not think this 'perfectly sincere' woman exists in all Er'Rets."

"Oh, she exists, my lady. And I *will* find her. Minstrels will sing of our love for years to come."

"Mercy. To think that I once wished to marry you."

This silenced Sir Rigil. He stared at Averella, his eyes wide and pondering. The fire crackled, painting shadow and light across his face. "Did you? Now that would have been a happy match. If only I had not lost you to the boy."

"If only you were not my uncle."

"Hmm. That too. Strange, that."

"Achan is *not* a boy," Gren said.

"Barely," Sir Rigil said. "Do not mistake me, the prince is a fine fellow, smart and brave. And you can trust him, which I feel is the kind of man you need most, my lady. But I've always felt a woman would be wise to marry an older man. For we have lived long enough to figure you women out. Years will pass before our steadfast young prince will know what to make of you, Lady Averella."

Heat flashed up Averella's spine. "And what of Lady Tara? Is her husband old enough to meet your approval?"

"Unfortunate situation, that. But Carmack will redeem her broken heart one day, for sturdy though he is, even Old Lord Gershom will one day perish."

Averella's mouth gaped at this statement. "You insinuate that Carmack Demry cares for Tara?"

"Oh, yes. He has loved her ever since he was placed on her guard. He was the only man I know who was disappointed to be promoted to his brother's Fighting Fifteen. For it meant he would no longer see Tara as much."

Averella sighed, stunned by this secret morsel. "So goes yet another tale of thwarted love."

"Always you focus on the dark side of things, my lady. You must focus on the light, for there is much joy to be had in this world. Open your eyes, and you will see it. And in time, all will be well—for all of us."

"You sound as if you truly believe that it will."

"Why shouldn't I? For Arman has given us the end of the story, has he not? Shamayim will be a wonderful home, even if this one remains dark. So fear not, and get some sleep. Tomorrow you shall see your young prince. And when you look into his eyes, just you see if you do not remember your true feelings."

Averella rolled her eyes at Sir Rigil, earning one more deep, hearty laugh from the knight. Then she settled back onto the hard ground. She focused on Gren's thoughts, curious what she was thinking after Sir Rigil's honest words.

Heavy sorrow pierced Averella's heart, bringing forth tears. She closed her eyes and looked through Gren's. She found herself staring at Bran's face, barely visible on the other side of the fire. Flame and shadow flickered over his skin. He *was* handsome. But Averella knew now for certain that she did not love him as a woman loves a man.

Tears stung her eyes, but they were Gren's. Then came Gren's thoughts.

Cetheria, why did you allow Bran to protect me if nothing was to come of it? If he doesn't love me, what will become of me and my baby?

Gren? Averella said.

Gren gasped and lifted her head, meeting Averella's eyes. *Do not do that without warning. It frightens me.*

I am sorry. I only wanted to say, take heart that Sir Rigil does not make Bran's decisions.

What he said made sense, though. I can see that Bran is still in love with you. What if he decides I would not be a good secondary match?

Why would you want to be anyone's secondary match? If he does not love you, then he is not the man for you, and you will find another—the right one.

Who else would possibly want me, a widow with child? I have no assets.

Why not Master Poe?

Harnu?

I think him quite charming. Once she'd gotten to know him better.

You think I should sacrifice a chance at happiness to marry someone practical, like Harnu?

I am only suggesting you consider it.

I will, if you consider Achan.

That is different.

Gren huffed a sigh and lay back down. *Why must everyone but you make sacrifices, my lady? Why can everyone be willing to love beyond rank except you? In cases of true love, station shouldn't matter. If it does, then the woman loves something else more than her suitor.*

This comment left Averella speechless. For if she loved Achan more than Bran, what did she love more than Achan?

A chorus of howls woke Averella. The chilled air clamped around her body, making her skin feel like that of a plucked bird. She pushed herself up to a sitting position.

The men stood shoulder to shoulder across the cave's entrance. Between the wide stance of Jax's legs, Averella could see a black wolf pacing outside.

She jumped to her feet and crept forward to peek over Sir Eagan's shoulder. Six wolves were outside the cave. Two paced back and forth. The others sat watching.

Averella's stomach boiled with the threat awaiting them. She whispered in her father's ear. "What will we do?"

His head turned a fraction until his eyes met hers. Warmth and assurance pushed aside her fear.

Thank you, Father.

He smiled. *That is the first time you called me Father.*

Is it really? Ever? Not even before my memory was lost?

The truth shocked you greatly.

Still, it seems I did not conduct myself in a manner befitting a noblewoman these past months. Forgive my coldness.

He took hold of her hand. *Of course I forgive, my dear. And I am sure you did your best.*

She winced, feeling undeserving of his kind words. *Are you? Memories have been coming to me these past days, and I am not convinced.*

I am sorry your mother chose to keep the truth from you.

Mother keeps many secrets. Part of being a duchess, I suppose. Perhaps watching her politics influenced my own.

Sir Eagan cocked his head. *How do you mean?*

From what I can piece together, the lie became so big that to cover it I had to lie again and again, until the truth was so far away it now seems impossible to find it at all, as if it too has gotten lost in the Veil.

He squeezed her hand. *It is never impossible, child. As we have been telling you all along, you must simply choose truth.*

She sighed. *You make it sound so easy.*

It is not easy, but it will set you free. That, I can promise.

"We will have to fight them, I fear," Sir Rigil said.

His words brought Averella back to the present.

The wolves.

"Better here, with our backs protected, than on the trail when they can come at us from all sides, separate us," Jax said.

"Still a half day's walk to Noiz," Peripaso said.

"It is a pity we do not have archers among us," Sir Rigil said. "We could pick them off one by one from here."

"Duchess Amal could storm them if she could find us," Sir Eagan said. "But I do not see how she could ever learn our location, especially in the dark."

Averella took a deep breath. "I could do it."

Sir Eagan gripped her shoulders and turned her to face him. "Your mother said you are not strong for storming."

"I am not. That is why you both must help me. I'll let Mother storm through me as we run."

Sir Eagan shook his head. "That will not work, Averella. To storm, you must remain stationary, as must your guard. That would mean you and I remain in the cave."

"Absolutely not," Sir Rigil said.

"Then no one will leave the cave until I have succeeded," Averella said.

"If you are weak afterwards," Jax said, "I will carry you."

"Thank you, Jax." Averella looked back to her father. As the highest ranking soldier, it was his decision to make.

He nodded. "Very well. Contact your mother."

And so Sir Rigil, Bran, and Gren packed up camp while Averella messaged her mother and explained the situation. Averella put her armor back on, and Mother gave instructions.

It will be just like before, dearest, in the forest with the black knights. You must relax and let me be your eyes.

Averella could not imagine relaxing at a time like this. *But I don't remember what I did before. And didn't I black out that time? What if that happens again before you can finish?*

I need your eyes for only a moment.

Would it be better for you to use Father's eyes?

No. He is stronger than you. Should you pass to the Veil, he can bring you back. You could not do the same for him.

Sir Rigil, Bran, and Jax stood at the mouth of the cave, swords drawn. Gren and Sir Eagan sat on either side of Averella, each clutching an arm for when she would undoubtedly fall. Noam sat to Sir Eagan's left, positioned to catch him if he fell in an effort to retrieve Averella from the Veil.

Averella's hands trembled.

"Do not fear, Averella." Sir Eagan threaded his fingers with hers and squeezed. "Arman will keep you safe."

"Thank you, Father. I know I have nothing to fear with you guarding me."

Are you ready, dearest?

Yes, Mother.

Relax, then, and let me step through you.

Averella lowered the shields around her mind. She focused on the largest wolf. It was simply sitting on the ground, watching, tongue lagging from its mouth. Sounds magnified in her ears now: the padding of the pacing wolves, the crackling fire, the clicking from trees, her father's breathing.

She felt nothing physical and had no way of knowing if her mother had begun, until the wolf yelped and collapsed. Something inside told her she should rebuild the walls around her mind, but she forced herself to ignore the impulse, to leave her walls down, her mind unguarded.

One of the pacing wolves tripped and skidded to a stop. The other stopped to sniff at his companion and whimpered. As the third wolf fell, an overwhelming peace filled Averella. At first she thought Sir Eagan had manipulated her emotions, but then her soul left her body as subtly as a flutter in her stomach.

She was floating up through the cave's ceiling, through dark rock that seemed endless, until a glimmer of lights shone in the distance. Noiz, perhaps? It looked closer than ever. She willed herself to float toward the lights, but something snagged her hand. Turning back, she saw Sir Eagan's transparent body floating beside her.

You must not leave us, Averella. We would like to reach Noiz as a group, and you with your body and soul as one.

Averella took one last longing look at the lights of Noiz and allowed her father to pull her back to the cave.

Your mother knows how to storm better than a thundercloud.

Mother. Veil warrior. Averella wanted to speak with her, but it would have to wait. Her weakness was pulling her toward sleep.

When she woke, Jax was carrying her through the forest. Branches snapped under his heavy footsteps. She could see Peripaso and Sir Rigil before them, moving down the trail. Light danced over the trees from Peripaso's torch.

Averella clutched Jax's shirt.

He glanced down on her. "Can you stand, Vrell?"

She looked up into his eyes and nodded. He set her on her feet, but kept a hand on her shoulder. He was so much taller, she felt like a babe with her father as she walked beside him.

They saw no sign of another wolf on the rest of their journey. The lights of Noiz became visible long before soldiers stopped them at the gate on the outskirts of the city. Sir Eagan declared himself, and the soldiers escorted their party through the army's tents, past a small village, and up a steep trail.

Averella had never visited Noiz, but now she remembered having heard stories of the kings who had spent time amongst the clouds. There were no clouds tonight. The stronghold glimmered on the mountain above. She wished she could see the land, for it was said that the view from Paniyn Gal was a breathtaking sight.

Perhaps another day. Once Darkness was gone forever.

This thought brought Achan's face to mind. He would surely visit the king's refuge more than once during his life. How handsome he had looked the day she found him wounded in the forest and tended his arrow wounds.

How like a Hadar he had appeared when Sir Caleb had dressed him for the Council meeting.

And how like a king in those clothes Sir Eli had provided in Mirrorstone. She recalled her anger when Jaira had kissed him. Such a manipulative creature, Jaira Hamartano, trying to steal the throne for herself with magic.

Averella suddenly recalled other women who had been taken in by Achan Cham's waggish smile.

A pretty red-haired girl in Melas.

Young Yumikak, who had danced with him all evening when their party had visited Berland. The girl had also snuck into his bedchamber to sing him to sleep that night.

Cousin Tara. The way Achan had walked with Tara on his arm. His glowing praise of Tara's character and wit. The way his eyes had gleamed when he spoke of his plans to propose marriage.

And then there was that barmaid in Tsaftown. But Averella did not want to think about her.

She recalled Achan's wide grin the day he had said, *"Oh, I see. All this time, all the strange things you've said on my behalf. Jaira, Ressa, Yumikak, Lady Tara, Beska. You were jealous."*

Averella had denied it, of course, for his words had been cocksure and provoking. But he had been right.

She had been jealous indeed.

Averella's legs were sore by the time they reached the entrance to Paniyn Gal.

A guard stopped them before they could enter into the great hall of the fortress. "Sir Eagan is expected. The rest of you must wait until I have instructions."

Sir Eagan squeezed Averella's hand. "Only a moment now." His endearing gaze made her smile. He passed through the doorway and started up a grand staircase without calming her emotions.

She peeked in the open doorway and up a grand staircase. From where she stood, she could barely see the tops of tables and the heads and shoulders of dozens of men and women who were eating in a great hall of sorts.

A familiar laugh pulled her gaze to the far left. And there, at the center of the head table, stood Achan Cham.

The sight of him sent a tremor down her spine. He was handsome as ever, wearing a fine ensemble of blue and gold. He walked to the top of the stairs and greeted Sir Eagan in a warm embrace.

Suddenly everything clicked. As if she had forgotten nothing, Averella remembered it all.

He had tried to kiss her under the waterfall. She had been afraid and swum away. But he had found her the next day in his chambers, begged her not to go, told her he loved her. She had brushed it aside. Too set on her agenda. Pining away for the shelter of home. Wanting to hide from her heart and the vulnerability the truth would bring to her life. Because she was embarrassed that she had lied to him.

The soldier at the doorway stepped aside. "You may all enter now. To the top of the stairs please."

Averella took a deep breath. Father was right. Only the truth would set her free now. And she longed for freedom from the bondage of her own lies.

Achan would be surprised to see her. Would he make a scene? The idea made her wince. She removed her helm from her pack. Better not to give him time to think it over as he watched her climb that steep staircase. She pulled her helm over her head and started up the marble steps, hiding behind her mask for the last time.

33

Achan stood at the top of the staircase. A half dozen people spilled into the foyer below. A woman led them up the center stairs. She wore a green dress with a bronze breastplate over it. A matching bronze helm covered her face. How bizarre.

"It's Iamos!" a soldier yelled from one of the tables.

Achan turned toward his men. Most had stood to stare down the steps as the newcomers approached.

"Aye, I saw her and Marpay healing men in Mahanaim," another soldier said from the end of the opposite table.

"They healed a hundred men," a man near Achan said.

"She healed me!"

"She scaled the sorcerer's tower and killed him."

Suddenly everyone was standing, beginning to move toward the newcomers.

Achan frowned. "Enough! Sir Eagan killed the Hadad. And there is no Iamos or Marpay. Any god but Arman is false." He turned his gaze to the woman, who was now halfway up the stairs. "Though you are a guest here and I owe you civility, if you claim to be Iamos, I say you're a liar."

The woman stopped. Her gaze, visible only through the slot in the helm, locked with his. "I *am* a liar, Your Highness, but I promise you, I never claimed to be Iamos."

The woman's raspy voice, muffled through the air holes in her helm, pulled Achan's eyebrows low over his eyes. "Then who are you, and what do you want?"

She removed her helm, revealing a tangle of black hair.

"Sparrow?" Achan's heart leapt. "Sparrow!" He started down the stairs.

She tucked the helm under one arm. “Not quite, Your Highness. I am not Sparrow or Vrell, as you have known me.”

Achan stopped so suddenly he almost fell down the stairs. “Sparrow, what game is this? I’ve spent more time with you than anyone. I have imagined your face every day we have not been together. I have made no mistake. You are Vrell Sparrow.”

“No, Your Highness, that is the lie I told you and everyone else.” She stood tall and seemed to be collecting herself. “I am . . .” She breathed heavily and started again. “My lord, I am Lady Averella Amal, formerly of Carmine. Currently without home.” She went down on both knees in the middle of the stairs and bowed her head low. “I pledge service to the true crown of Er’Rets.” Her next words were so muffled, he could hardly understand them. “If you will have it.”

A chill gripped every inch of Achan’s body. It was as if he was back at Ice Island, standing before the men in the Prodotez. The hall quieted. Achan could only stare at the top of Sparrow’s head. But not Sparrow. Never really Sparrow. Always Lady Averella Amal. He seemed to be melting into a pool of lava.

All this time? All along, Sparrow—and Scratch, and Vrell—all along she was really Lady Averella? He descended two more steps. “Sparrow, you—”

Wait. Wait! If Lady Averella were really Sparrow, then he was betrothed to her! He could marry Vrell! The girl who possessed his heart could truly be his wife.

No. He was no longer betrothed to her. She’d refused him. It seemed like all his old wounds hurt him at once, especially all his head wounds. It felt like he was the one who had lost his memory. He’d been betrothed to her, but now he wasn’t. She’d renounced her birthright. Wasn’t that it? Because Sir Eagan was her father she didn’t have the right or the heritage to be heir of Carm.

He descended another step.

Her true rank shouldn’t matter. It didn’t matter to him!

But the men had to have known! He turned back and looked up the stairs to where Sir Eagan stood beside Sir Caleb’s place at the head table. “*She* is your daughter?”

Sir Eagan bowed his head. “She is.”

Flames coiled within Achan’s chest. He looked back and forth from Sir Eagan to Sparrow. Why hadn’t he seen it? It made perfect sense. “And you knew all along?”

"From the night you freed me from Ice Island, Your Highness. Her face could not fool me."

Achan walked up three steps. He felt furious and elated and betrayed and relieved at the same time. He didn't know how to respond. At the moment, anger won out. "I see she gets her deceit from you." Then another wave of implications rose to mind. "Surely the duchess also knew?"

"It was not our secret to tell, Your Highness."

Achan barely heard him. He remembered the duchess in his room, in his mind, in the Veil, in her sitting room—training, teaching, encouraging—but never telling the truth. No wonder the duchess had never introduced him to her daughter. "I feel I have been betrayed by you all!"

Achan pinched the bridge of his nose. His own advisors had lied to him. Sparrow had lied! Blazes! He had never felt like a bigger halfwit in all his days. He twisted to look back on Sparrow. Her eyes watched him, wide and waiting. She was so beautiful. The object of his yearnings. Yet a duplicitous liar! And she had the nerve to make him feel bad for being tempted by other women. For all his weaknesses, he had always been honest.

He realized with a start that everyone in the great hall was staring at him. The intensity of every set of eyes and the deceit of his own advisors filled him with heat. He tried to contain his anger, but his limbs turned to fire. He ascended the stairs to get a good view of Sir Caleb. "What about you, Sir Caleb? Did you know this secret, as well?"

"I did *not*, Your Highness." Then Sir Caleb's stony expression broke into an incredulous smile. "But it does explain a few things."

Achan scanned the tables. Where was Sir Gavin? Right. He had gone down to talk with the Mârad general. Achan paced toward Sir Eagan. "Does Sir Gavin know?"

"Aye."

"Yet I suppose it was not his secret to tell either, was it?"

"Nay, it was not."

Achan walked back to the top of the stairs and looked down on Sparrow, who remained kneeling. Beyond her, scattered on the steps below, stood Sir Jax, Sir Rigil, a handful of Bodwin's guards, Gren . . . His heart softened to see Gren's teary face. Noam! He smiled at his old friend, who smiled in return. Bran Rennan, who looked completely exhausted.

Achan asked softly, "Did you know of this, Master Rennan?"

Bran's voice was almost a whisper. "I did."

Achan struggled to comprehend the meaning. His brain hurt, but he forced himself to look back over his entire past year, seeing it all in a new light. Lady Averella had disguised herself as the boy stray Vrell Sparrow in order to avoid marriage to Esek—so she could return home and marry her true love: Bran.

"Bran . . . I—I never knew! I—" Achan swayed on the steps and grasped the bannister to keep from toppling over.

Eben's breath! After all his prideful tirades against Bran for his mistreatment of Gren, and all along it had been Achan who had betrayed Bran. Fire burned within his chest. He sucked short breaths through his nostrils, hoping he did not lose control and fall into a rage. Or tears like a child. This was not his fault! He had not known who she was. She had kept it from him.

He closed his eyes. *Arman, give me wisdom.*

But he did not pause long enough to listen for any divine reply. He looked down on Sparrow again. It all came back to her. Despite his desire to hate her, a joy arose in him at seeing her again. Yet she had made him feel a remorse that she deserved more than anyone. He managed two words.

"Explain yourself."

They sounded cold and cruel and Esek-like, but he didn't care. He knew he was not the villain here. He wanted only to hear her speak.

Sparrow—his mind would not yet let him think of her by any other name—sat back on her heels. Her eyes, wide and green like Duchess Amal's, stared into his. "I went into hiding when Esek demanded to marry me. Macoun Hadar sensed my skill and sent the Kingsguard knights to fetch me. Jax and Khai. I was afraid to reveal my identity, so I kept up my charade, hoping Mother would know someone in Mahanaim who might assist me. Then you entered the story. And you know the rest. I was swept along with you on an adventure into Darkness."

Sparrow's emotional tone chipped at his anger, bored holes through it, piercing his heart from all sides. He wanted to run and take her into his arms and marry her on the spot. Where was Toros Ianjo? And yet, his heart was tentative, as if she might really be a black knight's illusion that would turn into a flock of gowzals any second and tear him to pieces. He steeled himself against her charms. "Why didn't you give me your true name? At least in Mitspah?"

Sparrow's eyes filled with tears. "Achan, please. Could we speak of this in private?"

He sucked in a sharp breath. "Answer my question."

She blinked, and a stream of tears ran down one cheek.

He towered over her like a marble statue, cold, hard, and paralyzed by his mixed emotions. He couldn't decide whether to comfort her or throw her in prison.

She sniffled. "I wanted to confess a hundred times, but I was afraid."

Her voice was a raspy whisper, yet Achan had no doubt that every ear could hear in the great hall. He felt a twinge of regret for forcing her to speak of such matters in public. He *should* have relocated to one of the council rooms. It was the proper, merciful thing to do. But he wasn't feeling very merciful at the moment. He folded his arms. "You were so afraid of me and my cruel intentions."

"No! Not really. I never truly believed you capable of such betrayal. But I— I was afraid that I loved you. Or afraid I only *thought* I did. Afraid I really loved Bran and was being unfaithful. Afraid that Bran no longer loved me. Afraid of being queen. Afraid that you would leave me or find a mistress or a whole harem."

She waved one hand in an arc as if accusing everyone present of being part of Achan's harem. "That was what frightened me most, Achan Cham—that I would hold your interest briefly but never your heart. That another more comely than me would traipse by, and you would be gone after her, as all of your forefathers have done. I couldn't bear to be only 'the wife' when a never-ending parade of women held your heart. *That* was why I never told you."

Sir Caleb. The knock came quickly, but Achan ignored it. He might never get Sparrow to speak so freely again. He would not stop her, no matter what she accused him of.

She squeezed her hands together as if wringing juice from an orange. "My father had told me of King Axel's reputation with women. And then you confirmed it." Her teary gaze met his. "You said I could be your m-mistress. I just—"

"That was just a stray thought, Sparrow! Can't a man's thoughts be private? I was desperate to have you in my arms but thought I had to marry someone else for politics, for the good of the kingdom. I only wanted to find a way to have you."

"But you thought it! It was my greatest fear, and you confirmed it." She gasped in a breath. "I did not believe it safe to give you my heart. I did not think you loved Arman. I am not beautiful enough or strong enough to be a queen. Bran left me. My father left me. Sir Rigil never cared for me in such a way. I just knew your head would turn from me as easily as theirs had. I could not stand to marry you and be cast aside."

Achan couldn't help but glance at Bran and Sir Rigil. Had Sparrow once cared for Sir Rigil too? Both men's eyes were downcast, expressions stoic. He looked back to Sparrow. "So you cast yourself aside in advance? To save yourself some hurt, you hurt yourself? What kind of way is that to live?"

She shrugged one shoulder. "A safe way?"

He released a gusty laugh. "Is this what you call safe? It's not a safe way, Sparrow, it's a pathetic and lonely way. Sparrow, sometimes life is scary. Get over it, and live." *With me!* he wanted to add.

She sniffled and tipped her nose, so small and red, in the air. "I am trying to, Your Highness. That is why I have come."

He scratched a hand through his own hair. "Well . . . good, then." He became aware again of how silent the room was and just how many people were watching them. Heat crept up into his face.

"Your Highness?" Sir Caleb said.

Achan wheeled around, nearly falling off his step. "Yes?"

"Why don't we move to the solar for Sir Eagan's report? We could have some food brought up. Those not attending the meeting are welcome to eat here."

Sparrow pushed to her feet. "Master Rennan needs a healer right away. He is wounded."

Sir Caleb bowed. "Of course, my lady."

Achan's eyes widened at the exchange, for Sir Caleb, who had disdained all talk of Vrell Sparrow for the past few weeks, now treated her quite differently. And Sparrow . . . No wonder she'd always been such a bossy little thing. Duchess Amal's daughter had been born and bred to rule Carm.

His stomach flipped in his gut. Oh, the things he'd said and done to this girl—to this noblewoman! Pig snout. He caught sight of the maroon sleeve on his arm out of the corner of his eye and looked back to Sparrow.

Arman? What exactly have You done?

It wasn't long before they were all assembled in the solar. Achan sat at the head of a table and watched Sparrow, who hadn't looked at him since her confession on the stairs.

She, Sir Eagan, Sir Jax, and Sir Rigil sat on one side of the table, eating like starved peasants. Sir Eagan sat on Achan's right, with Sparrow on the far end. Esper sat opposite Achan, just around the corner from Sparrow's place. Sir Caleb, Captain Demry, Inko, and Bodwin sat on the other side of the table. Shung and Manu stood by the door.

Bodwin's gaze fell on Sparrow and Esper, and his expression darkened. "Why are women being present for such a meeting? It's being bad luck to be having women involved in matters of war."

"Lady Averella is here at my personal invitation," Sir Eagan said.

Bodwin waved at Esper. "But Sir Caleb's wife . . ."

"Is here as my chaperone," Sparrow said. "Surely you must agree that it would be improper for a lady to be in a secluded meeting with ten men."

"That never stopped you before," Achan mumbled.

Sparrow's cheeks flushed pink, and when she spoke, she still did not look his way. "That is true, Your Highness. But I am turning over a new petal in an effort to become the flower you once proclaimed me to be."

This time Achan's cheeks flamed, more so when he caught Shung's smile. *Something funny, Shung?*

Shung's grin widened.

"So tell us the tale, Sir Eagan," Sir Caleb said. "How did you come to free the prisoners? And what brought you into the company of Lady Averella?"

"Well, Your Highness," Sir Eagan said, "my report goes thusly. I entered Mahanaim with Captain Demry's men. My mission was to slip up to the Hadad's tower and assassinate him. Little did I know what Lady Averella and her companions were up to. Her tale must come first. Just as Captain Demry attacked, Lady Averella took a boat to a secret entrance to the dungeon. Posing as Lady Viola, she was able to reach the cell with the guard's help. Then—and this part will please you, I suspect, Your Highness—Lady Averella took out the guard using a leg sweep." Sir Eagan raised his dark eyebrows and smiled. "What do you think of that?"

Achan tried not to smile. "I'm glad she learned something in her time with us *despicable* men."

Sir Caleb kicked Achan under the table.

Sparrow's spine straightened. She tipped up her chin, but looked at her trencher when she spoke. "Besides the leg sweep, Your Highness, I also learned to scratch, burp, and spit during my time with you. So I too am thankful to have learned *something* useful."

Esper held her hand over her mouth to suppress a giggle.

Achan drew in a breath, wanting to spit back something cutting, for Sparrow baited him like no other, but Sir Eagan clapped Achan's shoulder.

"Then Lady Averella challenged the freed soldiers to weaken Mahanaim from the inside. Shortly thereafter, she, Madam Hoff, and Noam met up with me atop the Hadad's tower. I pulled my knife on Lady Averella, for which I pray she forgives me."

"Of course I forgive you, Father. There was a battle going on, and I was wearing armor and a helm over my face."

Father. Achan looked from one to the other, seeing the similarities now. The hair, the round face, the light skin. How could he have missed it?

"How came you to wear this armor?" Sir Caleb asked.

"Noam and Gren scavenged it in the courtyard. We were helping some of the wounded as we made our way inside."

Sir Eagan chuckled. "Which is where she got the title Iamos, for the men believed they saw the healing goddess, her brother, and her maiden walking among them."

"I told them all that I was *not* Iamos," Sparrow said. "No one wanted to hear it, though."

"When I recognized Lady Averella, I put away my blade," Sir Eagan said. "The Hadad's tower was locked from inside. While Noam and I tried and failed to break down the door, Lady Averella went out the window."

"Of the watchtower?" Achan asked.

"Aye. Skirting the decorative ledge. Gowzals attacked her, but she still managed to dive in through the window and open the door. The Hadad awoke, though, and tried to control Averella, to make her kill me. But she fooled the old man and used Rhomphaia to finish him."

A gasp escaped Achan. Sparrow had killed Macoun Hadar? He glanced at Sparrow, then back to Sir Eagan. "But Sir Gavin told me you killed Macoun Hadar."

"Forgive me, Your Highness. I asked Sir Gavin to keep Averella's presence a secret in case . . ." He rubbed the back of his neck and shifted in his chair.

"Go on with the story," Achan said, not wanting to rekindle his anger at the deceit his advisors had carried on so long.

"When Macoun died, we saw the keliy for a moment. Strangest thing I ever saw. Then we got out of there. We met Sir Rigil, Master Rennan, and Sir Jax on our way back down. Then we found a boat and left Mahanaim."

Sir Eagan went on to explain their trip into Nahar Forest, a man called Peripaso who led them past Ebens and through the mountains, their trouble with wolves, and how they arrived in Noiz.

Achan desperately wanted to speak to Sparrow's mind, but something about the way she carried herself now intimidated him. And she would still not look his way. He forced himself to be patient. The words of her confession repeated like a song stuck in his head. All this time he had been betrothed to Sparrow! The fact made him turn away to hide his smile.

Then, as if he were having to go through it all again, he remembered that Duchess Amal had severed the agreement because her daughter had refused him. Sparrow had refused him. And he'd treated her horribly in the foyer.

Pig snout. But she had just said she was trying to be his flower petals, or something like that, hadn't she? He needed a moment alone with her to figure all this out. Yet he feared it as well. For it might be his last chance, and what if he squandered it? Win Sparrow, or lose her forever.

Arman, do I even want her? She's such a trial.

Yes, hang it all. For look how lovely she was. And fun. He missed her teasing barbs. Her nose in the air. Her captivating green eyes. Her pathetic use of a sword, though the fact that she had killed Macoun Hadar impressed him greatly.

Sir Eagan was still talking. Inko had asked him a question. "Going down one of the tunnels. Averella treated him."

"Master Rennan is having his wound looked at by a healer, or he would be here now," Sir Rigil said. "He has been a stalwart companion to us on this journey."

"I'll knight him as soon as he recovers," Achan said. "If you have no arguments, Sir Rigil."

Sir Rigil beamed. "None at all, Your Highness. The lad is due, in my opinion."

"And I shall knight the man called Peripaso and Lady Averella as well."

The room fell as silent as a calm sea.

Achan fixed his gaze on Sparrow, but she kept her head down, a torn piece of bread halfway to her lips.

"If not for Lady Averella—" Oh, how strange that name sounded on his tongue— "many of our knights would still be imprisoned, maybe eaten by the tanniyn. And Sir Eagan may never have found a way into the Hadad's tower or managed to kill him."

"But to be knighting a woman, Your Highness?" Bodwin said. "Has ever such a thing been happening?"

"Not that I've heard of." Sir Caleb cast a withering glance at Achan. At least he hadn't kicked him this time.

"Berland knights women," Shung said from his place at the door.

"And why shouldn't they?" Achan said. "Have not men been knighted for far less heroic deeds?"

"Be that as it may, Your Highness," Sparrow said, turning her green eyes to Achan for the first time since entering this room, "I am no trained warrior. I am simply a servant of my master. I thank you though, for you show me great honor in the offer. But all I have done is for Arman's glory. The Kingsguard knights, while brave and honorable and respectable, is not a place for me."

"Well said, my lady," Sir Caleb said, beaming.

Achan stared into those cat-like eyes. He had hoped his offer might at least make peace after having treated her so harshly in the great hall. Had it done that much?

The meeting went on. Sir Gavin had sent word to Sir Caleb that he had met with the Mârad general, and that Captain Chantry's ships were nearing Armonguard. Achan did not speak or ask questions during Sir Caleb's report, for he could focus on nothing but what had yet to be said between him and Sparrow.

"Unless you have something to add, Your Highness?" Sir Caleb said, drawing Achan's attention to him.

"No," Achan said, hoping he had missed nothing vital with his rambling thoughts. "Meeting adjourned."

Everyone but Achan stood. Sparrow and Esper inched their way toward the door behind Inko and Bodwin.

Achan stood as well. "Sparrow, may I speak with you?"

She stopped where she was. Esper stepped around her and met Sir Caleb on the other side of the table.

"Your Highness," Sir Caleb said, taking Esper's hand. "She is Lady Averella, and you must not speak with her without a chaperone present."

Heat flashed over Achan at Sir Caleb's implication. He said nothing, however, for in all his time in his role as a prince, he had never once wished to spend a moment alone with any noblewoman. Sir Caleb had trained him how to behave, but this was Sparrow. He suddenly felt oafish and beneath her, for she knew how poor his manners really were. All the time they had spent together, she must have thought his behavior so coarse, so common, so rude.

Esper stepped back toward the table. "I will remain with Lady Averella if she would like to stay."

"Thank you," Sparrow said with a small curtsy.

"Very well." Sir Caleb shot a warning glance at Achan and left the room.

And then there were four, since Shung remained beside the door and closed it behind Sir Caleb.

Sparrow hadn't moved since she'd stopped on her path to the doorway. Esper took her elbow and tried to see her face.

Achan stood at the head of the table, feeling completely exposed. He glanced at Shung. *Help me.*

What can Shung do?

Something. Anything.

"Madam Agros," Shung said. "We have not met." His tone was stiff, his words more formal than any Achan had ever heard him speak. "I am Sir Shung Noatak from Berland. I have been in the prince's service for several months now. I have much respect for Sir Caleb."

Esper curtsied. "I am pleased to know you, Sir Shung. Sir Caleb is the finest of men."

"Have you lived in Noiz long?" Shung asked.

Esper stepped closer to Shung. "For several years now."

Lady Averella. Achan pushed past her shields as if they were made of steam. Her name felt strange, even in his mind.

She turned her gaze to his. She was likely exhausted from her journey. Her skin seemed paler than what was healthy, and she looked quite thin. Her moss-colored eyes contained as much mystery as ever.

What might it be like to know this woman for real?

She cocked one eyebrow, and her lips curved in a small smile. *Yes, Your Highness?*

Words were lost within him. He only knew he didn't want to be parted from her, ever again. He couldn't very well say that. *I imagine you're tired.*

"I am indeed," she said aloud.

Her words were soft, the sound of her voice hypnotic. Only one thing really mattered. One thing Achan needed to know. "Did you . . ." His eyebrows sank. "Remember?"

Shung and Esper continued to talk by the door. Sparrow lowered her gaze to where her fingers fidgeted with a pleat on her gown. Her eyelashes were long and dark and fell like soft shadows over her alabaster cheeks. Why did his thoughts turn to poetry when she was around? He wanted to grab her, squeeze out a favorable answer. But he waited—for what seemed an eternity to pass—before she finally spoke.

"I did."

Small words to hold such power, but they emboldened him. "You became a man in order to avoid marriage," he said, tossing the words she had used to reject him back at her.

"To someone horrible." She reached into the neckline of her gown and pulled out a ring threaded on a length of twine she wore around her neck. She held the ring—his father's signet ring—on her palm and raised it between them. "You are not so bad, right?"

She had kept the ring, all this time. And she was using his own words. Playing along. Their gazes locked, taking Achan to another time and place. He finished what he had told her the last time. "And I love you."

She continued the exchange. "So it won't be like marrying a man thrice my elder or one who only means to use me."

"Nay." He grinned, changing her former rejection to, "It would be better."

Again her eyelashes fell to her cheeks, which were now flushed pink. "How can I know anything for certain? So much is muddled in my mind."

"What assurance do you need?"

"That you love me and not my title or inheritance. I have given it up, so it is unlikely you would get it anyway."

"Nothing has changed, Sparrow. I don't want your inheritance. Here." He took his father's ring from her hand, lifted the cord over her head, and set it on the table. Then he ripped her sleeve from his arm and dropped it on top of the ring. "I cannot renounce the throne, for that is Arman's call on my life, but . . ." He dug the gold coin with his father's likeness out of his pocket and slapped it on the table. He drew his boot knife and cut the coin in half, surprised how easily the blade sank through the gold.

"This is how peasants often do it, maybe not with a gold coin, but a coin of some sort." He held up the two halves, each pinched between his thumb and forefingers and hoped this would in no way offend her.

Sparrow's eyes focused on one half and then the other, and then his face. "I do not understand."

"Most peasants can't afford the pomp of a marriage celebration and feast, so the local smithy witnesses their promise to one another." He swallowed, wanting to say things just right. "You were right about me, Sparrow. I'm a man capable of unfaithfulness. I know because I was tempted recently. My father was such a man. And I am his son, so I could be just like him. I feel that weakness inside, calling to me. But I won't give it ears. You see, I have prayed that Arman will help me be a better man than my father. To make a different path for me and my sons. Arman has changed me, and I know that with His help, and yours, I will not betray you."

"Who tempted you?"

"A woman that Kurtz . . . Oh, Gâzar himself. Does it truly matter? The point is, I walked away and became stronger. And I pledge myself to you alone, forever, if you'll have me."

She bit her bottom lip. "Do you truly believe Arman is the One God?"

"Aye, and Câan His Son, who saved me from myself."

Sparrow's lips parted. "When did you come to believe?"

"The day you left Mitspah." He smirked. "I should thank you for leaving, I suppose, for if you hadn't, I might not have figured all that out."

Sparrow broke into tears then, weeping openly.

"Please don't cry, Sparrow. I promise to be a man worthy of your love."

"Oh, Achan. You already are such a man. As if *my* behavior has made me worthy of such devotion. I punished you for crimes you had not yet committed while I stood by, blinded by fear and lying like a rogue. But my lies never kept my heart safe. Please, do not believe your weakness is worse than mine. Arman does not put one transgression higher than another. All are disdained by him."

He took her hands. "We can help each other be strong."

"And you still wish to marry me?"

"Very much." He set one half of the coin on her palm and closed her fingers around it. "A token of my promise, from a stray boy named Achan to a stray girl named Vrell."

She looked at the coin. "I'd rather have the half with your face on it."

"It's my father's face, not mine. Though Sir Gavin swears they'll make coins bearing my likeness someday."

Her eyes flitted over his face. "What happened to your hair? Your ear?"

"During the Battle of Reshon Gate. A black knight—"

She reached up and ran her fingers over his ear. The sound of her skin on his magnified in his eardrum, like listening to the sea inside a shell. Her touch flustered him, excited him, and kind of hurt the blister that was forming there. The intensity of her green eyes weakened his knees.

"Please let me kiss you."

Her eyes widened. "Here? With our chaperones watching?"

Achan glanced at the doorway. Shung and Esper were still talking, about what he could not begin to guess. Achan bet Shung had never talked so long in his life. "They're not watching."

She inched back a step.

Achan had a sudden urge to wrestle her. But she was a girl—which perhaps explained why she'd never beaten him. "Meet me tonight?"

"Where?"

"In here." Achan pointed to two oversized doors on the far wall of the solar. "Those lead to a balcony that is said to have a magnificent view."

"Good thing we do not need a view, what with Darkness and all."

He stared at her for one long, stunned moment, then laughed. "Why do I feel as if you will always be jerking the mat out from under my boots?"

She picked up his ring from the table, hung it back around her neck, and tucked in into her neckline. A coy smile curled her lips. "Because I always will." She curtsied. "Until this evening, Your Highness. And do not forget my sleeve."

He bowed, and she swept from the room.

"Good day." Esper curtsied to Achan and Shung, then followed Sparrow.

Shung raised an eyebrow. "Well?"

What could he say of that conversation? He replayed it in his mind, though it had gone by like a lightning flash. "Only one thing is certain, Shung. She didn't say no."

When dinner ended that evening, Sir Caleb would not leave Achan's side, first insisting he visit the tombs of kings—which Achan did find fascinating—then demanding Achan get fitted for new clothes.

Achan sensed the man was distracting him on purpose and hoped honesty might work best. "Sir Caleb, must we fit new clothing now? I promised to meet Sparrow in the solar."

"Esper did not mention any such meeting."

"We did not invite Esper."

"Your Highness, I realize you and Lady Averella took many liberties whilst we all believed her to be a boy. But she is not one. And you cannot sneak off together without a chaperone. Knowing what I do about your experiences together, I am tempted to speak with Duchess Amal."

Achan frowned. "About what?"

"To either expedite this marriage or break the betrothal entirely."

Achan did not understand this man. Never would. "In case you've forgotten, we are no longer officially betrothed. Duchess Amal released me from my obligation when Lady Averella asked to be freed from it."

"But she had lost her memory." Sir Caleb tugged on the sleeve Achan now wore proudly on his left arm. "It's clear to *my* eyes that you both have moved past that."

"Then why would you ask to expedite the marriage?"

The look on Sir Caleb's face could smelt iron. "The last thing you need is a distraction. We are at war. I need you alert and focused on the task at hand, which is not sneaking off to steal kisses with Lady Averella."

Achan checked the shields around his mind, wondering how Sir Caleb could have known his plans so entirely without having read his thoughts.

Sir Caleb chuckled. "I was a young man once, Your Highness. I don't need to read your thoughts to know them. Now, if you promise to pay attention, you may invite Lady Averella to join us in the solar for a meeting. Sir Gavin would like to talk with all of us."

Not an hour later, a dozen or more men—and Sparrow and Esper—sat around the table in the solar. Sparrow had changed into a red gown that made her look like a flower in a garden. *You look lovely, Sparrow.*

Thank you. How unfortunate that all these people invited themselves to our meeting.

He matched her smile with one of his own. *Sir Caleb insisted. Esper and Shung are not chaperone enough to please him.*

Then he is a smart man, for I could disarm your Sir Shung with a leg sweep and Esper with hopps tea.

Might she be suspicious if you take down Shung then offer her tea?

Truly you are wise, Your Highness. I shall give them both tea and save my energy for you.

Achan laughed aloud, earning a glare from Sir Caleb. *You're a bold woman, Sparrow.*

If my thoughts offend you I shall keep them to myself.

By all means, I long to hear how you will spend your energy on me.

Why, by dancing, of course.

Dancing? Couldn't Shung and Esper be present for dancing?

Why, no, Your Highness, because you are so poor at it. I would hate to see you embarrassed in public.

We would do nothing more than dance?

Certainly not. You do not think I intended something sordid by my words? Really, Your Highness. I am a lady, well-bred and disciplined in such matters.

Well, I planned to kiss you as I did in Mitspah, until you grabbed hold of my hair for fear of the joy sending you straight to Shamayim.

How she kept a straight face after that comment, Achan would never know. *Now that would be entirely improper, Your Highness. Sir Caleb would definitely not approve.*

Which is why we are here and not on the balcony.

Yes. And you no longer have enough hair to grab hold of.

He ran a hand over his short hair and grinned.

Straight to Shamayim . . . Sparrow smirked. *You think very highly of your kisses. You believe they hold such power?*

At least that much. I am a cham bear, after all.

Little *Cham, so Sir Shung calls you. But how would he know the power of your kisses?*

Ha ha, my lady jester.

Sir Gavin Lukos.

Achan jumped so fast his chair scraped against the floor. He opened his mind to Sir Gavin. *Lo, Sir Gavin. How do you fare with the Mârad?*

Well, thank you, Your Highness. Sir Caleb tells me that Vrell Sparrow has made her way back to you.

She has. Achan met her eyes, and his stomach waged war within him. *But as you well know she is really Lady Averella Amal. No need to deceive me any longer. She has confessed.*

I am glad of that. Now that you know all, have you two reconciled?

Somewhat. Though Sir Caleb is careful not to leave us alone for even a moment.

I daresay he has his reasons.

Achan frowned. *The men appear restless, Sir Gavin. Might we start this meeting?*

I'm ready, if you will call it to order and be my voice.

One moment. Achan stood. "Could I have silence, please, as I offer this meeting to Arman for His guidance and glory?"

The men quieted, and Achan closed his eyes. "Arman, we come together to fulfill Your plans for Er'Rets. Thank You for bringing us this far. Guide us the rest of the way. Provide a plan to take Armonguard as peaceably as possible. So may it be as You decree."

"So be it," everyone said.

"Sir Gavin is watching through my eyes," Achan said. "I will speak for him." Achan raised a hand to command silence. *Speak, Sir Gavin. What have you to say?*

Captain Chantry's ships are currently anchored off the coast of Arman Duchy. They will wait for my order to time their attack with ours. We will march south toward Armonguard. Depending on Esek's army and how long it takes to defeat them, we will need to breach the fortress itself to open the gates so our men and Captain Chantry's men can get inside. This is no easy task.

Achan repeated Sir Gavin's words to the men.

"If we could get New Kingsguard cloaks, we could send a squadron down the Gadowl Wall," Sir Jax said. "They could join the enemy army and find a way inside."

"It leaves too much to chance," Captain Demry said. "First and foremost, the uniforms. Do you have the resources to create uniforms quickly, Bodwin?"

Bodwin shook his head. "I'm having seamstresses in the village, but not the cloth. We are having plenty of red . . ."

"Could we dye the red fabric black?" Sir Rigil asked.

"Possibly. I would have to be asking my weavers."

"Any other ideas?" Achan asked.

"What if we managed a dozen New Kingsguard uniforms, then took another dozen of our men down as if they were prisoners?" Sir Rigil said. "We get inside and—"

"Too risky," Captain Demry said. "They may not allow us to escort the prisoners inside. We might end up surrendering our men."

"May I speak?" Sparrow said.

Achan nodded to her. "Of course. For those of you who have not met her, this is Lady Averella Amal of Carmine."

She addressed the men in a confident voice. "Our group made it to Noiz due to the direction of a man named Peripaso. He knows the tunnels underground better than anyone. Years ago he took a tunnel out of Armonguard. With his help we might enter the castle from underground."

Bodwin laughed. "I've been serving Noiz as warden for thirteen years. Never have I been hearing of any tunnels."

"Nor had I until I met Peripaso," Jax said. "We would be wise to ask him, at least."

I've heard of tunnels under the fortress, Sir Gavin said.

Achan repeated Sir Gavin's claim, then said, "Send a man to fetch Peripaso, then."

Bodwin groaned and folded his arms, but Manu darted out the door.

"Thank you for your suggestion, Lady Averella," Achan said.

She bowed her head. *Bodwin son of Inko seems to have inherited his father's paranoia.*

I've noticed that as well. Have you thought any more about my offer?

Which offer do you mean, Your Highness? Your offer of a secret meeting no longer applies. And the offer of a dance was actually my offer to you. You could not mean that scandalous offer of kisses? Surely you were only teasing.

I was not *teasing.* He dug his half of their coin from his pocket and tapped it against his chin. *But I meant the offer that accompanied the coin I gave you.*

Oh, that. Well, I must confess it—

Children, do not forget that I am here, Sir Gavin said in a singsong tone. *And I hear your every word.*

34

Averella's face flamed. She could not look at Achan. Thankfully, Shung and Peripaso entered the solar, and the distraction spared her further embarrassment.

By the time she looked back to Achan, he bore no signs of Sir Gavin's rebuke on his face. He looked so different with short hair and a beard, and had grown much in confidence since she last saw him. How she had missed his company. But now that she had returned, being Lady Averella had only erected a different kind of wall between them. Protocol.

Sir Caleb would never permit them a moment alone now, especially if Sir Gavin told him what he'd overheard. It had never occurred to Averella how little time most couples spent together alone. Mother had trusted Averella with Bran more than she probably should have. And Sir Caleb would never give that freedom to Achan.

Shung set up a chair for Peripaso at the end of the table.

"You are Peripaso, I presume?" Achan said.

Mercy. Achan behaved so formally now, so educated and commanding. Sir Caleb had taught him well.

"I am, Your Majesty," Peripaso said. "It's an honor to make your 'quaintance."

"Likewise. I understand you have performed admirably, and I wish to knight you for your service to my men."

Peripaso ducked his head. "Many thanks, Your Highness, but I'm not a fighting man."

"Anything you desire, then. You only need ask."

Another bow. "You are most gracious, Your Highness."

"Can you tell us if there are tunnels that go underground from here to Armonguard? That exit inside the stronghold?"

"'Course there is, Your Majesty, sir. There's a river that'll get you there. One leads straight to the dungeon. You'd only need to break out of the cell, if it was locked. Other than that . . ."

"You have taken these tunnels recently?" Achan asked.

"Naw. Been ten years since I gone down that way."

"So the tunnels may have caved in?" Sir Caleb asked.

"Suppose they could've, though it ain't likely. I've been livin' thirteen years in the Nahar Caves. Only tunnels caved in was the ones I caved myself."

"Why would you cave in tunnels?" Achan asked.

"Keep the Ebens away from me."

Achan raised his hand to signal that Sir Gavin was speaking to him. "Sir Gavin wishes that Captain Demry explore the tunnel's entrance with Peripaso and submit a plan of attack." He dropped his hand. "Inform me when your plan is ready. Meeting adjourned."

Averella stayed in her seat as the men filed out of the chamber. She caught Achan's eye and sensed he was lingering as well. Perhaps he would get his chance to show her the balcony. She blushed at the thought, until she glanced up and met Sir Caleb's narrowed gaze.

"And now we have time to work through your wardrobe, Your Highness," Sir Caleb said.

Achan rolled his eyes at Averella. "Splendid. I was just thinking how I needed a dozen new pairs of trousers."

Captain Demry came to Achan's chambers to report that the tunnels were there, along with a dozen boats that could sit twenty each. Achan bloodvoiced Sir Gavin with Captain Demry's plan to enter Armonguard. The Great Whitewolf liked it enough to ask Achan to call yet another meeting where a final battle plan was hashed out.

Sir Gavin would lead their army and the Mârad out of Edom Gate and down the Gate Road. According to Duchess Amal, Veil Scout that she was, Esek's southern army had backtracked to the fields north of Armonguard. Whether they remained at that location or headed north up the Gate Road, Sir Gavin's army would meet them at some point.

The small group of soldiers in Noiz would divide into four squadrons and ride the boats on the underground river to the Armonguard dungeon. Upon arrival in Armonguard, Inko would command a squadron to take the northern gate, Captain Demry and his squadron would take the western gate, Sir Eagan and his group would focus on the eastern gate, and Achan and Sir Caleb would take their men to the watchtower, for that was where Duchess Amal claimed Lord Nathak and Esek spent much of their days.

The army was a day's ride closer to Armonguard, but the rivers should carry Achan and his group faster. Achan's group would seize the gates and keep them open so that Sir Gavin's army and Captain Chantry's men could get inside.

Achan's task, according to Sir Gavin, would be to kill Esek and Lord Nathak—and if possible rebuke the keliy.

And so the battle plan that would decide the fate of Er'Rets was set into motion. Achan adjourned the meeting and went looking for Sparrow before Sir Caleb could stop him.

But Sparrow had already gone to bed for the night.

The next morning, Averella discovered that the war council had met again the previous evening without her. She begged servants for details, but they claimed the meeting had been behind locked doors. She took to her bed to watch through her father's eyes and found him in his chambers, getting dressed in his armor.

She walked from her room to the great hall, looking for any familiar face, Achan's, especially. Soldiers were everywhere, dressed for battle. Something was going to happen, and soon.

She found Gren and Noam in the great hall eating breakfast. There was no sign of Achan at the head table. She sat down beside Gren. "Do you know where all these soldiers are going?"

"They leave for battle today," Noam said.

Today? But they had just arrived. "When?"

"I heard someone say within the hour."

"We're not permitted to go," Gren said.

"As well you should not," Noam said. "Nor should I, for I would only be a hindrance."

Achan Cham.

Averella opened her mind at once. *Achan, where are you?*

Me? It is you who haven't been answering, Sparrow. Last night you were asleep when I came to call, and this morning . . . still sleeping. I have been up since before dawn.

I heard that you will be leaving soon.

Very soon. Where are you?

In the great hall.

Can you come down to the tunnels to see me off? We won't be leaving for at least another hour, but Sir Caleb will not let me out of his sight.

He was leaving already? *Yes, of course I will come.*

She could hear the smile in his tone. *I shall count the breaths until your arrival.*

You are sweet. He would not likely be as sweet when he saw her.

Averella bid farewell to Gren and Noam and returned to her chambers. She had a servant bring her a man's uniform, then help her dress and attach her bronze plate armor. She loathed the idea of wearing it again but would be foolish to go without it. She had seen enough battle wounds to know the value of such protection.

Once she was dressed all the way to her helm, she donned her satchel, which Esper had replenished for her, put on her belt and sword, tucked her small knife into her boot, and followed the narrow rock path to her father's chamber.

She pushed open the door. Being a man with so much more armor than she had, Sir Eagan was not yet ready. She closed the door and leaned against it.

He caught sight of her and sighed. "Averella, you cannot come along. Your mother has already forbidden it."

"She does not have the right."

"She has every right. You are her daughter. And you said it yourself: you are not a warrior."

"But I am *able* to fight. And helping the wounded was the whole reason I came this far. I will not be left behind."

"A breastplate and helm is not enough armor for this battle." He addressed the valet who was attaching his breastplate. "We shall need some cuisses and greaves for the lady. A gorget as well, if you can find one small enough for her. And a shield."

The valet finished tying the points of Sir Eagan's breastplate and bowed. "I'll see what I can find, sir."

"It is doubtful Sir Caleb will allow this. The less you say the better. You will come with me. My task is to lower the southwestern drawbridge. Promise you will not leave my side?"

"I promise, Father."

"Good."

Soon she was walking stiffly after her father down so many flights of stairs that her legs began to ache. The valet had tied the leather armor to her thighs so tightly it pinched behind her knees, and her shield was heavy.

The sound of water made her hopeful that they were almost there, but they continued to travel down, down, down.

Just when Averella felt she might faint from fatigue, the tunnel walls fell away into a large cavern. Torches lit the scene. Two levels below where Averella and her father descended, the stairs emptied onto a rocky shelf that ran alongside an underground river. Hundreds of soldiers milled about, loading gear into a dozen boats that were tied to the shelf. The boats bobbed on the rushing current, front and back ends clunking against each other.

Though the boats were larger than the one she had taken from Xulon, Averella could not help but think of when she had first met Peripaso. She hoped the reekats were asleep.

Despite her aching legs, she kept on her father's heels. They finally reached the shelf and wove through the mob of soldiers. She wrinkled her nose at the stench of body odor. She doubted these men had bathed since Carmine.

Sir Caleb's voice grew in the darkness, and suddenly Sir Eagan stopped before him. Sir Caleb was dressed in full battle armor as well. He stood with a group of captains, Achan, and Achan's personal guards.

"You know, armor and water are a dangerous match," Sir Eagan said to Sir Caleb.

Sir Caleb hummed his agreement. "But the alternative is worse. The men have been told to be careful."

Averella stayed behind her father, hoping not to be seen, but she could not help looking at Achan. His armor looked impressive. His helm had a long nose guard, which allowed her to see his eyes, cheeks, mouth, and chin. Her maroon sleeve stood out against the brown leather armor on his arm and made her smile.

Shung whistled a sharp sound, and the crowd quieted.

Sir Caleb addressed the men in a loud voice. "You each know your captain. The first three boats will accompany Inko and Peripaso, so if you're on the mission to take the northern gate, move to the front. The second three boats are with the prince and myself. Our group will take the watchtower. Captain Demry will take the western gate, their boats are next. And those assigned with Sir Eagan to take the eastern gate will claim the last three boats. Make sure you're in the right boat before we cast off. Arman be with you all."

Averella stepped back to allow her father room to lead the way to the boats at the end of the line.

Sparrow.

She turned and met Achan's blue eyes.

What are you doing in that outfit?

She pulled back her shoulders. *Serving my prince.*

His lips pulled into a straight line. *I didn't ask you to fight. Just to see me off.*

I will not be left behind. I have proven that I can take care of myself.

Sir Caleb tugged on Achan's arm. "Your Highness, come this way and we'll get you into the boat." When Achan did not move, Sir Caleb followed his gaze until it settled on Averella.

"For the love of Arman, Eagan! What *is* this? Did your daughter forget she belongs in a dress so soon?"

"She has earned the right to fight," Sir Eagan said. "I have put her on my squad."

Sir Caleb groaned. "It isn't proper."

"I do not care whether it is proper," Sir Eagan said.

Sir Caleb shot him a scowl. "Don't use your calming tricks on me, Eagan. The duchess could not have approved this."

"The duchess is not her father."

Achan took hold of Sir Caleb's arm. "She can come." *As long as you promise to stay with Sir Eagan. And do not come looking for me.*

She sighed and tossed her head. As if he was the only reason she wanted to go. *Why would I come looking for you?*

He cocked his head to the side as if it were obvious.

Tears formed in her eyes, and she blinked them away. *You really want me to stay away?*

Only if you wish me the best chance of life.

What does that *mean?*

Sparrow. I can do nothing but stare at you whenever you are around. Your mere presence owns my full attention. If you're beside me, I shall be cut down in an instant.

She twisted her lips. *Not if you're trying to protect me. Then no one could stop you.*

But that's just it. What good is my objective when you might be in danger? I would think of nothing but protecting you. This battle belongs to Arman. I must give it my full attention.

You are right, of course. I will stay by my father's side.

"Thank you." He swiped at the strap under his chin that secured his helm, but his metal gauntlets only scraped against the edge of his helm. "It seems I am a prisoner inside my own armor." He stepped up to her and rested the forehead of his helm against hers. The steel clinked together. His closeness doused the light, and she could barely see the reflections that were his eyes.

"Be safe," she whispered.

"You as well." He set his hand on her shoulder. His gauntlet scraped over her bronze armor. He lowered his arm and stepped back. Their eyes remained locked together until Sir Caleb stepped between them and guided Achan away. Achan shot one last glance in her direction before he was lost in the crowd.

"Let us find our boat, Averella," Sir Eagan said. "My men will be awaiting their captain."

She followed her father down the rocky shelf. *Will I be a distraction to you too, Father? Should I stay behind?*

I am not concerned. My objective is safer than the prince's. Once we achieve it, we only need hold it.

Do not tell the men who I am. I do not want anyone fretting over me.

He sent a wry smile her way. *Very well, Averella.*

Her father took her arm and helped her down into the boat. She felt the soldiers' eyes on her, wondering what pathetic soldier required assistance to climb into the boat. She considered pulling away from her father's grip, but her armor was so heavy she feared she would topple overboard.

She settled beside Sir Eagan in the front of the boat on a bench that curved around the left side. She tucked her shield between her knees. A torch had been set into a notch in the nose, warming the left side of her helm. *How long since these boats have been used, Father?*

Who knows? But they were checked over as soon as Peripaso and Captain Demry discovered them. They are sound.

The rocky shelf was now completely empty but for a handful of servants who had carried down supplies.

"For Arman!" Achan's shout resonated through the cavern, warming Averella's heart and igniting her courage.

A chorus of "Arman" answered, followed by manly roars and cheers. A moment later, the rope was lifted from the tether and the current sucked the boat into the dark tunnel.

She reached out for Achan and was surprised to find his mind still open to hers. *That was an inspiring call to arms.*

Thank you. I only hope Arman will make it clear what I am supposed to do.

She could only imagine what he must be going through. *Still uncertain?*

Aye. Darkness is not a beast I can fell with a sword.

Perhaps rebuke it as you did in Barth?

Perhaps.

The soldier beside Sparrow knocked into her, laughing about something the man next to him said.

Sparrow?

Yes, Your Highness?

I'm glad you've come along. I've missed you.

She smiled. *I have missed you as well, though I did not know it was you I was missing for some time.*

That's funny, coming from you.

What do you mean?

You say you didn't know it was me you missed, and yet until now I've never known who you *really were, though I missed you specifically.*

Hmm. Yes, I suppose that is amusing.

But how did you manage to come? I am surprised Sir Caleb did not put his foot down.

You gave me permission. Did you forget you outrank Sir Caleb?

I often forget.

Well, perhaps he hopes I will be killed and spare you a marriage to a woman with so little decorum as to wear trousers in public.

You agree to marry me, then?

She grinned wide and tipped her head down to avoid questioning stares from her boat mates. *I did not say* that, *Your Highness.*

You did not refuse, either. Do you have your coin?

I sewed it in a pouch and added it to my necklace.

It's in a safe place, then.

Yes. Very safe.

The boats moved swiftly down the underground river. The journey was long and cramped. Averella dozed off, and when she woke, her legs had fallen asleep.

How long will it take us to get there, Father?

A day and a half, so Peripaso told me.

So long?

The men sang songs and told jokes to pass the time and fight tricks of Darkness. Averella kept to herself, but joined them for meals of dried meat and bread. Not knowing there was a lady present among them, the men spoke freely about the battles they had fought in the past days, lingering over gruesome details of wounds and deaths, green fire, chams, black knights, and tanniyn. The whole thing made Averella shiver, but the ride was otherwise so boring she could not help but listen in.

Peripaso had no intention of stopping for the night or even to stretch one's legs. The soldiers relieved themselves over the side of the boat whenever the urge struck them. It seemed a cruel fate to Averella. She felt as if she were back on the road to Mahanaim with Jax and Khai. Thankful she had not drunk much water before leaving Noiz, she was careful to only sip from her water skin.

A day and a half later, they finally stopped along a sandy bank. Her father bid her take a moment to herself while he organized his men. By the time she returned, Inko and Captain Demry's groups had both left. Achan and Sir Caleb's squad was crowded in a circle to the left of an opening in the rocky wall.

"We must keep our voices down," Sir Eagan said. "The dungeons should be empty when we reach them. We must move swiftly, for more guards may have arrived by then. We will exit into the northern arc of the keep, straight across from the eastern gate. Any questions?"

No one spoke, so Sir Eagan raised his torch and said, "Then we go. Follow me." Sir Eagan led the men through the dark opening in the rock.

Come back to me, Sparrow.

Averella looked over her shoulder and locked eyes with Achan. She lifted her armor-clad hand. *You as well.*

The distraction had lost Averella her place in line. She waited for the men to pass so she could fall in at the end. But Jax gripped her arm and pulled her in front of him. Their eyes met, and she opened her mind to his knock.

We shall be partners, Vrell. You watch my back, I will watch yours. Agreed?

Yes, thank you, Jax. I am glad you are in this squad.

From that moment on, everything happened in silence. Averella entered the dark tunnel in the rock. It led upward over jagged ground until letting out into a large cell. The iron-barred door hung open. Averella jogged in line through a maze of dirt pathways in the smelly dungeon and up a curling stairwell that emptied into a dark stone corridor inside the mighty Armonguard fortress.

They turned twice in the corridors and spilled out into a dark night. A cool breeze blasted her face. She barely had time to look around as she sprinted to keep up with the men. A screech cut through the darkness. A gowzal.

She shivered and told herself, *Do not think on it. Focus on the gate.*

Dark shadows circled the ground. She glanced up to see swarms of gowzals gliding past the torches on the sentry walls. Even in darkness, the whitestone walls of Armonguard shone bright against the dark bodies of the creatures.

A battle already raged around them. She passed by a man in a dingy red Kingsguard cape who was screaming, clutching his arm. She slowed her steps and reached for the strap of her satchel, but a firm grip on her shoulder changed her mind.

Jax towed her away from the injured man. *First we must achieve our objective, then you may help the injured.*

The decorative wrought-iron arch that marked the gate loomed ahead, a lacy tangle of charcoal thread against a black sky. Men in New Kingsguard cloaks shot arrows down from the sentry wall on either side of the gate. Jax pulled Averella behind his shield. She held up her own just as a heavy thud knocked it against her head. She didn't dare move her shield to see what had hit it.

She ran blindly after the soldiers until her shin struck something solid. She looked down to see the bottom rungs of a wooden ladder. She raised her shield to see more of it.

Jax grabbed the back of her belt and lifted. "Up you go."

Averella climbed awkwardly, the heavy shield and armor weighing each step. Something glanced off the right side of her breastplate, knocking her sideways. Her foot slipped mid-step, and she fell, holding on with one hand.

Jax's strong hands grabbed her legs and boosted her back up. She scrambled to find hand-and-footholds, then climbed as fast as she could.

It seemed strange that there was not more resistance to their climb, but when her eyes crested the parapet and she saw an enemy soldier crumple without having been touched, she knew her mother was helping them from the Veil.

Averella heaved herself over the parapet and drew her sword. She stood just north of the eastern gate on one arc of the scalloped sentry walk, looking out over the wall. Torchlight and the ghostly grey castle reflected off the inky black surface of Lake Arman, which surrounded the castle like an impassable moat.

To her right, Sir Eagan and his men occupied the gatehouse. Clanking chain signaled they were lowering the drawbridge. A half dozen bodies lay on the wall between the ladder and gatehouse—all enemy. She spun around to look inside the castle walls. Below, red and black cloaks swirled, swords clashed, men screamed, birds cawed.

She cringed at the cacophony. Shifting shadows on the ground lifted her gaze back to the skies. Gowzals swarmed like houseflies overhead, the thickest cluster over the distant watchtower, which glowed at the top with eerie green light. Her heart clenched at the idea of Achan going up there. Who would he find at the top wielding that light?

"Look sharp, Vrell!"

Jax's voice pulled her attention back to where she stood. A line of New Kingsguard knights approached from the north along the curved sentry wall like a line of ants. There must have been a hundred or more, all coming their way.

She looked back to the gatehouse. Jax stood outside the doorway, waving her in. She skipped sideways for a few steps, then ran inside.

"Bowmen!" Sir Eagan stood in the center of the gatehouse. "Two in each door. Quickly!" Three men ran to the southern doorway. Sir Eagan lowered his voice and grabbed the third man's arm. "Kates, you on this side."

Averella pressed back to allow Kates, a bearded, red-headed man, to kneel just outside the northern door. She glanced through the opposite door and saw just as many enemy soldiers advancing from the south.

"We must keep the bridge down for Captain Chantry's men," Sir Eagan yelled. "Take aim and await my signal. And consider the curve of the wall when you shoot."

The floor trembled under Averella's boots. The distant clatter of footsteps sounded like rain. But the thudding of her heart proved this was no spring shower.

"Shoot! Now! Take them down!" Sir Eagan pushed a quiver of arrows into Averella's chest. "When the men run out, fill their quivers with these."

Averella set down her shield and took the quiver. She sheathed her sword and moved to the doorway. The *shuck, shuck, shuck* of arrows leaving the bowmen's strings was constant and methodical. Kates was a quicker draw than the soldier beside him, but both seemed to never miss. Black-cloaked men fell before their comrades and were trampled or tossed over the wall. Still the enemy advanced.

Kates drew his last arrow, and Averella pushed a handful of arrows into his quiver before he managed to raise his arm again. He never had to wait. She did the same for the other bowman. Both shot arrows until there were no more.

"I'm out!" Kates jumped to his feet, swung his bow over his arm, and drew his sword so quickly Averella lunged out of his way.

"Hold the gate!" Sir Eagan yelled. *Averella, stay back if you can, at least until the melee passes.*

Averella glanced at her father, but he had turned to the southern doorway. She picked up her shield and drew her sword. Her heart drummed inside her head, melding with the beat of the approaching footsteps. She pressed back into the corner of the gatehouse, peeking out an arrow loop beside the northern doorway.

The archers had felled many, but they were still greatly outnumbered. Jax stood at the front of seven men on the northern side of the gate. Averella counted the heads of the enemy and got lost after twenty-three. There were still more than twice that many charging, swords raised.

Why had she wanted to come along again?

Jax drew his axes and crouched. Kates and the others raised their swords.

"For Arman! For our king! Hold the gate!" Sir Eagan yelled.

Averella looked over her shoulder to see her father pacing at the back of the line on the southern entrance, sword raised to the dark sky, yelling so loud his face was red.

This was no time to be timid. Averella stepped through the northern door and stood in the same position as her father. She lifted her sword high.

The enemy was close. Twenty yards. Fifteen. Ten. A man fell at the front of their line, tripping two. The enemy trampled over the top of them.

Well done, Mother. Averella smiled, though the act felt oddly cruel.

Jax stuck down the first man to reach him. Two more rushed past. Kates lifted his sword. Metal clashed. Men growled. Screamed.

A man in black sprinted through their line, headed right for the door. Averella put her weight behind her shield and rammed into his side. He bounced off the wood and stumbled, screaming as he lost his footing and fell over the parapet and into the water below.

The fighting went on. Rather than swing her sword, Averella continued to take advantage of the tight space at the door, knocking men over the edge of the wall. She tried to knock them into the water, rather than to the ground inside the bailey, but it did not always work.

A few paces before her, Kates fell to his knees. A black knight stepped over his body and raised his sword to Averella. She lifted her own and did not miss the fact that her blade trembled.

He swung at her head. She lifted her shield to block, but his sword flipped around and cut at her legs. She crouched into the attack, but the blade struck her shield, knocking her back into the doorframe. She dropped her sword and slumped inside the doorway.

The black knight's trousers swished as he stepped over her. She pulled the knife from her boot and stabbed it into the back of his knee, between the ties in his armor. He screamed, whirled around, and kicked her, flipping her on her side. A prick under her arm turned her head. The black knight stood above, the point of his sword set under her arm where he could drive it through to her heart.

But the man stood still, grimacing, eyes darting about, face pale. He grunted. His sword arm trembled, rattling his gauntlet against the chain mittens he wore underneath.

As he crumpled to the gatehouse floor, Mother's voice said, *Now, take more care, dearest. I am most displeased to find you here.*

Averella released her pent up breath. *Thank you, Mother.* But she did not take care. She pushed to her feet and ran out the door. She grabbed Kates under the arms and dragged him inch by inch into the gatehouse. His body left a swath of red blood on the whitestone sentry walk.

It turned out to be a stab wound in his thigh. Most men died in battle from leg wounds. Not this one, if she could help it.

She reached over to the stormed black knight and pulled her knife from the back of his knee. She cut off Kates's leather cuisse, then cut through his trousers so she could see the wound. It was not a stab at all, but a slice to the bone. She did her best to wrap it.

When she finished, she dragged him against the inside wall of the gatehouse, sheathed her boot knife, lifted her shield and sword, and ran back outside.

There were only eight left fighting on the northern side of the gatehouse. Four red cloaks, four black. The black knight closest to her cut down the last of her squad that stood between the enemy and her and kicked him over the side. He turned to face her—Khai Mageia.

She gasped. "But you are dead!"

"We'll see about that, boy!" His nasally voice brought a flash of memories that coated Averella's palms in sweat. He raised his massive sword, which was as long as Averella was tall, and lunged.

She scooted aside, keeping her shield in front. The blow struck her shield and knocked her through the air. She crumpled against the parapet and hit her head. Her helm slipped off. She scrabbled to pull it back on, but the damage had been done.

"*You*," Khai said. "You thought you killed me that day in Mitspah." He cackled. "It's true, my lady. You did. Just as your lover killed my prince by lopping off his arm. But our master cures even death."

"You are *not* cured," Averella said. "You will still die someday, and then you will have to face Arman."

"Doubtful. For today, Arman will lose once and for all."

"You always did brag too much, Khai." Jax stood behind him with the two remaining Old Kingsguard soldiers. All but Khai had been defeated.

Khai sighed extra loudly. "Don't think you can beat me because you're a giant. It'll take more than the four of you to fell me."

"Everything with you is always an exaggeration," Jax said. "The boasts from your lips, the length of your sword, the strength of your so-called gods . . . You cannot compensate for your shortcomings with deception. The truth is always revealed in time."

"Let it be revealed, then." Khai screamed and charged.

Jax and Khai spun in a whirl of strikes and parries. But once they had turned halfway round, Khai retreated, running north up the sentry wall. Jax took off after him. Averella followed, not wanting to lose sight of Jax.

At the apex of the scallop that wrapped around the gardens, Khai turned to face Jax. He chanted, hand outstretched, but Averella was too far back to hear. Jax stepped slowly toward Khai, but before he could strike, a green ball of fire shot from Khai's outstretched hand and into the sentry walk, right where Jax stood. Another struck the battlement. Averella cowered under her shield as the chunks of stone and sand rained down like hail. When the sound stopped, she looked out.

The whitestone floor crumbled like sand under Jax's feet and spilled into the water. Jax stumbled, and the wall caved under his feet. He reached up to grab the nearest merlon, but it broke off in his grip, and he fell down into the dark water.

Averella's heart seemed to fall with the giant. She glanced across the destruction to see Khai lower his hand.

"You coward!" Averella yelled.

"Don't like my style?" Khai extended his arms and bowed. "Come fight me yourself then, *my lady*." He turned and fled up the sentry walk toward the watchtower.

35

Achan ran up the spiral stairwell from the dungeon, breath heavy from the weight of his armor. Sir Caleb led their squad, followed by Sir Rigil and Bran, then a half dozen soldiers Achan didn't know, then Cortland, Manu, and himself. Shung, Toros, and Cole were directly behind him, and the rest of their squad brought up the rear.

Achan hadn't thought it fair to deny anyone his or her place in fighting for their freedom, not even Sparrow. So Cole had been put in charge of carrying the banner of Armonguard.

Achan tried to focus on the task ahead as if it were merely a training. Take the watchtower. Nothing more. Nothing less. Simply take the watchtower. But his thoughts bounced down trails like a jackrabbit.

Had he grown up here, as he should've, would this stairwell be familiar?

Was Prince Oren lost? Or would he return to his body?

This was Achan's home. Unless he failed.

But Arman was with him, so he couldn't fail, right?

If Darkness didn't recede when Lord Nathak was killed, would Arman explain how to push it back?

Achan craved Sparrow's encouragement. She had left her mind open to his, a fact that bolstered his hope for their future. He dared a peek through her eyes. She stood on a sentry wall behind a kneeling bowman, who fired into a charge of New Kingsguard knights.

Achan's foot caught on a step and he stumbled. Shung grabbed his belt, saving him from crashing against the stone steps. *Thanks, Shung.*

Let the fear strengthen. Let it bolster your sword.

Fear. Was that his problem? Was he afraid?

As if there were any doubt.

At the top of the stairs, they ran through part of Castle Armonguard. Again Achan's mind imagined scenes of a young boy and his parents walking together, talking. What part of the castle was this? Where would his bedchamber have been? Not likely on any ground floor.

They exited into a courtyard filled with the clamor of screams, clashing steel, and horses' cries. From the number of red cloaks, Achan guessed the gates had been won and Sir Gavin had been let in. Achan followed Manu. The watchtower stood in the distance. A beacon calling him to arms. Green mage magic lit up the tower's roof.

Achan ran past overturned carts, burned cottages, drooping tents, fighting men, dead men, and a few dead horses. Gowzals circled overhead. Some swooped down and perched on the dead, feeding off the carnage. Achan kept his gaze fixed on the watchtower, until a great roar pulled his focus to the gate on his left.

Barthos, the beastly idol from Barth, swirled around the gatehouse. Achan could barely see Inko's grey head as he stood before the beast, hands raised, no doubt chanting a rebuke.

Achan kept pace with his line as they ran around a charred structure and past a deserted blacksmith's forge, snaking around dead men. They slowed down when they reached a grassy clearing. The whitestone watchtower loomed above, hundreds of men tangled in battle at its base. Esek would be up there. And Lord Nathak.

A chorus of "Lee-lee-lee-lee-lee!" and a line of Eben warriors charged, most waving long spears and shields, their pale foreheads marked with three black lines.

Achan crouched. He held his shield before him and set Ôwr's flat against the edge, peeking over the pointed top. Cortland and Manu met the first two Ebens. Achan bounced on his toes, ready to meet the next one, but Toros darted in first and slashed at the Eben's bare legs.

Four other Ebens circled to Achan's right. Achan turned, watching them. Shung stood ready behind Achan, and Cole—covered in gleaming silver armor—clutched the Armonguard standard, his eyes peeled wide through the slot in his helm.

Stay back, Cole, Achan told him.

Three of the Ebens ran at Shung. Apparently, they found Shung the bigger threat. Achan couldn't blame them. Shung expertly deflected each jab.

The last Eben clutched a club the size of Achan's leg. He swung high. Achan kept his shield at middle guard, flinching as the wood arced toward his face. But as he hoped, the Eben reversed his swing and batted at his legs. Achan shifted his shield into low guard in time for the club to beat against it. Achan hacked over the top of his shield. His blade just missed the Eben's elbow.

The giant swung for Achan's legs again. Achan lifted his shield, expecting this to be a feint, but the blow stung his legs through his armor.

Achan stumbled and turned in time to block a spear thrust at his face. Another spear slid across the back of his neck. He rammed his shield against one spear, parried a jab from another, and raked his blade against the club on his backswing.

The Ebens were trying to separate them. Achan needed to get back with Shung. He lashed out and cleaved for his attacker's legs. The Eben staggered, tripped over a fallen body, and fell onto his rear. He raised his shield over his head. Achan circled him, raining blows like an axe on a log. Splinters of wood and paint went flying. Three of Achan's soldiers ran up and relieved him, so Achan sidestepped back to Shung and waved Cole to follow.

Sir Caleb's voice boomed in Achan's inner ear. *Do not engage unless you must. We must get inside the watchtower, for that is where the wielders will be.*

And Lord Nathak. His half-brother.

Go, Little Cham, now! Shung yelled as he finished the last of the three Ebens. *To Manu.*

Achan ran toward Manu's dark hair and red cape. And the line was moving again. It lost form as they tried to pass through another melee. Manu stopped to deflect a blow. A man shrieked. Achan darted around Manu, safely out of the arc of his cousin's sword. He peeked at the tower just as a green orb sailed toward him. He leapt back, knocking into Shung. The fireball thudded into the grass, sending singed grass, soil, and silent tendrils of smoke into the air.

Shung gripped Achan's arm and tugged. *This way.*

Achan followed Shung through a gap in the fighting. As they neared the tower, the enemy defense came into view. A wall of rectangular shields and mantlets circled the bottom of the tower. They were decorated with three black stripes or painted gowzals. All had a slot or hole of some kind at the top. Arrows and balls of green fire flew out from those openings. An occasional boulder sailed over the top.

Achan lifted his shield to his nose. *They've got mangonels, Sir Caleb. They're hurling stones.*

I see that. Where are you?

Shung and I are straight out from the entrance. We need a way past the blockade.

See if the duchess can aid us. I'll gather the men to you.

Agreed. A boulder flew through the air straight at Achan. With no time to dodge it, he crouched and braced his shield. The rock hit, though not with the force he'd expected. He peeked over his shield to see a man's head rolling away.

A jolt of nausea gripped him. He closed his eyes and focused on Duchess Amal's pleasant face. *My lady? We could use your assistance.*

An enemy soldier charged. Achan pushed to his feet and raised his sword, but Shung darted forward and met the attack. Achan turned in a quick circle and saw only Sir Caleb and a handful of his squad approaching.

Duchess Amal's voice filled his ears then, music to his anxious soul. *How can I be of service, Your Highness?*

If Sir Eagan can spare you, we need help accessing the watchtower. They've barricaded us out.

I see it. I will take out the men at the entrance. Be ready.

Sir Caleb reached Achan's side, panting. "What news?"

"She's attacking now. We must be ready to charge."

Sir Caleb gathered the men into three lines. The center line consisted of Sir Caleb, Bran, Cortland, Achan, Shung, and Toros. "We all charge together. The outer lines protect the center. Once the center enters the watchtower, do what you can to take the shields and guard the door."

Now, Your Highness! Duchess Amal said.

"Now!" Achan yelled.

The men charged, shields before them, swords ready. They met no resistance, thanks to Duchess Amal's storming, and Achan's line ran inside the tower and up the stairs. Sir Caleb, Bran, Cortland, Achan, then the rest. Shadows on the wall preceded three New Kingsguard knights coming down from above.

Like all towers, the stairs rose on the left, circling to the right. This gave the defender the advantage as his right arm faced the outer wall. Sir Caleb struggled a moment as his blade was obstructed by the center pillar. He switched his sword to his left hand and pressed upward. Achan already held Ôwr in his left hand.

But the narrow stairs allowed for no more than one battle at a time. And when Sir Caleb managed to fell one opponent, only Sir Caleb was able to meet the next. There was nothing the others could do but wait.

Sir Caleb killed the second man and stepped over his body to meet the third.

An external force shook the tower. Sir Caleb's opponent stumbled and slid down a few steps on his back, his plate armor gliding over the stone. Sir Caleb darted aside and bashed his boot against the man's head as he went by. Shung finished him off.

The tower shook again. This time the wall cracked at an arrow loop, right where Achan stood.

A snakelike head bashed through the wall, sending bits of whitestone and dust over the stairwell. It knocked Bran down, curled up the stairwell and snapped at Sir Caleb, then swung back, pushed over Cortland and Manu, and screeched.

A tanniyn!

The creature's breath was a hot putrid wind in Achan's face. He cowered against the central pillar, hiding behind his shield. *Duchess! The tanniyn!*

The tanniyn's next screech was laced with pain. Achan peeked over his shield to see Shung wrench his sword out from the creature's neck. The tanniyn bashed its head into the steps above, then smashed down through the steps the men stood on. Whitestone steps crumbled underfoot. Cortland fell down the new hole. Manu tumbled down the stairs. The tanniyn nipped at Achan's shield, then hissed, its maw open wide.

Hold on, Your Highness! Duchess Amal said.

Achan wanted to strike, but the beast's mouth pressed the shield so tightly against the pillar he could not move, its breath a rotten puff of air. Sir Caleb grabbed one of the creature's fangs and yanked its head away from Achan. Shung stabbed the tanniyn's neck again, and it drew back from the hole like a coil of rope. Sir Caleb went with it, still gripping its fang.

"No!" Achan dropped his weapons and grabbed Sir Caleb's leg. His grip slid down to Sir Caleb's boot, paused, then tugged free. Achan fell against the pillar, clutching Sir Caleb's boot. *Duchess! The tanniyn has Sir Caleb!*

I see him, the duchess said.

Achan couldn't move. He stared through the dusty air at the hole in the tower wall but could see nothing but Darkness. He waited for Duchess Amal to speak again, but she did not.

Averella paced, studying the broken sentry wall. The interior edge appeared solid, though it was only as wide as her foot in several places. She should go back to Sir Eagan and the gatehouse. Instead, she sheathed her sword and stepped toward the jagged edge of the sentry wall.

Someone needed to stop Khai. She had done it once. She could do it again.

She threaded her shield over her head and arm so that it hung off her back. She stepped carefully, arms outstretched to help her balance. She had walked the pine log fence at the Rennan home many times. This was no different. Except that she could not see her feet through the tiny slot in her helm. She took it off and left it on the sentry walk. She would have to survive without it.

Her first few steps were scoots, keeping her feet on the stone. Once her courage was bolstered, she moved her right foot in front of her left. Her top-heavy armor and shield pulled her forward faster than she wanted to move. Control slipped away. She ran the last steps before diving onto the sentry walk.

Her armor scraped over the stone. She lay prostrate, panting. Once her lungs strengthened, she pushed to her feet and jogged down the sentry walk toward the watchtower.

She rounded two scallops and had started out on the long section of wall that circled the watchtower when she spotted Khai sitting against the battlement on the narrow curve. He faced the tower, eyes closed. Gowzals fluttered over his head, squawking. Had someone killed him?

She slowed her steps and drew her sword, hoping to sneak up on him, if possible.

A great cry brought Averella to the crenellation. She looked over the side just as a tanniyn rose from the lake, its neck curled like a ringlet. Averella crouched as it sailed over her and rammed its skull halfway up the tower.

The sentry wall under Averella's knees shook. Water rained off the creature onto her head. She pressed against the battlement and watched the tanniyn pull back and ram the tower again. This time its head broke through. Bricks of whitestone and dust fell to the bailey below. A man inside screamed. The creature's long neck writhed.

A haunting thought gripped Averella: Achan's squad was assigned to the watchtower.

She stood, legs trembling, and inched toward the place where the beast's neck rested between two merlons. She didn't have the strength to sever its head, so she drew back her sword and stabbed.

The creature's screech chilled her arms. She tried to wrench her blade free, but it was stuck. She braced her feet against the battlement and pulled with all her weight. The beast shifted. The sword's grip ripped from her hand, snagged on a merlon, then snapped the merlon off, as the tanniyn slithered backwards.

Averella dropped to her stomach and peeked at the tower. The beast drew back from the hole, writhing, a man in its mouth.

Merciful heart! Arman, help him!

The serpent's neck retracted over the crenellation, knocking the man free before it sank out of sight.

The man dropped onto Averella's legs and rolled off. She twisted to see him draw onto his hands and knees then collapse, gasping in deep breaths of air. Averella crawled to his side and pulled off his helm. A thatch of frizzy blond hair puffed out.

"Sir Caleb!"

He groaned, and his eyes fluttered until his gaze settled onto hers. "My lady?"

"Are you hurt?"

"I don't think so." Yet his body slumped unconscious.

Averella! Her mother's voice made her jump. *What are you doing here? You were to stay with Sir Eagan.*

I have to stop Khai. He is just ahead of me on the sentry walk. Can you see into his mind?

I am uncertain who Khai is—wait. The man sitting near you? He is the tanniyn's wielder. I just stormed him. Kill his body before he gets back to it.

Kill him?

Try your best. Your father needs me. I shall return.

Averella ran to Khai's body. The tanniyn had taken her sword, and Khai sat on his in such a way that she could not free it from its scabbard. She drew her boot knife and held it to his throat. Her hand shook so badly that the blade blurred, so she sheathed it and grabbed Khai's boot.

She dragged him, one tug at a time, past Sir Caleb's body, to the place where the tanniyn had broken the crenellation. She pushed until his leather armor scraped over the broken stone. His body slid away, but just before his head went over he caught himself on the sides of the wall.

Averella gasped. She peered over the edge and stomped on Khai's gauntlets, but fiery green wind from his lips blew her back to the other side of the wall.

The green wind swirled around her like a cage, keeping her pinned, whistling, screaming. Averella watched, mortified, as Khai climbed back onto the sentry wall.

"I don't care who wants you." Khai stepped toward her and pulled off his gauntlet. "You're far too daft to stay where you should. This is a war. Death happens. My prince will have to find another way to take Carm."

He reached through the funnel of wind, grabbed her throat, and squeezed. His touch sent a fire down her throat that seemed to coat her insides in ash.

Arman, help me! Lungs void of air, she choked. A plume of black smoke puffed from her lips. How? Drops of water fell on her head. Was it raining? She glanced up to see what seemed like a tree trunk of scales curling overhead.

The tanniyn had returned. It plucked up Khai in its maw and rose, taking him into the air like a morsel and pulling Khai's grip from Averella's neck. She fell to the sentry walk. The wind ceased. Averella panted in long breaths of moist air. Should she hide? Run? Would the tanniyn eat her next? If Khai was not controlling it, who was?

Khai's scream drew her gaze skyward in time to see his feet vanish into the creature's mouth. The beast lowered its head, and in an instant its long neck coiled around Averella, encircling her like yet another cage. The beast's golden eyes stared into hers as if asking permission to eat her next.

"How do you fare, Vrell? Did he hurt you?"

The familiar voice came from just above the tanniyn's head. Averella blinked. The darkness obscured her friend's face but not his large body sitting atop the tanniyn's neck as if riding a horse.

"Jax!"

He slid off the side of the tanniyn and jerked his head to the side, and the tanniyn slithered back over the crenellation.

Averella embraced him. "I thought you were dead. I thought—"

"Aw, it takes more than a fall to best Jax mi Katt."

"But you said animals were not your strength."

"Not *your father's* strength. I can't storm, but I have a way with water beasts." He frowned over her shoulder. "Is that Sir Caleb?"

Averella turned and crouched at Sir Caleb's side. "He is breathing, and I see no flesh wound, but he is obviously injured. Perhaps he hit his head or passed out from fright? He was fighting the tanniyn."

"I hope his sleep is peaceful, then," Jax said.

Averella glanced up to the watchtower. Achan had asked her to stay away. She must grant him that request, but what if he were hurt? *Your Highness? How do you fare?*

She winced and waited for his reply.

The tanniyn had taken Sir Caleb. And Cortland had fallen. Achan turned from the hole in the tower wall and glanced down the stairs. At least six steps had been knocked away. Toros and the men stood at the lower part of the gap. Only he, Shung, and Bran were above the break.

Achan peeked through the gap. No sign of Cortland. His shield lay on the steps below. Pig snout. Achan picked up Ôwr. Well, he preferred a longsword, anyway. Hopefully he might find his own shield later. Behind him, Bran groaned. Shung crouched and helped him stand.

"Can you go on, Bran?" Achan asked.

"Of course," Bran said. "Head stings a bit. I'll be fine."

"What is your order, Highness?" Toros asked.

"Take out as many of the enemy as you can."

Toros grinned. "Arman be with you."

"And you as well." Achan started up the stairs, but Shung cut him off.

"Shung will lead. Boar will follow Cham."

Bran's eyebrows almost leaped off his face. "I'm a boar?"

Achan laughed and it lightened his mood. "Very well, Sir Shung. You may lead the way, but the entire source of this war awaits us on the tower roof. The task is left to us. Are we ready?"

"Shung is ready."

"As am I, Your Highness," Bran said.

Achan nodded to Shung. "Lead on, Sir Shung."

They had barely climbed one rotation of the tower stairs when Sparrow spoke to him.

Your Highness? How do you fare?

Achan smiled. She seemed incapable of knowing what to call him since the problem with her memory. He wasn't sure which he liked better, the exasperating, argumentative Sparrow or the respectful, polite Lady Averella.

I am well, though we have lost many. And you?

Alive. I wondered if I may be of service.

Achan stopped and held up a hand to Bran. Shung turned back and paused. *Aren't you with Sir Eagan?*

No. Khai took control of a tanniyn, but mother and Jax fixed them both. Is your squadron missing Sir Caleb?

Yes! Did he survive? Achan rushed to the nearest arrow loop.

He is breathing but unconscious. There is nothing I can do but let him rest.

Achan looked down on the northeastern gate and sighed. *I cannot see you. This arrow loop points the wrong direction.*

I do not mean to stall your mission. I only wanted to check—To see whether you need anything.

I need you.

You do? There was a smile in her voice.

He needed her to live. He hated to ask anything of her, but she was too valuable an asset to ignore. *If you can get down, and if it's safe, go to the base of the watchtower. See if you can help the injured. And look for Cortland. He fell.*

Yes, Your Highness. I will go right away.

Achan winced. *Sparrow?*

Yes, Your Highness?

From now on, call me "Achan," please.

A long moment of silence stretched on. *We shall see.*

He rolled his eyes and grinned at Shung and Bran. "Both Sparrow and Sir Caleb live. Let us finish this."

36

Averella backtracked along the sentry walk with Jax until they found an abandoned ladder. They climbed to the back of the watchtower and ran around the side. Sounds of battle slowed their steps, and they found themselves behind a wall of shields where Achan's bowmen were shooting through arrow loops in the wood. Between two shields she could see a ground battle raging in the distance. The archers were keeping the enemy back from the tower.

Behind the shields, a standard-bearer, who seemed quite young, waved the Armonguard flag back and forth. She spotted Sir Rigil beside the young man, pacing in front of the tower entrance.

She approached him. "Sir Rigil, I have come to aid the wounded. Do you have any?"

"My lady Averella! Jax! All my joy to see you well. Was Sir Eagan successful at taking the eastern gate?"

"He has taken the gate and holds it still," Jax said.

"The prince asked me to check on his men. A man named Cortland, specifically," Averella said.

Sir Rigil winced. "Last I saw, Cortland had passed out from the pain. I am no healer, but I fear his legs are broken."

"Show me."

Sir Rigil led her just past the doorway. A young man lay on his back, his right leg twisted at an odd angle. His left knee looked to be bent naturally, but the blood coating his trousers led her to believe there was a protruding bone. This would be tricky to set.

She took a deep breath and took in his appearance. Wild blond hair and a familiar chin. "My, he resembles a young Sir Caleb."

"Cortland is Sir Caleb's nephew," Sir Rigil said.

She looked to the young man's face again. "Oh dear. Jax, will you help me?"

"I'll do all I can, Vrell."

Shung slowed his steps on the tower stairs. *Doorway is around bend.*

Duchess Amal? Achan called. *Can you tell us who is atop the watchtower and where?*

Certainly. Lord Nathak and Esek are looking over the edge of the tower. Sir Kenton is in the center on the roof, pacing about. And two guards stand by the doorway.

"Five against three," Achan whispered to Shung and Bran. "Not my favorite odds."

Five against five, Duchess Amal said. *For you have me and Arman to help you.*

Thank you, my lady. "Duchess Amal says we are even when we count her and Arman."

"She is a wise woman," Bran said.

I sense a great and dark power in Lord Nathak, the duchess said. *I confess, I do not know how to fight the keliy. I am at a loss, Your Highness.*

Can you storm the guards?

I can do that easily.

Start there. Then go after Sir Kenton. I wager he is the best swordsman of the three. Let us know when you succeed.

Achan relayed the plan to Shung and Bran. He kept his gaze fixed on Shung's face, which was focused up the stairwell. *Arman, help me know what to do.*

A hot flash gripped Achan's body. Arman did not speak, but his warmth instilled a confidence Achan had been lacking. *Thank You, Arman.*

A sword clattered down the curved whitestone steps. *I have stormed the guards, Your Highness,* Duchess Amal said, *but Sir Kenton is protected by Lord Nathak's dark magic. I know not how to help there. Arman be with you.*

Then we will have to defeat him with steel. Thank you for trying, my lady. Achan pushed against Shung's shoulder. "Now."

Shung ran up the final steps. Achan darted through the doorway behind Shung and out onto the circular whitestone roof. His legs quavered as the tower vibrated under his steps and he sensed how high up they were. A waist-high whitestone parapet circled the edge. Icy wind whirled around him and seemed to slow all movement. It chilled the surface of his skin but did not penetrate, for Arman's heat inside him acted as a shield. A tangle of gowzals swarmed overhead, squawking and flapping in the wind.

Just as the duchess had said, Sir Kenton stood in the middle of the roof. Lord Nathak and Esek were at the battlement's edge. Bran ran toward Sir Kenton, and they clashed swords. Achan and Shung circled the duel, headed toward Esek and Lord Nathak, who no longer wore a leather mask over half his face. Who no longer had half white hair and beard. Who now had two working eyes.

"I should have known." Esek flashed a cocksure smile Achan's way. "Your brother is looking well, don't you think? Uncle? At least now I understand why he kept you alive."

Achan held up Ôwr and looked from Esek to Lord Nathak. "The keliy healed you both. But why did it wait so long to heal you, Lord Nathak?"

"Jibhal and Macoun's method of keeping me in my place all these years. They are dead now, and I am the Hadad." Lord Nathak lifted his hands to the sides. "*Machmâd pârar.*"

Six green streams of light shot out from his palms, igniting bonfires evenly spaced around the roof's perimeter. The fires died down, leaving a Lord Nathak in each place.

Six Lord Nathaks in addition to the real one still standing beside Esek.

Achan and Shung turned their backs to each other, swords outstretched to the multiple Lord Nathaks. In the roof's center, Bran and Sir Kenton continued their duel, their blades clashing in an erratic rhythm.

My lady, can you help us? Achan asked.

They are but apparitions, Your Highness. I can only pray Arman's protection on you.

Achan blew out a long breath. They were on their own. *We eagerly request your prayers then, my lady.*

You shall have them, Your Highness.

"My coming to your procession was a mistake," the original Lord Nathak said. "If only I'd known that hours later my master would die and his master would come to me. And my new master assures me that killing you now will make me even stronger. You no longer have any power over me, boy. *Lawcham!*"

The six apparitions of Lord Nathak drew their swords. Ghosts or not, the sound of steel against wood stabbed shards of ice through Achan's warmth. He rocked from one foot to the other and squeezed Ôwr's grip in two hands. He turned his back to Shung. *Just like the practice melee in Carm.*

Aye, we will triumph.

Achan wished he had Shung's confidence. He reached for Lord Nathak's mind, hoping to glean something useful, but pain stabbed his skull. He drew up his shields, wary of the dark magic Duchess Amal had sensed. A gowzal squawked overhead. *Arman, give me strength to fight this enemy. Help me to do Your will.*

The apparitions attacked. One thrust a blade at Achan's chest, which he blocked with Ôwr. It certainly felt like real steel against his blade, with real mind and muscle behind it. Before he could regroup from the first attack, a sword glanced off his leather rerebrace, another cleaved into his left greave. Frustrated, he lashed Ôwr out in an wide arc, shocked to see the silvery blade pass through all three apparitions. Where was that steel and muscle now?

It was nothing he shouldn't have expected. How did one kill an illusion? Last time Duchess Amal had stormed the wielder, but this wielder was too strong.

Achan could only defend himself. Before long the apparitions separated him from Shung, circled around, stabbing and hacking their misty blades. They didn't seem stronger than regular men. Just invincible. Achan swung Ôwr wide again, failing to take any ground. He adjusted his footing, concentrated, and cut for the nearest apparition's leg. Like nicking a tree branch, his sword made contact with something.

The apparition transformed into a gowzal. The bird squawked and flapped over Achan's head, then began to rematerialize as Lord Nathak to his left. Achan struck the creature before it could fully form.

A short screech and the gowzal fell to the roof, flapped a few paces, and stopped to screech one last time. Achan had cut off its wing. He lunged toward the creature and kicked it down the stairwell.

Shung! He spun around in time to block a strike from another of Lord Nathak's apparitions. *Concentrate on the mind within. There is a gowzal in each. You can kill them. The birds, I mean. Strike at the mind, and then when the bird appears, kill it. You must kill the bird. A rebuke helps you see it.*

A shriek turned his head. A puff of feathers drifted over Shung and two remaining apparitions. *Ahh. Very wise, Little Cham. Shung will fix them now.*

By instinct, Achan kicked his attacker. His foot passed through its body, bringing an icy chill with it. The apparition pushed him aside and cut across Achan's neck. His gorget blocked the strike, but it still knocked Achan down. The tower shook under his body. He rolled back to his feet and got into position again.

A sword scraped against Achan's armor from the back. He ducked and ran past where Bran and Sir Kenton fought to the edge of the roof. His two attackers split up. One came after him. The other went after Shung, who was still fighting two Lord Nathaks of his own.

They were still trying to keep Shung from helping him.

Achan's attacker managed to nick the side of his knee between his cuisses and greaves. Achan rebuked himself. Here Shung fought three to Achan's one, and Achan still got hit.

His rebuke reminded him of the words Inko had used on Barthos. It couldn't hurt. Achan repeated the words aloud. "Arman hu elohim, Arman hu echâd, Arman hu shlosha be-echâd. Hatzileni, beshem Câan, ben Arman."

He wasn't completely sure these were the right words, but they did seem to have an effect. The apparition shimmered. Only a dark blob in its head seemed more solid. Achan swung for the dark spot, and his sword hit something solid. This Lord Nathak vanished. And the gowzal plopped to the roof, dead, feathers floating on the air.

Achan ran across the tower roof toward Shung and his three opponents, but Bran and Sir Kenton crashed through Shung's battle. Sir Kenton pushed Bran back with a series of strikes from side guard. Bran grunted with each parry, as if his arms might give out at any moment.

Achan started toward Bran. Sir Kenton snapped his blade around Bran's shield, and Bran's scream slowed Achan's steps.

Bran crumpled to the roof. Sir Kenton kicked Bran's sword over to where Esek stood, then turned his dark gaze to Achan, his curtain of hair flowing like a cape. He approached, one slow step at a time.

Achan kept back from Sir Kenton, tentative, trying to see if Bran was still alive. He knew better than to think about Sir Kenton's strength and skill, but his head told him he would be wise not to engage. To defend only. Shung was still blocked off by three Lord Nathaks, so Achan was on his own. And despite his fear, he couldn't simply defend. He had to defeat Sir Kenton. He had to win.

He sniffed a long breath through his nose, willing strength to his body. He might not have enough skill to beat Sir Kenton, but Arman did. "Arman hu elohim, Arman hu echâd, Arman hu shlosha be-echâd. Hatzileni, beshem—"

"Your words do not frighten me, boy. I'm no demon."

Achan nodded to where Esek stood with Lord Nathak. "Yet you keep company with them."

"Don't kill him, Sir Kenton," Esek yelled. "Just tire him a bit for me. I want to be the one to end his life."

"Are you too much of a coward to face me yourself?" Achan yelled to Esek, almost hoping to fight him instead.

"I'm simply tired of all these games. Rant about my laziness if you must. But I have no qualms about letting Sir Kenton tire you."

A gowzal shrieked. Shung had defeated another.

Achan let Sir Kenton take the first swing. A jab to his gut. Achan stepped aside, parried, and raked Ôwr over Sir Kenton's arm on his backslash. The sword sliced into Sir Kenton's rerebrace, bolstering Achan's courage.

Sir Kenton growled and swung for Achan's neck. So Achan ducked and swung for Sir Kenton's feet. One step ahead, that's where he needed to stay.

Sir Kenton straightened, then lunged forward with a direct thrust to Achan's chest. Achan side-stepped and chopped Ôwr over Sir Kenton's extended arms, not hard enough to do any damage, though.

Easily twisting free, Sir Kenton released a series of blows that weakened Achan's arms. The last one came so quickly Achan only just managed to parry it.

Blades crossed, Sir Kenton slid his sword along Ôwr toward Achan's neck. The blade made a thick sound as it sliced against Achan's leather gorget.

Achan made use of Sir Kenton's closeness to grab hold of his wrist and chop Ôwr over Sir Kenton's arm again, this time with more force. Sir Kenton lunged back and shook out his arm as if that last blow had stung.

Even so, cutting wasn't working against Sir Kenton's armor. Achan needed to find a place to stab. He took a deep breath, but Sir Kenton whipped out his blade with one hand, stunning Achan with a blow to his shoulder.

Achan staggered, and Sir Kenton stepped close and shoved his hip into Achan's side, the weight of man and armor enough to knock Achan off balance. A blow to the back of Achan's leg skidded past his armor and bit into the back of his knee. Achan screamed and skipped aside.

Hold on, Little Cham, Shung said to Achan's mind.

Sir Kenton grinned at Esek.

Despite his injured leg, Achan darted forward and grabbed the hood of Sir Kenton's cape. He yanked the man to the ground, dropped a knee to his groin, and drove Ôwr through his exposed armpit.

Sir Kenton sucked in a sharp breath, shuddered, and lay still, staring into the sky. The circling gowzals reflected on his glossy eyes like lost ants. The icy wind swished his black hair over the whitestone roof.

Achan trembled, aghast that he had succeeded against Sir Kenton. He took hold of Ôwr and pulled it out. The white blade, coated in bright blood, didn't come out as easily as expected.

A curse from Esek snapped Achan's head around.

To the left of the roof, Shung growled and took down the last apparition.

Achan pushed to his feet, putting his weight on his right leg, for hot moisture stung his left. "Give up, both of you." Achan panted, but just as he stepped toward Shung, another six balls of green flame shot out from Lord Nathak's hands.

The green fire mirrored in Lord Nathak's eyes. "Take your time, stray. My only real goal this day is to kill you, and I am in no rush to do so."

"Let me deal with him, Father." Esek crossed the roof and drew a black blade from the scabbard on his hip.

"Don't be a fool, son. Let the magic do it."

Esek snorted. "I don't need the magic now. Look at him. He's wounded. And I won't lower my guard like Kenton did." Holding his sword loosely, Esek swung the blade in a circle and jutted his chin at Sir Kenton's body. "My Shield will be brought back to life, you know."

His black blade flashed. Achan jerked Ôwr up, and the swords rang together.

Achan tried to sweep out Esek's leg, but his left leg buckled, unable to hold his weight on its own. Esek laughed and slashed at Achan again.

Achan parried, faked a cut to Esek's head, and cut for his feet. Esek blocked the strike, which left his torso free. So Achan spun his sword upward and tried a cut from high guard, which would slice Esek open down the middle.

Except Esek jerked back out of reach.

"You really should consider armor." Achan glanced at Esek's arm, the one he'd cut off.

"I don't *need* armor, stray."

Esek swung wide and deep, twisting his arm so his blade came toward Achan like a hook. Achan's instinct was to dart aside, but he turned into it instead, meeting the strike with Ôwr's flat.

Esek stumbled but recovered with ease. His feet glided over the roof, his blue eyes locked with Achan's. Achan limped. The bottom half of his right leg felt like a numb stump. When Esek sprung forward with a cut from side guard, Achan almost missed the block.

Esek's blade came down again and knocked Ôwr away, then cleaved down on Achan's shoulder.

Achan's breastplate crunched. He lost his feet, lurched over the carcass of a gowzal, and spilled to his knees. His left knee screamed, and he put his weight on his right.

Esek bared a nasty grin as he stepped in close and tore off Achan's helm. He pressed his blade to Achan's throat, just above the top edge of Achan's gorget. "Am I king, Uncle? Call me king, and maybe I'll let you live."

Then he fell forward, brow furrowed. His blade scratched Achan's neck, all force gone. He grabbed Achan's shoulder with his free hand and sank to his knees, eyes wide with shock, grunting mouse-like sounds and curling into Achan's lap.

Bran stood over Esek's crumpled form, clutching a small knife in a trembling hand. Bran!

Following Bran's lead, Achan pulled his own boot knife and stabbed Esek in the side of the neck. A moan gurgled from Esek as he twisted over the rest of the way and thumped to the roof, eyes closed forever.

37

"No!"

Achan turned on his knees to see Lord Nathak, the real one, marching toward him, hands raised, green mist swirling from his palms. Achan's chest heaved. He stood, his left leg burning and stiff. "Your heir is dead."

"No matter," Lord Nathak said between clenched teeth. "I will resurrect him."

Again? "How many times does he have to die?"

Lord Nathak grinned. "That is the beauty of the power of the keliy. Nothing is ever too far."

Achan had felt its power that day at the Reshon Gate when he had possessed the black knight. He picked up Ôwr. "The keliy's power is a trick. It brought Darkness upon us, and I am here to send it back."

"And how will you do that, little brother?" Lord Nathak's lips twisted in a sneer. "You don't know, do you? Well, I taught you to obey me once. I can do it again."

A hot knife stabbed Achan's skull. It had to be Lord Nathak's bloodvoice gripping his mind as in a vise. He dropped his sword and tried to clutch his head, but his body betrayed him. Despite his throbbing leg, he dropped to his knees and leaned forward, bowing before Lord Nathak.

A brief memory of himself at ten years of age in Lord Nathak's solar, experiencing a similar pain and lack of self-control, flickered in his memory. He had made himself forget.

Lord Nathak hummed his approval. "Now that's much better."

Achan fought the grip on his mind. Arman had spoken to Achan, not Lord Nathak, as king. And Sir Gavin had said that Achan was stronger than any other bloodvoicer. With Arman's help he could defeat Lord Nathak and rebuke Darkness. He knew he could. He focused on Lord Nathak's mind.

Suddenly he saw himself through Lord Nathak's eyes. He looked small and weak, kneeling on the tower roof. Behind him, Bran sat clutching his shoulder beside Esek's body, looking half dead himself. Across the roof, Shung fought the new host of Lord Nathak's apparitions.

Achan concentrated on Lord Nathak, trying to leave part of himself in his own body. *Step backward.*

Lord Nathak grunted as if surprised. His feet shuffled. Inched back.

Achan planned to send another command, to trick Lord Nathak to jump off the roof, but he remembered his promise to Duchess Amal. He was not to control anyone, even Lord Nathak.

Achan pulled back his control a bit, unsure what to do now. In his moment of indecision, Lord Nathak lunged forward and punched Achan's body.

Achan fell back on the roof, in his own head again, jaw stinging.

"Nice try, boy. I didn't know Sir Gavin had taught you such dark magic. Clearly you have not yet mastered it."

And he never would. Achan reached for Ôwr.

But a bolt of green lightning shot it across the roof. "I am not through with you," Lord Nathak said. "Renounce Arman, and all will be well."

A pressure rose at the back of Achan's head and grew. Achan concentrated on shielding himself, but the pressure stabbed. "I won't. Arman spoke to me. I will not refuse Him."

Lord Nathak's face contorted, angry. He stepped over Achan and gripped the side of his face with his bare hand.

The pain spiked. Nausea gripped Achan. His limbs shook.

"Renounce him, and I shall stop," Lord Nathak said.

Achan clenched his teeth and fists, and changed focus. He tried to get inside Lord Nathak's mind again. But doing so somehow lowered his own defenses, causing the pain to seize every pore. He fell onto the ground and writhed, trying to get away from the anguish. If only he could shake it off.

Sir Gavin's voice came first. *Achan, what's happening?*

Your Highness, Duchess Amal said, *you must shield yourself. Do not allow him inside your head.*

Fire and ash! Inko said. *Be closing your mind, boy!*

Achan! Sparrow's voice, panicked. *What is wrong? Achan, be careful!*

Achan panted and met Lord Nathak's dark gaze. He tried to relax, but the torment made it impossible.

Closing his eyes, Achan recited the words, *Arman hu elohim, Arman hu echâd, Arman hu shlosha be-echâd. Hatzileni, beshem Câan, ben Arman.*

The pressure began to fade from his head.

Lord Nathak stared down, his eyes wild. "If you will not serve me, you will die."

A dull thud turned Achan's head. Shung had again defeated Lord Nathak's apparitions. His gaze flickered to Achan. He started toward them. "The little cham will not die this day."

Lord Nathak lifted his hands to Shung, green fire trailing around the edges of his fingers.

Shung reached back his sword arm. "He will live as long as Arman determines." He swung his sword, but Lord Nathak's green fire caught the blade mid-swing.

Shung trembled, shook his head like a wet dog, and screamed, then cut the blade down toward Achan.

Achan rolled to the side and grabbed Ôwr. *Don't let him control you, Shung. Call on Arman.*

Achan stood on shaky legs and raised the old sword. "Arman hu elohim, Arman hu echâd, Arman hu shlosha be-echâd. Hatzileni, beshem Câan, ben Arman."

Lord Nathak extended a smoking green hand toward each of them. "Machmâd pâr—"

"Arman!" Shung screamed, cleaved his blade down from high guard, and cut off Lord Nathak's left hand.

"Câan!" Achan swung Ôwr at Lord Nathak and severed Lord Nathak's right hand.

Blood oozed from Lord Nathak's veins. The man's eyes bulged. Shung kicked him in the chest. White-faced, Lord Nathak stumbled backward. Shung stepped up to him, swung his blade in a wide arc, and cut off his head. The grotesque torso collapsed to the floor beside its severed pieces.

Achan looked away, wheezing to catch his breath. All was silent. Lord Nathak's body lay in four bloody pools on the roof.

Could it really be over? How did a keliy die? Who was next in line? The thought made Achan twist around toward Esek's body, but it lay still in the midst of a dozen dead gowzals.

Achan looked upward. "Why is it still dark? What else do we have to do? Perhaps it is nighttime?"

Shung shrugged, then motioned to Bran. "Can anything be done for the boar?"

Achan ran across the roof and used his right leg to kneel at Bran's side. The squire's eyes were closed, but choking breaths seeped in and out of his lips. Bran still clutched his opposite shoulder, blood seeping between his mailed fingers.

There was blood everywhere.

Bran's eyes opened. He sucked in a wet, gurgling breath and his arm twitched. "Take care of her."

"Of who?" Achan asked.

Bran croaked a near silent laugh, though his eyebrows pinched together. "Who indeed. Don't let her . . . run away. She tends to . . . to run. A lot."

Sparrow. "I won't let her run, Bran. I promise you."

"Good." Bran's brow softened. "And tell Gren . . ."

But he never finished that sentence.

Achan fell to his rear and looked into the dark sky. "Why, Arman? Didn't I do everything You asked? Where is the light?"

"Achan."

Achan looked toward the entrance to the stairwell. A woman in a red dress stood there. Sparrow.

How had she gotten up the broken steps? Achan glanced from Bran's body to Sparrow and back. He pushed to his feet and stepped into the line of sight between Sparrow and Bran. "I'm sorry, Sparrow."

She walked out onto the roof. The wind blew her skirts against her legs, the hem flying out to the opposite side like a flag.

Achan approached and took her hand. It was as cold as the floor in Ice Island. His were sticky with blood. "How did you get up here?" He frowned. "Weren't you wearing trousers and armor?"

The corners of her mouth curved up, and when she spoke, the voice was not her own. "I *was* wearing my green doublet with the ermine trim, but you ruined it."

Achan dropped her hand and stepped back. "Lord Nathak?"

Sparrow's skin darkened. Her hair began to grow, curl, and lighten to a chestnut color. Her body morphed, stretching the red dress wider and longer.

Gren.

Achan shook his head. "Stop that."

"But you preferred this face, did you not?" Lord Nathak said, and Gren melted and reformed into Lady Tara.

Achan limped back to Bran's body and picked up Ôwr.

Tara's musical laugh made him cringe. "I'm beyond human form now, dear brother," Lord Nathak said in Tara's voice. "A sword cannot harm me."

Help me defeat this foe, Arman. "Arman hu elohim, Arman hu echâd, Arman hu shlosha be-echâd. Hatzileni, beshem Câan, ben Arman."

Tara walked toward him, shimmering, each step changing her appearance. She swelled and stretched. The dress twisted into britches and a linen apron until a huge man stood before Achan, hunched and balding. Tara's voice spoke first, then changed pitch until Poril's voice came forth. "Poril was easy to manipulate, he was. Enjoyed beating you."

Please, Arman. Help me. Achan inched back and raised his voice. "Arman is God, Arman is One, Arman is Three in One. Deliver us in the name of Câan."

Poril's body shrank to the stately image of Esek. Achan looked from Esek's illusion to his dead body, then glanced at Shung, not knowing what to say or do.

Pray. Shung waved a hand Achan's way. *Call on Arman. The little cham is His chosen.*

Achan opened his mouth to argue, but his mind was an empty pot.

Call on Arman, Shung said again.

And say what else? I'm just one man, Shung. There's nothing special about me. Nothing I can do that you can't. I've asked His help, but nothing has changed.

"Esek made a better Crown Prince than you," the keliy said. "He always craved power."

Little Cham can bloodvoice better than any man. Or woman.

Achan stepped back from Esek's likeness. He *did* have a strong ability to bloodvoice, but how could he use that? *Cover me, Shung.* He forced his eyes shut, though his senses screamed he was a bigger fool than Esek for doing so.

Arman, I am but a man. I cannot defeat this enemy by my own strength. I barely have strength left. Achan fell to his knees and stifled a cry at the pain in his leg. *Please banish the Darkness, Arman. Bring back the sun. Defeat this enemy before me. Let Your light shine again, over all Er'Rets. In the name of Your Son, Câan, I ask this of You.*

He opened his eyes. The sky was still dark. Nothing had happened. Arman had not answered. Shung now stood between him and the keliy, which had taken the form of an adolescent Berland boy.

"Arluk wanted to live," the boy said. "To be squire for Koyukuk."

Arluk. The friend Shung had killed in his youth.

Shung mumbled a prayer. "Arman God. Arman One. Arman Three."

Ôwr shook in Achan's hand. Soon the keliy would wield its green fire and he and Shung would fight until they fell.

Achan? Sparrow's voice rang inside his head. *What is happening?*

The mere sound of her voice boosted his morale and stilled his trembling hands. *I called on Arman, but He does not answer. What more can I do?*

Perhaps you can give Him an offering.

Arman doesn't need my offerings. Gold cups and coins are for idols like Cetheria. All I have is Ôwr and half a gold coin.

Not riches, Achan. An offering from your heart. Arman deserves more from you than demands.

Of course. Achan recalled Toros's advice. *"Arman does long to hear your prayers, but He also deserves your praise and worship. Your allegiance."*

Achan closed his eyes. *Arman hu elohim, Arman hu echâd, Arman hu shlosha be-echâd. You are my god. You are my creator. You are holy beyond all comprehension. Mightier than the fiercest cham. Stronger than the tallest Eben. You are wise. Worthy of more than I know how to give. You're my deliverer. My father.*

Heat swelled in the pit of his stomach. Heat that could do miracles. If only all the people could feel Arman's power. How could they doubt the truth then?

He sucked in a quick breath of cold air. The lyrics of a song the worshippers in Melas had sung came to him now.

No darkness have we who in Arman abide.
The Light of the world is Câan!
We walk in the light when we follow our Guide.
The Light of the world is Câan!

Achan carried Arman inside him. He was part of Arman's light. So was every man, woman, and child in Er'Rets who believed. Alone, as one man, Achan could not succeed. But if all the people joined together . . .

Because the temple of Arman was His people.

Achan lowered the shields around his mind completely. Voices gushed into his thoughts, drowning out one another. Millions of voices. He winced at the level of noise. At the pressure. The pain.

He gritted his teeth and spoke to all the people at once. *Lo, this is Achan Cham, born Gidon Hadar to King Axel and Queen Dara.*

The din in his mind softened a great deal. He could hear the keliy speaking to Shung, feel the cold wind whipping around Arman's warmth within him. *I stand at the top of the Armonguard watchtower facing Lord Nathak, the man responsible for my parents' death, the man responsible for ushering the reign of Darkness over Er'Rets. Arman has set me as king over this land.*

Some voices protested.

He ignored the curses and growls and raised his voice. *I come to you for help. We've been silent far too long. Many of you have turned your backs on Arman. Many never bothered to know Him at all. But Arman is the One God. He created Er'Rets and everything in it. He gave each of you life and purpose. He loves all of you as His own sons and daughters.*

To defeat Darkness, we must unite our faith. We must worship the One God, Arman. We must call out to Him for mercy. Though He hears my prayer now, my voice alone is not strong enough. I am only one man. But together, we are mighty. I ask you to join with me now. Worship Him.

And Achan began to sing.

Er'Rets was lost in the darkness within.
The Light of the world is Câan!
Like sunshine at noonday His glory shone in.
The Light of the world is Câan!

In his mind he could hear scattered voices singing along.

No darkness have we who in Arman abide.
The Light of the world is Câan!
We walk in the light when we follow our Guide.
The Light of the world is Câan!

Ye dwellers in Darkness with tar-blinded eyes.
The Light of the world is Câan!
Go, wash, at His bidding and light will arise.
The Light of the world is Câan!

More and more voices joined, until he was leading a mighty choir.

No need of sunlight in Shamayim we're told.
The Light of the world is Câan!
For Câan is the Light in the city of gold.
The Light of the world is Câan!

So loud were the united voices, Achan could no longer hear the hecklers. A tremor danced in the air around him. A warm breeze swirling with the cold.

Arman hu elohim, Arman hu echâd, Arman hu shlosha be-echâd. Hatzileni, beshem Câan, ben Arman. Say it with me and mean it with all your heart! Arman is God, Arman is One, Arman is Three in One. Deliver us in the name of Câan.

The wind grew louder in its battle of cold and heat. It began to howl. The roof trembled beneath Achan's knees. The people continued to chant in unison. Achan opened his eyes. The wind had color now, black and green and what looked like . . . light. It swirled around the figure of the boy Arluk and Shung, who had tears streaming down his hairy cheeks. The boy turned his angry gaze to Achan, morphing back into Esek.

"Am I king?" Esek's voice warbled through the wind. His hair whipped around his face, and he suddenly screamed in an unworldly voice.

Like Ôwr's shining blade, a beam of light pierced the dark sky and stabbed down, lancing Esek through the chest.

Esek shattered into a flock of gowzals. The birds flapped in the heavy wind, squawked, and vaporized into mist.

Achan looked deeper, for he could see that the gowzals had not vanished at all, but gone to the Veil. And somehow Achan could see both places at the same time.

Two beings stood before him, side by side. Lord Nathak and a pale, thin creature with gangling arms and legs, black eyes, black lips, and black horns that coiled like those of a ram. The keliy. The Hadad's master. A minion of Gâzar. The lance of light continued to beam down from the clouds.

"Be gone from here in the name of Câan!" Achan yelled. "Both of you. Your time in Er'Rets has ended."

The keliy snarled like a rabid dog, but its legs slowly twisted into a funnel of wind. The creature reached out and grabbed Lord Nathak's arm.

"No!" Lord Nathak cried. "I don't want to die!"

The beam of light coming down from the sky swelled and crept along the roof until it met Achan's boots. Achan could see dust and feathers floating in its golden glow.

The wind funnel spun faster. Lord Nathak and the keliy became indistinguishable from one another. The light beam grew, now encompassing Shung and Bran's body, then Sir Kenton's body, the entire watchtower roof.

And beyond.

The funnel sucked away. Vanished. To the Lowerworld, perhaps?

All was silent. Daylight poured from a widening hole in the clouds. And the sun continued to spread its light over the water and land below.

Achan limped to the battlement and looked out over the land. Twilight. The cover of Darkness was now nothing more than dark storm clouds. The sun shone through them, casting a riot of color in the sky.

Cheers chorused in Achan's mind and rose up from the ground below.

Thank You, Arman! Achan closed his mind and offered a private echo. *Thank You.*

PART 5

IN THE LIGHT

38

The sun shone down on Castle Armonguard as if it were the first day of creation. But Averella had no time to enjoy it.

She and Jax recruited every healthy soldier to help transport the wounded to the lawn south of the watchtower. More than four dozen wounded had been brought there already, lined up like corpses on the grass. Sir Eagan joined them, and together they did all they could.

When two soldiers dragged Kurtz onto the grass, Averella thought he was dead. He had taken an arrow to his lower neck, just above the collarbone. It was remarkable he still breathed. She removed the arrow with the help of an elderly soldier and the arrowspoons her father had given her, and she bandaged his throat.

A man's shadow fell over Kurtz's face and stretched out on the bright grass. Likely Sir Eagan checking on Kurtz. "I can do no more for him than this," Averella said, hoping Father would not point out an obvious mistake.

"He is blessed to be in your care."

Still crouching, Averella spun around on her toes. Achan stood at Kurtz's feet. The sun behind him made his outline glow. She could hardly see his expression, but shiny gashes all over his breastplate gleamed and caught the light.

A flutter passed through her stomach. "Achan!" He extended a hand. She reached out and slid her hand into his and found it sticky, coated in drying blood. "Are you injured?" Her eyes studied him. One leg was coated in blood from knee to boot.

He pulled her to standing, harder than need be. She flew up from the ground and slammed against his breastplate. He held her there with a hand at the small of her back. She could do nothing but gaze into his eyes. His hair, wet with sweat, frizzed out like the rambutan fruit from Nesos. The blisters on the top edge of his burned ear had mostly healed now.

"Achan?"

But he only stared, the hand against her back trembling. A single tear streaked down from the corner of his eye and vanished under his ear, painting a clean stripe through the dirt on his face.

"You did it, Achan! I heard your voice. I sang with you. You brought all Er'Rets into fellowship with Arman. I have never been so proud of anyone."

He grimaced, as if the compliment pained him. "Sparrow—"

"We asked the soldiers to bring the wounded here. Do you think that will do? I do not know this castle well enough to take them inside. Besides, the fresh air will help to—"

"Vrell!" Achan swallowed. "My lady Averella." His hand clenched behind her, taking the back of her tunic in his fist. He closed his eyes. "Bran is dead."

A chill fell over her as if the sun had passed behind a cloud. She shook her head. "No, I— I can still sense him." But even as she said it, she knew she could no longer feel Bran's presence.

"He saved my life," Achan said. "I realize you might not consider that the best exchange, but . . . I am sorry."

She tried to pull back, but his grip was too strong. The world spun around her, everything blurred, green, white, silver, red.

Achan spoke to her, a low, muffled sound she could not interpret. Her feet left the ground as Achan lifted her just before she fell.

She woke in a chamber brightly lit by sunlight streaming through a set of opened double doors that led to a balcony. She lay on a double tester bed canopied in white organza linen that shifted in a breeze sweeping through the doors. She wore a nightgown. One of her own. Mercy. It had been ages since she'd worn this.

Where was she? This was not her bedchamber. How had she come to be here? She sat up and slipped out of bed.

The chamber was large, curved on one side, likely on the perimeter of one of the arcs of the Armonguard keep. She frowned. Did that mean the war had been real? And what Achan had told her of Bran . . . ?

The walls were bare on one end of the chamber, covered in colorful tapestries on the other. Two servants stood where the tapestries ended, working together to hang more tapestries. A maid stood beside the door.

"Good morning, dearest."

Averella turned and found her mother sitting in a wicker chair on the other side of her bed. "Mother!"

By the time she reached the chair, Mother had stood. They embraced. Averella started to cry.

"I am so sorry, dearest. He was a good and brave young man."

This declaration ended all communication on Averella's part, for all she could do was sob into her mother's chest. She searched her memory to recall what her last words to Bran had been.

She could not remember.

This only made her cry harder. Mother helped her back into the bed. She did not know how long she lay there before she drifted off to sleep.

When she woke again, her curiosity grew stronger than her grief. She turned onto her side and drew the organza curtain aside. All the tapestries had been hung now. A maid stood by the door. The wicker chair was empty, but Averella's mother stood on the balcony, looking out over the lake.

"Mother?"

Mother jumped, then walked to Averella's bedside. She placed her hand on Averella's cheek. "How do you fare?"

"Forgive me for my self-pity. What a fool I have been."

"Not a fool. Grieving is necessary when a loved one is lost."

"How many nights have passed since—"

"Only one. We gave you hops tea to help you rest."

She felt hollow. "I am hungry."

"Then I shall have something brought up." Mother nodded toward the doorway, and the maid scurried out the door.

"I am in Castle Armonguard? It is still standing then?"

"Oh, yes. The battle did no damage to the main keep. They are already repairing the sentry walls."

Averella pushed up onto one elbow. "I should get dressed and help Father and Jax with the wounded."

"You will do no such thing. There are now over twenty healers in the bailey working on the wounded. Each army had some of their own, you know. You, Jax, and Sir Eagan are not the only healers in Er'Rets. Relax. All will be well."

Averella lay back on the bed. "Sir Caleb?"

"He is fine."

"Esek and Lord Nathak?"

"Defeated." She looked out the balcony again. "Utterly."

"How did you get here so quickly? I thought you remained home."

For once, Mother looked almost sheepish. "I confess I could not. I boarded one of Captain Chantry's ships as it passed Carm. I've been sailing for the past week."

Averella squeezed her mother's hand. "I am glad you are here. I am so sorry for all the trouble I caused."

"Think nothing of it. I forgive you." She brushed a soft kiss on Averella's forehead. "Are you feeling well enough to receive guests?"

Averella ran a hand over her tangled hair. "I must look a fright."

"The prince is not among those waiting. He paced outside your door half the night until Sir Caleb whisked him away. He is likely sleeping now."

Disappointment washed over Averella. But Achan deserved rest. "Who *is* waiting?"

"Gypsum and Syrah are in the solar just outside your chamber. Shall I let them in?"

Averella sat up. "Of course. What about Rioja, Terra, and Mariel?" For Averella wanted to see all her sisters.

"They are on an outing with Sir Eagan. I shall fetch Gypsum and Syrah at once." Mother left the room and returned a moment later with Averella's sister and maid.

Gypsum ran to Averella's bedside and took her hands. But Syrah remained beside the door, ever the reserved servant.

"Oh, Vrella!" Gypsum said. "We had to stay on the ship when all the soldiers came ashore to fight. Mother said you would have stayed in Noiz, but I did not doubt you would sneak away with the men. To see you well . . ." She kissed Averella's cheek. "I am so thankful."

"I did not *sneak* anywhere. I put on trousers, yes, but I went straight to my father's chamber and received his permission to go along."

Gypsum frowned at this. "Mother told me about her and Sir Eagan. I still cannot believe it." Her eyes lit up. "You have not heard the latest in regards to Sir Eagan's love for Mother. But I shall let her tell it." Gypsum turned aside so that Averella had a clear view of where Mother stood with Syrah.

"You have news, Mother?" Averella asked.

"Sir Eagan and I intend to marry."

Merciful heart! "Oh, Mother! How exciting! When will this take place? Right away?"

"No, dearest. Not until after . . ."

"After what?"

Gypsum sat on the edge of Averella's bed. "The date of Mother's wedding depends entirely on you, dear sister."

"How so? If you are seeking my approval, Mother, you need not."

"I do not wish to upset you."

"Impossible. What greater joy than to see my parents wed. I give you both my happiest blessing. What a celebration it shall be! Name the day."

"Mother and Sir Eagan cannot marry until they return to Carmine," Gypsum said. "It would be a scandal not to marry there."

"Well, of course you would marry in Carmine," Averella said. "I did not mean to imply otherwise. Only that it should be soon. You have been parted for too long."

Gypsum sighed like an exasperated tutor. "Vrella, you are thicker than a redpine. None of us will be leaving Armonguard until Prince Achan is crowned. And if he is to marry, that will likely happen first. So, dear sister, am I to marry Prince Achan or are you?" She raised her eyebrows and flashed a wicked smile.

Averella laughed. "Merciful heart! I see the problem now. Thank you, Gypsum, for saying it so plainly, but rest assured, *dear sister*, it will not be you."

"I do not believe you know the prince's mind that well," Gypsum said, a haughty grin on her face. "For I spoke with him last night at dinner, and he paid me a nice compliment. If you still harbor doubts, I would be happy to fulfill Mother's promise."

"You must know that Mother rescinded that offer."

"Yes, but the prince has not yet given me an answer," Mother said, fighting a smile.

"See?" Gypsum bounced on the edge of the bed. "So there is still a chance I could marry him."

Averella couldn't keep a deep laugh from escaping. "Then perhaps Mother's wedding date depends on you and not on me, Gypsum."

"Oh, enough teasing, please!" Syrah said from her place at the door. "I can't bear it. Tell us, my lady, please."

"First, Syrah, come and give me a hug."

The maidservant rushed to Averella's bedside, and the two embraced.

"I was so worried about you, my lady. When your mother said you were lost . . ."

"None of that, now. I am perfectly well. And to ease your mind I shall tell you all that Prince Achan and I did speak before leaving Noiz." She removed her necklace and slipped the half coin from its pouch. "Not only do I still carry his father's ring, but he gave me this." She held the coin up on her palm.

Mother, Gypsum, and Syrah all leaned in, eyes wide.

Syrah squealed and clapped her hands like a delighted child.

"Half a coin?" Gypsum frowned. "I do not understand."

"Peasants sometimes split a coin as a token of an engagement," Syrah said. "Because they cannot afford rings. But never with a gold coin, my lady."

Averella studied the coin. The idea of marrying Achan soon, of being able to see him every day—without a chaperone!—sent a thrill from her head to her toes.

39

Achan sat at a table in a vast chamber. It was yet another meeting, but this time only Sir Caleb, Sir Eagan, Sir Gavin, Shung, and Prince Oren were present.

Dozens of reports had come in from allies across Er'Rets, who had until now been living in Darkness. People were celebrating, singing and dancing all hours of the day. An extraordinarily high number of people spent time outdoors, enjoying the sunlight and how nature was budding and blooming like spring. There would be one more hard winter there, but next fall would bring the first harvest western Er'Rets had seen in thirteen years.

There were also reports of people hiding from the light, as if the sun was a different kind of curse. Many Poroo and Eben tribes and some entire families from Melas and Mirrorstone were said to have gone underground, locked themselves indoors, or moved into caves. Achan wondered if they would ever recover from the influence Darkness had left on their minds.

Sir Caleb had recovered from his blow to the head. Achan and Duchess Amal had gone into the Veil, searching for Prince Oren's stormed self. It took two days, but they had found him wandering the tombs of the kings in Noiz. Together, they had managed to reunite Prince Oren with his body. He had lost half his left leg from the green fire. A wooden cone was attached to his thigh and tapered to the floor. He moved about with a cane. He had lost a good deal of weight and his face was gaunt, but he was in good spirits. He'd accepted Achan's thanks for saving his life, but refused to allow Achan to blame himself for the loss of his leg.

"What of the Council of Seven?" Prince Oren asked.

"I'd like to keep it," Achan said. "But they will meet here three times a year. Do you think that reasonable?"

"Why keep it?" Sir Caleb asked.

"I think it's important to leave some things as they were," Achan said. "And the people of Er'Rets are familiar with the Council. I realize it was to be disbanded once the prince came of age, but I cannot see what goes on in Therion or Carm or Barth. Keeping the Council is a good way to know what's happening elsewhere in Er'Rets and to see the dukes and Duchess Amal on a regular basis."

"I think you are wise to keep the council, Your Highness," Sir Eagan said. "But *you* should appoint the members. And you must also appoint your Great Officers."

Achan had never heard of that. "What are they?"

"The men who will serve you here, in Armonguard," Prince Oren said. "Your staff, so to speak."

"Are there men serving in these positions now?"

"No. The positions have been vacant for years," Prince Oren said.

And so, with a little help from the knights and Prince Oren, Achan spent the next hour appointing his Great Officers. Prince Oren would serve as Lord High Steward, which meant he would manage Er'Retian property and financial affairs.

Sir Eagan would serve as Lord High Chancellor, or secretary to the king, until he could train Manu Pitney, as Sir Eagan wished to return to Carmine with Duchess Amal and travel to Zerah Rock to reconcile with his father.

Achan could think of no one better for the position of Lord Great Chamberlain, officially charging Sir Caleb with the management of the king's living quarters, wardrobe, and general well-being.

Achan appointed Sir Gavin as Lord High Commander of the Royal Armies, which Sir Gavin had been doing already.

Duchess Amal became Lady Chairman of the Council of Seven. But due to Cela Duchy's rebellion, Achan divided Cela duchy in two for the time being. Half the land went to Barth Duchy and half went to Nahar Duchy. If the Hamartano women could not be reasoned with, perhaps the Council of Seven would become the Council of Six. Or there could be another war. Only time would tell.

Duchess Amal would remain duchess over Carm Duchy, Lord Orson over Therion, Duke Pitney over Allown, and Lord Dromos over Nahar. Inko son of Mopti would become Lord Mopti and rule over Barth Duchy. With the strife there, it would not be an easy assignment.

As king, Achan would preside over Arman Duchy. He left Lord Levy in Sitna for now. And he decided that Prince Oren's son, Donediff Hadar, would move to Mahanaim as ruling lord, and Donediff's second in command would be promoted to warden of Eret's Point.

Achan appointed Toros Ianjo as Lord High Priest.

Which left only one position undecided: The Lord High Master of the Horse. Unfortunately, the stablemaster and his assistant had both died in the battle for Armonguard.

"I would like to appoint Noam Fox," Achan said.

"The stray?" Sir Caleb said.

Achan could only stare at Sir Caleb.

"Forgive me. I mean no disrespect, Your Highness. I only wonder how much this young man could know about running a stables for a palace like Armonguard."

"Noam has run the stables in Sitna for the past five years," Achan said. "He is young, but I have no doubt in his ability to care for and train horses."

"I'll vouch for him," Sir Gavin said. "He took masterful care of my horses when I was in Sitna."

"I shall draft official letters of appointment and send them to each individual appointed this day," Sir Eagan said.

"I'd like to take Noam's letter myself," Achan said.

"Very well," Prince Oren said. "If you do not have anything further to discuss, I would like to show you the how the repairs are coming along."

So Prince Oren led Achan and the knights to a balcony overlooking the northern arc of the keep.

Achan turned in a circle, taking in the view now that he had the chance. The sunlight cast glittering diamonds over Lake Arman and warmed Achan's head. The lake surrounded the whitestone castle on all sides with three bridges leading back to land: north, east, and west. The Gadowl Wall stretched across the western land like a line drawn in charcoal. To the north, the Gate Road wound up the Cela Mountains. In the distance beyond, he could see the peak of Mount

Bamah, which stood halfway between Armonguard and Barth. The King's Road twisted off over the eastern prairie until it vanished into the Nahar Forest on the horizon.

Below, the bailey swarmed with movement. Men towed carts filled with supplies into the stronghold through the northeastern gate. Hay and rushes, food, firewood, lumber, and stone. Directly below the keep wall, two peasants sprinkled seed on the ground for a flock of chickens that fluttered about, clucking and pecking up breakfast.

At the foot of the watchtower, masons mixed sand, straw, lime, and water in a square trough, making mortar to repair the holes. Soldiers used a basket hooked to a rope to raise new stones up to the broken wall. A faint chorus of "The Pawn Our King" carried over the sound of building below.

Achan should feel happy. The curse of Darkness had gone. He would soon be inducted as king. He was home, finally. Home for good. But the knot in his stomach consumed this thoughts. Would Sparrow blame him for Bran's death? If only he had tried to help Bran sooner.

"Armonguard has been home to the royal family since Echâd Hadar first came to Er'Rets," Prince Oren said. "It will be so again."

Achan met his uncle's measured gaze. "It's a big house." Much bigger than a cottage in the woods.

Prince Oren chuckled. "It is what you make it, nephew. Would you like a tour of your home?"

"I would like that very much."

And so went the rest of the morning. Prince Oren took Achan around the bailey, through the northern arc, into the western arc, and finally into the southern arc of the keep. They toured the dungeons, the kitchens, the stables and barn, the temple of Arman, the great hall, and the gardens.

It all left Achan dumbstruck, especially the gardens.

And then Prince Oren led Achan from the gardens into the foyer of the southern arc, passing under the grand staircase. This was the most ornate room yet. The ceiling rose two levels high. Eight whitestone pillars ran side by side, holding up the vaulted cathedral ceiling, which was a turbulent ocean of white plaster and dark walnut ribs and bosses. Intricate murals were painted onto sections of the walls. Achan made a note to study each painting another day.

Prince Oren hobbled through the foyer and turned to face the grand staircase of red mosaic tile with a gold leaf banister. The rails were the same dark walnut as the wood on the ceiling.

The staircase mirrored itself and swept up both sides of the room. It curled around the contours of the arched wall and met back in the center on the second level. There, a balcony wrapped around the room with a half dozen corridors leading out from it. Underneath stood the doors they had entered through. The doors to the gardens.

Prince Oren led them up the stairs, down one corridor, and through a double doorway.

"The throne room."

Achan's pace slowed until he stood in the middle of the room. It was also two levels high with a flat coffered ceiling of gilded squares. Scarlet fabric lined the walls and was divided by gilded pilasters and gold torch sconces. Mosaic tile in a combination of porphyry, alabaster, shell-pearl, and turquoise covered the floor and sparkled in the torchlight.

Two thrones sat side by side on a raised dais at the end of the room. The chairs had high backs and were upholstered in white satin that was embroidered in gold with the crest of Armonguard. Behind them, another dais, this one higher, held a simple altar crafted from walnut.

"Would you like a moment here?" Prince Oren asked.

"No." Though Achan could not help but wonder who would sit on the chair beside his. Sparrow would, wouldn't she? He wanted to go see her.

Prince Oren led him to the king's quarters next. The room was as large as three of Sitna's cottages, but all the furniture and walls were draped in sheets of white linen. It was like walking through clotheslines. An ornate canopy bed stood against one wall. A fireplace occupied the opposite wall. To his left, on the arched wall, were a set of double doors. Two single doors divided the right wall into three.

Achan lifted a linen sheet from the wall and found a mural beneath it. "You never used this room?"

"I was not king," Prince Oren said.

Achan walked to the double doors and pulled one open. The linen sheet covering them swung out, revealing doors paneled in stained glass. They led to a large balcony that hung over where the northern arc's wall met the southern arc.

"King Axel liked to watch the sunsets from here."

Achan could only imagine. An image of Esek on the balcony in Sitna ran through his memory. He shuddered and went back inside. "Where do these other doors lead?"

"The one in the corner is a privy. The one in the center leads to the queen's quarters."

Why would the queen have her own chamber? Achan walked through the door. The walls were whitestone. No tapestries, no linen drapes, no furniture save an oak canopy bed stripped of even its mattress. "Why is this room not preserved like the king's chambers?"

"The queen did not sleep here," Prince Oren said.

"Who did?" When no answer came, Achan turned and caught Prince Oren exchanging a glance with Sir Gavin.

"Me?" Achan asked, recalling how Sir Gavin said King Axel carried his son everywhere.

"Nay," Sir Gavin said. "King Axel used this chamber for his mistress."

A chill flashed over Achan. "What was her name?"

"There were many, Your Highness," Sir Caleb said, "as we discussed before."

Achan's stomach twisted. "Did my mother ever sleep here?"

"She did," Prince Oren said. "In the beginning."

"And she slept where at the end?"

"The northern arc, Your Highness," Prince Oren said.

"Way over there?" Unbelievable! For the northern arc was across the castle. "Show me."

Prince Oren took them another way, twisting through a labyrinth of corridors. Achan's anger grew with every step that carried him further from the king's chamber.

Why so very far away?

They finally entered a room preserved as the king's chambers had been. Achan fell into a chair draped in linen, sending a poof of dust around him. "Where did I sleep?"

Prince Oren pointed to a narrow door gilded in gold. "Through that door, with your nurse."

"A nurse." So formal. So cold. So . . . depressing. After having waited so long for a child, could his mother not handle him on her own? "Was I a difficult child?"

"Oh, no, Your Highness," Prince Oren said. "You were a very pleasant babe."

Yet his mother clearly hadn't been preoccupied with his father's attentions, either. "What did she do all day?"

"Busy being queen," Prince Oren said.

"Too busy to mother her own child?"

"Course not," Sir Gavin said. "You were Dara's joy."

"You are forgetting, I fear, that royalty, even nobles, do not live as peasants," Sir Eagan said. "A nurse is a common thing amongst the upper class. And that does not mean your mother did not care for you herself. Simply that she had help."

"But my father? Sir Gavin, you said that they were more in love than ever at the end. You told me—"

"Aye, but it was a long road back to repair all the hurt that had been done," Sir Gavin said.

Achan took this information as a lesson from the father he would never know. He would not make that mistake for himself. "Take me back to my chambers."

When they reached the king's chambers again, Achan pulled down the sheet that covered the bed, then the one that covered the balcony doors. Dust clouded the room. He opened the balcony doors and waved in fresh air. He looked to Prince Oren. "Am I permitted to make some changes?"

"Of course," Prince Oren said. "Change anything you like. We could remove the tapestries, repaint the room. All the furniture needs reupholstering anyway. I'll have some swatches brought up and call the carpenters."

Achan held up a hand. "All that can wait."

"What, then, do you have in mind?" Prince Oren asked.

Achan peeked through the door into the queen's chamber. "Put this bed elsewhere. Make this into a solar."

Silence filled the room. Achan turned to see the men watching him. "Can I do that?"

"You *could*," Prince Oren said.

"I beg your pardon, Your Highness," Sir Caleb said. "But do you plan to marry Lady Averella soon?"

Achan felt for the coin in his pocket. "I honestly don't know."

"Perhaps we should wait on such a major change until we know for certain," Sir Caleb said.

"I don't see why," Achan said. "If I don't marry her, I shall have a relaxing solar. If I do marry her, then *we* shall have a relaxing solar." He grinned.

"So you would like your queen to have your mother's chambers?" Prince Oren asked, his tone flat. "On the northern wing? I thought they displeased you."

"They did," Achan said. "My dear advisors, whomever I marry will share *my* chambers."

Sir Eagan's thin lips drew into a line. Sir Gavin's eyes twinkled. Prince Oren hid a smile. And Sir Caleb honked out laughs like a goose.

"What is so funny?" Achan asked.

"The queen will be expecting her own space," Sir Caleb said. "Privacy."

Achan frowned at whatever it was he was missing this time. "Privacy from her husband?"

"Undoubtedly," Sir Caleb said.

Achan shook his head. "No. That won't be necessary."

Sir Caleb laughed heartily now, as if Achan had asked Sparrow to live in the privy chamber. "You cannot surprise Lady Averella Amal with no chamber of her own."

Achan massaged the back of his neck. He did not understand any of this. If he was to be married, why wouldn't he and Sparrow live together? They would have in his cottage in the woods. So why not here? "Very well. Sir Eagan, send a message to Lady Averella making this known."

"With all due respect, Your Highness," Sir Eagan said. "It is customary that the queen have her own chambers."

Achan set his jaw. "Why?"

"Because noblewomen are used to having space of their own," Sir Eagan said. "For their maids and gowns and such."

Sparrow had grown up in a castle. She was used to such luxuries. "But I want us to share the same space."

"Once you are married, there is no impropriety in your sleeping in each other's chambers," Sir Caleb said, "but you should still have your own."

Achan raised his voice. "And still I ask why?"

"It has always been this way with the upper class," Sir Caleb said. "One of the benefits of the wealthy."

"For Lightness' sake, don't coddle him." Sir Gavin fixed his gaze on Achan. "It's done so that your wife won't know who you take into your bed. There lies the tradition."

Which was exactly why Achan wanted to share a room.

"Gavin, that is not the only reason separate chambers are favored," Sir Caleb said. "Think about bathing and getting dressed. It would not do for the king's servants to be around the queen in those circumstances. Nor would it be proper for the queen's servants to be around the king."

Achan clapped his hands together and grinned. "Then we will finally be able to dress and bathe ourselves."

"It will also put pressure on your new bride," Sir Caleb said. "If she knows she will share a bed with you nightly, it will look as though . . ."

"You're in a hurry to produce an heir." Sir Gavin winked.

Achan's cheeks blazed. He straightened, but could not look at anyone, Sir Eagan, especially. His next words came out as a croak. "That's not at all what I intend to imply."

"Achan," Prince Oren said. "It's natural to be nervous about marrying. Do not make things harder than need be."

"All of you mistake my meaning entirely." He fought to put his feelings into words. "My father failed my mother. He's to blame for this . . ." he waved his hand around the empty room . . . "arrangement. There's much infidelity in my family line, so I must do what's necessary to keep such temptations away. If I start my marriage with such distance—with even one wall between us—how will I be able to grow closer to my wife? And if I do not grow closer, how will I fight temptation when it appears before me?"

"Where would she keep her gowns?" Sir Caleb asked.

"You think she has that many?" Achan asked.

Again Sir Caleb laughed. "Likely ten times as many gowns as you have ensembles."

That seemed quite excessive. "Build a bigger wardrobe?"

"It will be terribly awkward to share one room, I should think," Prince Oren said. "Wouldn't you feel crowded?"

"I slept under an ale cask for thirteen years, Uncle. This room is bigger than three cottages in Sitna Manor." Achan sighed. "Look. Peasants do not have the luxury of putting their problems across a castle or even in another room. Most homes only have one bedchamber. Why should my queen and I live differently from our people? If we are to succeed in this union, we must be forced to tolerate one another always."

"I see wisdom in your choice, Nephew," Prince Oren said. "But since you know your bride already, I suggest you speak to her about this so she is not surprised when her maid tells her where her belongings were taken."

Achan clarified Prince Oren's wording. "Her maid?"

"Syrah came with one of Lady Averella's trunks," Sir Eagan said. "Duchess Amal tells me the other trunks and servants will come in the next few weeks."

A maid and a trunk arriving with more on the way seemed a good sign of Sparrow's intentions, but all this had happened before Bran's death. Achan had never seen a woman faint over such news, until Sparrow.

"If we've a wedding to plan, it should come before the coronation," Sir Caleb said. "No sense in crowning you king, marrying you off, then having a third ceremony to crown your queen. Unless you'd prefer it that way."

"What is my other option?"

"To be married, and then crown both of you together."

"I think the people would like that," Prince Oren said. "What say you, Nephew?"

The mere thought relaxed Achan. That he might not have to suffer the coronation alone. "If Lady Averella will have me, I'd very much like us to be crowned together."

"Then we must determine whether or not Lady Averella will have you, once and for all," Sir Caleb said.

Achan took a deep breath. "I shall ask her at once."

40

"Sit down, Vrella, you are making me dizzy."

Averella sat on the stool beside Gypsum and picked up her embroidery. Though Gypsum was busy on her project, Averella did not touch her own. She stared at the balcony. The heavy curtains were pulled back, but the organza ones were drawn, the wind billowing them into the room every so often. "What is taking him so long, do you think?"

"Likely walking across this beast of a castle." Gypsum twisted her lips and took a stitch. "Be thankful his boy came first so Syrah had time to make you presentable."

"My presentation has never bothered Achan before."

Gypsum rolled her eyes. "Calm down, then. It is not like you have never seen this man."

"Stop lecturing me. You do not know how I—"

"My lady?" Syrah stepped inside and curtsied. "Prince Gidon has arrived. Will you see him?"

Averella and Gypsum both stood. Averella waved her hand at Syrah. "Of course. Send him in right away."

Syrah departed and returned a moment later. "His Royal Highness, Prince Gidon Hadar."

Averella brushed away the creases in her skirt and straightened her posture. Sir Shung entered first, followed by another guardsman, then Achan, walking as stiffly as a scarecrow. Two more guardsmen followed him.

Merciful heart. They made a commanding entrance.

Averella and Gypsum curtsied together. Averella had not seen Achan so clean and fashionable since their dinner in Mirrorstone three months past. He wore a red satin doublet, black trousers, and a golden cape. His short hair was combed neatly and his scruff of a beard was trimmed.

Achan's eyes—clear blue and bright—met hers, and he seemed to relax some. He bowed swiftly. "Lady Averella, Lady Gypsum, thank you for allowing this visit."

"As if you need permission to visit me, Your Highness," Averella said.

"Oh, but I do. I thought once I made it here to Armonguard, I'd be free to roam a bit. Alas, I still need permission to visit the privy."

Gypsum giggled, which seemed to cause Achan to grimace. "Forgive me. That was crude." His voice whispered in Averella's mind. *How I wish we could meet elsewhere, Sparrow. I've never been suited for such decorum. I always say something foolish.*

You are doing fine. She motioned to the wicker chair. "Would you care to sit?"

Achan stepped toward the chair, then stopped. "No." His hands formed fists at his sides. He glanced at Sir Shung. "Might Lady Averella and I have a moment of privacy?"

Shung stomped his foot and nodded.

"But we aren't to leave him unchaperoned," one of the other guards said to Sir Shung.

"Shung will guard with his mind." Sir Shung gripped the man's shoulder and steered him to the door. All four guards left, though the one who had spoken up looked reluctant.

"He's new," Achan said. "He's replacing Cortland until his legs are healed."

"How is Cortland?" Averella asked.

"Grateful to you. Sir Caleb totes him around in a cart until his legs heal." Achan glanced at the stool where Gypsum was sitting again.

Syrah stood just behind her, peering over her shoulder at the swiftly growing work of art.

"Gypsum?" Averella asked. "Might you and Syrah run to the kitchen and inquire if Master Poril could make strawberry tarts for dinner?"

"I assure you, he is more than able," Achan said. "Now that I have made him master of the kitchens, he is outdoing himself to show I didn't make a mistake. There is plenty of gingercake to be had."

But Gypsum simply took another stitch and said, "Syrah does not need my company to complete that task. Go ahead, Syrah."

Syrah curtsied and left the room.

"Gypsum?" Averella said, hinting as best she could with the tone of her voice.

Gypsum tugged her needle. It scraped through the fabric until the stitch was snug. "Yes?"

"Might you give us a moment alone?"

Gypsum glanced at Averella. "You know I cannot."

"*Gypsum . . .*"

"It is my duty to act as your chaperone, as no other female is present."

Achan chuckled. "To think of how many times we shared a slab of dirt before a campfire without a chaperone, huh, Sparrow? And a few chambers too."

Averella blushed and shot a scowl his way. *Do you want a moment alone or not?*

What? He grinned innocently. *It's the truth.*

Gypsum made a short hum of disapproval. "Only because my sister was lying to you, Your Highness. Had you known the truth, that *never* would have happened."

Averella closed her eyes a moment. Only Gypsum would have the gall to scold her in front of the Crown Prince.

Achan cleared his throat. "Would you object, Lady Gypsum, if Lady Averella and I stepped onto the balcony alone?"

Gypsum lifted her chin. "Only if you are there too long."

"We shall be quick about it, then, for your sake." Achan took Averella's hand and tugged her through the organza curtains. The outside warmth clapped onto her skin. The glorious sun hung high overhead, proclaiming victory over Darkness. Averella's balcony looked southwest over the vast blueness of Lake Arman. Two high lounge chairs were all that furnished the balcony.

Achan helped Averella sit on one of the chairs, then sat on the edge, facing her. "Are you well?"

The full weight of Achan's blue eyes made her stomach dance. "Very."

His eyebrows puckered. "You are not angry with me?"

"Whatever for?"

His mouth opened, closed, opened. "I . . . Bran?"

"Oh, Achan. That was not your fault. You do not blame yourself, do you?"

"Well, yes, actually. And that I have caused you pain."

"Rest assured. Of course I will miss Bran greatly. He was a dear friend. But he is with Arman now, and we both know how lovely that is."

Achan glanced down and took her hand. "Yes." He rubbed his thumb over her wrist. "I toured the castle."

"Have you?"

"Aye. The king's chambers has a balcony three times the size of this one and stained glass doors rather than curtains."

"It sounds lovely."

His voice lowered. "I want to share it with you."

Share it? She cocked her head to the side and forced a serious expression. "Share a balcony and glass doors?"

"The entire chamber. If you'll marry me." He slipped his half of their coin into her hand. "Prince Oren said my parents had separate chambers. But I don't want to be separated from you ever again. Live with me?"

She could not help but smile at the way his brow wrinkled as he awaited her answer. As if he really didn't know what her answer would be. "But, Achan, that's not how things are done. Nobles always have their own bedchamber."

"So? This castle is too big for a home. Let's take up residence in only one room, like Trajen and Ressa. You can have as many rooms as you want for your gowns and changing and a solar. Have a room for every shoe and piece of jewelry if you want. Only . . ." he cupped her face in his hands, leaned in, and lowered his voice . . . "I don't want any walls between us. Never again." His eyes were so close that hers lost focus. "May I kiss you?"

Oh, she wanted him to. "But what of Sir Shung?"

He's not really watching. A small smile. "May I?"

Averella's eyes fluttered closed. "Yes, and you need never ask again."

His lips met hers softly, and she could feel them trembling. He released a breath and drew back, staring at her mouth. "All this time you were Lady Averella." His eyes flashed to hers and he smirked.

"From that day I first saw you in my cell in Mahanaim. Sitting in the corner, so small and scrawny."

Averella batted his arm. "It is not kind to tell a lady she is scrawny."

His smile lit up his face. "You're anything but scrawny."

She lifted her chin. "Well, I first saw you walking in Esek's procession. You called me Scratch."

"Arman was putting us together."

Averella looked past his face, out to the lake. "I almost ruined it."

Achan set a hand against her cheek and turned her face back to his. "We both made mistakes. But Arman knew we would figure it all out."

He kissed her again. His arms slid around her waist. The heat of the day seemed to heighten with their touch. Their minds connected, and all Averella could hear him say was, *My Sparrow. My Sparrow. My lady Sparrow.*

She ran her hands up his arms, over his shoulders, and rested them at the nape of his neck, which was moist from the heat of the sun. He hummed and pulled her tight against him, threaded one hand in her hair.

She grabbed his shoulders and pushed him back with a gasping squeak. "Achan, please."

His chest heaved as his breathing slowed. "I'm sorry, Sparrow. I've dreamed of you for so long. I never thought things would work out between us at all—and never that they would work out so perfectly as this."

"Perfectly, perhaps. But your passion must not consume us."

His lips, swollen from kissing, curved in a mischievous grin. "I wasn't raised with your scruples. Sir Caleb has taught me some decorum, but I'm a stray at heart and a passionate man."

This time Averella could not keep from laughing. She loved how Achan could always make her smile. "My lips can attest to your passion, but such passion did not bring favor to my parents' actions."

"Did so." His grin darkened. "Their passion created you."

"Achan, really!" She swatted his chest.

"If I promise to behave, will you allow me to court you?"

"Court me?" Her eyes flew wide.

Achan's smile dwindled. "I'll wait, if that's your wish. But Sir Caleb said I must be crowned soon. He says if you're willing, we should be married first so we might be crowned together. Otherwise, there'll be a separate ceremony to crown you after we're married."

"And you prefer we be crowned together?"

"I hoped we could be. It would be much more pleasant that way." His brow furrowed. "I guess that's pretty quick, huh?"

She sighed dramatically. "Well, if it makes things easier on Sir Caleb, I suppose we must skip the courting. But you must rein that passion until we are married."

He breathed out a laugh. "I will. But are you sure, Sparrow? I don't mean to pressure you. What with your lost memory and having been stormed . . ."

"Do not think on it a moment longer. For without your knowing it, you have been courting me since I first clapped eyes on you. And if you make me wait much longer I shall be very cross."

He smiled and kissed her again.

41

Most strays never received a manhood celebration different from any other day of birth celebration, and some never even celebrated that. Achan wanted things to be different for Cole.

For the time being, Cole and Matthias shared a chamber across the hallway from the king's bedchambers. Achan gathered Shung, Toros, and—against his better judgment—Kurtz, for the boy looked up to the man despite Achan's attempts to keep them apart.

After hours of planning in Achan's chambers, the men crept into the room that Cole and Matthias shared. Achan and Shung both carried torches, but Shung extinguished his and waved the smoky stick beneath Cole's nose. Not as good of a restorative as tobacco, perhaps, but more convenient.

The boy squirmed in his bed a bit and rolled over.

Achan fought against his smile. *Shung, however did you and the knights keep a straight face when you woke me?*

A warrior does not smile for this part of the ceremony.

I guess you have more self-control than I do.

You are realizing this only now?

Achan smirked at Shung. *How will you wake him now, O wise one? For he has turned his back to you.*

Shung poked Cole in the back with the end of his torch.

Cole, wearing nothing but undershorts, shot up to sitting. He had been rail thin when Achan had first met him, but he had meat on his bones now, and muscle too. He held his hand between his eyes and Achan's torch, wincing in the light. His voice came raspy. "You need a horse, Highness?"

Achan mustered as deep and manly a voice as he could. "Cole Tanniyn, do you wish to enter into the bonds of manhood?"

Cole yawned so long he groaned. "Bonds of what?"

Achan frowned. He'd practiced that line over and over until it sounded official and exciting. He should have known Cole would be confused. Simple was best with Cole. Achan tried again. "Want to know what it takes to become a man?"

Cole's eyes flashed as white as chicken eggs. He pushed onto his knees and glanced from Achan to each of the other men, then back to Achan. "Yes, Your Highness, I do. Will you tell me what I need to know?"

"Get dressed and come with us, and we'll tell you."

One might have thought the castle was under attack, as fast as Cole dressed. When he was ready, Shung held open the door. Toros and Kurtz went through, then Cole. Achan started toward it but caught sight of a set of eyes watching him from the other side of the small room.

Matthias.

Achan winked at the boy. "Someday, Matthias, you'll get your turn."

Matthias grinned.

The next morning was a day for visiting old friends. Achan found Poril in the kitchens. The old man wept and begged forgiveness, but that hadn't been Achan's reason for the visit. He wanted to start over with Poril, and to make sure that Poril understood he was not to beat whatever lad served him in the kitchens. By the time Achan left, Poril had fed him all the gingercake he could eat.

Next, Achan and his guardsmen exited the western arc of the keep, headed for the stables. Achan had not seen Noam since that day in Noiz when he had lost his temper with Sparrow. He also needed to make time to speak with Gren. He hated to summon any of them, but he might have to resort to that with Gren. The knights gave him so little free time these days, he might never get a chance to see her before his wedding. He hated to only bloodvoice her.

A flash of heat passed over him at the very thought. He was going to be married. To Sparrow. He would praise Arman for the rest of his days for the way it had all worked out.

They stepped inside the stables. Achan had passed outside them on his tour with Prince Oren but had not come in. The structure was three times the size of the Sitna stables. He sensed hundreds of animals inside. A few chickens roamed the dirt floor. And one piglet, which made Achan think about Mox, the scrawny barn boy who'd been there the day Sir Gavin had first spoken to Achan.

He peeked down the first row of stalls, which seemed to house only pigs. Where were the horses, then? "Noam? You in here?"

Footsteps plodded over dirt, nearing, as if someone were running his way. Achan's guards stepped around him.

And then Gren appeared, cheeks pinked, looking pale in her black mourning gown that seemed a little too tight over the belly. She also looked to have gained some weight in her cheeks. "Achan!" she squealed. Her eyes darted to Achan's guards, as if she didn't know what to make of them. He would see her now as well. Perfect.

"It's only Gren," Achan said. "Sir Shung, meet Gren."

Shung grunted and the guards fell back. Shung nodded to Gren. "Pleased to know you."

"Sir Shung is my Shield and friend," Achan said.

Gren lunged up and hugged Shung. "Oh, thank you for keeping him safe, sir!"

Shung's arms remained stiff at his sides. *What a puppy the fawn is.*

Achan grinned, but before he could respond to Shung or Gren, Noam stepped into the open.

"Achan." Noam glanced at the guards and lowered his gaze. "I mean, Your Highness."

"No, Noam. None of that from you." Achan pulled his old friend into a rough embrace and clapped him on the back. "How are you!"

"Fine, thanks. Unreal how the gods deceived us all. No wonder you were such a fighter."

"I see you have put the stables back together."

"Oh, Noam has done everything," Gren said. "There were a few stable boys who used to work here, but none knew as much about the animals as Noam."

"I figured as much," Achan said. "Which is why I came to ask you to be Lord High Master of the Horse."

"Master of what?"

"Lord High Master of the Horse. It is an official position. Means the management of the Royal Stables and all matters of horses and hounds fall to you. Breeding, care, feeding, things like that. What say you?"

"You think me worthy?"

"Are you not doing the job already?"

"Well, I suppose . . ."

"It is settled then, unless you wish to return to Sitna."

"No!" Noam said. "I wish to stay here."

"Very well then, Master of the Horse. Welcome home."

Noam grinned, then laughed, then hugged Gren and swung her around.

"Achan, that's wonderful!" Gren said. "But what of me?"

"You are welcome to live here, Gren."

"What about my parents?"

"You think they would like to move here?"

Her eyebrows sank. "I don't know." She reached out and touched the edge of Lady Averella's sleeve that was tied to Achan's arm. "I heard Duchess Amal absolved you from your agreement with Lady Averella."

"Aye, she did," Achan winked, "though I think she and I shall keep the bargain anyway."

Gren's face paled. An awkward silence descended. Noam walked over to Shung and the guards and struck up a conversation.

"You really love her?" Gren asked Achan.

The thought of Sparrow made Achan smile. "Aye."

Gren did not smile. "Well, I think she's a fool for treating you the way she did."

He folded his arms across his chest. "She had her reasons."

She poked a finger against his chest. "Don't you defend her. She was being a fool."

He laughed and snagged her wrist to deflect any more knife-like jabs. "Fine. She was a fool."

Gren sighed and pulled out of his grip. "I like her too." She stepped back and leaned against the first pigpen. "She's so smart."

Achan huffed a sarcastic laugh. "Too smart sometimes."

"I thought maybe you'd still want me."

Achan's face tingled as the blood drained away. "Oh, Gren. We talked about this back in Carmine."

"You always wanted to marry me, and now that you are king, you can do anything you want, right?"

"Within reason."

"And what is unreasonable about marrying the woman you love?"

"Gren."

"You don't love me anymore."

The words struck Achan's chest like a fist. But he had to be honest. "I'm sorry."

Her bottom lip trembled.

"Nor do you love me in that way, Gren, so do not play games." Achan looked over her black dress again. "Who do you truly mourn in this gown? Riga or Bran Rennan?"

A rosy flush crept over Gren's cheeks, but she whispered a laugh. "Is it not ironic, Achan, that you'll marry Bran's former love and that I might have married . . ." She sucked in a long and quivery breath. "Was there any chance he'd have married me? I was certain he cared. I could see it in his eyes."

Achan took her hand in his. "He did care, Gren."

She clapped her free hand over her mouth and squeezed her eyes closed. This did not stop the tears from leaking past her eyelids and trickling down her cheeks. Her other hand settled protectively over her unborn child.

Achan took her into his arms and held her tightly. She sobbed and trembled, and he stroked her hair with one hand and rubbed her back with the other.

Gren pulled away and met his eyes, her cheeks wet and glossy. "What will become of me? You were always my hero. You always stepped in to save me."

"I cannot save you anymore, Gren. No man can save you always. We're too flawed."

"You're going to tell me that your Arman god can?"

Achan shrugged. "Not if you already know it."

"What you did to bring back the light . . . I've never seen anything like that."

"There is no one like Arman, Grenny." Achan told her then of how he had found Sparrow at the gates of Shamayim, of the glorious pull of that place, of meeting Câan in Mitspah. Of his choice to serve Arman above all things.

"Please, Achan. If you won't marry me, take me as your servant. I can work in a kitchen. Let my child grow up in the castle where he'll be safe and provided for. I can't go back. The people in Carmine disdain me. And no one I know lives in Sitna anymore. Please, have mercy."

"Harnu plans to return to Sitna."

She snorted. "Harnu . . ."

"Harnu also asked me for my blessing."

"To marry *me?*" She rolled her eyes. "That man."

"I wonder if we have both misjudged him."

Her mouth gaped. "Achan, you can't be serious."

"If he were any other man, how would you interpret his actions since Riga's death? I'm told he maintains your cottage. And that he left his duty to his father to assist you and Sparrow on a foolish crusade. He risked his life for you both. He also fought in my army and earned a promotion."

"Write a song about him, then, why don't you?"

"Don't let your childhood prejudices taint who he's become. I beg you, consider his offer. I want to know that you are being taken care of. I'll move your family, Harnu's, the smithy, and your entire cottage to Armonguard, if need be."

"I thought no man could save me?"

"That's not what I meant. Promise me you will think about Harnu?"

Gren twisted her lips into a reluctant smile. "I will think about it. But I promise nothing more."

42

A lot went into planning a wedding—even more so for planning a joint coronation. Achan allowed himself to be dragged along by Prince Oren, Sir Caleb, Sir Eagan, and Duchess Amal, agreeing to whatever they liked best.

Red velvet would be best? Very well.

Achan's officers should carry an organza canopy? Fine.

The garden would make a lovely place to be wed? The garden it would be.

Achan simply wanted to be married. But Sir Eagan informed him that Duchess Amal had selected a date for the wedding that was still two weeks away. Achan desired no grand party. When he asked why he must wait two weeks, Sir Eagan said it had something to do with Lady Averella's being a woman. Then Achan was sorry he'd asked.

He saw Sparrow only at mealtimes in the great hall. The duchess had her daughter on a strict schedule that involved bizarre beauty treatments, diets, and baths. Achan found this a waste of time. No amount of bathing in rose petals could improve perfection. Besides, he'd seen her reposed in trousers and an orange tunic—and liked her then.

Prince Oren took him to where the royal jewels were kept, in a locked, secret room off the king's chamber. Here Achan marveled over crowns, swords and shields, rings, brooches, and more types of jewelry than he ever imagined existed. After spending hours looking over everything, Prince Oren suggested he choose something to send to Lady Averella as a gift. Something she could wear in the wedding. So Achan chose one of his mother's crowns, and Sir Caleb had it sent.

Achan would have rather taken the crown to her himself.

One other task occupied his free time. He had grown up believing a man had one responsibility to complete before he could marry: he had to build a home, a place for his bride to live, a place to build a family.

Since Achan now owned Castle Armonguard, he didn't *need* to build a home, so he poured all his efforts into remodeling the king's chambers and the adjoining solar.

The two weeks flew by.

The night before his wedding Achan lay awake tossing and turning in his bed. Then at last a sudden calm came over him. He sat up and looked to the door. "Sir Eagan?"

But it was Sparrow's voice that filled his mind. *My father taught me his little trick. Lay back, and I shall help you sleep.*

Achan obeyed, but Sparrow's attentions, no matter how calming, would never help him sleep. *What are you—?*

Shh. I have a song for you.

A song?

Pity on my heart from the day I first saw you.
    Your pleasing face burns—

Really? From the day you first saw me?

Yes. I was enamored with you. I simply could not figure you out. A stray soldier. You were a mystery.

Achan left his body and passed through the Veil until he floated above Sparrow's bed. She wore a white gown. Her blankets were pulled up to her waist, and she smelled sweet. There were no chaperones in the Veil. *What did your mother make you bathe in today?*

Rosewater and olive oil. Then I had to have yet another sea salt and honey scrub. And just when I thought it was over, a horrible, tortuous sugar and lemon paste.

How is a sugar and lemon paste tortuous? It sounds delicious.

But they don't let me eat *it. They use it to rip off my hair.*

She didn't look to be missing any hair. *You're ripping off your hair? Whatever for?*

Not the hair on my head, goose. The hair on my legs and arms . . . Every place but *my head. I am so soft you will be able to fold me up and put me in a satchel.*

The thought of touching her skin sent a thrill through his body. *You smell like almonds.*

She gasped and pulled the blankets to her chin. *Achan, go back to your room. You have no business being here.*

Why not? If you're going to talk to me, I'd much rather see your face.

She growled, but it sounded so much like a purring kitten that Achan laughed.

So, why do you smell like almonds? Achan asked.

Syrah washed my hair with crushed almonds. It is supposed to make it silkier.

Achan couldn't see any difference in the dark. *Really?*

You can tell me what you think tomorrow.

I wish you were here now.

It is only one more day.

It may as well be one hundred.

You poor dear.

He watched her eyes flicker around him, never quite looking in the right place. *Are you nervous?* he asked.

A little. Are you?

I don't like being stared at by a crowd of people.

I will call it off, you know, if you want me to. There is still time.

Very funny, Sparrow. I want to show you our home. I built it for you . . . sort of.

A home?

The king's chambers. I think you will like it.

Is there an open place where I can practice my leg sweep on you?

He chuckled. *As a matter of fact, there is.*

Excellent. I shall bid you farewell, then, Achan. Please let go of my mind so I can sleep, or I will have no energy for leg sweeping tomorrow.

We mustn't have that. Sleep well, Vrell Sparrow. Until the cock crows.

Until then. Good night.

Achan fought the temptation to remain in her bedchamber and watch her sleep. After tonight, he would never be parted from Sparrow again.

He returned to his body and stared at the organza canopy above his bed. He could never rest now without help, so he reached out for Shung's mind, heard the man's heavy snoring, and relaxed, drugged by his Shield's deep sleep.

Averella could not breathe. "That is too tight!"

"Once more and I will be done." Lady Coraline Orthrop pulled the ties of Averella's corset again.

Averella swore she heard a rib crack. "I will not be able to walk."

"Pish posh. A corset does not affect your legs."

"If my brain can only think of the pain and lack of air, it will not have time to tell my legs to move."

"You are terribly dramatic, Averella. How ever will the king put up with you?"

"The same way every man finds a way to put up with his wife, I suppose. Are not all women dramatic at times?"

"Just you remember to show him respect."

"Oh, he knows I respect him. But how will a tight corset matter? I can tell you now he cares little for these things."

Lady Coraline smiled. "He may think he cares little now, but once he sees you in it, I have no doubt he will ask you to wear it again."

Averella rolled her eyes. "All the more reason he never see me in it. Then he will not be disappointed when I burn it."

"At least you will not have to wear it for long."

Lady Coraline's singsong tone brought a flush to Averella's cheeks, but she held her tongue. The less she reacted, the less Lady Coraline would provoke her.

"Let's get your dress on now." Lady Coraline gathered the sides of Averella's wedding gown and held it down on the floor. "Step in."

Averella put a hand on Lady Coraline's shoulder and stepped into the gown. Lady Coraline pulled it up, twisted it the right direction, then helped Averella get her arms into the sleeves.

Averella had to admit, the gown was lovely, even if the waist was two sizes too small. The dress was all blue, as blue symbolized purity, peace, loyalty, and trust.

It had a fitted bodice, long fitted sleeves, and a flowing skirt made of pale blue brocade heavily embroidered with golden thread and pearls. Embroidered blue brocade accented the gown with a cuff around each upper arm, an inlay on the top of the bodice, and a loose belt that dangled in front.

Mother said Achan would be wearing blue as well. Averella could not wait to see him.

Once Lady Coraline had laced up the gown, Syrah fetched the matching blue cape that was lined in gold satin. It attached with two sapphire brooches that clipped to the front of the dress just below each shoulder, allowing the cape to drape off the shoulders and trail on the ground. A third sapphire brooch clipped onto the belt in the center front.

Lady Coraline had already attacked Averella's hair. It was down, as a bride's hair usually was for her wedding. But Lady Coraline had curled much of it with an iron rod that was still perched in the embers of the fireplace.

Now that Averella was dressed, Lady Coraline set a gold circlet on Averella's head. It was encrusted with sapphires and rubies—a gift from Achan that had belonged to his mother.

Lady Coraline attached a two-layer white organza veil to the circlet then turned Averella to face a full-length mirror. "There now. It is not trousers, but it is blue."

"It makes me look as though I have a figure."

"You look radiant, and you do have a figure."

"If only something could be done for my voice."

"The prince loves you as you are, so you told me. You would not be you with another woman's figure or voice." Lady Coraline peered over Averella's shoulder and met her gaze in the mirrorglass. "Are you ready, my dear?"

"As ready as a girl can be on her wedding day, I suppose."

"Are you frightened about the ceremony?"

"No."

"About the celebration?"

"No."

"About tonight?"

Averella turned her head and met Lady Coraline's eyes. "I am nervous, but not afraid."

"You are fortunate to be marrying someone you love."

Averella looked back at her reflection in the mirrorglass and sighed. "I know."

A pressure squeezed in on Averella's mind and her mother said, *It is time, dearest. Are you ready?*

Yes. "Mother is coming," she said to Lady Coraline.

Lady Coraline scowled. "I hate it when you do that. You and your mother and your bloodvoices."

"*And* my husband."

Lady Coraline rolled her eyes. "Yes, child. Your children will likely have it too. What ever will I do?"

"Get used to it."

Achan couldn't breathe. It wasn't the layers of blue silk and velvet he was wearing, though he wondered at the cost of his outfit. If silk and velvet were cheaper than coats of chain, maybe he could outfit his army in wedding ensembles. They felt equally thick and brought the same inescapable heat.

Or maybe the heat was due to his situation.

He stood deep in the temple garden at the end of a white wood pergola that was so draped in vines and flowers the scent was overpowering. Shung stood at his side, then Noam, Sir Gavin, and Sir Caleb. Across from him, Lady Gypsum and two maidens were dressed in blue and white gowns. Lady Gypsum grinned at Achan as if she knew some secret.

He glanced away.

Hundreds of chairs had been set up in the gardens, and not one was empty. The audience was divided by an aisle that ran from the double doors at the back of the southern arc of the keep to where Toros, Achan's priest, stood at the end of the aisle, facing the audience. Achan glanced down the aisle again.

Nothing.

He released a shaky breath and thought of the handful of mentha leaves he'd stashed in his pocket. He'd already eaten so many his tongue felt raw, but his stomach had yet to settle, so eating a few more wouldn't hurt. At least Sparrow would not be able to accuse him of having stink breath.

He reached into the narrow pocket in his doublet. His fingers did not find mentha leaves but his half of the coin. He drew it out, squeezed it, and tucked it back into his pocket.

His left-hand pocket furnished him with another store of mentha. He stuffed two leaves into his mouth as stealthily as he could and took a deep breath.

Arman, give me peace, I beg You.

The gardens *were* beautiful. The valances were thick with vines and white blossoms. Achan glanced at his future mother-in-law. The woman's eyes were also fixed on the entrance.

Bang!

He jumped as the doors at the back of the keep swung open. A man and woman stood in the open doorway.

Father and daughter.

A murmur ran through the crowd. A man to Achan's left began to play an eerie tune on the pipes. Achan shivered. What kind of song was this? It felt more like a death march than a wedding song.

His bride started forward. She was draped in what looked to be blue and gold gemstones. Her veil was so thick he couldn't even see her face.

Is that you under all those stones, Sparrow?

Does it look like someone else?

Can you even see where you're going?

No, but thankfully Sir Eagan can be my eyes.

Achan chuckled, thankful for bloodvoices and the chance to speak with his friend. *How long is the garden walk, anyhow? Can't you take normal steps?*

Whatever is your hurry?

I feel as though everyone is staring at me, and I do not have a veil to hide behind.

You cannot see it, Your Highness, but I am rolling my eyes at your sad situation. And I cannot take normal steps because my gown is a vise tighter than an Eben's fist.

Mercy. Well . . . it looks quite nice.

She was still inching toward him. *It had better look better than "nice," or you shall pay later.*

You promise?

But Sir Eagan and Sparrow had reached the end of the pergola, and she said no more.

Toros spoke to Achan, drawing his gaze away from the heap of silk and jewels that was Sparrow. "You come here today, my prince, of your own free will to marry this lady?"

"Aye, that I do."

Sir Caleb shot Achan a dirty look, likely due to Achan's saying "aye" rather than "yes," but Sir Eagan smiled.

Toros addressed Sparrow. "Lady, is it true that you come here today of your own free will to be married to this prince?"

"Yes, it is true."

"Whose blessings accompany you?"

"That of her father and all her family." Sir Eagan kissed Sparrow's hand, then stepped behind her.

"Please join hands with your betrothed," Toros said.

Achan held out his hand, and Sparrow slipped hers into it. His heart leapt at her touch, despite them both wearing gloves. He readjusted his grip by sliding his fingers between hers and squeezed. *Why did they make us wear gloves?*

It is proper to wear gloves at formal occasions.

I still cannot see your face.

Perhaps I am Lady Jaira, and you will not know until our vows are sealed.

Now I'm truly frightened. Should I run?

You had better not.

"Above you are stars, below you stones. As time goes by, remember . . . Like a stone your love should be firm. Like a star your love should be constant. May the wisdom of your minds guide you. May the strength of your wills bind you. May the power of love and desire bring you joy. And may the strength of your dedication make you inseparable.

"Be free in giving affection and warmth. Be close, possess one another, but have understanding and patience. For storms will come, but if you obey Arman, they will pass quickly.

"Your Highness, I have not the right to bind you to the lady Averella. Only you have this right. If it be your desire, say so at this time and place your ring in her hand."

"It is my greatest desire." Achan lifted Sparrow's hand and pressed the man's ring he had chosen from the vault in her palm. He folded her fingers over it.

"Lady Averella, if it be your desire for Prince Gidon Hadar to be bound to you, place his ring on his finger."

Sparrow's head tipped down, and she patted the air in search of Achan's hand.

He reached out and touched her fingers. *Looking for this?*

Oh, hush up. She slid the ring onto his finger. The gold gleamed against his white glove. His chest tightened.

"Lady Averella," Toros said, "I have not the right to bind you to Prince Gidon Hadar. Only you have this right. If it be your desire, say so at this time and place your ring in his hand."

"It is my desire." Sparrow reached out, and Achan helped her by meeting her hand. He couldn't help but smile at her blindness as he took the ring from her.

"Your Highness, if it be your desire for the lady Averella to be bound to you, place her ring on her finger."

Achan took Sparrow's hand and slid the gold band onto her finger.

"Repeat after me: I, Prince Gidon Hadar . . ."

Achan said, "I, Prince Gidon Hadar . . ."

". . . in the name of Arman that resides within me . . ."

". . . in the name of Arman that resides within me . . ."

It continued that way, with Achan repeating everything Toros said.

". . . by the life that courses within my blood, and the love that resides within my heart, take you, Averella Amal, to my hand, my heart, and my spirit, to be my chosen one. I promise to love you without restraint, whether sick or healthy, whether in plenty or in poverty, until Arman parts us in death."

Then Toros asked Sparrow to repeat the same to Achan. When she had finished, Toros said, "By the power vested in me by Arman and the future king . . ."

A low laugh passed through the crowd.

". . . I declare you husband and wife. May your love so endure that its flame remains a guiding light all your days."

Toros stepped before them and placed a hand on each of their heads. "Arman is one. Arman is three. Arman is three in one. Bless, preserve, and keep this couple, look upon them with mercy and favor, fill them with wisdom and grace, that they may live together in this life, and that in the world to come they may have life everlasting. May it be so."

The audience echoed with "So be it" or "May it be so."

"Your Highness, you may kiss your bride."

Achan lifted the veil over Sparrow's head and smiled down on her lovely face. "There you are."

Her brow crinkled, as if she were about to say something smart. He pressed his lips to hers before she could speak. The scent of almonds flooded his senses. He took her face in one hand and held her steady, laying his claim in front of every witness present. So warm and sweet. He hummed, joy bubbling over. One more quick kiss and he pulled back.

The crowd cheered. Achan felt his face go flush. Sparrow's did, as well. Tears teased the corners of her eyes.

Toros turned Achan and Sparrow until they faced the crowd. "Here stands before you, Prince Gidon Hadar and his bride!"

The crowd cheered again. Achan took Sparrow's hand in his, kissed the back of it, then they walked hand in hand down the aisle.

People showered them with seeds and grains of wheat to wish them prosperity. He had to inch along to keep pace with Sparrow, for she was barely moving. Then she tripped.

Achan swept her up in his arms and carried her the rest of the way.

He entered the keep under the grand staircase. The banquet would be held in the great hall. But instead of taking the stairs up, Achan carried Sparrow through the foyer and into a solar on the first level. He kissed her, twirled her in a circle, and set her down. "I don't want to go to a banquet and stuff my face, Sparrow."

She set a hand against her stomach. "I doubt I could eat a thing. There is no room in this dress for anything else."

"Let's leave then. Why must we sit through another formal banquet?"

"Because you are the future king and—"

"And you are queen."

"Yes. And your people—"

"Our people."

"*Our* people want to celebrate with us." She punched for his arm.

But he caught her fist and tucked her hand around his neck. "Such a violent wife I have. You don't have any weapons on you, do you? Perhaps a knife?"

"I told you, there is no room in this dress. Not even for a little knife."

"Perhaps I should check." He ran his hand from her waist and up her side.

She slapped his hand away. "My dear husband, this is not the time or place." But she raised onto her tiptoes and kissed him.

Your Highness? Sir Caleb's voice.

Achan groaned. *What is it you want, Sir Caleb?*

The guests are hungry. They are seated in the great hall, but there is no sign of the prince and his bride.

Achan drew back from Sparrow and stared into her eyes. *Say that again, Sir Caleb?*

Say what?

His bride.

The guests are waiting, Your Highness. The sooner you eat, the sooner the banquet ends.

Hmm. Point taken. Achan took Sparrow's hand and led her to the door. *We are on our way.*

They feasted on roasted quail, venison, fish, ale-flavored bread, stewed cabbage, tarts and custards, dates, pistachio nuts, and spicy mulled wine. Achan lost count after five courses. Sparrow, as she'd predicted, hardly ate a thing.

A minstrel sang several songs about Achan and Sparrow, including "The Pawn Our King" and a new song titled, "The Sparrow that

Was a She." There were other entertainers including a juggler, an acrobat, and a man with a dancing dog.

When it came time for people to dance, Achan was quickly parted from Sparrow in order to dance with Duchess Amal, Lady Gypsum, and Lady Gali. Achan was surprised to see Sir Gavin dancing with a pretty grey-haired woman.

He somehow managed to get free and spotted Sparrow. She was standing near the wall, surrounded by a group of men. Achan nudged his way across the room, but someone grabbed his arm.

"Best wishes to you, Pacey," Kurtz said.

"Thank you, Kurtz." Achan braced himself for a comment about the wedding night, but Kurtz surprised him.

"I like what you did for Cole the other night, Your Highness, and that you included me. My father . . . he didn't talk much. Too busy with the guardsmen. And he made a sport of women as if they were hawks or dice. Guess that and the sword was all I learned from him."

Achan dug for something to say, but Kurtz went on.

"What you said about the code, of honoring women and protecting them. I figured it out, I did. That's why Gavin left me out of your ceremony. I was a bad influence, I was. But you included me in Cole's night. I guess you see something good in me, eh?"

"There is much good in you, Kurtz. You are friendly and brave and strong. And you remind me to not take things so seriously always."

"How did a cub like you get so smart, eh?"

"Good friends. A girl named Gren loved me when no one else would. And a fellow named Noam. But I give Gren most of the credit."

"You've done the same for me, you have. By asking me to mentor Cole. I won't let you down, Pacey. I won't."

Sparrow stepped up behind Kurtz, and Achan held his hand out to his bride. She took it, and he pulled her close. "Look who is here, Sparrow. It is Kurtz. And he is not dancing! What do you say about that?"

"He must be ill," Sparrow said.

"I'm as well as water, my lady. But I cannot pass myself off as a wild stallion anymore. I fear my limp is here to stay. And no woman would look on me now. Not with a scar like this on my neck."

"On the contrary," Sparrow said. "Many women will be drawn to your battle scar. To think you fought for the freedom of Er'Rets. You are a hero to this land."

Kurtz beamed. "Now, I like that, I do. You've put the right spin on it, my lady. I'm a hero, I am. All have pity on the hero who's me, eh?"

Sparrow giggled, and Achan pulled her back to the dance floor. Her cape was so long he had to twist it up and over her arm so she would not trip.

Midway through the dance, Duchess Amal called them over to where Poril had set dozens of small cakes on a table. The duchess stacked three cakes on the floor between Achan and Sparrow. "Let us see if you can reach her, Your Highness, without knocking down the cakes."

Achan leaned over the cake and kissed Sparrow.

Duchess Amal and Sir Eagan took turns adding cakes to the growing stack between them. Before long, the cakes were piled so high that Achan could see Sparrow's head only. He bounced up on his tiptoes and leaned over the swaying tower of cake, but his chest knocked into it and the cakes fell against Sparrow. She squealed as the cakes knocked her down in a pile of crumbled sweetness.

Achan leapt to her side and helped her up out of the mountain of cake. "Sorry, Sparrow. I did my best."

"I think that twenty cakes is enough prosperity, do you disagree?"

"You are all the prosperity I need."

Duchess Amal swept up to them and took each of their hands. "My dear daughter." She kissed Sparrow on the cheek. "And my son." She kissed Achan. "Are you happy?"

"I have not been so happy since Sir Gavin asked me to train as his squire," Achan said.

Then Sparrow said, "Mother, I am overjoyed."

EPILOGUE

Achan felt as though the weight of the land rested on his shoulders, and no crown had been placed on his head yet.

Not the official one, anyway.

Sir Caleb had sent Matthias in to wake him before dawn to get him ready for his coronation. And now he was dressed in clothing that weighed twice what his wedding ensemble had weighed.

He wore a red brocade doublet with a navy stripe sewn from his right shoulder to his left hip. Cream-colored trousers and no shoes. Achan found this strange, but the king being barefoot was part of the ceremony.

Then the cape: ermine over red velvet with a train longer than a bride's. The thing was also trimmed and fully lined with ermine fur. All the weight of his garb was in the cape. Sir Caleb had tied it to Achan's doublet at his shoulders to keep the strings from strangling him.

Achan stood in an antechamber off the foyer, just down the hall from the throne room, waiting for his queen. If they had dressed Achan in this much garb, he doubted Sparrow would be able to stand under the weight of her gown.

At least she'd gotten to sleep in.

But when she arrived, he was surprised to see that she wore a simple white dress embroidered in gold thread. Until Sir Caleb put a matching cape on her shoulders.

Sparrow tugged the ties at her throat. "It's so heavy!"

Achan smiled at her worried expression. "Consider it a feat of strength."

"I told you I have no desire to join the Kingsguard."

"Aye, but think how the captains will berate any weak men who enter their ranks. 'Even the queen can do this!' Men will have no choice but to step up to the challenge."

She rolled her eyes at his humor. "I doubt any captain will ask his men to don such a cape for training."

"Likely not." He nudged her leg with his bare foot. "At least you get shoes." He stepped before her and kissed her lips. "Did you sleep well?"

"Yes, and you?"

He kissed her again. "As well as possible with you claiming the entire bed."

"I did no such thing."

"No matter. That bed is far too big. It is a relief to be crowded again."

The next hour passed quickly. Achan and his queen were escorted to the throne room by a squadron of uniformed men. Sparrow walked beside Achan, on his arm, which was only possible due to the dozen men carrying the trains of their capes, three on each side of his, and three on each side of hers.

Some sort of grandstands had been constructed on each side of the throne room, creating an aisle up the center. The stands were packed with people dressed in finer clothing than Achan had seen, even at his wedding.

In the far right corner, an orchestra played a majestic anthem on harps, pipes, lutes, flutes, bugles, tabors, bells, and cymbals. A choir of robed minstrels accompanied them. The beautiful, regal song brought a shiver to Achan's soul. Sparrow squeezed his arm.

He patted her hand. *That's quite a song, huh?*

It is the most beautiful thing I have ever heard.

The soldiers escorted Achan and Sparrow down the aisle. The mosaic tile was bumpy under his feet. The throne room had never looked so huge. The scarlet walls were meant to bespeak royalty, but they made Achan think of all who had shed blood and even died for him to be here. His parents, Lord Livna, Riga, Bran, thousands in battle . . .

Each step that took Achan closer to those white-and-gold chairs seemed a dream. He swallowed, careful not to make eye contact with any of the people standing so close on the sides of the aisle. *And how about all these people?* Achan asked Sparrow.

Not so different from when I walked up the garden path at our wedding.

The memory made him smile. *I thought you couldn't see anything.*

That lace veil had a few cutouts here and there. I could see in places. When I stood still.

Well, thanks for sparing me from having to walk up that aisle, at least.

I did not design the wedding ceremony, Achan. Nor this one.

The floor is cold. Why can't I wear my boots?

The footprints are part of the ceremony.

Right. I've not had this many people stare at me since Sir Gavin dragged me before the Council.

I am glad he did.

Achan sighed and shook his head at all that had led to this moment. *As am I.*

Finally Achan and Sparrow reached the satin-upholstered thrones. The chairs sat side by side on a raised dais of solid whitestone. Achan glanced at the impressions in the stone. The footprints of King Echâd Hadar.

"You come to lay claim to this throne and realm?" Toros Ianjo's voice pulled Achan's gaze away from the footprints. Toros stood on the upper dais, behind the thrones, dressed in white robes embroidered with the three interlocking red circles on the front. He also wore a tall, golden hat.

Achan lifted his head. "I do."

"Identify yourself."

"I am Achan Cham, born Gidon Hadar to King Axel Hadar."

"King Axel was king before you. You come to take his place?"

"I do."

"Then stand in his steps and in the steps of his forefathers all the way back to King Echâd Hadar, the first king of Er'Rets."

Achan gave Sparrow's hand one last trembling squeeze, then had to release her so they could turn around. They faced each other a moment as they rotated slowly, allowing their train-bearers to move those massive capes over the arm of each throne.

Once they faced the audience, Achan took Sparrow's hand again, then they stepped backward up onto the whitestone dais. Achan slid his feet back over the smooth stone until he felt the indentation of the footprints. He glanced down, matching his feet to the grooves like pieces of a puzzle. Heat trickled down his spine to his toes.

King Echâd had stood in this place, as had every other king of Er'Rets, some two dozen men.

And now him.

Arman, help me.

BUT YOU, MY SERVANT, ACHAN, WHOM I HAVE CHOSEN, I TOOK YOU FROM THE ENDS OF ER'RETS, FROM ITS FARTHEST CORNERS I CALLED YOU. I SAID, 'YOU ARE MY SERVANT'; I HAVE CHOSEN YOU. SO DO NOT FEAR, FOR I AM WITH YOU. I WILL STRENGTHEN YOU AND HELP YOU; I WILL UPHOLD YOU WITH MY RIGHTEOUS RIGHT HAND.

Achan shuddered in the heat of that promise. *Thank You, Arman. You are so good to me.*

Toros walked down Achan's side of the dais, circled where Achan's cape lay spread on the mosaic pavement, and stopped before the thrones, facing the audience.

The music ceased.

Nausea rolled about in Achan's stomach. He squeezed Sparrow's hand. *I think I might be ill.*

Be ill later in your chambers.

Our chambers.

She sent him a look as if to say, "You exasperate me."

He grinned.

Prince Oren, Sir Gavin, Sir Caleb, and Sir Eagan walked before Toros in a diamond formation and turned their backs to each other so they were facing outward. The drums started in on a military march, and the men began to walk. Prince Oren limped down the aisle with his cane. Sir Eagan took three steps and stopped, facing Achan and Sparrow. And Sir Caleb and Sir Gavin marched straight until they reached the east and west walls.

The drumming stopped.

Toros spoke then, his voice loud and authoritative. "I hereby present unto the people of this great land, King Gidon Hadar, the Great Cham, Ransomed by Câan, Servant of Arman, Son of Axel, and your undoubted King. Beside him sits his bride, Queen Averella Amal of Carmine. Wherefore all of you have come this day to pay homage and service to this king and queen, I ask you, land of Er'Rets, are you willing to do the same?"

The entire congregation shouted, "Arman save the king!"

Achan jumped. Sir Caleb had prepped him for this, but the chorus of voices, in unison, all proclaiming him king made him tremble.

Then Toros said, "I ask you, land of Er'Rets, are you willing to do the same?"

Prince Oren, still facing the door, yelled, "The people from here to the south say they will."

Sir Caleb said, "The people from here to the east say they will."

Sir Gavin: "The people from here to the west say they will."

And Sir Eagan said, with a wink to his daughter, "The people from here to the north say they will."

The four men turned and walked back to the center, then returned to their original places at the front of the audience.

Toros turned to face Achan and smiled. "Will you, King Gidon Hadar, son of Axel, solemnly promise and swear to govern the peoples of Er'Rets according to its laws and customs?"

Achan said the first of several lines Sir Caleb had made him memorize. "I solemnly promise to do so."

"Will you cause law and justice, in mercy, to be executed in all your judgments?"

"I will."

"Will you to the utmost of your power maintain the Laws of Arman and the true profession of the Book of Life?"

"All this I promise to do, so help me, Arman."

Prince Oren then approached, carrying a thick book. *The Book of Arman*. He handed it to Achan, who took it in both hands. "Here is wisdom and the mouthpiece of Arman, the most valuable thing this land has to offer."

Achan slid the book onto a shelf under his throne, then said, "Upon Arman's word I will always sit, stand, and rule this land. For it is the only foundation that is unshakable." Achan looked to Sparrow, nodded, and together they sat.

Then Prince Oren, Sir Gavin, Sir Eagan, and Sir Caleb returned, this time each holding a pole of a square canopy made of golden brocade. They positioned themselves so that the canopy covered Achan and Sparrow.

A servant carried a glass jar to Toros, who held it up, then stepped before Achan. "King Gidon Hadar, by the authority of Arman, I anoint you with oil that has been consecrated. As King Echâd, the first king was anointed, so be you anointed, blessed, and consecrated King over all the peoples of Er'Rets, whom Arman has given you to rule and govern, in the name of Arman, may it be so." He tipped the jar over Achan's head. The cool oil tickled Achan's scalp, ran down behind one ear, down his left cheek, and streamed off the front of his hair.

Toros then placed his hand on Achan's head. "King Gidon Hadar, by the authority of Arman, I lay my hand upon your head, seal, and confirm the anointing and herby pronounce a blessing upon your life and reign."

Toros closed his eyes and began to pray, "Holy Arman, the exalter of the humble and the strength of thy chosen King, bless and sanctify Your servant Gidon, who by Your call and our agreement was anointed with this oil and consecrated King. Grant Your servant the spirit of wisdom and government, that being devoted to You with his whole heart, he may govern wisely, that his time in this office may be in safety, persevering in good works unto the end, and by Your mercy and timing, come into Your everlasting kingdom. May it be as I have said."

The audience voiced their agreement.

Then Toros anointed Sparrow and prayed a similar blessing over her. She squeezed Achan's hand the entire time, but did not speak to his mind.

Prince Oren and the knights carried the canopy away. Toros then faced the audience and asked them to stand.

A young man approached carrying a pillow with a huge crown on top. The pillow had a strap, which the man wore around his neck. The crown looked heavy indeed, made of gold and red velvet and encrusted with hundreds of jewels. A second young man followed, gripping a staff in one hand. It was as tall as the man carrying it, made of dark wood and topped with an ivory carving of the two-headed eagle, the symbol of the Hadar name. Golden rings were spaced around the staff, one for every king who had ruled Er'Rets.

Toros took the crown from the pillow and lifted it in the air. "Arman, we offer up this crown, and Your servant Gidon upon whose head You will place it, as a sign of royal majesty, that he may be filled by Your abundant grace and all kingly virtues. In Your eternal name, may it be so."

Toros placed the crown on Achan's head, simultaneously stealing Achan's breath. The crown was stiff and heavy. It sank onto his head, stopped by some inner lining that kept it from falling over his eyes.

Toros then took the scepter from the boy and held it before Achan. "Arman, we offer up this scepter, and Your servant, Gidon, in whose hand You will place it, as a sign of his authority, that he may rule with this scepter and not a sword. In Your eternal name, may it be so."

Toros passed the scepter to Achan. He took hold of the smooth wood.

Another young man approached from Sparrow's side. He too held a pillow that carried a crown almost identical to Achan's. Toros took the crown and offered a prayer for it, then placed it on Sparrow's head.

A layer of tears coated Achan's eyes. He blinked them away and squeezed Sparrow's hand, thankful she sat beside him, loved him.

Toros said another prayer, or maybe he was talking to the audience. All Achan knew was that he had no more lines to recite. He stared ahead into nothingness, ready for this service to end, remembering all that had taken place to get him here.

A chorus of "Arman save the king! Arman save the queen!" jolted Achan's mind back to the present.

Toros turned and knelt before the thrones. "I, Toros Ianjo, priest of Arman, will be faithful and true, and faith and truth will bear unto you, my Sovereign Lord, King of this Realm and Defender of the Faith, and unto your heirs and successors according to law. So help me Arman."

Then, one by one, the audience came to swear fealty.

At first it was humbling, like that day Prince Oren, Sir Rigil, and Bran had sworn fealty to Achan in the Council chambers in

Mahanaim. But the numbers never seemed to dwindle. Drowsiness plagued Achan. He tried to disguise his yawns and keep his eyes from drooping, but kept failing.

The trill of the drums and heralding of the bugles was mercy indeed.

Achan and Sparrow stood and exited the throne room. The day was far from over. Now it was to the great hall for the coronation banquet.

How fare you, my king? Sparrow asked.

Desperate for sleep.

Food will hopefully bring you the energy you need to make it through the rest of this day.

I hope so. I would hate to fall asleep on my trencher.

Sir Caleb promised me a week of rest starting tomorrow.

He promised me as well, and I intend to hold him to it.

She stepped closer to walk beside him through the doorway leading out to the grand staircase. *Then hold on but a little longer, my king. For we have the rest of our lives to rest, but only this one day to celebrate our crowns.*

Mine is heavy. Is yours?

It is a weight I can bear only with you by my side.

Achan smiled. *I would kiss you, but I fear the crown would fall off. Can you imagine it rolling down the stairs?*

That would be a sight to behold.

You *are a sight to behold.*

She pursed her lips. *With words like those, we shall never rest.*

I can live with that.

THE END

A Note from the Author

Thanks for reading *From Darkness Won.*

As always, I love to hear from you. E-mail me at info@jillwilliamson.com with your thoughts on the book or questions about writing.

Please join my Facebook fan page or sign up for my author ezine at www.jillwilliamson.com to stay posted on new projects.

If you'd like to help make this trilogy a success, tell people about it. Loan your books to friends, give them as gifts, and ask your library or bookstore to order it. Also, posting a review on Amazon.com, Goodreads.com or BarnesandNoble.com is always very helpful.

Acknowledgments

Thanks to God, Brad, Luke, and Kaitlyn, who love me in spite of my numerous flaws.

And thanks to: Jeff Gerke, a fabulous editor and writing instructor. To Nicole O'Dell, Shirley Fruchey, Stephanie Gallentine, Adele Haijeck, Leighton Hajicek, Ness Hajicek, Chris Kolmorgen, Amy Meyer, Xavier Meyer, Diana Sharples, and Kathy Tyers for reading my book and/or helping me make it work. To my ladies' Bible study group for praying for me. And to Greg Bremner, whom I forgot to thank in book two for all his help with hunting birds and killing bears, and for his help with fires in this book. Greg, you are a gold mine of information. You are John Wayne!

And to my readers, thanks for reading Achan and Vrell's story.

Q&A with Jill Williamson

The following is part one of a two-part interview of questions sent in by readers. The second half of the interview can be heard online. See the end of the interview for details on the podcast.

Q: What made you decide to write the Blood of Kings trilogy?

I saw a tree in the front yard of a burned-down house. The part of the tree that hung over the fence and above the street was leafy green, rocking and rustling in the wind. But the branches of the tree inside the yard were charred and stiff. I couldn't wait to write a story about a land that was partially cursed in darkness and went home and Photoshopped the image of the tree on my author website.

Q: How did you come up with the idea for bloodvoices?

I needed a way that my girl character could learn that my boy character had royal blood. I thought it would be cool if those with royal blood had some telepathic ability to sense others like them. I first called it Blood Vision. Then I changed the name to Qoldam, which is Hebrew for bloodvoices (qowl—voices, and daum—blood). But Qoldam was difficult to pronounce, so I ended up calling it bloodvoicing.

Q: Why did you use Hebrew instead of inventing words like so many fantasy writers?

I stole the idea from J.K. Rowling. She used Latin for many of her character names and most of her magic spells in the Harry Potter books. I thought that was clever, so when I was brainstorming this book, I looked on my bookshelf and saw a French dictionary and a Hebrew/Greek concordance. I thought Hebrew/Greek sounded more like a fantasy novel. Plus, I liked the idea of using words from the Bible.

Q: The whole "storming" idea is very similar to Native American shamanistic beliefs, where if someone was sick, the shaman had to leave his body and go find their spirit. Did you get the idea from a similar source or invent it?

I know nothing about Native American shamanistic beliefs. Storming came about as a natural progression of the magic of bloodvoicing. In each book, characters proclaimed a bit more about how the magic worked, then I had to work out the details.

Q: Why is Vrell fair when so many others are tan? What is her lineage? It's not Kinsman, right?

Vrell's heritage is part Kinsman, part Poroo. I created five races of people for this series. Native to Er'Rets are the Poroo (white skin), who inhabited the north, and giants, who lived in the south. Kinsmen (brown skin) came to Er'Rets from the southeast, the Chuma (olive skin) came from the southwest, and the Otherlings (grey skin) came from the northwest.

Q: Is Er'Rets an island in the middle of a huge ocean? Are its inhabitants aware of any lands beyond?

Yes and yes. At first I thought of Er'Rets as more like a continent, but based on my map scale, the land is only a bit larger than the state of Nevada. Some Er'Retians know there is land beyond since King Echâd came to Er'Rets from elsewhere almost 600 years before the story takes place. I never really thought about what else is out there, but I suspect the pirates in Hamonah could tell you.

Q: How is Achan such a nice person when he was abused and neglected in his childhood?

Achan's friendship with Gren Fenny had an incredible influence on his life. She rescued him from being alone. She taught him to swim and was kind to him. Told him that he should be treated well. That he was worth more. And that inspired him. He wanted to be to others what she had been to him. Plus, he saw her parents interact and how they loved each other and hoped that he might have such a family someday. Agape love is a powerful thing.

Q: There is so much detail in your world, how do you keep track of it all?

I have a large, 3-ring binder in which I keep everything important. I have maps, a timeline, family trees, sketches, character charts, city charts, lists of herbs and their healing properties, lists of Hebrew words and translations, pictures of weapons, facts about horses, and notes about medieval architecture. I go to that binder often to reference details for the story. It's a great tool. I have similar folders for other books I've written, though only the Blood of Kings trilogy has needed to move to a 3-ring binder.

Q: When you wrote the ending did you think you might be giving too much detail after the story was basically over?

Yeah. Jeff and I talked about whether to cut out the wedding and coronation. But we ultimately decided that the readers had earned the chance to be there after so many pages of Achan and Vrell not being together. And my teen readers wanted me to leave the ceremonies in, claiming they provided the perfect time for the reader to calm down without making the ending feel abrupt.

Q: Will you write more books about Er'Rets?

Perhaps. There are so many interesting places we never got to see: Jaelport, Hamonah, Nesos, Cherem, Magos, Land's End… I always thought a story about the war between Cherem and Magos would be fun to write, as would a story about Jibhal Hamartano and the start of the black knights. We'll see.

To hear more fan questions answered and more behind the scenes information check out this podcast interview with Jill Williamson from the folks at Life Story:

http://www.lifeisstory.com/interviews/
interview-with-jill-wiliamson-the-blood-of-kings/

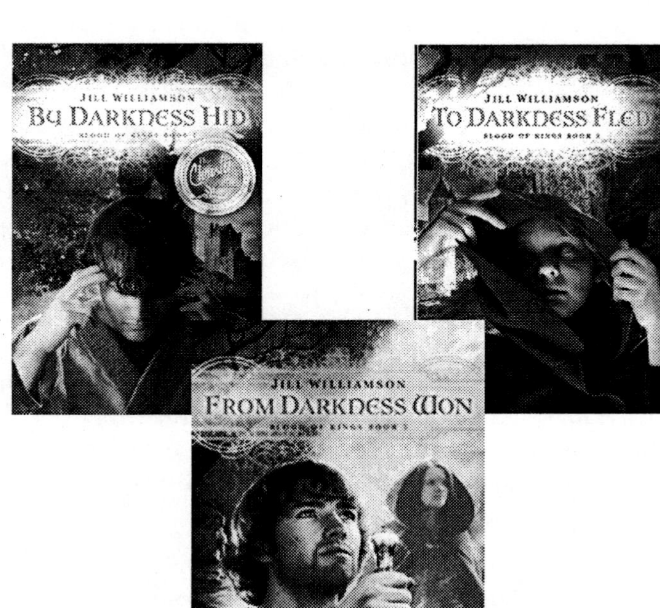

Read the Entire
Blood of Kings
Trilogy